Cover original design by Mollie Gibbs

SPITALBROOK

Beverley E Gibbs

Copyright@2025 Beverley Gibbs
All Rights Reserved

First Published 22 November 2025
ISBN – 9798296443861

All characters featured in this book are fictional, and any resemblance
to any person or persons in real life is purely coincidental.

Dedication

This is for my family, near and far, past, present and future.
My inspiration comes from all of you.

Chapter 1	LONDON – 1951
Chapter 2	NORFOLK – 2024
Chapter 3	NORFOLK – 2024
Chapter 4	AT SEA – 1951
Chapter 5	NORFOLK – 2024
Chapter 6	NORFOLK – 2024
Chapter 7	NORFOLK – 2024
Chapter 8	AT SEA – 1951
Chapter 9	NORFOLK – 2024
Chapter 10	NORFOLK – 2024
Chapter 11	BARNET – 1952
Chapter 12	NORFOLK – 2024
Chapter 13	NORFOLK – 2024
Chapter 14	AUCKLAND – 1952
Chapter 15	NORFOLK – 2024
Chapter 16	NORFOLK – 2024
Chapter 17	NORFOLK – 2024
Chapter 18	NORFOLK – 2024
Chapter 19	NORFOLK – 2024
Chapter 20	NORFOLK – 2024
Chapter 21	NORFOLK – 2024
Chapter 22	NORFOLK – 2024
Chapter 23	AUCKLAND – 1954
Chapter 24	NORFOLK – 2024
Chapter 25	NORFOLK – 1954
Chapter 26	NORFOLK – 1954
Chapter 27	NORFOLK – 2024
Chapter 28	NORFOLK – 2024
Chapter 29	NORFOLK – 2024
Chapter 30	NORFOLK – 2024
Chapter 31	CHRISTCHURCH – 1970

Chapter 32	NORFOLK – 2024
Chapter 33	NORFOLK – 2024
Chapter 34	NORFOLK – 2024
Chapter 35	NORFOLK – 2024
Chapter 36	CHRISTCHURCH – 1994
Chapter 37	CREWE – 2024
Chapter 38	CREWE – 2024
Chapter 39	NORFOLK – 2024
Chapter 40	NORFOLK – 2024
Chapter 41	NORFOLK – 2024
Chapter 42	NORFOLK – 2024
Chapter 43	NORFOLK – 2024
Chapter 44	NORFOLK – 2024
Chapter 45	NORFOLK – 2024
Chapter 46	CHRISTCHURCH – 2024
Chapter 47	NORFOLK – 2024
Chapter 48	NORFOLK – 2024
Chapter 49	NORFOLK – 2024
Chapter 50	MID-FLIGHT - 2024
Chapter 51	NEW YORK – 2024
Chapter 52	MID-FLIGHT – 2024
Chapter 53	AUCKLAND – 2024
Chapter 54	ROTORUA – 2024
Chapter 55	WELLINGTON – 2024
Chapter 56	CHRISTCHURCH – 2024
Chapter 57	CHRISTCHURCH – 2024
Chapter 58	CHRISTCHURCH – 2024
Chapter 59	CHRISTCHURCH – 2024
Chapter 60	SOUTH ISLAND – 2024
Chapter 61	LONDON – 2024
Chapter 62	NORFOLK – 2024
Chapter 63	NORFOLK – 2024
Chapter 64	NORFOLK – 2024

Acknowledgements:

Thanks go to my lovely friend Claire, who read the first draft chapter by chapter, provided constructive feedback and ultimately gave me the nod to believe that Tilly's journey was worth pursuing to publication.

Secondly, I must thank my proofreaders, Mollie, Manda and Jon for diligently proofreading my first printed draft. To Jon who would not normally read this genre, but was the first to finish it and found so many things for me to edit! To Manda who pointed out my obsession with the comma as well as providing me with key details gleaned from her extensive travel experience. There are probably still too many commas though! Finally, to Mollie who gave me the benefit of her keen teacher's eye for detail – I learnt so much doing the edit. I am grateful to you all. I hope any remaining glitches don't spoil the story!

I also want to thank Mollie for her cover design, which gave us more than one sleepless night, but I'm so pleased we stuck with it.

1

LONDON - 1951

'Goodbye,' her anxious cry, swallowed up among so many other desperate voices, drifted on the wind, then disappeared, absorbed by the choking smog and drizzle.

As the giant, steam driven vessel moved out of the London docks, Violet looked up from the quay and strained to see her sister. A small dot among so many faces. Faces mostly streaked with tears. Her sister. Young, vulnerable and alone. She waved her handkerchief hard, alongside so many other emotional relatives, of passengers fleeing, in a mass emigration from a tired and broken country. She wept. For her sister. But also, for herself. How had this happened to their happy, post war family? Violet turned to her husband and buried her face in his heavy, woollen overcoat. Would she ever see her sister again?

Sighing, they turned and made their way home. Violet was the lucky one. A loving husband, a warm home. Yes. Fortune had been kind to her. And she knew it.

Once they were back home Violet's husband Ronald took her coat and guided her to the armchair. A solid upright pillar of the community, Dr Stillman was her rock. She shivered and battled to keep the emotion from her voice.

'Thank you love,' she looked up at her husband and smiled. How had she been so lucky to find Ronald, when Temperance had had the opposite luck? He smiled back.

'How about a nice cup of tea Vi? I think you need it.' Ronald, a practical and calm man, had been qualified as a GP for six years now and was well established in the community. Their home doubled as Ronald's surgery, where Violet worked on the administrative side. They were fortunate enough to be able to afford a cleaner, who came in for an hour each evening to help Violet. They also employed a nursing sister Mary, who worked 3 days a week alongside Ronald. Their large front parlour had been converted into the surgery and with a lovely bay window, it was open and light, giving the room a comfortable feeling. On the opposite side of the hall, was the snug; a compact room now used as a waiting area. Vi had been careful to decorate it with brightly coloured posters, featuring happy healthy people.

At 26, Violet was 2 years older than her sister Temperance. Together with their two younger brothers, Hector and Joseph, they had grown up in a big sprawling home in the Norfolk countryside. Happy times had been spent with their cousins who had visited often in the summer months. Long warm evenings were spent lying on their backs on the hay bales, gazing up at the stars and dreaming of nothing more than their next adventure. Carefree, innocent days.

When Violet met her beloved Ronald at the village dance in West Snoring, in the December of 1946, she knew instantly he was 'the one.' They danced for several hours; eyes only for one another, then Ronald walked her home. Under the moonlight, at the end of the driveway, they shared their first kiss. Their future was sealed.

Ronald was still living at home with his parents and older sister Daphne in the adjacent village, but being 10 years older than Violet, their paths had not crossed before. Violet's mother was naturally concerned about the large age gap.

'He's a man' she would say to Violet. 'A proper man. Why don't you find yourself a nice boy, of your own age?'

But Violet was in love with her man. Ronald was the one. They made plans for their future which took them south, away from their tiny village to the outskirts of London where in Barnet they settled.

To begin with, they rented a small flat above a parade of shops, while Ronald, established himself as Doctor Stillman, in the emergency wing of Barnet General. Within a short time, an opportunity arose for Ronald to take on his own practice and their hunt for a suitable property began.

Their new home in a pretty, leafy lane, had roses at the front, and an old air raid shelter in the large back garden. With space for the surgery to allow Ronald to begin practicing. They put down all their savings as a deposit and with a mortgage, secured their dream home.

Oh, how Violet now wished she had brought her sister with her. Her poor Temperance was heading on the high seas, for a land, and a new life, so far away. Violet pulled the handkerchief from her sleeve and dabbed at her eyes. Regrets were futile. She now had to wait for that first letter.
The dusting would not do itself, and worrying did no-one any good. Violet finished her tea and pulled herself together. She was heading into the surgery when the newly installed telephone rang out from the hall. She lifted the receiver.

'Hello Barnet 3524.....'. Violet sat down heavily on the hall seat
'Father? I am sorry, but I do not want to speak to you.' With a deep breath, Violet replaced the receiver in its cradle, leant back against the wall, closed her eyes, and sighed.

2

NORFOLK - 2024

It was a regular day on the water for Tilly. She was looking forward to a relaxed day with her art palette and easel. Tilly, full name Matilda Jean Montgomery-Brown was a confident and independent, 26-year-old. Attractive, easy going, and popular among her close friends.

Tilly's houseboat was moored in a serene spot on the canal. Close enough to the village to enjoy a social life with her besties, but far enough out, to ensure the peace and tranquillity of life in the country.

Her boat, 'Georgie', was her pride and joy. Carefully restored and decorated by her own fair hands, it contained an eclectic mix of old, antique, and collectable objects. Life on a houseboat required an organised mind, and for Tilly, and her cat Marmite, that hadn't always been easy. Yet Tilly had gradually learnt how to be frugal with her possessions to make best use of her limited space.

'Georgie' - you decide whether male, female or other – had been divided into 3 small sections. The middle was a space dominated by a small, wooden church pew, which Tilly and best friend Melody had rescued from a skip. It had been lovingly renovated with the help of Melody's carpenter husband Sam. The village church had, like so many, replaced their seating with more comfortable and versatile modern chairs. The pews had then been sold off to raise much needed funds. Tilly's pew was badly damaged at one end: hence it's rejection. The church was happy for Tilly to rescue it, in return for a small donation. Thanks to Tilly's artistic skills and Sam's practical help, it had been given a new purpose.

With space tight, Sam had fashioned a useful storage box under the pew. Here, all her art materials were stored, and other odds and ends. It was a little bit muddled, but Tilly knew where everything was....most of the time!

Her table was an old cabinet door. Fixed to wooden pedestals, it did the job and fitted perfectly. Opposite this social space was the galley kitchen area and moving to the back of the boat a tiny doorway led out to the bathroom and exit. The doorway was so low that most had to duck, but not Tilly. At just five foot tall it did not cause her a problem.

Her favourite space was her bedroom. Nestled at the front of the boat, she enjoyed the dual aspect windows, where she could fill her internal happiness pot on the new sunrise; drift off into a dreamy sleep lulled by the sounds of calling mallards, and in between, gaze at the lapping water in a happy mindfulness stupor.

Her bedroom was colourfully decorated in true Tilly style. A very slim windowsill doubled as a dressing table and her clothes lived everywhere. Mainly on the floor.

Tilly had lived on her houseboat with Marmite, since the tender age of twenty-one. She attended university at eighteen, keen, excited, and a little apprehensive, looking for something new to fill a huge void in her life. Following the death of her father in a tragic work accident when she was just 15, things naturally changed at home.

Growing up in a comfortable, council house, life had been just like those of her friends. Her parents were not too strict, and she'd had a few boyfriends when she was younger, but nothing very serious. Once her dad had passed, she was left with her mum to grieve. As a teenager, her emotions ran high. Her father's passing just increased them tenfold.

University was to be an escape for young Tilly. While she was studying, her mum had met a new man. A businessman, with lots of money. David Kennedy had shown little interest in Tilly. She didn't like him much either, but her mum did, and they were married mid-way through her second year. They moved to a big modern home, on a new estate, and Tilly felt uncomfortable whenever she returned. She made the decision that she did not want to return to live with her mum and Dave once her university life was over.

This is where 'Georgie' came in. The boat she called her saviour. With the help of her best friends Kit and Melody, and Melody's husband Sam, she had made the perfect home in Georgie. Bought with some of the money her dad had left her, she settled on the local canal. Tilly was forced to mature rapidly to cope with her catapult into adult life.

Life was steady. A part time job doing the paperwork for a small plumbing company took up 3 days of her week. As a family business, the manager and his wife took Tilly to their hearts and let her work her hours to fit around her other hobbies and indulgencies. The money she earned from her 3 days was just enough to keep things ticking over, and allowed time to focus on her other passion, art. Tilly would often sell directly from her boat, but sometimes in local exhibitions too. She also had a permanent display in her favourite coffee shop, An Extra Slice.

With Kit and Melody, Tilly had become a popular customer at An Extra Slice, and the three were regularly treated to half price cakes by Brenda the owner, who had a soft spot for the girls.

Tilly also volunteered at the village charity shop 'Cat Care'. A charity close to her heart, and, as the name suggested, they rescued unwanted or stray cats and kittens. Cat Care had rescued her beloved Marmite from a building site when he was a tiny kitten. She could not imagine her life now without her cheeky, furry friend. His unconditional love provided all the company she needed.

Tilly was happy with her life and appreciated what she had. As she drew the curtains and hunkered down in front of her small wood burner, with her latest crochet project, and the radio for company, her phone sparked into life; a bright flash of blue, and familiar vibrating rumble. It was a text. And it was from her mum.

3

NORFOLK - 2024

'Call me please,' was all the message said. Tilly put her phone to one side and tried to ignore it. Her mum rarely contacted her, and Tilly wasn't in the mood for an argument. She tried to concentrate on the crochet pattern but found herself glancing over to see if there had been any updates. Phone on silent, but always on vibrate, she couldn't avoid it completely, unless she turned it off. Just as her curiosity was about to get the better of her, the phone sprung into life and juddered at her side. 'MUM Mobile' flashed on the tiny screen. She grabbed the moving gadget and pressed agitatedly at the green phone symbol.

'Tilly, didn't you get my message?' Her mother's anxious voice barked. Tensing slightly, Tilly tried to respond casually.

'Yes mum, I was busy, I have only just seen it.' The small, white lie sat uncomfortably with Tilly, but she wanted the upper hand. 'What is it?'

'It's Uncle Hector - he has been in touch with me. He's asking to see you Tilly. I fear his health may be failing. He didn't sound quite with it.' Tilly took a deep breath. 'Did you hear m..'

'Yes mum' interrupted Tilly, 'I was trying to think.' She paused momentarily, 'Okay, I'll call the home.' Tilly felt suddenly flustered. Shocked at her initial reaction.

'Well dear, if you need anything, you have my number,' and with that, her mother hung up.

Tilly looked at her watch. It was only 7.40pm. Not as late as she had thought. There was time to contact the home.

Uncle Hector was not actually Tilly's uncle, but her mum's uncle. Tilly's great uncle. But Hector and Tilly had always had a connection. When she was a little girl, Hector would tell her about his adventures, exaggerating his exploits, as a single man with an exciting job in the art world. Her mum and dad would take her to meet Hector when he was back in the country, usually in posh London hotels, where Hector seemed very at home. As she grew up, they corresponded, and in the past few years, since his retirement to a very up market care home, she had visited him often.

Hector had told her a bit about his early days. He had grown up with his three siblings in an idyllic location; a 12-acre family farm. His father had cultivated potatoes, and his mother took on small needlework jobs for people in the village of West Snoring. Hector remembered his early days as happy ones; long summers filled with laughter. His cousins regularly joined them to camp under the stars and play in the small brook that ran along the edge of their boundary. Always told they were not to go any further than the brook, Hector and his brother Joe would push that limit by climbing down into the shallow water. So many hours they had spent catching tiny sticklebacks with cans tied to sticks. These were the main things that Tilly remembered from the stories Hector relayed - those and the art. He loved his art, and it had become a quite lucrative career for him, taking him all over the world.

Tilly struggled to think straight, these memories of happy times with her great uncle raced around her head. Why did her mum have so little interest in Hector? He was her uncle after all. Yes, he liked to exaggerate, but that was the Brown way. Her Aunty Jean was similar. Tilly walked into the living space in her boat and plucked her address book from the small bookshelf. Opening it at 'H' for Hector she found the number for 'Sunny Days Care Home' and dialled.

'Hello, Sunny Days, Pat speaking, how can I help you?' The receptionist was bright and cheery. Tilly smiled.

'Hello Pat, my name is Tilly and I am calling about Hector Brown. He is my great uncle, and we have received a call from him. My mum was concerned that he may not be well?' Tilly realised she was rushing, and gulped as her mouth dried, faltering over her words.

'I'll have a look for you love, but I don't have anything on the notes here at reception. Can I take your number and I'll give you a call back?' Tilly gave Pat the information she needed and then, wanting to keep busy and reduce the negative thoughts, she put the kettle on.

Without realising it, Tilly drifted back into reminiscing. It had been a while since she had last visited Uncle Hector and a bit of guilt surfaced. The lovely Sunny Days care home was just a 20-minute drive from her mooring on the canal and, although Tilly didn't have a car, her friends would always drive her if she needed to get there quickly. There was so much going round in her head, when just minutes later her phone rang and she was brought abruptly back to the current. She grabbed the mobile, keen for news.

'Hello Tilly, it's Pat here from Sunny Days. How are you?' The friendly patter threw Tilly a bit. She was feeling anxious and just wanted to know the news about Hector.

'I'm ok, thank you Pat, yes, fine. Is Hector? Fine I mean. Is Hector..er, ok?' she stuttered, her words garbled. She took another breath.

'He's just fine love,' said Pat in a calm friendly voice. 'Absolutely fine. I have seen him and spoken to him. To be honest I think he was feeling a bit lonely and would welcome a visit from a familiar face. He is sorry if he worried you.' Tilly let go of the breath she had been holding, relief flooding through her body like a miniature tsunami.

'Thank you. Oh, thank you so much. Yes, I will visit him, as soon as. Can you tell him that please?' Tilly started to plan before she had even finished the call.

'Of course I will Tilly. Glad to help. Bye now love.' Pat hung up and Tilly's arm dropped. Hugging the phone to her chest, she sighed again, muttering her relief under her breath.

Tilly finished making her tea and took it into her bedroom. She sunk into the large cushions on her bed, dimmed the lighting, and texted her mum back to update her. She was meeting with Kit and Melody the following morning for coffee at their favourite café, so she was sure she could get a lift with Kit to Sunny Days then. She had hoped to do a bit of painting, but that could wait. She quickly fired off another text and her visit was sorted.

Now, where was she with her crochet?

4

AT SEA - 1951

Straining behind crowds of bodies, Temperance ached for that last glimpse of her sister. Her family. Her beloved family. Yet family she was being forced to part from, possibly forever. She pushed through one layer of the crowd; just one more push and she would be at the barrier. She was only slight, and turned sideways, edging forwards into a non-existent gap.

'Sorry, excuse me....er..thank you, oh yes, please can I just get through?' She wasn't waiting for answers, but the words poured from her, apology on apology. She felt it was all she could do to absolve herself of the guilt that washed over her as she pushed to the front.

Once there, a mass of tiny faces greeted her. Tiny white hankies in tiny hands, waved furiously up to their departing friends and relations. In there somewhere were Violet and Ronald. She knew they were standing near a large pile of crates, newly offloaded from a ship that had arrived from the east. Probably containing spices, or some other exotic cargo. She could see over to the right, the crates, and yes, could that possibly be Violet in her best winter wool camel overcoat?

'Violet,' she shouted at the top of her voice. No-one noticed. Everyone around her was doing the same. Calling, waving, and crying. Temperance felt an emotion, but no tears emerged. She had done all her crying, and now she had to look to the future. Her future, in a far-off land. 'I'm here Violet, over here,' and along with everyone else, she waved furiously and just hoped they could see her.

As the large steam ship, the SS Magnificent, edged out of London docks, on that early November morning, bound for New Zealand, via New York, Temperance stood on deck until all the faces were dots in the distance. She had a small bag which she clasped to her chest and turned to push back through the throng of people. Excited family groups, individuals, mostly young. All heading for an unknown land.

She found the steps that took her down to the lower decks, then paused, to retrieve her ticket.

Deck: Lower 2, Corridor 4, Room 7B.

Looking at the large map of the ship's layout located at the top of the stairwell, she realised she had several more flights of stairs to descend before she reached Lower 2. She continued her descent alongside many others.

'You alone love?' Temperance turned to face the voice. 'Elsie, pleased to make your acquaintance.' The girl Elsie was holding out her hand. Temperance shook it, smiling.

'Oh, yes.' Temperance hesitated momentarily. 'How do you do Elsie; my name is Penny. Well, my actual name is Temperance, but call me Penny and yes, I am on my own. Are you?' Reassured by the offer of friendship, Temperance perked up. 'I am heading down to my cabin, on Lower 2.'

'Oh lovely, me too. Yes, I am on my own. Up for an adventure, me. Like the sound of the 'New Zealand' and exploring other places on the way.' Elsie giggled. 'Let's get moving to find our rooms.'

The girls continued down to Lower 2, then stopped again to assess the layout. By luck they were in the same corridor, and just 4 rooms apart. The cheapest inner cabins, but at least their own personal space. One up from the dormitory type rooms with six bunks but nothing much else. They really were the very cheapest option, but Violet had insisted her sister had her own space and had contributed from her own pocket to the slightly more expensive ticket. There wasn't a window, so no natural light, but a bed, dressing table with small drawer for clothes, and a cupboard containing a small bowl for washing, a jug for water and a chamber pot. An essential for nighttime. She unpacked her small bag, then sat back on the bed. Hard, and rough, but her home for the next six weeks, so she would have to get used to it.

Once both girls had sorted themselves out, with Temperance being much quicker than Elsie, they ventured back up on deck to gather with fellow travellers. There was an air of excitement, and busyness and Elsie led the way to find the centre of everything. A long dark dining canteen area, where queues were growing. Some chairs by the porthole windows were vacant and Temperance turned to stake their claim. The travellers had all been allocated meal and drink coupons to use on the journey. Much like the food ration vouchers they'd had in the war. Temperance suddenly felt quite weary, and a wave of emotion swept over her, catching her quite off guard. As tears brimmed in her big blue eyes she looked to Elsie for reassurance.

'I need to sit down Elsie. I really need to.' Thinking that perhaps she had been carried away by her new friend's enthusiasm, she was partly regretting the return to a higher deck. If she could just sit down and close her eyes for a while, she might rally. Elsie wasn't stupid and saw the look in Temperance's eyes. One of homesickness or perhaps longing for something she no longer had.

'Don't worry love, I'll get us both a nice cup of tea, and you just relax there. Pass me your coupon, dear. I'll be two ticks.' Elsie took off, and ensconced herself in the queue, as Temperance settled by the window, with her thoughts.

When Elsie returned with two steaming cups of hot milky tea, Temperance was almost asleep. The gentle rocking sensation of the ship was actually quite soothing, and she had been happy to sit with her eyes closed while waiting. The tea perked her up, and the girls faced one another on the hard seats, to enjoy their tea. Elsie was the first to speak.

'So tell me Penny, where do you come from, and more to the point, why are you emigrating when you clearly don't want to go? I saw those almost tears earlier love; you can't fool me.' Elsie's smile was gentle, and concern for her newfound friend genuine.

'I *do* want to go,' said Temperance, a bit too quickly to be convincing. Elsie cocked her head sideways, and screwed up one eye, as if to say *I don't believe you.* 'I do,' she said again. 'I am looking to broaden my horizons.' Temperance left it at that. She couldn't speak the truth. Violet and Temperance had made a promise to each other that the truth would never be spoken. Perhaps Elsie was showing interest, but Temperance felt she was being nosy. She was uncomfortable sharing personal information, so early on in their friendship. She thought for a moment, then said.

'I have a sister Violet, but my parents are dead. So, I was living with Violet and her husband in Barnet. He is a doctor, you know. A proper medical one. But in the end, I didn't think it was fair to take a room in their home. Intrude on their lives. When I saw the 'Ten-pound pom' adverts, I decided that was the answer. Vi, you know, my sister, she helped me with the fare, and then both Violet and Ronald drove me to the dock. Because I haven't anyone else. So, you see, there really isn't much for me to stay for.' Temperance looked away, out to sea through the tiny porthole window. Unable to hold her new friend's gaze as she told her blatant lie. After a pause to compose herself, she turned back to Elsie.

'How about you?' Elsie didn't push it. It was clear to her that Temperance was hiding something, but it was her secret to keep.

'I am looking for something new and exciting,' began Elsie, in her confident way. 'My oldest brother Bob emigrated two years ago to Australia, with his new bride. I was left at home with dad, but now dad has a new lady in his life, I decided it was my turn. That's it!' She seemed very honest and her story plausible. Temperance still wasn't ready to share anything more, and smiled, continuing to sip at her tea. 'I'll miss our old dog Rex, but me and dad, well, we didn't always see eye to eye, so once I had the money, I was booked onto the next available boat. Didn't care where it was going, I just wanted to be on it. So here I am. Don't you worry love, I won't pry. You don't have to tell me anything you don't want to. We've got six weeks on this big beast together, so we don't want to fall out now do we?' Elsie pushed back her shoulders and smiled confidently, holding Temperance's gaze, teasing 'come on gal, let's have some fun while we're here. Might as well make the most of it love. We can't get off now - well, not unless you are a bloody good swimmer!' They both had a giggle and Temperance visibly relaxed.

Temperance knew her reaction was a little unusual, but Elsie was right. It was going to be a long trip and so they had to make the best of it. She resolved at that moment, that when the time felt right, she would tell Elsie the truth.

The girls spent the evening in the communal lounge, people watching, until they eventually retired to their respective cabins. As Temperance pulled the thin, rough blanket tightly up under her chin, her head swayed with the life-changing events of her day. Fighting the inevitable sleep, as her eyelids weighed down in the dark gloom of her windowless cabin, she was eventually wading through vivid dreams, as sleep overtook her. There was no going back for Temperance. She was on her way to a new life and with it, hope.

5

NORFOLK - 2024

'Woohoo Kitty, over here,' waved Tilly to her friend stood at the door of the café. Tilly had arrived first and looked across at Brenda smiling. Brenda, the café owner ushered her to the best table and brought her a regular cappuccino - Tilly's coffee of choice. Tilly, Kit and Melody had been friends since school. People said that two was company, three a crowd, but the girls had always found their relationship worked perfectly.

Kit was the clever one. Slim, with beautiful shiny auburn hair and a strong determined personality. As a buyer for an upmarket clothing company she worked hard to climb the ladder, flying all over the world.

Kit moved to London, where she bought her own flat with space to keep her prized sports car. Bright red, sexy, sleek and fast. Just like Kit.

Melody was the opposite to Kit. A homely girl, dark blonde unruly curls, worn long and usually tied back. She was married to the lovely Sam who she met at the local technical college. Sam was training to be a carpenter, while Melody studied beauty and hairdressing. They met in the college canteen over a bowl of crispy fries. Eyes locked and that was that. Proper love at first sight stuff. They married the year after they qualified and now lived in a flat close to Tilly's houseboat, with their 18-month-old daughter Lois.

Melody was a mobile hairdresser, which was particularly good for Kit and Tilly as they benefited from discounted haircuts, and nails as a bonus. Tilly also managed to wangle eyebrow shaping every three months at 'mates rates'. Melody had a gentle kind nature, much like Tilly, and loved their girly catch ups. Not always easy with a youngster, but Kit and Tilly loved Lois almost as much as her parents did. Luckily, Sam worked for his dad's carpentry business and was free to look after Lois whenever needed. Otherwise, the little one just became one of the girls and joined in the coffee get togethers. Brenda was only too keen to spoil her with chocolate brownies and Melody always came well prepared with baby wipes to deal with the aftermath!

Today it was just the three of them. Tilly arrived first followed by Kit. As she pulled up outside the shop, the car turned a few heads. As Kit took her seat at the corner table, Melody appeared looking a little flustered.

'Hiya Mel, you okay?' Tilly got up to hug her friend.

'Hello Tilly, Kit. I'm fine just lost track of time with Lois needing a last hug before I left. What about you two?' She smiled at Kit who shuffled into her seat and shrugged off her jacket.

'I'm fine thank you lovely. Quite an easy drive down. Makes a change for a Saturday. Shall I take your coat, and hang it with mine?' Melody handed Kit her coat and took a seat on the far side of the table. Job done Kit sat back down.

'I see you started without us Tills?' teased Kit, pointing at the empty coffee cup. Before Tilly could respond, Brenda was at the table to take their order.

'Now what'll it be ladies? The usual all round, or do you fancy something different? I also have some tasty tray bakes, cakes and pastries.' Smiling, Brenda paused with her notepad and pencil. No modern tablet gimmick for taking orders, just old-fashioned pen and paper is how Brenda liked to run her establishment.

'I'd like some of the pecan and toffee flapjack please Bren, and I will stick with my latte as usual.' Kit's sweet tooth meant she rarely enjoyed a coffee without cake of some kind.

'Noted young Kit, and what about you two?' glancing towards Melody at the back of the table, Melody was looking at the menu.

'I actually fancy a herbal tea please, and a toasted teacake if you have one?' The other girls looked at her with mock surprise.

'Herbal tea - seriously?' teased Tilly. 'Oh, I guess it is ok on this occasion, but don't make a habit of it. I am definitely having more caffeine. Another cappuccino for me please Brenda, and a plain croissant. Can I have it warm with butter and jam please?' Brenda winked as she turned away.

'Coming right up.'

It had been a couple of months since their last proper get together, and this one had been planned for some time, so it was particularly handy it had coincided with the call the previous evening from Uncle Hector. The girls started to chat about what they had been doing in the intervening weeks since their last meeting, and it was not very long before their drinks and cakes arrived. As Tilly buttered her croissant, she turned to Kit.

'Kit, I know it might be a bit of a cheek without pre-warning you, but I wonder if you would give me a lift to the care home when we finish here please?' Taking a bite of her croissant, she looked at Kit, eyebrows raised.

'No probs, are you seeing Uncle Hector?' Both of Tilly's friends were familiar with her closeness to her uncle Hector, especially since the death of her dad.

'Yes, thank you Kit, I wouldn't normally ask without warning, you know that, but yesterday he called my mum. Long story short, mum called me.' Tilly finished her croissant, licking her fingers clean of butter and jam.

'Your mum called you?' Melody sounded shocked.

'Yes, basically Uncle Hector contacted her in a bit of a state by all accounts, so I called the care home, and they reassured me that he is fine, just a bit lonely. So, I said I would visit 'ASAP'. I hope you don't mind, but as you have the car - and I always love a ride in your car, you know that - I thought I would be cheeky.' The girls laughed.

'It's no problem at all Tills, I will drop you on my way back.' Kit had nothing to rush home for. So the girls spent another two hours chatting, drinking and eating tasty treats before they parted company.

Arrangements were made to meet up the following month. Sometimes Kit was out of the country or called away last minute, but they always made a date and agreed that if it was only two of them, they would still stick to their plan. Kit and Tilly hugged Melody goodbye, then got into the sports car, with the postcode for 'Sunny Days' plugged in to the satnav, Tilly waved as Kit took expertly to the road in a rather speedy fashion.

6

NORFOLK - 2024

Tilly waved goodbye from the steps of the care home, as Kit disappeared in a flash of red. Tilly did think that perhaps Kit drove a little faster than was permitted, but that was Kit. She lived on the edge. Tilly wasn't an experienced driver, so couldn't really comment. She decided it probably just felt faster in the low-down sports car, than in Sam's work van! But Tilly considered herself lucky to have friends who were mobile and generous enough to give her lifts, for the times when she couldn't manage with the bus, so she never complained.

She walked up to the care home's wide sliding doors, which opened automatically. A lady on reception smiled at her.

'Hello love, how can I help you today?' A broad smile accompanied her friendly welcome.

'Oh hello, you're Pat, aren't you? I recognise your voice.' Tilly smiled back. 'I'm Tilly - we spoke last night about Uncle Hector..er..I mean Hector Brown'

'Of course, Tilly love. I remember. Come this way, and I will take you through the security doors to his room. He is up and sitting in his chair. He will be glad to see you Tilly. He has been a bit down.' Tilly followed Pat towards the section of the care home that housed the bedroom apartments. Uncle Hector's was number 7.

'Ah, here we are.' Pat knocked, then pushed open the door straight into a living room. She stepped aside so that Tilly could go through. 'You've got a visitor Mr Brown. Look who has come to see you today.' Pat smiled at Tilly. 'I'll be at the desk if you need me.'

The main room was large, bright and airy. Wide French doors framed with heavy, red, velvet curtains led straight out onto the garden. The private care home was not a cheap place to reside, but it had been Hector's choice, and he had lived there happily for twelve years since his retirement. In addition to the sitting room with two armchairs and a small television, his bedroom was generous, boasting an ensuite shower room, modelled on the matrimonial suite of a cruise ship, the Sunny Days Care Home's high-end accommodation was the Ritz of residential care for the elderly, and Hector had chosen it for that reason.

Hector's suite contained just a few of his most personal possessions. In his bedroom, he had a man's traditional oak wardrobe, with hanging rails on one side, and small drawers on the other. A small dressing table was positioned in the centre of one wall, the surface covered in ornately framed photos. As Tilly entered the main living room, Hector struggled to his feet to greet her, using his stick to steady himself, he was determined to give Tilly a big hug.

'Hello my lovely Tilly, oh how wonderful it is to see you, my dear,' Hector was visibly beaming, his delight in this long overdue meeting with Tilly evident. She quickly moved forwards to support him, as he reached out to hug her. Still a tall man, if a little stooped, he gave a strong bear hug each time they met.

'Please don't worry about getting up Uncle Hector, come on let's get you back to your armchair.' She eased him back to his seat and took the seat next to him.

'Would you like some tea or coffee Tilly? I'll call for refreshments.' Hector reached over to his side table.

'I have just had coffee with my friends, thank you. It was my friend Kit who dropped me off.' Tilly wasn't sure she could manage another coffee just now. 'Perhaps a glass of water - if you are having something yourself?' Tilly shifted forwards in her seat to face Hector. 'Do you need me to call Pat?'

'Ah, no I have this bell here,' he raised his hand to reveal the emergency bell resting on the side table. 'If I just press this, I can speak through the intercom, and order whatever I want, to be delivered to my room.' Hector pressed the bell. Just as he had described, the intercom sparked into life; a disembodied woman's voice asked how she could help him.

'Please can you bring me a glass of water, and an Americano with warm milk, and brown sugar. Can I also have some egg mayonnaise sandwiches please; enough for myself and my young guest.' Hector paused and looked across at Tilly, who smiled. 'Yes, I think that is all, thank you.'

'Very good Mr Brown, it will be sent through to you shortly' came the reply, and the voice rang off.

'Wow Uncle Hector, I didn't know you had room service. It's like a posh hotel.' Tilly's voice couldn't contain her surprise. She didn't remember it being quite so upmarket on previous visits.

'It's good here Tilly. The management has recently changed, and it has got even better! Now, I am glad you came and didn't leave it too much longer as I have things I want to talk to you about.' Hector smiled and leant back in his armchair. Tilly gave an apprehensive smile. She knew what was coming. Keen to find out how Hector was feeling, she got in first and asked him. She thought he sounded a little breathless.

They settled down to chat about his health. Hector insisted he felt fine but didn't remember texting Tilly's mother the previous day. He seemed more anxious than usual to talk on his favourite subject. Family. Especially history and his childhood.

'Did you know, young Tilly, that I had two sisters, as well as a brother Joe. There is something I have never been able to talk about. As I get older, I think it is bothering me more than it used to. I really want someone to talk to about this and you are the one I trust. You are my family, Tilly.' Hector looked at Tilly earnestly.

Tilly felt a bit uncomfortable. 'What about mum, or Aunty Jean?' Tilly suggested, but Hector made a face and waved away that option.

'No Tilly, it's you. I have always known you are the one. You are kind and caring, and you are interested in family. You are the one, love, to tell my story to.' Hector was firm and determined.

'Okay then Uncle Hector, this sounds a bit more serious than usual. I am all ears.' Not quite knowing what to expect now, Tilly adjusted her position in the big armchair. It felt like the visit was going to be longer than she had anticipated. 'Tell me what it is about the family that is bothering you.'

And so he began.

7

NORFOLK - 2024

'Have I ever properly talked to you about my childhood?' Hector turned to look at Tilly. 'Have I Tilly?'

'Yes, Uncle Hector, you know you have.' Tilly tried not to sound patronising. Hector's memory had clearly deteriorated since their last chat, but that had been some months ago.

'I know we have chatted before Tilly. I know that. Of course. But I mean in detail Tilly. In detail. I have so much I want to tell you, but I have gaps. Bits missing. Bits that are a mystery; that I never knew. Things my parents never gave me an answer about.' Hector was rambling and seemed anxious.

'I like hearing the stories about your childhood Uncle Hector. Tell me again.' She smiled at the old man encouragingly. He was more confused; his conversation jumped from one thing to another, without actually finishing anything.

'It's not just about my childhood though. It's what they did Tilly.'

'Who are 'they' Uncle Hector?' He was agitated, with something serious on his mind that he needed to share.

'I think they sent her away. My sister. I think that is what they did.' He paused.

'You had two sisters, Uncle Hector. And a brother. You have told me that already.' Because of his confusion, Tilly decided it might be best to try and steer him back to the familiar happy memories he had shared with her in the past. She didn't mind hearing it all again. If it made him happy. 'Tell me about your time on the family farm.' Tilly spoke encouragingly and leant forward.

But Hector clearly didn't want to go back over old stories.

'Yes, I do.' He paused. 'I mean, I did. Oh, I don't know. I don't know if it's *did* or *do*. That's the problem Tilly, I just don't know.' Hector looked sad.

'What don't you know?' Tilly's voice was calm, and she reached out to touch Hector's hand, which was resting on the arm of his chair. Did he have tears in his eyes? She thought he had. 'Tell me Uncle Hector. I'm here. I will help you if I can.'

Hector relaxed a little. 'I had two lovely sisters. Temperance and Violet. Older than me. Both beautiful. Violet, well she married Ronald. She died a few years ago now. They moved around quite a lot and ended up living down in Kent. He was a doctor you know. Her husband.' He seemed a bit brighter remembering his sister. 'But Temperance.' There was a long pause. He sighed deeply. 'Oh, lovely Temperance. Such a beautiful girl. I don't know what happened to her. She just went away.' His eyes glazed over. 'Just disappeared.'

'Just disappeared?' said Tilly, repeating Hector. She was quite lost for words. It wasn't the story of his happy times as a boy on the family farm, that she had been expecting. Instead, whatever he had on his mind, was clearly serious, and troubling him. As she struggled to know what to say, he broke into her thoughts.

'This is what I meant, when I said I had something to tell you. You see it wasn't always happy on the farm. Oh, as small children it was nothing but happy. But as we grew older, and the girls grew into young women, then things changed.' Tilly sat in silence, gazing at the old man. He hesitated, and looked out of the patio doors, eyes searching, as if the answer was out there.

'In what way did it change, Uncle Hector?' Tilly gently encouraged.

'Our Violet got married and moved away. Her husband Ronald was a nice man. She did well there. Us boys, Joe and I, we missed her. Once she was settled in her new home, we were allowed to go and stay. We'd go on the bus - the Green Line, and we got off in Barnet High Street and walked down to the factory where she worked. She used to make darts you know. Put the flights on the ends, and then into the box. Violet would meet us when she finished, and we would get another bus home. Or walk. If it was a nice day. A Summers day.' Hector was rambling again, but it was nice for Tilly. She liked to hear him reminiscing. He seemed to be transported back to those early days of his youth. The memories so clear. 'We started to go often. Father would pack us off. Sometimes Mother would go away too, but never Temperance.' He became subdued again, mentioning his sister's name.

'Tell me about Temperance, Uncle Hector.' Tilly knew her request might touch a nerve, but Hector turned to Tilly.

'I can't tell you anything more about Temperance, because she was sent away when I was just 14, and I don't know where. I don't know why. And it has troubled me. I'm sure my parents engineered it. Or my father anyway. Oh, but it's no use raising it now. So many years have passed. I don't suppose she can be found?' He was looking at Tilly, the question hanging in the air. She looked down at her lap for inspiration, then back at him.

'Maybe. It might be difficult. No, it will be difficult, but with the Internet- you know, the World Wide Web, we might be able to find something out.' Tilly was just saying something to give Hector hope. She didn't really know how you traced people who had disappeared 60 years ago.

'Oh, Tilly love, would you try that for me?' Tilly nodded, suddenly overcome with emotion, she swallowed willing the rapidly forming tears, to remain hovering on her lower lashes.

'I will try Uncle Hector.' Tilly didn't know what else she could possibly say. She had to give him hope. 'You will have to give me a little information to get started. I don't know much about our family history. Actually, I don't know anything. But one of my best friends loves all that, so I know she will help me. Can you tell me her birthday, and your parent's names?' Tilly rummaged in her bag for her notebook. She always had several notebooks, or sketch books in her large cotton bag. 'Perhaps where you lived at the time would be useful.' She knew it was 'the farm' but hadn't any more detail than that.

There was a knock at the door, but not waiting for it to be answered Pat appeared with a tray containing the egg mayo sandwiches, coffee and water. The crockery was prettily decorated with pastel flowers, old fashioned and fluted at the edges. The sandwiches sat on a matching bread plate, and Pat placed the whole tray on the coffee table in front of them both.

'Okay my loves, enjoy. If you need anything more, just call.' Pat left them with a wave.

As they ate, Tilly asked Hector again for anything else he might remember that would help in her search. He gave the bare details he could recall, and Tilly keenly noted them in her book whilst balancing the tea plate on the arm of the chair. He only knew things he had been able to get his sister Violet to tell him. He knew it was 1951 when she was sent away, somewhere overseas. He didn't even know where.

Hector ate slowly and seemed to enjoy his tasty lunch. Once finished, she noticed his eyes closing. Time to go, she thought. He seemed to have forgotten about his earlier anxieties, but Tilly decided she would have a go at googling Temperance. How many people called Temperance could there possibly be, she thought.

She gently kissed Hector on the forehead, and as he stirred, impressed on him to stay in his seat. He didn't argue and she let herself out of his apartment. At the desk, Tilly asked Pat to add Tilly's name and number to his contacts. She stressed that, as his great niece, and probably only visitor, it was she who should be contacted, and not her mother, in the event of any news. Pat wrote down the details and said she would see what could be done.

Tilly left Sunny Days, crossed over the road and headed down to the bus stop, feeling quite drained. Glad she had made the effort to visit, but knowing she would be relieved to get back to her cosy floating home for an evening with Marmite in front of the fire. She resolved to call Melody about the google search. It could wait until tomorrow though.

The bus appeared bang on time. Tilly jumped aboard, tapped her phone on the paying machine as she entered, then settled in the corner back seat, put on her headphones, jumped to Spotify and closed her eyes.

8
AT SEA - 1951

After several weeks on board the SS Magnificent, both Temperance and Elsie had got to grips with life on the high seas. They had experienced one particularly bad storm which had confined everyone to their cabins for a whole day. Temperance had found this a distressing experience, and her sea sickness mixed with homesickness had been at its worst. She had tried to sleep throughout the storm. When it had eventually calmed, she was unwilling to venture out. It took some persuasion, but eventually Elsie would no longer take no for an answer and demanded she joined her for dinner on the top deck.

The days slowly became easier for the timid Temperance, and she started to chat to other travellers, and made more acquaintances. More time spent in the social areas meant less time to dwell on what she had left behind. She did, however, keep a very detailed diary of the mundane as well as the quirky parts of the trip. The journal helped her feel connected to reality. Always before bed, she wrote up the day in detail, but also during the day if she had a bit of quiet time, she could be found with pen in hand, never far from her precious notebook. Elsie called her 'Little Miss Cleverclogs' whenever she saw her writing. Temperance didn't mind this, but this particular afternoon, while they were sitting together on the top deck, in the 3rd class tea lounge she challenged her friend on the subject.

'Don't you like to write, Elsie?' Temperance noticed Elsie's usual wide smile drop into an almost worried half frown.

'What do I need to write for?' Challenged Elsie back. Temperance looked at her newfound friend with compassion. It crossed her mind that perhaps Elsie couldn't write.

'But you can write?' Temperance questioned. Elsie paused. Looking for the right words to respond.

'The truth Penny is that my handwriting is poor. I can type. I'm a really good typist - 60 words a minute you know. I know my words and I can read, but I don't find it that easy to write. At school they didn't help me. I wanted to use the wrong hand, you see. They made me use this one.' She held up her right hand. It made sense. Poor Elsie was left-handed, but she had been made to use her right hand at school. No wonder she was put off.

'I can't type; would you be able to teach me? I can then teach you to write. With your left hand, if that is what feels right for you.' The grin on Elsie's face returned, and she nodded enthusiastically.

'I'd like that very much Penny. You have a deal.'

The remainder of the trip had a proper focus from that day onwards. Each day they found time to do a bit of writing and a bit of typing, although they were limited on paper. Elsie had made friends with a young chef, who she seemed quite sweet on. He had somehow found her paper in return for…well, Penny didn't know what, but she had a fair idea. It meant the remainder of their journey to New Zealand, via New York where they had changed boats, was a full and productive one, and both girls gained an extra skill. It bonded them in a way nothing else had. A shared experience which brought them closer, and for Temperance, that little bit nearer to feeling like she could share her secret with her new friend.

The SS Noble, the replacement ship they were moved onto in New York, eventually docked safely in New Zealand's North Island city of Auckland. A journey that had taken them six weeks, to the other side of the world. A new world. Their new life had begun.

9

NORFOLK - 2024

Tilly had pondered on what it would be possible to discover about the mysterious Temperance, and her secretive disappearance. She hoped to find something she could take back to Hector within a short space of time, but only if her friend was willing to help her.

'Hello Melody, it's Tills, are you free to talk?' Tilly had spent her morning on the laptop searching for information about people who had emigrated in the 1950s. That much she had worked out from the slim pickings of information Uncle Hector had shared. She hadn't got very far, although found it interesting and kept getting sidetracked with engaging and sometimes curious snippets and facts. She had to keep dragging herself back to the job in hand. 'I need your help with something I'm doing for Uncle Hector. I need help to trace my family history. Could we meet, do you think?' It was lucky that Melody lived close by, and that Sam or her mum could look after Lois at the drop of a hat. Today, however, neither were necessary as Melody was free.

'Of course Tilly, I am free now if you like. Where would you like to meet – how about the library? It's warm, we can get free coffee, and the librarian Judith is lovely. She knows her stuff and is a whizz on the internet.'

'That sounds perfect Mel, thank you so much for this.' Tilly filled Melody in with a bit more detail on the conversation from the previous day with Hector. She felt a relief that she was no longer on her own. The weight of burden shifted.

Time and venue agreed, Tilly put her laptop into her rucksack and just had time for a tidy up before she left. The library was in a small parade of shops only a mile from her mooring, and a similar distance for Melody. When she got there, Melody was already inside talking to the librarian at the main desk. A tall slim lady in her mid-fifties, with glasses on a cord around her neck, and an unexpectedly hippy style of dress.

'Hiya Tilly, I was just telling Judith about your challenge. We have been discussing passenger lists and Judith knows which websites to search, if you can give her a bit of information to begin with.'

'Hi Mel, hello Judith, thank you for offering to help me with this.' Tilly took her rucksack off her back and placed it onto the nearest table. 'I have my laptop here, and my notebook. Basically, we are looking for a 'Brown'.'

'Oh dear, that makes it a bit more challenging.' Judith smiled. 'But we like a challenge girls, so let's go over to the desk top computer in the small side room. No-one has booked it out today, so you can be on there for as long as you like.' It sounded promising, Judith's enthusiasm for her job evident and infectious.

The girls followed her into the side room, which was not only secure, but more private so easier to chat without upsetting anyone.

'We don't have as much information as you'd find in a full records office, but we have more than you can get from generally trawling the net.' Judith smiled and pulled out a chair. Tilly sat at the computer, with Melody at her side. Judith stood behind while they got logged on, then disappeared briefly.

'You were right Melody, Judith is really helpful - but I suppose that is the nature of the job! And I guess I won't be needing this!' said Tilly pointing to her laptop. 'I also have a notebook, so perhaps I will just make notes to begin with.' Melody nodded, as Judith reappeared with a sheet of paper in her hand.

'Here is a list of useful websites, with our log in details. I would start with this one which holds passenger lists. I know that, because I have used it myself for family history research.'

'Oh brill,' exclaimed Tilly, quite excited to get going now, 'I am feeling positive. I hope I can find some news I can take back to Uncle Hector.'

'I'll leave you two to it then, just give me a shout if you get stuck.' Judith went back to her desk and the girls started their search.

There were lots of people called Brown, and lots of them were women, but none were called Temperance. Most were travelling in family groups. After an hour, Tilly was becoming despondent.

'Come on Tills, you can't give up after just an hour. Searching for family when you are building a proper family tree can take days, months even years of research. Shall we ask Judith if she has any ideas?'

'Well let's look at what we know first. Her name, Temperance Brown, it was 1951 and she was single. We assume she sailed from London on a big ship. That's it. We don't know where to, but we know it was overseas, and she wouldn't have flown.'

'Do you definitely know it was from London then?' questioned Melody.

'He said Violet, that's his other sister, and her husband went with her, but he didn't say any more. I know they lived in Barnet, because my mum's dad also moved to Barnet and that is where mum met dad, which is close to London.' Tilly paused 'so it's an assumption, but we have to start somewhere.' Tilly added with wavering conviction. 'Okay, let's ask Judith for some suggestions.' Tilly had thought she would be able to do this alone, but in the end why pass up the offer of help from an expert? Melody went out to fetch Judith who joined them immediately. They filled her in on the searches they had done, and the fact that, so far, they had drawn a blank.

'Right girls, what we need is to eliminate the ones who we know are definitely not your lady and see who we are left with. I would suggest, if she was escaping something, might she have changed her name, do you think? Or perhaps just called herself something different? Have you thought of that?' Judith sounded positive.

'I hadn't thought of that, no, so you mean she might not show on the list as Temperance Brown at all, and we might have seen her, but not....if you see what I mean?' Tilly laughed, this idea filled her with renewed hope. 'Okay, I am going to start again and narrow it down by writing down all the 'Browns', then all the ladies.' It was going to take a while, but Tilly wasn't needed anywhere else today.

'Perhaps I will leave you to it Tills, I really need to get back for Lois and Judith is here to help you - but let me know what you find, won't you?' Melody got up and put on her jacket. 'Remember. Call me or text.' Tilly didn't look up, but lifted her left hand in acknowledgement, her right hand busily scribbling names onto a clean page of her notebook.

Another hour passed, and the light was starting to fade with pinkish hues seeping in through the library windows. The sure sign of a beautiful sunset, and nice weather to come in the following days. Tilly leant back in the chair and stretched. Her shoulders ached; the result of two hours hunched over the library computer. She sighed and looked down at her list. She had narrowed it down to seven people across four boats. Two boats to New Zealand, one to New York and one to Canada. She started to think dreamily about the adventures of these young Brown women, adventuring off to unknown lands, and felt quite jealous of their bravery.

Coming back to the reality of her search she started to analyse them. Starting with the boats destined for New Zealand, there was Millicent Brown who was a lady's maid, and Joan Brown a seamstress, and perhaps a little older than the demographic she was looking at. She counted both out. The second boat to New Zealand had a Beatrice Joy Brown and an Ethel Brown. They looked like a mother and daughter, and neither name was even remotely like Temperance. She discarded them both too. This left two ladies on the boat to Canada, and one on the boat to New York. She was veering towards the New York boat, so wanted to leave this until last. The ship to Canada had a little bit more information on the list. An address. Only a region, but more than she had found on the earlier lists. The writing was quite small and faint. She zoomed in to expand the writing. It looked like Winifred Brown, Wandsworth. That wasn't her. One left on this list, Mary

Brown, Woking. Another discard, in Tilly's opinion. So that left the boat to New York.

The final image loaded to the screen, and Tilly leant in, to peer closely at the monitor, hopeful it was going to give her the answer she was looking for. Halfway down the page, listed in surname order, the name Brown jumped out - forename Penny. Penny Brown. Tilly's heart sank. She had built up her expectation and was now feeling a sense of disappointment and failure. She scrolled across to the far-right hand side of the page. It was another different lay out to the previous passenger list, and Tilly noticed another column. Family contact. Zooming in she could just make out the name, 'Mrs V Stillman, Barnet'. A brief flutter of excitement ran through her. There was something Uncle Hector had said. She knew there was a Barnet connection. She rummaged through her bag to find the notebook she had taken with her to 'Sunny Days' and hurriedly opened it, to find the notes she had made with him that day. Something that had seemed unimportant at the time, jumped out at her. She had scribbled down 'sister Vi married a doctor, called Ronald Stillman, lived Barnet'. That was it, surely? The 'V' that was Violet, his older sister. Penny Brown, perhaps that could be a pet name for Temperance. Temperance had wanted to disappear, and until now, she had. Tilly was feeling almost tearful with joy. She was pretty sure she had found Hector's missing sister Temperance and would now be able to take Uncle Hector the news. What a great feeling this was, and grinning from ear to ear, she grabbed her phone. She just had to tell someone.

'Melody...you will never guess what?'

10

NORFOLK - 2024

Tilly excitedly relayed the final moments of her discovery to her friend Melody, then put her phone away, gathered up her papers and laptop, and stashed everything hurriedly into her bag. As she reached the desk, Judith looked up and raising her eyebrows, asked how she had got on. Tilly's beaming smile said it all really.

'Oh my goodness Judith, I have just had the most nerve-racking, but also exhilarating time researching those Passenger Lists; who knew such things existed? I really am so grateful to you for setting me on the right path.' Judith was pleased she had helped another happy customer.

'It was my pleasure Tilly. You know where we are now, if you need any further help.'

'Thanks. I will remember that - just in case I go family history mad - but it isn't something in my immediate plans.' Laughing, Tilly picked up the rucksack and left the library with a brief wave.

As she wandered back along the towpath to Georgie, a few ideas were going around in her head. The main one being a return visit to the care home, to deliver her exciting news. But Tilly needed to spend a day on her boat painting, and then the following days would be at the plumbing supplies shop where she worked as a part time administrator.

The family firm 'Water Works Ltd' run by father and son Donald and Paul Hardy, was a popular local company with their offices in the high street. It was a good half hour walk from the canal, so on a nice day that was Tilly's preferred mode of transport, but otherwise she would cycle. It seemed like the visit to Uncle Hector would need to wait a few weeks.

She realised, as she climbed down into her floating home, that she was feeling quite hungry after her mornings research. First job was to get the kettle on, then a sandwich prepared while it boiled. Cream cheese and cucumber, on her favourite seedy brown wholemeal, and a cup of ginger and lemon herbal tea. She took it through to her bed and lounged back on the cushions, flicking on the radio for background noise. Radio 4 being her station of choice. The girls teased her about her old-fashioned ways, saying it was an old person's channel, but Tilly enjoyed the variety and the talking, especially while painting. 'The Archers' were her favourite, and she would listen every day, as well as the omnibus on a Sunday morning. She would laugh about it with the girls - and was convinced that one day she would convert at least one of them!

After lunch, Tilly couldn't immediately muster the energy to move from her cosy spot. Marmite had joined her and was curled up on her feet at the bottom of her bed, and the sun was streaming in, to brighten the space she inhabited. She decided to grab her sketch book and make some preliminary drawings; designs for the latest enamel ware. She had a large collection ready to decorate, and as spring moved into summer and weather improved, she would start to get custom at the boat, so needed to build up her stock. The summer season brought welcome visitors holidaying in the area and that was always good for business. Holiday makers always bought gifts to take home. Expanding her range to include some jewellery, she also made some designs in preparation for a jewellery making session.

'Come on Marmite, we need to get up and do some proper work.' He looked up at her with a cat smile, then yawned and tucked his head back into his body to continue sleeping. Tilly climbed off her bed, knowing she couldn't put off her painting afternoon any longer, however comfortable she felt. 'Okay, just me then,' she said, giving him a quick scratch on the head, then finding her mojo she swept out of the bedroom to start an afternoon of art in the middle of the boat. Her happy place!

11
BARNET - 1952

Violet was in her husband's surgery waiting area, showing a patient to her seat, when the postman knocked. Most days there was a delivery for the surgery of one kind or another, in addition to any personal post. For this reason, they had become quite friendly with their regular postie Jim.

'Hello Jim, nice day today,' as Violet opened the door, the friendly Jim was beaming as he handed a large pile of post to Violet.

'Good day to you Mrs Stillman, isn't it glorious? A perfect spring morning. How are you and the good Dr Stillman today?' Not pausing for breath, or perhaps even expecting an answer, he stood for a moment. 'There's an interesting one in there.' He pointed to the pile now in Violet's hand as she sifted through. 'An airmail.' He paused. 'You know, one of those thin blue letters, folded and stuck together, without an envelope.' He was clearly interested, as he would normally hand over the post and be on his way.

'Ah, ok, well thank you Jim, I'll sort through and look out for that one.' Not wanting to look rude, but keen for privacy, Violet stepped back and started to close the door. 'Good day to you Jim and thank you again.' She closed the door fully and took her post straight to her small kitchen, away from the surgery.

Violet was keen to find this letter Jim had referred to, assuming it was contact from her sister. Since Temperance had set sail some three months previously, she had heard nothing from her, so this would be the first contact. Violet found her hands shaking as she tried to filter through the mail. Unable to think clearly, she pulled out the small pine kitchen chair and sat down with a sigh. 'Come on Violet, pull yourself together,' she whispered under her breath, a harsh admonishment. Then she found it, tucked between two larger white paper envelopes addressed to the surgery. The thin blue paper, with the pre-printed Air Mail stamp on the front, above her own address, and next to a pretty stamp with brightly coloured flowers, and 'New Zealand' 2d in tiny letters. A mixture of relief and fear washed over her. She turned the letter over. Confirmation of the sender evident on the back.

SENDER :Penny Brown, Box 422, Auckland, New Zealand.

She read it over and over. Her little sister, now living on the other side of the world. It seemed impossible, but this was the proof that

Temperance really had travelled all that way on her own and succeeded. Violet realised she would not know that Temperance had succeeded until she had read the letter. She couldn't put it off any longer and took it to her dining room. There she found the ornate letter opener in her writing desk and gently slipped its blade under the lip of the blue paper, where it instructed her to 'cut here'. As she unfolded the letter, she could immediately see it was tightly packed with writing, in her sister's neat and quite elegant script. She walked to the window noticing that Temperance had dated it at the top, Sunday, January 24th, and then she began to read:

Dearest Sister,

I dearly hope this letter finds you well? I think of you and my beloved family daily, so far away in my home country. Yet here I am now in the most beautiful of places, and I am sure you are keen to hear how I have fared since we parted at London Tilbury docks, so many months ago?

To begin with, I must tell you that I made a friend. Elsie is her name. We met on board the SS Magnificent, and our rooms were on the same lower deck as one another, and very close. It was the one thing that got me through the journey, knowing someone else in the same position as me. Perhaps not in exactly the same position - I didn't tell her about you know what - but we are both spinster ladies travelling alone to a new country, with very few possessions. Elsie is a typist, and promised to teach me, as she had brought her portable typewriter with her on the ship. She is very confident and is not afraid to talk to anyone she meets. She is also very pretty, with golden curly hair, cut short. She even wears ladies slacks. Elsie really is quite a rebel, and I like her. She has already started to teach me to type.

We arrived in New York and there was a problem with our boat. But don't worry, they moved those of us heading further afield, to another ship. The SS Noble, which took us first to Australia where most passengers disembarked, and then the rest of us, including Elsie, were brought from Australia to where I am now settling, in New Zealand. Elsie and I have been given a room together in a kind of hostel. It's clean and warm. Well of course, it's summer here in January, and we are enjoying glorious sunshine, while exploring the spectacular countryside.

Violet, you would love the beautiful trees and bushes, like nothing you have in England. So much open space, they call 'The Bush' and we are told not to go off on our own, as we could get lost in the thick forests. The city of Auckland, where we are currently living, has areas where the city is more built up, but is very similar to London. I am meeting a lady on Monday who is going to interview me for a job cleaning the council offices where Elsie is working. Please don't be disappointed that I will be doing such a menial task. I am hoping that when I have learnt how to type properly, I will get a better job. Possibly with Elsie in the typing pool.

That brings me on to money, and I really do hate to ask, but please Violet, could you see your way to sending me out some money? I think father owes me that at least, and I thought you would be able to find your way to get something from him. I wouldn't ask if I wasn't desperate, but I really have nothing left. My money was all but spent on the journey, and now I must pay rent as well as buy food and clothes.

I know you will do your best for me, dearest. Please don't leave it too long before responding.

Your loving sister, Penny.

p.s. I am calling myself Penny Brown, and only use Temperance on the official papers, where I need my passport for verification.

Phew. Violet felt quite exhausted reading the tightly packed writing. She read it through a second time, and then a third before folding it up and tucking it into her apron pocket. She had lots to think about and digest. Deciding she needed to discuss it with Ronald, the only thing she could do was get on with her day. Her thoughts were broken by the loud ringing of the surgery telephone. Yes, it was definitely time to get on with her day.

12

NORFOLK - 2024

It turned out to be a beautiful spring and Tilly had managed to get stuck into her art. With a forthcoming exhibition inked into her diary, she was working hard on developing a saleable portfolio. Her theme for the exhibition was 'Canalside' and in addition to her paintings, she had also produced some proper old fashioned Canal Art. Trawling antique fairs and junk yards, she had managed to acquire plenty of enamel jugs, vases, pots and plates, to decorate in her own unique style. Her actual painting ranged in size, price and subject matter. She was particularly pleased with a series of small square frames featuring spring flowers. She hoped they would sell as a set of four, with daffodil, crocus, grape hyacinth, and her favourite; the snowdrop.

Work at the plumbers had also been busy and Tilly had even managed to do a bit of overtime. The end of the tax year had meant lots of paperwork. As a family business, the father and son team didn't need any extra plumbers, but young Paul was clearly quite fond of Tilly and would hang around the office on the days she was at work. Sadly, Tilly didn't feel the same. Paul wasn't really her type. In addition, he was a youthful twenty-one. Too young for Tilly, she preferred a more mature boyfriend. She was always polite, but just lately he had invited her out twice, and she had turned him down both times, giving an excuse that she was busy. She knew that soon she would have to tell him she wasn't interested.

Tilly wanted some downtime, after a busy two weeks of almost non-stop work. Then Kit had messaged her and Melody late that night to say she would be visiting the next day. She had some business locally and asked if they had time to catch up. Of course, Tilly wasn't going to turn down an opportunity to meet up with her best friends and had sent her response. Melody was a little later in responding. After a bit of back and forth it was agreed they would meet at 11 at An Extra Slice.

A naturally early riser, it meant Tilly had a few hours to herself before their rendez-vous. One thing she had been meaning to do was sort out two or three small watercolours to take to the café. Brenda had been in touch to say she had sold two in the past week. This was an ideal time to replenish the stock. In addition to her 'Canalside' portfolio for the upcoming exhibition, she also kept simple watercolours that she could sell cheaply. She enjoyed still life, and these sold well. She put two into her bag to take with her later.

The girls arrived together and sat down at their usual table. Tilly handed Brenda the two watercolours. The café wasn't very busy, meaning Brenda had time to put them straight up on the wall in the gaps left by the sold paintings. She then brought the girls a full lunch menu each. It had been a slow morning, so Brenda was hopeful for extra sales.

'Thanks Bren.' Kit took the menus. 'My treat this morning ladies, I'm celebrating a new job.' The girls congratulated Kit keen to know more about the new role. 'It's a promotion to Head Buyer within my current employer. I am going to be travelling a bit further afield, with a regular trip to New York.'

'Oh well done Kitty Kat, you are so clever.' Tilly was genuinely pleased for her friend, knowing it had been her childhood dream to reach this position.

'I can't imagine all that flying Kat, is it tiring?' said Melody interested, but glad it wasn't her who was the actual highflyer.

'Not as tiring as looking after a baby, Mel. You could do it; you just need more confidence in yourself.' That was certainly something Kit had in buckets full. 'Come on ladies, have whatever you like - I think we can call this brunch, don't you?' The girls smiled and huddled round the menu. Brenda did wander over to see if they were ready, but Tilly waved her away, saying 5 more minutes please.

They eventually decided on a bacon and egg bap, blueberry compote pancake stack and smashed avocado on toast with poached egg and halloumi. Kit wanted a croissant to go with her bacon and egg bap, so they ended up ordering one each, plus coffees all round. Brenda was pleased with the extra custom but happy to look after her regulars and treated them all to a small piece of homemade short bread straight out of the oven. Proper melt in the mouth stuff, Kit asked Brenda to put some aside for her to take with her.

'Why are you down this way again so soon?' Tilly was curious about the new job, and why that should mean an extra trip 'back home' for Kit.

'Well, I mentioned New York, and I was telling the truth when I said I will have regular trips there.' Kit clearly had more news.

'And?' questioned Melody 'what else aren't you telling us?'

'And....well, I am going to be going straight out at the weekend just to set everything up. I will be doing my training from the New York office.' Waiting for a reaction, Kit smiled at her friends. 'Then I am coming back a week later to properly sort out leaving my flat and car, and, well anything you have to sort out if you are going to live in another country for....well, at least four months, possibly six.'

'SIX MONTHS!' exclaimed Melody and Tilly in unison.

'Yeah, I know. I was surprised too. But it is an opportunity I can't turn down, so I am here to see my dad and sister and my gran to put them all in the picture, before I go. And you two of course.' Kit looked a bit hesitant. It was a big step, even for this confident young woman.

'Come here and give us a hug.' Melody leant over and grabbed her friend for a friendly squeeze. 'We understand. We will miss you, that's all, won't we Tills?'

'Oh loads, Kit we are gonna miss you so much…I mean…who is going to pay for the coffees?' They all laughed, each with their own thoughts about how their cosy dynamic was about to change.

The girls continued to chat, ordered a refill for their coffees, and Tilly told Kit about the search in the library computer system for Uncle Hector's missing sister. 'I now need to go back to the care home to pass on my findings to Uncle Hector. I think I will go in a few days, after I have had a day to myself. It has been non-stop work.' Tilly's idea of non-stop work was not quite the same as Kit's, but Kit kept quiet. Tilly worked to live, whereas Kit, the workaholic career girl, tended to be the opposite.

Soon enough it was time for Melody to go and collect Lois. An Extra Slice was starting to fill up with lunch time guests, so the girls took their leave and parted outside the door, with hugs all round. Then extra hugs for Kit.

'Remember to text,' said Melody 'plus we can facetime you when we are in the café.'

'I will. But remember there is a time difference and bear in mind I will be working. Don't just call me without checking. I might be in some important meeting…' Kit was teasing, although semi-serious. She didn't really know what to expect, but she was excited. 'Anyway, I am only going for a week to begin with. I will call when I get back and we can have a proper 'au revoir' dinner for me.' The girls laughed, and hugged again, then went their separate ways.

Tilly took the scenic route along the tow path back to her boat. As she walked, she got out her mobile and dialled.

'Hello there, is that 'Sunny Days'?

13

NORFOLK - 2024

After a week of painting, walking and enjoying proper 'me' time, Tilly woke with just one thing in mind for the day. Her visit to Uncle Hector at Sunny Days, to share the news that she had found details of his missing sister Temperance. It had been more than three weeks since her previous visit. Tilly was feeling excited to see Hector, and to be able to tell him about her research, in addition to hearing more of his stories. She was up early, with a plan to catch the 10.33am bus. Notebook and pen safely stored in her rucksack she left at quarter past, leaving Marmite sunning himself on the roof of the boat.

The bus was late. A little annoying, as Tilly had told the care home to expect her at 11. It turned up at 10.45 and she took the front seat. A practically empty bus, with a driver who had no interest in apologising, or explaining his delay. Tilly decided it wasn't worth making a fuss and plugged herself into Spotify to pass the time.

On arrival, a different lady, whose name badge said 'Jane' in large pink lettering, was on reception. Tilly introduced herself and was told Hector was in the day room with the other residents. Taken in a different direction, away from the bedroom apartments, Tilly followed Jane down the oak panelled corridor to a pair of glazed double doors. She was shown through to the shared lounge area, where Hector was sitting in the corner, next to the window, where he had a perfect view of the busy bird feeder.

The room was bright and airy, with large patio doors that opened out onto a secluded seating area, paved in colourful slabs and adorned with ornate metal garden benches. A perfect sun trap in the summer, Tilly thought. There were 8 residents in the large room. Seated on traditional wing backed armchairs with a cosy wood burner filling the room with warmth. A large bookcase, full of books, stood by the doors. How nice the residents had something so homely to share. It looked like some of the books were large print. They really had thought it through in this establishment.

A group of three residents were comfortably dozing on the far side of the room. There was a large television on one side, but it wasn't on. Classical music - she would guess Radio Three - was playing quietly.

'Mr Brown, you have a visitor,' Hector turned to Jane and smiled, but looked a little vacant. 'It is your….er, Tilly?'

'Great niece,' chipped in Tilly, 'He is my great uncle.' Tilly smiled to Jane as if to say, 'you can go know'. Jane took the hint.

'Your great niece Tilly is here to see you, Hector.' Turning to Tilly she said, 'I'll be at the reception if you need me.' Tilly thanked her, and she left the day room.

'Hello Uncle Hector. It's Tilly.' She paused as Hector studied her face, as if he was trying hard to recognise her. He seemed to have deteriorated since the last visit, but perhaps he was just tired, Tilly thought. Then almost like a switch had been pressed, his face lit up with recognition, and he put up his arms for an embrace.

'My darling Tilly, hello. How wonderful of you to visit me.' He wheezed, then coughed fumbling in his pocket for a handkerchief. He motioned to the seat next to him with the other hand. Tilly handed him the glass of water that was on the table in front of him, and he took it gratefully. Eventually composing himself, he sat back in the big armchair with a sigh. 'What brings you here, young lady?' Tilly felt a little uncomfortable. She wasn't sure he remembered her last visit so needed to broach the subject, thinking that might jog his memory.

'I came about three weeks ago, do you remember?' She paused, but there was nothing coming from the old man. 'Oh, that doesn't matter, if I tell you about our special chat, it might come back to you.' She nodded, hopefully, willing him to do the same.

'I'll try love. It is lovely to have a visitor. You try and remind me.'

'Well Uncle Hector, you told me about your missing sister. Temperance. You asked if I could try and find anything out about what had happened to her.' She looked at him in earnest.

'Ah yes...I think I do remember that conversation, young Tilly. Yes. Oh yes, I have had my sister Temperance on my mind for some time now.' It was like watching an awakening; a flower slowly opening, or a sleeping cat uncurl itself. He was remembering, and Tilly was flooded with relief. 'So. Have you found her? Have you found my Temperance?' Hector's rheumy eyes looked expectantly to Tilly, as if she was going to produce his sister like something from 'This is your Life'.

She started to explain the journey she had been on, to get to this point.

'I went to the library, where a very nice lady helped me look some things up on the internet.' She paused, but Hector was nodding. He probably didn't know what the internet was, but she kept going. 'It was fascinating Uncle Hector; all the historical records are stored on computers now. You can practically look up anything you like.' Hector was more alert by this point. 'The good news is, I found that Temperance went on a ship called the

SS Magnificent, from Tilbury Docks, in 1951.' Hector leant forward in his chair.

'Oh well done Tilly. That would be the right time. Our Violet was married and had already moved with her husband Doctor Stillman, to Barnet. ' He seemed to be far less vague as the distant memories of his youth returned. 'I wonder if she knew?' He appeared a little more subdued as his thoughts took him to his other sister, and to his distant past.

'Well, I can tell you that too. She *did* know, because I think she was there. Anyway, if she wasn't there, she knew about it because she was named as next-of-kin. Do you want me to tell you where the ship was destined?' Hector was keen, so she decided to push on. 'The ship was bound for New York, Uncle Hector. Can you believe that? The other side of the Atlantic Ocean.'

'New York? Well, I'll be blowed,' said Hector. Then proceeded to cough again, waving to his glass. Tilly gave it to him, then sat forward as he drank and cleared his throat. 'New York you say? I don't think I was expecting you to say New York, young Tilly. Australia, or New Zealand maybe, but not New York. But I visited New York. On more than one occasion when I was in the art business. I used to accompany fine pieces of art around the world, to hand deliver to the new owners. To think…I could have seen her, had I only known.' The talking brought on another wheezy coughing fit, which was worse than the previous one. Tilly looked around for help, as Hector eventually controlled the cough, but his breathing continued to sound wheezy and laboured.

Tilly glanced at the other residents in the room. All much as she imagined residents of a care home would look. Elderly, helpless and weak. Not at all like the picture conjured up by Richard Osman's books, which she particularly enjoyed. No-one at Sunny Days looked remotely 'with it' enough to be able to solve a murder. Perhaps she wasn't being fair. The two ladies at the back of the room, chatting whilst engrossed in their individual knitting projects, were most definitely on the ball. Her attention came back to Hector. He didn't seem well enough to do a lot of talking, so she sat looking out at the birds. His eyes started to close, just as a lady with the tea trolley arrived.

'Tea, ladies and gents? Who needs a little caffeine to give them some oomph this bright spring morning? Lunch will follow shortly, but I can only drive one trolley at a time.' She laughed at her own joke, and the knitting ladies chuckled along with her. Hector's eyes opened and Tilly smiled to 'Paula' another large pink badge giving away her name.

'Yes please, we would both like tea.' Paula served the two ladies, then came to Tilly and Hector next.

'What's all this then young Hector, entertaining young ladies today in the lounge. You be careful the other residents don't get jealous.' Paula laughed again, as she teased Hector.

'This is my niece Tilly. To be absolutely correct, she is my great niece. She's my only visitor. Isn't she lovely?' Hector was proud, and Tilly felt a guilt for visiting so infrequently. Realising how much it meant to him; she mentally resolved to try and visit more often.

'I love to hear Uncle Hector's stories of the old days and the family,' said Tilly, taking Hector's and then her own tea from Paula, and putting them onto the table. 'My own grandad died before I was born, so Uncle Hector is like a grandad to me, aren't you Uncle Hector?' Paula put a friendly hand on Hector's shoulder, winking at Tilly.

'You've got a good'n there, young man, definitely got good genes.' She stepped back to her trolley. 'Now I can't stand here chatting to you two all day, but I'll be back soon with lunch.'

Continuing her rounds, Paula gently woke the other residents in turn to administer the regulation morning tea or coffee. Tilly looked round the room again, wondering if any of them had become friends, not liking the thought that Hector might be lonely.

'Uncle Hector, there are lots of other people here with you at Sunny Days aren't there? Do you enjoy each other's company?' She was struggling to think of the appropriate way to ask him, what he actually did every day. She knew from previous visits that there were clubs. Chess and Bridge were two she knew about, but she also knew they did not interest Hector.

'Oh yes Tilly, I get on well with George. He did his National Service in Egypt, the same as me. He worked on the payroll, because in civilian life, he had worked in a bank. Then after his National Service he went back to the bank, rising to Bank Manager. He married, but his wife died young, and they didn't have children, so he remained on his own. Much like me...' He stopped and seemed to be thinking.

'Tell me about your National Service Uncle Hector. I am interested. You didn't marry though, like George?' Tilly had never felt able to ask Hector why he hadn't married but now seemed an appropriate time.

'Oh young Tilly, things were different in those days. I did have a sweetheart. We met at school. Her name was Joan.' He smiled remembering the distant past. 'But she didn't wait for me, and while I was in Egypt, she found herself another fella, and that was that.' Matter of factly he seemed to end the subject.

'You never found another love?' Tilly pushed a bit, to see if he could be encouraged, but he stayed firm.

'You see, there were other things going on. Our Temperance had gone, our Violet was married, and Mother wasn't well. I had lots of other things to think about at home. So you see, there was never another opportunity for me. My National Service was an escape for me. From the goings on at home, and some independence for me too. I was only 18, you know.'

'Okay, can you tell me about your National Service? That sounds exciting for a young man, travelling out to Egypt.'

'Yes, it was exciting. It was going to be my first time abroad. We had to do training in this country first of course, with leave to visit home. I had to attend an interview in London. It was in a square off Southampton Row, near the British Museum. Do you know it?' Tilly didn't but nodded, and Hector continued. 'Then we had a medical before we got the call up proper.' Tilly could see Hector was enjoying the memories of those far off days. His eyes sparkling with the recollection. 'They asked me what regiment I wanted to be in, but I hadn't a bloody clue. I had heard of the Royal Engineers, so I said that, because I didn't know any better. So that is where I ended up.'

'After your interview, what happened then? Is that when you went to Egypt.' Tilly was following Hector's explanation with interest. He was so deep in his memory that it was like he was talking about something in the present.

'On the 7th March 1957 I went by train to Farnborough, the Royal Engineers Training Base in Hampshire, with just a small suitcase. It was a Thursday I recall.' Tilly smiled at the detail he was able to recall. 'We were given a uniform, and our hair was cut short, if it wasn't already short, that is. There were twenty or so in each barrack, and we had a bed and a locker each. We were there for basic training, but I didn't do that.'

'Oh, what did you do then?' Tilly was intrigued.

'Well, they gave me an aptitude test, and from that I, plus three or four others, were pulled out because we were bright.' Hector's face lit up animatedly as he retold the story. 'I was selected to go to Chatham for the Royal Engineers Deputy Military Mechanics, for three months. Regulars took 18 months to do the course. We had to do it in just three months. Basically, we were back at school. Maths first then an exam and they weeded out those that failed. Then we worked on designing power stations, then in a factory. After each bit, we did an exam. But I failed at the end, I failed the last exam. I didn't revise enough because I kept going home at weekends.' Hector's face dopped as the memory replayed. 'Well, the truth is I didn't go home. I used to go and stay with Violet and Ronald. Sometimes, I would go home to see Joan - the girl I was sweet on, or my old friends. We used to go to the speedway. I hitch hiked. Sometimes I didn't have a pass to get out of the Chatham area so I went to the local speedway and back in the same night. I was interested in motorbikes. I had to dodge the 'redcaps' when I came back. Everyone was in uniform – army redcaps were military police, and they patrolled the railway stations, checked you were smart and if you were pulled up they'd ask to see your pass. Bob my best mate did his National Service in the Air Force in Yorkshire. When he was home, we arranged to meet at Haringey speedway. If I had weekend leave, Friday evening to Sunday evening, 48 hours, or Saturday lunchtime to Sunday evening, 36 hours, then I went home to Violet's or to see Mother and Father in Norfolk. If I didn't have a pass, I skipped off.'

'Did you get in trouble if you skipped off, Uncle Hector?' He laughed.

'I never got caught, Tilly. I was a wily young thing. Ducked and dodged those redcaps and always got back into the barrack without being spotted.' Hector chuckled.

'So when did you go to Egypt then, Uncle Hector?' Tilly wasn't bored, but she had assumed it was just all about Egypt. Clearly there was so much more to National Service than just going abroad.

'They knew I wanted to get out of the country. I had made no secret of the fact. When a call came through one day, to my senior officer, with news that someone had dropped out of the next Egypt contingent, and they needed to fill the space, he nominated me.' Hector remembered like it was yesterday. The delight on his face as he recalled that moment, said it all. 'I was so happy. At last, I was going to be seeing something of the world. That had always been my ambition - not a specific job, but just something that would allow me that opportunity. So of course, I said yes when asked, and they immediately gave me a one week pass to go home and say my farewell to the folks.' Hector paused and took a sip of his tea.

'Can you remember any more?' Tilly's question, innocent enough. But Hector was quick in reply.

'Of course. I remember it all Tilly, it was truly the best experience of my life. After National Service, there was no going back. Knowing my sister had gone away, assuming abroad, but not knowing why, it hadn't felt comfortable at home. I didn't take the full week I had been allocated. I was so keen to go, I was back and ready in plenty of time. Together with the other lads. You know.' He said nodding. 'A ship took us to Malta first, and then on through the Suez Canal, to Egypt. That was our destination. Then two happy years.' He looked vacant again, steeped in his memories.

'What did you do in Egypt, Uncle Hector?' Tilly managed to bring him back to the now.

'Oh, well I worked in the stores. Stock keeping, and all that. I learnt a few phrases, and some songs in Arabic. I also started to smoke cigarettes. Of course, we didn't know they were no good for you back then, and we all smoked because they were free. Part of our monthly rations. Once you start, you see, it's hard to stop. Don't you go taking up that nasty habit Tilly. Now I have this blessed wheeze and cough.' Tilly shook her head. On cue, Hector started to cough.

'It's ok Uncle Hector; I have no plans to start smoking. Go on...' Composed, he was about to continue, when Paula returned with the lunch trolley. Making a noisy entrance - Tilly presumed this was so that those harder of hearing roused themselves. 'Uncle Hector, I think your lunch is here now, and probably time I left you. You will be needing a nap after all this chatter.' Tilly teased.

'You're not wrong there, young lady. I am feeling quite tired. But it has been so lovely to have you with me this morning. You will visit again soon?' He questioned.

'I will, Uncle Hector, don't you worry. I definitely will!' Tilly got up when Paula approached.

'You don't need to go love, we can rustle up something for you, if you like?' Tilly shook her head.

'He is quite tired actually, so I think I have worn him out with talking about the old days.' Paula nodded and moved out of her way. Tilly gave Hector a kiss and assured him again that she would be back soon. She left the lounge giving a little smile and wave to the knitters, who lifted their needles in acknowledgement.

Tilly left by the main doors, out into the unseasonably warm April afternoon. Feeling pleased with herself and satisfied that a good deed had been done that day, she skipped along to the bus stop and jumped straight on a waiting bus.

14

AUCKLAND - 1952

Temperance returned home to the small room she was renting in the high-rise apartment block in Auckland. She had done a late shift cleaning in the council offices, followed by a two hour evening class, and was feeling exhausted. The caretaker Bert was at the door as she arrived, and pushed it open for her, tipping his hat.

'Good evening, Miss Penny,' his usual greeting, whatever the time of day.

'Good evening to you Bert and thank you.' Temperance went through to the lift and pressed the call button, unbuttoned her jacket, and dropped her bag to the floor. The lift arrived in a matter of minutes, and the doors opened. A gentleman Temperance hadn't seen before stepped out, glancing at her from under the rim of his broad hat, he smiled widely, winked and lifted his hat in acknowledgement.

'Miss' was all he said, as he briskly brushed past her. Temperance couldn't help herself take a backwards glance, just as he did the same. Flushed, she hurried into the lift and pressed the button for floor six.

As she opened her door, she saw a bulky brown envelope partly protruding from the letterbox. Excited to see what this first bit of post was, she quickly closed the door behind her, grabbed the letter, and clutching it tightly went through to the small living space she shared with Elsie. The letter was definitely hers - clearly addressed to Miss T Brown. Without removing her coat, she sat down on the armchair and studied the item. Post marked United Kingdom, with her sister's address on the back, she wasted no time in tearing open the end.

Inside the envelope was a further envelope which she put to one side, and a letter written on airmail paper. She began to read.

Dearest Temperance,
It was a big relief for us to receive your letter. Ronald and I are glad to hear you have found somewhere to stay and have made a friend in Elsie. We make no judgement on the work you will be doing and are pleased to hear you have a plan to better yourself.

It is interesting to hear about the natural beauty of your chosen country. It does sound very much like I would enjoy the flora and fauna surrounding you, but it is unlikely I will ever see that beauty for myself, and so I welcome your detailed descriptions when you write to me dear. You sounded happy in your last letter and for that I am grateful. I hope it means that in time you can forget about what happened and dismiss the trauma that you felt at the time. I still feel a guilt that you couldn't stay with me, dear. That might have worked in time, but I understand your need to get as far away as possible.

Over the question of money, this has put me in a difficult position my dear. You know I gave you everything I could spare, and Ronald was good in supporting this. It has created a conundrum for me with Father, but in the end, I did approach him. He was able to give ten pounds, and this I have enclosed in one-pound notes, enclosed in a separate envelope. I hope you have the means to get this changed into New Zealand dollars, and request that you do not ask again for money. It is not appropriate, and I am unable to provide any more from my own purse.

Please do spend it wisely and keep me updated with your work situation. Perhaps put a little aside to buy stamps and letter writing materials.

I am sure you will obtain something with a little more ambition as soon as you are able.

I will finish now to catch the post.
Fondest love,
Your sister Violet.

Violet had sent her the money she had pleaded for. It was something. As she folded the letter, Elsie waltzed in through the front door, full of smiles and Elsie type joy.

'Hello love, oooh, what have you got there?' Not one to miss anything, Elsie spotted the letter as Temperance tried to tuck it away into her pocket.

'It's just a letter from my sister. Just a letter that's all.' Temperance felt a sudden need to keep knowledge of the money a secret from her newfound friend. Not that she had any reason not to trust Elsie, but they were yet to learn very much about each other. That would come in time, Temperance was sure of it, but since arriving in New Zealand there had been very little time to do anything but work, eat and sleep. Elsie went out at weekends, but Temperance had so far avoided the extra expense that came with socialising. Elsie made quite a bit more money in her job than Temperance did, but she was hopeful that the next secretarial job would be hers if she kept up with the evening classes and continued to make good progress. The class teacher said she was a natural and was currently up to 40 words per minute. She expected her to be on 60 words per minute by the end of the term, and that would be enough to secure her a position in the council secretarial pool.

The girls had a small kitchen, and generally shared the duties, but Temperance was by far the better cook. A traditional meat, potatoes and two veg meal was rustled up most days, and the girls ate at a small breakfast bar in the kitchen. This doubled up as a dining space, with a view straight into their small lounge area, which was sparsely furnished. The room contained a two-person sofa, plus a small hard chair, coffee table and standard lamp. They had a wireless, but didn't want to use up too much electricity, so saved it until the evenings. Temperance had crochet hooks and wool and was slowly making granny squares to sew together as a blanket. She had brought her hooks with her and a little wool, and Elsie had managed to obtain more wool for her from some of her work colleagues. Some evenings when they were at home together, Temperance tried to teach Elsie how to crochet, but Elsie didn't have much patience, and chose to read or do her nails, especially if she had splashed out on a bottle of nail varnish, which she sometimes did on payday.

It was nice to have made a friend, Temperance thought. But it wasn't like having her sister, and getting the letter from Violet today, had reminded her of home. Sighing, she took her envelope into her bedroom and tucked it into the inside pocket of her travel case. She wasn't ready to share her secrets with Elsie. Not yet anyway.

15

NORFOLK - 2024

'Mum? It's Tilly.' She didn't know why she introduced herself by name. Clearly her mum would know that, but it was her automatic response. It gave her some thinking time. She was always apprehensive when contacting her mum as there hadn't been regular contact since Celia's marriage to her stepfather David.

Tilly had chosen to give her mum a call. Their relationship had always been a little frosty, but after her most recent visit to Uncle Hector, she felt she needed to talk to her mum. Hector was Celia's uncle after all. Celia showed little affection for her uncle but everyone was different, and that was borne out by their own less than loving relationship.

'I thought I'd come over, I have been to see Uncle Hector again and you might be interested in hearing a bit about my visit?' There was a pause, then her mum replied.

'Yes Tilly love, of course. When were you thinking? Perhaps it would be best to come when Dave is away?' David worked away occasionally and Tilly was very happy to visit when he wasn't going to be there. Theirs was not a comfortable relationship either.

'I am free today actually mum. If David is at work, I could come over now. I'll bring some lunch.' Not wanting to give her mum an excuse to say no, she rounded off the conversation, pushing her mum into a corner, where she couldn't say no.

It was a dry day, so Tilly decided to cycle to her mums. Panniers loaded up with a flask of home-made leek and potato soup, and half a loaf of bread made the previous day, she set off along the canal path. Her mum and David lived in a modern house on a large new estate. Tilly once had a small bedroom in their previous home, but now the rooms in their four bedroomed luxurious modern abode were all very much accounted for. A lovely bedroom for her mum and David, a sewing room for her mum, where she also did the ironing, an office for David, and the last bedroom a 'guest' bedroom. She wasn't aware they had friends to stay, but at least there was a space for her in an emergency. That is how Tilly saw it anyway.

A thirty five minute cycle ride, and she pulled up on the drive, locking her bike in the side alley. It seemed like a nice enough area, but she didn't want to risk losing her only means of transport. Her mum had seen her and opened the door before Tilly had a chance to knock. Her mum was smiling, unusually.

'Hello Tilly.' She leant forward for an air kiss. Tilly tried to embrace her mum, feeling a bit of warmth in her welcome. But as always, it was as pleasant as hugging an ironing board, and she pulled back quickly, embarrassed, but determined to stay positive. 'Come through to the conservatory - it's new. Did I tell you?' Tilly's mum, Celia, had never had very much in material things, but they had been happy when Trevor, her dad was alive. Once David came along, he was able to provide Celia with whatever she wanted, so Tilly was pleased for her mum, that she now had a nicer standard of living. Well, nicer from Celia's point of view. Tilly wouldn't swap her Georgie for a fancy conservatory any day!

'I have some fresh bread and home-made soup mum. I'll just pop it in the kitchen.' She took her pannier and emptied the contents, noticing the kitchen also looked different. 'A new kitchen too mum? I thought the other one was smart - and not that old?'

Tilly followed her mum into the conservatory and sat down on the new wicker sofa.

'It wasn't to Dave's liking - you know, the wooden effect kitchen. He wanted white gloss. He does like to cook, and I didn't mind.' Her mum seemed to be trying to justify the unnecessary expense, knowing what Tilly would be thinking about it.

'It's nice mum. I'm glad you have nice things. The conservatory is nice too.' There was a pause. Sitting adjacent to her mother, meant no eye contact. Tilly didn't prefer this way of talking, but she knew her mum would be more comfortable. 'So, I've been to see Uncle Hector again. I thought you might be interested.'

'Oh yes?' Celia tried to sound interested. 'How is he?'

'I think he is genuinely quite poorly mum. That is the real reason I wanted to come and see you. It's very comfortable in his care home and the staff are lovely. So friendly. But he has a horrible cough. Sometimes it's uncontrollable. It was certainly worse the second time I visited.'

'You've been back?' Tilly's mum sounded surprised.

'Yes mum, after my initial visit, I told him I would do a bit of research on the whereabouts of his sister Temperance. He seemed quite distressed at the time. He also seemed quite forgetful. Not about the distant past, but definitely about the present. I don't think he recognised me when I went the second time, and he didn't remember our chat about Temperance.'

Tilly poured out the story of her research at the library with Melody. It was nice to be able to share it with someone who was family. Her mum showed some interest when she got to the passenger list details, which was encouraging for Tilly, and she continued.

'New York?' questioned her mum. 'I don't think that is correct Tilly. I am sure my dad had been sent letters from New Zealand. Perhaps you should research a bit further.' Tilly was a bit taken aback but welcomed her mum's interest.

'Oh really mum? What else do you know about the family?' Tilly saw an opportunity to get her mum talking.

'There are a few bits.' Her mum's face lit up as she recalled. 'I have a place I call my 'Special Things' box where I keep, well, old special things. Shall we look at it over lunch?' Tilly smiled and agreed that would be nice. Her mum hadn't really taken on board her concerns for Hector's health, but this was a start.

They prepared the soup together, then Celia brought her box to the table. Some very old memories were safely preserved within the small, old fashioned, lady's vanity case. It was white, or rather, had once been white but was now quite yellowed with age. Inside, it was lined with red nylon and sported a small mirror on the inside of the lid. It was rammed with papers, envelopes and at the side, small objects had been tucked down into every small gap. Her mum proceeded to take things out - holding them momentarily as she remembered. A time, or a place perhaps. She was clearly transported. Not unlike her Uncle Hector's reminiscing. A small pair of white, silky, baby booties. Tilly's first 'shoes' according to her mum.

'This box will be yours one day Tilly. Lots of history in these letters. Your school reports, some letters from your dad when we were courting. Of course, we never married, but that didn't mean we didn't love each other, we just didn't feel the need.' Tilly had never heard her mum speak in this way about herself, or her dad. It brought a lump to her throat.

'Tell me more about where things came from mum. I'm really interested in the family history now I have done that little bit of research.' Her mum rummaged down to the bottom of the case and pulled out an old paper bag. Wrinkled, and torn at the edges, but quite thick brown paper with 'Spicer and Son Men's Outfitters' printed diagonally across it, it bulging with equally vintage envelopes, presumably containing letters. Tilly leaned forwards, keen to get her hands on the envelopes, but resisting until offered.

'Ah, here they are. Letters passed to my dad when his parents passed on. My dad died young, as you know, but I kept the letters. I was interested. I did look through them a long time ago, that is why I remember New Zealand. I liked that old stuff like you do. Here, look at this one, see?' Celia held up a thin blue airmail envelope with a very pretty stamp on the front, very definitely from 'New Zealand. 'I think they are all the same Tilly. Some ornate stamps.' Tilly took the envelope and turned it over. The sender's address was faintly written, but she could make out 'P Brown, Christchurch,

NZ' in small, neat handwriting. She started to open the envelope, when her mum quickly took the letter back.

'No, Tilly. No reading. You can do that when they come to you. Not before.'

Tilly slumped back into her chair. A little frustrated. Just when she had felt a thaw creeping into their relationship, she was brought back to reality with a thump. Celia hurriedly gathered the bits back together and piled them back into the box.

'So you see, New Zealand - that was what you wanted to know wasn't it? Not New York.' Celia closed the case and locked it. 'Actually, I think Dave might be home shortly. You know, in case you don't want to bump into him.' Returning to her daughter, Tilly got the message and got up to collect her flask.

'Yes mum,' she said matter of factly. 'Okay, well that was useful, but I'll go now. Like you say, don't want to upset anything. Remember what I said about Uncle Hector though. You might want to visit him. I, for one, will be going back more often now.'

There was no response to this from Celia, and Tilly left without an ironing board hug. As she cycled home, she went over the course of events in her head. Glad she had made a bit of progress with her mum, but she knew her mum wouldn't change now. Not now she was married to David. He was the one in charge there, and there was nothing Tilly could do to change that. A fast pedal took her back home. Back to Georgie and Marmite. Back to her happy place.

16

NORFOLK - 2024

As her only daughter cycled away, without a backwards glance, Celia leant back against the closed front door and sighed. Momentarily, feelings of regret surfaced. Feelings she could not deny but was generally able to suppress. Her time with Tilly today had been enjoyable yet tinged with sadness at their disconnection.

Going through the 'Special Things' box, had brought back very happy memories of her past. Memories so distant now, it felt like another time. As if those things had happened to someone else, not her, Celia. Overwhelmed by emotion, she had closed the box and in doing so also shut out memories of the happy times. The fear of opening old wounds and letting sadness back in was too great. She wasn't ready for that, and something had taken over. It was done.

She took herself back to the conservatory and sat down. The vanity case was still on the table. She stared at it. What harm would it do to take another step back into her past, to live some of that happiness once more? Edging forward, Celia carefully unlocked, then lifted the lid letting it fall open once more. Pausing, thoughts spiralling, but not quite out of control, she again stared. This time at the contents. The mounds of papers, bulging envelopes, trinkets, and various other ephemera which all screamed 'memories' to Celia.

Celia's family were country folk, and things had been happy until her father died suddenly of a hereditary but undiagnosed heart condition, when she was very young. She had no memories of him at all, but her mother was left bereaved and with two tiny children, Celia aged three and baby sister Gilly moved in with her parents to their three bedroomed bungalow. There, Celia and her sister shared a small bedroom, and money for the multi-generational family was tight.

Celia had been just fifteen when she met Trevor Montgomery at the local youth club. He was seventeen and already working at the docks. Celia was at secretarial college, learning shorthand and typing. It was what most girls did back then. It was approaching the end of the course, when, over the long, hot summer, Celia and Trevor fell head over heels in love.

Celia, much to the dismay of her mother and grandparents, moved out to 'live in sin' with Trevor Montgomery in a small, rented bedsit. The scandal of her actions was short lived, and whilst the Brown family didn't exactly approve, they eventually accepted Celia's life choices, when young Matilda came along in 1995.

They had been so happy. Just the three of them in their small council terrace. A move up from the rented bedsit, Celia didn't think she could be any happier. Trevor worked all hours to give his family the life they deserved. Life was perfect. Until it wasn't.

Celia would never forget that late night knock on the front door. Two uniformed officers, delivering the devastating news that her beloved Trevor had been found drowned in the dock. A tragic accident, they said. That was that. Her perfect life over. Tilly was fifteen at the time and that is when the relationship between herself and her only daughter changed.

Celia heard a key in the door, and hurriedly closed the case, putting it down by the side of the chair out of view.

'Hello darling, I'm in the conservatory.'

17

NORFOLK - 2024

Tilly had been stewing all night about the mistake she had made with the New York connection. She went over and over in her mind, the day spent with her mum. In the end, she concluded that further digging was needed. Although still not wholly convinced she was wrong, she had to admit the letter seemed pretty conclusive evidence that Temperance was at some point living in New Zealand. She had no choice but to go back to the information obtained at the library. She felt a little embarrassed that she had given Hector the wrong destination country, and thinking about it, he had seemed a bit surprised. Had he known all along? The whole Temperance issue was becoming more complicated, and she just wanted to get this research over and done with - the idea of tracing the whole family history was becoming less appealing, and the novelty of the idea waning. She would need to update Uncle Hector if the news she had delivered was wrong. She just wanted to get it sorted now and go back to see him as soon as possible.

The following day was what she called her 'Charity Tuesday.' Her once a fortnight volunteering stint at her favourite charity shop. Sometimes it was a short day if there were lots of volunteers, and regardless of the number, they always closed at 4pm. Tilly decided she would go back to the library after work. A bit more research might put her active, curious mind at rest. She needed to get to the bottom of it, plus Judith was so helpful, she didn't think she needed to bother Melody. The library was the next step on the ladder to solving more of the mystery.

The cat protection charity staff were all so friendly, it was a highlight of Tilly's fortnight to spend time with them. She couldn't think of anything better than rooting through someone's preloved items, to discover hidden gems for the charity to sell - and to get first dibs on, if she was lucky. This Tuesday she was one of three volunteers in the backroom, sorting the donations. There were lots of bags to be gone through that had been donated at the weekend. Between three of them they didn't take long to log everything and pile them up ready to be priced. A job the shop manager, Wendy, reserved for herself and would not allow others to be involved in. Something Tilly found a little annoying, but apart from that, she liked Wendy. In a box of books, a New Zealand travel guide caught her eye - a sign perhaps? It gave her a bubble of excitement in her tummy, and a feeling of hope for her library visit later.

The shop was quite quiet all day, and Wendy let the back-room staff go at 3 o'clock. Tilly grabbed her bag and made the short 5-minute walk round the corner to the library.

Bursting into the library quite breathless, Tilly announced her arrival to Judith at the front desk, who was delighted to see her again.

'Are you on your own Tilly?' said Judith, as she took her through to the research room.

'This time, yes Judith. I was hoping to pick your brains if that's okay? It is all a bit last minute, as I have been given a bit of extra information from my mum, which suggests Temperance - you know, the lady I was trying to trace - didn't actually go to New York, but instead to New Zealand.' Tilly's reason for returning so soon, tumbled out in garbled dialogue. Judith smiled.

'That's fine, no explanation needed, you are allowed back here as often as you like. Get yourself logged on to the computer, and I will be back in a minute.'

Tilly got set up quickly and as promised, Judith was back to help in no time. Judith's advice was to look at arrivals in New Zealand rather than departures, explaining that it was quite possible that her ship had stopped over in New York, en route to the southern hemisphere. Tilly realised potentially she had another few hours of searching ahead of her and started focusing on the New Zealand websites for 1951/2 arrivals. SS Magnificent was not on any of the lists, which was a blow. It meant she had the laborious job of picking through every ship, and there were several each month. Tilly had done it before, so she was determined to do it again - it was just a question of time. Knowing what she was looking for this time, she settled down to a couple of hours focussed internet searching.

Tilly looked at her watch. She had been at the library almost two hours. The library would be closing in 15 minutes, and it didn't look like she was going to be successful. She packed away and logged off the computer. Feeling deflated again, knowing a return visit was going to be needed, she stopped at Judith's desk on her way out.

'No luck Tilly?' Judith realised from the expression on Tilly's face, that the search had not been a successful one.

'Not this time. I don't know if I missed something, I am feeling pretty tired, but I just couldn't find her.' She shrugged, giving an audible sigh of frustration.

'Would you like me to have a search? I sometimes have a bit of spare time between my regular jobs.' Judith generously offered her time and expertise. Tilly was quick to accept.

'Would you really? Oh lovely, thank you Judith.' Tilly put her bag down. 'I'll write down the key points for you - basically her name and the year she left London. Thank you so much Judith. Oh, and here is my number.' Tilly left feeling a little lifted and walked slowly back to her boat.

Settling down for the evening, Tilly cuddled up close to Marmite and opened her book. A keen reader, she picked up her current read– Wuthering Heights. She planned to work through some classics, starting with Bronte novels. After some time, her eyes began to close. Reading always made her sleepy, and fighting the sleep, a ping from her mobile phone brought her back to her senses. A text from an unknown number.

I think I've found her - Judith

18

NORFOLK - 2024

'Good morning, Sunny Days Care Home, Margery speaking, how can I help you?' Tilly hadn't spoken to a Margery before at the care home reception. She sounded very efficient - perhaps a little terse. Tilly hesitated, before speaking.

'Oh, er I was calling about Mr Hector Brown.' She had barely finished speaking when Margery interrupted.

'Oh yes, Mr Brown has completed all the paperwork you left him. I have it here for you to collect.' Tilly was puzzled.

'I'm sorry. What paperwork are you referring to please Margery?' Tilly waited.

'You are Miss Howard from Gently and Coombs Solicitors, are you not?' Tilly felt the receptionist was quite rude in her tone.

'Not!' said Tilly firmly. 'I am Mr Brown's niece, Tilly. I just called to see how he is, and to let you know I want to visit him again this week. I am now concerned that he seems to have had a visit from his solicitor. Is that correct?'

'That is correct. His business with his solicitor, however, is private and confidential. As far as his health is concerned, Mr Brown has been having more spells of confusion. We have also had the doctor visit due to a dizzy spell, and a small fall. He is an elderly man. You must be aware these episodes will continue until….well, until the end.' Margery was offensively blunt, and Tilly was taken aback.

'Really, well, I thought somebody would have called me. You do have my number.' Tilly had regained her composure, but it didn't take away from the fact that she was now feeling renewed anxiety for her Uncle Hector's health.

'I am agency cover while the care home recruit a permanent receptionist. I don't have access to contact numbers for the residents. You can visit….'

'That figures,' said Tilly under her breath and hung up, unable to bear any more.

Tilly was worried that Hector was genuinely poorly. She couldn't leave it. With the new facts she had received from Judith, which were quite exciting she wanted to see him that day. She decided not to make arrangements with the home following the call with Margery the agency worker.

'Hello mum. I'm going to visit Uncle Hector. Would you like to come with me? Tilly was hopeful that their time together recently, might have warmed her mum to the idea of visiting her uncle.

'Oh no, I'm afraid I'm busy today Tilly. Sorry. Perhaps next time?' Celia sounded quite matter of fact. Tilly wasn't surprised by the response but continued.

'He's been getting worse mum; there may not be a next time.' A little short, Tilly couldn't help herself. 'Okay, never mind.' Tilly hung up. She had to do what she knew was right and get herself up to Sunny Days.

Tilly decided to spend the morning finishing off some housework on the boat - a general tidy up was very much overdue. She couldn't leave it another day, but would give it a blitz, then go out after an early lunch. Marmite was being particularly affectionate as Tilly swept through the galley, getting under Tilly's feet.

'I'll be back this evening for a cuddle Marmite, but really you are not helping me.' Marmite meowed on cue and jumped up onto the pew to pummel a cushion, before curling up for the rest of the day, to sleep.

The bus, thankfully, was on time and Tilly got a seat at the front. She still felt a childlike thrill when getting the front seat on a double decker, but why sit anywhere else when the view from the front was so clear and wide? A beautiful day, the trees were blossoming and the road where the care home was located, was particularly leafy, with a row of lime trees lining each side. What her dad used to refer to as a 'Typical French Road'. She got off the bus quickly and walked the short distance to the care home, apprehensive at what she was going to be greeted with. As she pushed open the main door, she was greeted by Jane at the reception. Surprised, but pleased Tilly greeted her with a smile.

'Jane, hello. Boy, am I pleased to see you here. I was expecting someone else.'

'Hello, Tilly isn't it? So who were you expecting?' Jane started looking through some papers on the desk.

'This morning, I spoke to a....er, well a not very helpful lady, when I called. Her name was Margery.'

'Oh yes Margery. Don't worry she was let go at lunchtime when I arrived. There had been a couple of other complaints to the agency about her. We won't be having her back.' Jane rolled her eyes. 'I expect you have come to see Hector. Very wise.' Jane wrote Tilly's name in the visitor's book.

'Why do you say 'very wise' like that? Has he been very poorly? I know Margery said you had to get the doctor because he had a fall, but apart from that I thought it was just a memory problem?' Tilly knew it was more than a memory problem; she just wasn't ready to voice it out loud.

'I'll take you down to his room love. Now, you must be prepared that he has deteriorated since you last visited. Yes, we have had the doctor to see him, but I am afraid he can't fix the mind, just the body, and there are limits with that at his age.' Jane edged in front of Tilly in the corridor and opened Hector's door. 'Go in love.' Tilly went ahead, with Jane just behind her. 'Call his name gently love, so that he knows you are here,' Jane whispered.

'Uncle Hector, it's me, Tilly. Remember?' Hector was in his bed. His eyes were open slightly, and a lost, vacant expression met Tilly's, but he wasn't asleep.

'I'll be at the front desk if you need anything love or ring the alarm. Be patient with him, he's not what he was.' Jane left quietly, and Tilly moved to the side of his bed, and sat down on a large, red, leather, wing backed armchair. It was cold to touch, but the room was anything but cold. A feature, Tilly supposed, of care homes in general. She reached out and touched his hand, which was placed over his turned down bed linen. He slowly moved his head to face her but said nothing.

'Uncle Hector. It *has* been a few weeks.' Tilly felt choked and struggled to find the appropriate words. Feeling out of her depth, she took a deep breath and paused, as she thought through what to say next. This gentle old man was clearly fading away, and her one wish was to be able to give him some happy news. Come on Tilly, she said to herself, now is not the time for self-pity. 'Look what I've brought you.' Her voice stronger and unwavering, as she put on her bravest face. 'Some grapes, which I know you like. Some chocolate - your favourite dark bar.' There was a flicker of interest, as Hector was handed the chocolate. He lifted his hand and turned to Tilly with a smile.

'I had a fall. I'm stuck in my bed. Who did you say you are? I'm sorry love, I think I've seen you before.' It was just a little bit heartbreaking for Tilly. She grasped his hand, and he let her.

'I'm Tilly. I'm your Great Niece. When I visit you, we like to talk about the old days. We talk about Violet, and about Temperance.' She paused, as he raised his hand in a gesture of recall.

'Oh my sisters Violet and Temperance. You know them?' He seemed a bit brighter. She decided to stick to the topic. Whether it was going to be the right time to bring any new news, she wasn't sure.

'Yes, you've told me lots about happy times on the farm with your brother Joe and your two sisters. We talked about Temperance going away. Do you remember that chat?' Tilly was so desperate to bring a little of their conversation back to Hector. But Jane had said be patient with him. Everything was working so much slower. He did seem to be warming up.

Unlike the last visit though, there had so far been no spark of recognition. Tilly thought about the time she had with him. Comparing it to her last visit he had clearly deteriorated very quickly, without any real explanation. Tilly didn't know what a dying person looked like, but in her heart, she knew he wasn't going to be around a whole lot longer. So today it seemed less important to deliver news about how his long-lost sister Temperance, had made her way from London to New Zealand, as Hector had presumed and as Judith had confirmed with her extra contacts. But more important to spend time bringing back happy memories that would stay with him, once she had gone home.

'Would you like a hot drink Uncle Hector? I can call the staff like we did last time I visited you in your room.' She wasn't sure if that might trigger a memory, but she fancied a hot chocolate and thought it was worth a go. Plus, a distraction to simply sitting.

She made the call and ordered coffee for Hector. Paula arrived shortly after the call with two hot drinks and a plate of biscuits. She winked at Tilly as she left. Sitting Hector up, he seemed quite weak, but with the small hospital like table that could be rolled under his bed, he was able to enjoy his coffee without help, helping himself to several custard creams.

'You know the tin is in the airing cupboard. I have told you that before.' Tilly looked at her great uncle puzzled at this random statement.

'The airing cupboard?' She repeated, not really knowing what he was talking about.

'Yes, you will need to reach down inside. It is on the secret shelf where we always put the key.' The biscuits were giving him a bit of energy, but the conversation content was wholly confusing for Tilly. What airing cupboard was he talking about, to start with, never mind a tin.

'What tin are you talking about Uncle Hector.' She sipped at her hot chocolate and tried to sound casual.

'It's in there. In the box. The letters. The answers. For when the time comes. Good girl. You will sort that out for me. Promise? You remind me of my sister Temperance you do. The letter is there, and the key. Find the box. Find my Temperance.' Tilly patted his hand.

'I will Uncle Hector. Don't worry. You don't need to worry about anything. Just drink your coffee and relax. Look at the birds on your bird table.' Wanting to distract him from a subject that seemed now, to be causing him some anxiety, her thought was just go with whatever he wanted. She didn't understand what that was. He didn't have a house, so no airing cupboard, but he must be remembering something from long ago. If she could reassure Hector, hopefully he would remain calm. He began to cough, then wheeze, pointing to his water which she passed him.

'We used to try and hit the birds, when I was a lad. Joe and I. And the rats. We had sling shots. You know, you probably call it a catapult. We never did hit them though.' The coughing caught Hector again, causing him to retch. Struggling to get his breath, Tilly got up concerned, ready to pull the alarm, but Hector waved at her and shook his head. He took another gulp of water which seemed to calm the cough. Lying back on the bed, supported by a mound of soft feather pillows, he said 'You're Celia's girl?' Surprised at this unexpected statement, Tilly quickly acknowledged that she was indeed Celia's girl. Boosted at last by the return of some of his memory, Tilly returned to the armchair. Hector was smiling up at her. 'You really are a Brown, young lady. Beautiful smile, just like my Temperance. It is so lovely of you to visit me. An old man like me. I do feel very fortunate you know.' It felt to Tilly like the old Uncle Hector was slowly emerging. 'I've had a good life. Don't be sad when I've gone, will you. None of that stuff and nonsense.'

'Please don't you talk like that Uncle Hector. You've got years in you yet.' Tilly looked at the man she had known all her life. Wrinkled brows and sagging jowls. Age marked hands, slightly arthritic; long, bumpy fingers, curled in a half grip, tendons tight. She wondered what it felt like when you got to a point in your life when you couldn't really do anything anymore. All the things she loved to do and didn't imagine life without. Her painting, her boat, meeting friends, cycling, visiting the coffee shop. Just normal things she took for granted every single day. She couldn't imagine it and didn't want to. It conjured up feelings she didn't want to feel. This was the life Uncle Hector now led. Looking down at him she realised his eyes were closing. It perhaps was time to make a move.

'I'm going to go now Uncle Hector and let you rest.' He opened his eyes and smiled up at her as she kissed his forehead. He lifted his hand in a wave, as she left the room. She couldn't look back. A single tear escaped and ran down her cheek. She wasn't sure there would be many more visits with her gentle old relative. Overwhelmed, she left the care home, briefly waving to Jane on reception as she left.

The afternoon was still bright, and Tilly needed some fresh air to gather her thoughts. She walked for a mile or so before catching the bus from a later stop. Before heading back to Georgie, she dropped into the Spar to buy a bar of chocolate then on to the Chinese takeaway. Special fried rice and a portion of crispy chilli beef was her go to. She really couldn't face cooking and just wanted a relaxed evening.

Back at the boat with her hoard of comfort food, Marmite yawned, looking up at her from the pew. His day had been very relaxed as always, but he was as pleased as Tilly was, for the evening company.

Preparing to eat her food straight out of the foil container, a gin and tonic in hand, and Marmite close by, she put one of her favourite films into the DVD player. A bit of Bridget Jones was the tonic she needed to lift the spirits, and she settled at last in her own cosy, safe space, to immerse herself in her evening.

19

NORFOLK - 2024

Tilly woke with a bit of a sore head. Empty takeaway containers on the shelf, and a gin glass lying on its side beside them. She had dozed off during the film, clearly in need of her sleep. Nature was calling and Marmite was standing over her, wanting to be fed. She glanced at the clock radio. 7.15. Plenty of time. She was in no hurry to get ready for the day and returned to her bed after satisfying Marmite's hunger and a quick visit to the bathroom.

Checking her phone, there was a message. It was Kit on the 'Best Buddies' chat saying 'hello'. It reminded Tilly that Kit was heading out to New York in two weeks. She felt proud of her friend. Kit had worked extremely hard to get to this position, but perhaps even the confident Kit was having a bit of a wobble and needed her friends for reassurance. Tilly pinged a reply, then checked her social media before eventually getting herself prepared for the day.

The morning at the plumbers, the afternoon to do a brisk food shop. If Melody was free, she thought a catch up at An Extra Slice would be the tonic she needed to shake off the worries about Uncle Hector. Another message sent, over a bowl of porridge with goji and blueberries, and she was ready for her day.

The sun was out, but there was an early summer chill in the air, so Tilly marched briskly to the office in the high street where the plumbing company was based. On arrival Valerie was waving a duster out of the upstairs office window. Strange, Tilly thought. Val didn't usually help with cleaning - well, anything really. It was a family business, but Tilly did paperwork, and telephone calls. Val's husband Donald spent most of his time pricing jobs, but when a big job came along, he would work alongside his son Paul. In general, Paul did most of the jobs which could be done single handed. Having only recently completed his apprenticeship, at twenty four, he was late in qualifying, but he had been plumbing with his dad since he was sixteen. Either he didn't want to pursue higher education or didn't have a choice. He seemed happy though, and always had a big cheery grin and a friendly nature. Tilly had never asked him if plumbing had always been his dream, because she didn't want to encourage his attention. She knew he was a bit fonder of her than she would like. His sister Belinda was at University in Newcastle studying Italian. Tilly had the feeling Belinda wanted to spread her wings and definitely wouldn't be returning to the family business once she had graduated.

She was met at the door by a flustered Valerie.

'Oh, Tilly I am pleased to see you. Everything is going wrong.' Valerie still had the duster in her hand. 'The internet has crashed, Donald has been called out to an emergency broken boiler, and the cleaner has called to say she has another job, and she hasn't given me any notice.'

It explained the duster and pinny. Tilly never really understood why they employed a cleaner anyway; it was only a bit of hoovering. Then again, Valerie could probably do the administration that Tilly did, if she put her mind to it, so why employ her? Ultimately, Valerie preferred to be a lady of leisure, and the business had always been able to afford her that luxury. Donald, an easy going fifty something, indulged his wife, and it seemed to work. Today, Tilly didn't mind what she did. She was being paid, so anything went.

'Don't worry about that Val, I can pick up the cleaning if you want me to.' Smiling, she stepped in past Valerie and put her bag down by her desk.

She was the first point of contact in the office, and, although they didn't get many walk-in customers, she did sell the odd tube of sealant or bath plug, both popular with do-it-yourselfers.

'Would you?' Valerie didn't wait for a reply, 'thank you love.' Her tone was almost of expectation. Before Tilly had a chance to take off her coat, Valerie was taking off her apron and handing over the duster.

'No worries,' said Tilly, managing to keep a smile on her face, through almost gritted teeth. 'You get off and I will carry on here. Are we expecting Paul in today?' Tilly pulled out her chair and switched on her computer, grabbing a pile of post before sitting down to open and log it. A job she didn't need the internet for.

'He has a small, leaky sink job on Swan Crescent, followed by a replacement cistern at the council flats. He should be back by midday, so that is before you finish. He will lock up, but perhaps you can put the hoover round before you leave?' It wasn't a question, and Valerie by now had her own coat on, her very expensive handbag over her shoulder and was standing by the door.

'I said I would. You get off now Valerie.' Tilly repeated. The truth was she could concentrate much better when Valerie wasn't around, so the sooner she had the place to herself, the better.

The morning flew, and Tilly was soon feeling up to date and ready to log off for the day. Right on cue Paul arrived, bright eyed, and full of smiles he bounced into the office like an excited puppy.

'Morning Tilly,'

'Er, afternoon Paul. Drop any paperwork into the top tray please, and I will sort it out next time I'm in. I'm just going to quickly vacuum in here, before I head off.' Tilly had the vacuum cleaner already plugged in and ready to go. Paul tried unsuccessfully to start a conversation, but could not be heard above the noise, so gave up. Less than 5 minutes later, Tilly was exiting by the front door, waving her goodbyes to Paul before he had a chance to engage her any further. Poor Paul, Tilly thought as she headed up the high street, but he just wasn't her type. What was her type? She didn't really know, but right now, she didn't have the energy for a relationship, and even if she did, it most definitely would not be with Paul.

Melody was already at An Extra Slice waiting when Tilly arrived. She waved to Brenda at the counter as Tilly joined her breathless, at the corner table.

'Sorry Mel, I had to do a bit of cleaning before I left the office.' She dropped into her seat with a grunt.

'Cleaning?' Melody exclaimed.

'I know, long story. Anyway, how are you?' The girls caught up quickly with the latest news. Lois could now say a couple of sentences - amusingly and coincidentally the sentences were 'More cake' and 'cake please' among others also food related. Melody had already updated Brenda; so proud she was of her little girl. Tilly filled Melody in on the latest 'Uncle Hector' news.

'At yesterday's visit, his health was a real concern for me. I was hoping my mum would want to visit him, but she isn't showing any interest yet. However much I stress to her, the real change I see each time I visit.' Tilly slumped, remembering the previous day.

'And you really thought she might?' It was a rhetorical question from Melody. Tilly's friends knew what her mum was like. 'You just keep doing what you're doing Tills. You love him, and even if he can't always remember you straight away, I am sure he appreciates you being there. You said yourself he is always happy to have visitors. You've told your mum the situation, and you can do no more. It isn't your responsibility.' Tilly knew Melody was right. There was nothing more she could do, apart from keep visiting, and that was her intention.

'So Tilly, what do you think we should do for Kit? She's leaving in less than two weeks, but I did think she might be expecting a nice send off. One of Brenda's speciality cakes with a message iced on it. What do you think?' Tilly felt a pang of guilt. Kit had not been on her mind, like she clearly had been on Melody's.

'That's a lovely idea Mel, shall we call Brenda over?'

'No need, I've already done it. Ready for Friday evening when she is popping back to see her dad and sister.'

'Bless you Melody, and here am I all wrapped up in Uncle Hector, while you're having to think of everything else.' Tilly was glad to be able to leave that bit of organising with her friend. It meant her focus could stay on Uncle Hector. As she leant forward to pick up her coffee cup, her mobile vibrated in her jacket. Struggling to remove it from her pocket, she was too late, and the call went to voicemail. 'I'll listen to that later,' she said to Melody.

'I probably should be going now anyway Tills; mum has Lois and I don't like to take advantage! I'll call Kit if you like, then let you know the arrangements for Friday?' Again, Tilly was grateful to her friend, and they parted with a hug and a wave at the café door.

Tilly had planned to do a bit of painting that evening, with a fresh canvas set up on her easel. She walked casually back along the canal, planning in her head the picture whilst dialling in to her voicemail.

'Hello Tilly love, this is Jane at Sunny Days Care Home. Please can you call me as soon as you get this message? Thanks love. Bye.' Tilly stopped. Her heart leapt, skipping a beat. Why was Uncle Hector's care home calling her? Fumbling, she dialled to return the call, her heart racing as it rang.

'Good afternoon, Sunny Days Care Home, Jane speaking, how may I help you?' Jane's bright happy mood was conveyed easily to Tilly's ears.

'H..hello Jane, it's Tilly here. You asked me to call.' Tilly realised that she had stopped walking, and was also holding her breath, in anticipation.

'Oh Tilly love.' Jane paused, and Tilly could hear her taking a deep breath. 'Tilly, are you sitting down?' It was just what Tilly did not want to hear.

'No, I'm, oh, what am I doing?' Tilly couldn't articulate exactly what she wanted to say.' I mean, no, I'm walking, I'm on my way home. Just tell me please. Is it bad?' She wasn't sure if she was ready for this news. She just knew she needed Jane to be straight with her.

'I'm very sorry love. There isn't an easy way to say this. Dear Hector passed away peacefully this afternoon.'

20

NORFOLK - 2024

'Hector passed away peacefully this afternoon.' The words hung heavily in the air. Tilly didn't remember the last part of her journey home. It was a blur, physically and figuratively. She didn't fight the tears, as they flowed easily, soaking her cheeks. Briefly brushing them away, she stepped down into her boat; her safe space, climbed onto her bed, and let her emotions take over.

Marmite was by her side, a sixth sense that all was not right. And all was not right. Tilly couldn't think logically. She pulled Marmite to her, curled up under her duvet, and eventually dropped off into a fog of sleep.

Roused some hours later, by the dull tone of her mobile phone, calling to her from the depths of her rucksack, she raced, head thumping to answer it. It was an unknown number. She realised her heart was pounding, as the memory of her previous call came flooding back. The pain almost winded her. She glanced at her watch; it was just after 5. Not as late as she had been expecting. She sat up straight on the bed, Marmite pushing his nose into her side, demanding affection.

'Hello, Tilly Brown speaking.' There was an almost pause, before the voice of a gentleman greeted her.

'Good afternoon Miss Brown, my name is Ashley Coombs, of Gently, Barker and Coombs Solicitors. I am acting on behalf of your great uncle, Mr Hector Brown. I am sorry to call you so soon after the sad news of his passing. Are you free to talk?' Mr Coombs cleared his throat. Tilly thought he didn't sound very old, and perhaps a little nervous. Now fully awake and alert she found her mind was still catching up with the last few hours and trying to make sense of it all.

'Hello Mr Coombs. Er..yes, I'm free.'

'Ashley, please. How are you Tilly, do you mind me calling you Tilly?' She thought he sounded friendly. Calming down, her heartbeat slowing, she took a deep breath and sighed audibly. She took herself to the pew and sat down.

'No, that is fine….um..Ashley. How can I help you?' At last Tilly was coming to her senses, and logic began to return.

'That's good. Now Tilly, I've been Hector's solicitor for the past six years and managed his financial affairs since he became unable to do so himself. You may be aware that he has recently changed his Will, and it is lodged with my firm?' He didn't pause for a response, yet Tilly had never even considered what Uncle Hector had in his Will; in fact, that he even had a will. It just wasn't something she had thought about. Ashley continued. 'It was Hector's wish that his wake would take place at the family home. The old farm 'Spitalbrook', and he entrusted the job to you to organise it. Are you able to come into our offices in the next day or two for me to give you more details?' Ashley had stopped speaking at last, and Tilly was trying to comprehend what he had just conveyed.

'His funeral?' Tilly said, suddenly overwhelmed by the reality of Hector's death.

'Oh, pardon me Tilly, no. I do apologise, I have misled you. No, the funeral is all planned. Hector did that and we will make the arrangements. It is just the wake, at the former family home, that he wants you to manage.'

He made it sound very simple, with his calm efficient tone.

'Ah…ok. I can come tomorrow. Where are you? It's a lot for me to take in Ashley. I still can't believe Uncle Hector has gone. I only saw him yesterday.' Tilly felt herself welling up again, as she thought about the day. 'I haven't even told my mum yet. I need to call her.'

'Don't worry yourself thinking about it now, you come into our offices at 10am tomorrow and we will discuss it. We'll help you Tilly, you are not on your own. We're in the High Street next to the Co-op. I'll see you tomorrow.' Mr Coombs hung up and Tilly stared momentarily at her phone, again trying to work through everything that had just happened.

Painting was no longer an appealing way to spend her evening, but after an unplanned early sleep, she knew she wasn't going to feel tired. She couldn't put off her first job. That was to call her mum. She chose to call Celia's mobile, not wanting to get David. Celia answered immediately,

'Mum, it's Tilly. I've got sad news.' She paused, thinking her mum might say something, but silence filled the void. 'Uncle Hector passed away this afternoon.' Tilly's voice broke as she voiced the news out loud.

'I suppose it was inevitable.' Her mum seemed unusually unfeeling. Tilly composed herself, assuming David was in the room with Celia, which might account for the lack of sympathy in her response. Or maybe it was just the shock.

'Well please can you pass the news on to Aunt Gilly, and….' The words caught in her throat. Tilly needed to compose herself and took a deep breath. 'And anyone else you know who might need to be told?' Tilly then felt nothing more could be said. The brief conversation had felt cold and without emotion on her mother's side. Tilly wasn't completely surprised by her mum's response but had hoped for a bit of understanding or empathy for how she might be feeling. It was clear, surely, that she would be upset - perhaps even need comforting, but there was nothing. Tilly decided not to bother telling her about the call from the solicitor, and hung up, agreeing to 'see you soon' which she thought unlikely.

Tilly popped open a bottle of Lidl pink prosecco, deciding Tuesday was as good a day as any to open it. Toasting her great uncle with the pink bubbles, more tears escaping, she picked up her phone, opened WhatsApp and messaged in the Best Buddies group.

Hey guys, I am really sad to tell you that today, my uncle Hector died. I know you would want to know. As you can guess, I'm feeling pretty low. I'll call you tomorrow.

Taking her glass back to the comfort of her bed, she flicked the TV on for company, sat back with her glass of bubbly and went over the day once more. Thoughts still spinning, of what a visit to the solicitor might bring, she gradually drifted off into a deep sleep.

21
NORFOLK - 2024

Tilly woke to messages from both Kit and Melody expressing their sincere condolences. It seemed oddly formal from her closest friends, but then she thought, what *do* you say to a friend when someone close to them dies? She wasn't sure she would know either, and was grateful for their sympathy. Melody wanted to come round that day, and Kit said she was prepared to come earlier than Friday if she was needed. Tilly pinged a message back to the group:

Thanks girls. I'm ok. Uncle Hector's solicitor rang me yesterday afternoon and said I'm to organise the wake. I think he made a mistake, as he said it's to be at the former family home (what family home, I am puzzled!) Going to Solicitor at 10am today to find out what I really need to do. Will let you know after the appointment what comes out of it, but think I am going to need your help. Love you guys, Tills xxx

She immediately received replies from both girls, who said they were there for her if she needed them. The reality still hadn't sunk in, but there wasn't time to dwell on it. Tilly got herself dressed and cycled up to the High Street in plenty of time for the 10 am appointment. A parade of shops she had visited so often, yet she had never previously noticed the half-glazed door, nestled between the shop fronts, with the name 'Gently, Barker and Coombs Solicitors' stencilled in gold on the glass.

With her bike parked and locked safely in the conveniently positioned bike rack, she pushed open the door. The steep, straight staircase, enclosed by a wall on each side, heavily patterned in dull 70s style paper, was dark, except for the light coming through the door glass. The carpet was old, but clean. The whole stairwell musty smelling. Apprehensively, she started to climb.

At the top of the stairs, a door to the right was labelled *Mr Gently*, the one to the left *Mr Coombs*. Tilly wondered what had happened to Mr Barker but knocked on the door to the left. A young female voice responded with a sharp 'come in'.

Tentatively, Tilly pushed open the door. The room was old fashioned. It had a lavender smell - Tilly guessed it was the young lady's attempt to cover the mustiness. Sat behind a heavy, old, oak desk, she greeted Tilly with a smile.

'Good morning, is it Miss Brown?' She wore tortoiseshell rimmed glasses, and a dated cream blouse with a big, billowy bow at the unfashionably high neck. Below that, Tilly could not see. She guessed the uniform for a solicitor's secretary was frumpy and old, whatever your age. There was an ancient, electric fire plugged in to the wall opposite the desk, which Tilly thought looked suspiciously unsafe. Its grey and white twisted flex was frayed along its length. Tilly nodded. 'Please take a seat,' said the young woman - Tilly could now see a name plate on her desk introducing her as 'Miss Angela Howard'. She pointed to a high-backed armchair, covered in threadbare, woven, tapestry fabric. Everything had seen better days, Tilly thought. 'Mr Coombs will be out to meet you shortly.' The secretary went back to her typing and Tilly sat down stiffly.

It wasn't long before Mr Coombs came out to greet Tilly. He offered his hand, and she shook it firmly.

'Pleased to meet you Tilly. Ashley Coombs. Please call me Ashley.' As she had suspected, he was much younger than one expects a solicitor to be. Perhaps early 30s, possibly even younger. He had a nice smile and ushered her in to his office.

'Angela, can you bring us some tea please?' Angela had a slightly resentful look on her face, thought Tilly. She nodded, nonetheless.

The office was much the same as the rest of the building. Ashley explained that he had been a partner in the company for 8 years, since the demise of Mr Barker. That explained the missing solicitor, Tilly thought. It was his first job after qualifying and he had been dealing with Hector Brown's affairs for the past six years, as he had explained on the telephone. Tilly sat politely and nodded where appropriate. At that point, Angela brought tea in on a wooden tray. Bone china cups and saucers, in a floral pattern, with sugar bowl and milk jug to match. The old-fashioned theme followed through, thought Tilly. Ashley thanked Angela, and she was quick to leave the room, without a word.

'So now we come to the nitty gritty Tilly. How have you been coping since the news of your uncle's passing?' He seemed genuinely interested. Tilly said she was still coming to terms with it, and that she presumed it might take a while for it all to sink in. 'Of course.' Was Ashley's response. 'You may not be aware, but we very recently visited Hector at the care home on his request. He wanted to make some alterations to his will and had written other bits and pieces in a letter. He was, in our opinion, of sound mind, and so we made those adjustments. The Will is to be read out after the funeral. I explained to you on the telephone that Hector had made all the plans, didn't I? The music, the readings, and all pre-paid. There is nothing you need to do there. However, he does stipulate his wish was for the wake to be held at the old family farm, and he specifically requested that you, Tilly, were to prepare the farm for this.' Ashley stopped speaking, but Tilly didn't know what to say. 'Has that come as a shock Tilly? You are looking a little blank. We are here to help where we can, so money will be no object.'

'I...well, yes, it is a shock. I didn't know there was a family farm. I mean, I knew there *was* a family farm. You know, in the past, but I didn't know it was still in the family.' Tilly needed to get things straight in her head; to be sure what was being asked of her.

'Oh yes Tilly, there is a family farm, in Norfolk, just outside the small village of West Snoring. About a 40-minute drive from here. He had it closed up many years ago, before I was dealing with his affairs. When he was still a working man. He left the key with the solicitor. I have it here.' Ashley Coombs pulled open the heavy wooden drawer of his desk and pulled out a large, bulging, paper folder. From this he produced the oldest key Tilly had ever seen. Large and ornate, it looked like something out of a fairy story. 'I believe it may be boarded up and so will need those boards removed. I will arrange for the electricity and gas to be turned on, and you will then be able to go in and give it a good clean. You will probably need to remove dust sheets. The funeral is going to be two weeks on Thursday. It hasn't taken long to get that organised. As I said, Hector had done most of the planning already. It was simply a case of the date.' So matter of fact, thought Tilly, the job of a solicitor. So blunt.

Ashley poured the tea, and they sipped it in silence. Tilly felt a bit awkward, not really knowing what to say. She felt there must be questions to ask in these circumstances, but nothing was coming to mind. The fact was that Tilly was required to sort out this old house, in a little over two weeks. She already felt out of her depth, but as a tribute to Hector she was keen to get it right. She finished her tea, put the cup back onto the tray, thanked Mr Coombs, then asked for more details of the house.

'Of course, Tilly, the address is Spitalbrook, West Snoring, Near King's Lynn, Norfolk. The locals will know it, so drop in to the local pub, The Chequers Inn, if you are stuck.' Ashley seemed like he had delivered all the information he had for now. 'If you have any other questions, just give me a call.' He handed her his business card. 'You can hire a car, and we will re-imburse you.' He then rummaged again in the envelope which had contained the large old key. 'Ah, and one more thing Tilly. There is a letter here, which was deposited by Mr Brown relatively recently. It was to be given to you prior to the will being read. We don't know its contents until after the reading of the will, when we will be able to open our copy. You can keep the key until after the wake, and then it will come back to us. Do you think you can manage all that?' Tilly took the envelope, addressed to

'Miss M Montgomery-Brown.' What could she say? She had to manage. She thanked him, shook his hand again and left.

She was relieved to get back out into the fresh air, after the stuffiness of the office. Tilly tucked the envelope into her pocket, where it would be safe for the journey home. She then collected her bike and pushed it back along the towpath to her beloved boat. Marmite was waiting for her on the roof, he meowed, then stretched as he crept towards her for a fuss. Tilly locked up her bike and went onboard. To read the letter and then to contact her friends. After doing so, her message to the girls was simple.

'Help'

22
NORFOLK - 2024

Tilly,

My dear Tilly. You will never know what joy I have felt, these last few months with you by my side. Your smile lights up a dreary room, and your enthusiasm for life is infectious. In fact, I think you have given me the energy to go on, far longer than I would have, had you not been here. You have been like a daughter to me, and I will be forever grateful.

I am, however, not going to live forever, and that is why I have made the very easy decision to change my Will and to leave some of my most treasured and personal possessions to you, my dear. The things that mean something to me. You will find everything in my room at Sunny Days. All of my favourite items I brought with me to the home. In addition, I will leave you the sum of £10,000. There is a reason for this which I will come to. I have put it all in my Will, which is lodged with the solicitor. But of course, you will know this by now. Please do not allow any busy bodies, whether family or not, to interfere. These are my wishes.

Now regarding the £10,000. This is to help you carry out my request. You may not need it, in which case it's yours to keep. But I didn't want to make demands and leave you without the means to carry them out.

So my dear Tilly, this is what I must ask you to do please, to fulfil my wishes and for the requirements of the Will to be carried out fully. A key sits in the writing desk. It's a mystery. I would like you to try everything you can, to find out what it is for – important or not – I have always wondered but never had the energy or made the time to find out. You need to do this for me. I have one other request too and this might be where you need the money. Please can you try to find out what happened to my sister Temperance? Nobody spoke about her after she ran away. I feel ashamed that I didn't try to find her. I have a box, given to me by my older sister Vi. There may be clues there, but I have never felt able to look in it, so I left it at the old family farm. I think, sadly, that I have been running away all my life. If you can find her, or if she has passed on, then find her final resting place for me please, I want you to tell her she has always been in my thoughts.

There really should have been some family money, but it never materialised on our side. The 'Brown' family were always private, British 'stiff upper lip' sorts. Now unless my father drank or gambled away a significant inheritance, then it must have gone somewhere. You know what I mean. I know you do; you are a sensible girl. But the money which should have come down to you, through your father, I want to put that right. So lastly, can you find our missing money? Is the mystery of the money and my missing sister connected? That is what I have always wondered.

Now lovely Tilly, I know you are a clever one. I know you will unravel our family history. No skeletons in my cupboard as far as I am concerned, but you may have to do some digging (and I don't mean with a shovel, ha ha) to get to the bottom of the mystery surrounding our Penny - that is Temperance's pet name. You will need to build a family tree to know what really happened to all the Brown ancestors, and this might help you unravel the mystery. I suggest you start by building that. You will learn something in the process, and it might even be fun!

Once the mystery is solved, you can settle down, enjoy your life and forget about me. Tilly, may it be long and happy and full to the brim with laughter.

Always your loving Uncle Hector
xxx

Melody arrived at the boat within 10 minutes of reading the message. Kit was apparently already on her way, and likely to arrive in the next thirty minutes. Melody and Kit had been corresponding since that first message from Tilly, and after some consideration, Kit had contacted her new employer, and they had agreed to her delaying her trip to New York until after the funeral.

Tilly was overwhelmed that her friends had just dropped everything for her. She was still reeling from the sad news, although wondered to herself why she felt so surprised. Hector had deteriorated so much in the last few weeks; it was surely to be expected. Then the call from the solicitor followed by the most surreal meeting in that odd office of his.....and now this letter.

Tilly had opened the letter once settled back on Georgie. Whilst still processing the news that Hector wanted her to organise the wake at the family home - a home she hadn't even appreciated still existed - she now also had a letter written in his own shaky handwriting. But not just any letter, he was sharing with her the details of part of his will. That he wanted her, Tilly, to receive his most personal possessions, but not only that, also a sum of £10,000 to enable her to solve some mysteries about his past. Yet again, the overwhelming feeling of apprehension swept over Tilly. More thoughts started to whirr, then breaking into those thoughts came a knock on the roof.

'Hello Tills, it's me.' Melody came in through the small entrance and met her with a giant hug. Tilly couldn't help herself and burst into tears. A release of her pent-up tension. Melody was also tearful, and the girls stood embracing for several minutes, silently supporting as close friends do. Eventually, Tilly drew back and sat down on the pew, Melody joined her. Tilly grabbed a large box of tissues from the shelf and blew her nose loudly, while her friend dabbed at her own eyes. Tilly exhaled loudly.

'Thank you, Mel, for coming so quickly. Perhaps I was being a bit silly, but I couldn't think straight.' Looking across the table she smiled, and Melody reached out her hand.

'You know we're here for you Tilly, both Kit and I, plus Sam too. He sends his love.' She gave Tilly's hand a squeeze. 'We will do everything we can to help.'

'I know you will. I really am so lucky to have such lovely friends. So now I just need to plan a wake.' She paused briefly. 'This is something way out of my comfort zone Melody. You and Kit are my lifeline.' Tilly wasn't exaggerating how grateful she felt to not be on her own.

'It's going to be good Tills, my Mum is happy to have Lois so that I'm free for you. Don't worry, troubles are always better shared. If this is a trouble? We just need to work out a good send off for your great uncle.' Melody was always so positive, and generally bright and bubbly. In the circumstances, a little more subdued, but still positive. Tilly knew that Melody would be the level-headed one, who would keep them on track.

'It isn't just organising a wake though. We....well, technically I, must visit the family home, in a place called 'West Snoring' about a 40 minute drive away. I was hoping you'd come with me?' Tilly gave her most pleading look.

'You know we will. I'll get Sam to drive us, and Kit can drive you. She should be here soon, shall I put the kettle on?' Without waiting for a reply, Melody got up and filled the kettle.

They had only just poured out their coffee when Kit arrived, sweeping on to the boat, in true Kit style making her presence known. Tilly got up for a hug but Kit, less emotional than her friends, stayed composed. Tilly ushered her behind the table to a place on the pew and got her a mug. They had a brief catch up about Kit's journey, and the change to the New York plans, where Kit brushed off the appreciation, saying it was no big deal.

Tilly then picked up the letter and read it out loud. The girls passed it round, each reading through the letter, before it was returned to Tilly and placed on the table in front of them all.

'I don't know where to start. The funeral, the wake and a family tree to build so that I can find his sister. After all that work we did in the library Melody, and now I have a whole lot more to do. But he wants me to have £10,000, so that I can find her.' Tilly looked from one to the other of her friends questioningly, whilst nervously clasping her hands together.

'Shall I say what I think?' began Melody.

'Please do,' said Tilly, and Kit concurred.

'Firstly, the family tree can wait. The positive is you have a bit of a lead on where she went. Secondly, the wake. That is the priority. I say we take the key and go straight over to West Snoring. Once we have seen the house and assessed how much there is to do in advance of the funeral. It will just be simply sorting out some food and drink.' Melody smiled widely. 'I said that Sam would drive...how about going now?'

'Now?' said Tilly, quite alarmed at the immediacy of the suggestion, but calmed by her friend's logical assessment of the situation.

'Good idea Melody, why not Tilly? I can drive us too. You said yourself that it's only 40 minutes away, no time like the present - as they say!' Kit was on board with the idea, and picked up her car keys, keen to make it happen.

'Ok...yes, okay guys, you win. Let's do this. What is it..' Tilly looked at her watch. 'Just gone 12.30. Is Sam free now?'

'I'll call him. I know he is free, so I'll just get him to come over here right now. He's probably waiting for my call.' Melody had the phone to her ear as she reassured Tilly. They didn't want to give her any excuse to delay any further. Time really was of the essence.

'So we go to the house with the key,' Tilly patted her hip pocket. 'But it might be boarded up, the solicitor said.'

'No problem, Sam has tools to sort that out. Come on let's get outside, he'll be here in a few minutes.' They shuffled along the pew and edged out with Tilly locking the door behind her. The sun had come out and was unseasonably warm. Kit's sports car was parked alongside the canal, and while she was unlocking and putting down her hood, Sam pulled up in his van and jumped out for a quick hug with Tilly.

'Can we have the address Tilly? The postcode should be enough.' Sam had a modern satnav in his van, and Kit had the same on her phone. They got into their respective vehicles, and Sam took the lead. Feeling nervous excitement, Tilly accepted her friends were helping her, and she was grateful. With no further delay, they were on the road and heading to

Spitalbrook in West Snoring. The mysterious family home of Tilly's ancestors.

23

AUCKLAND - 1954

Temperance had done well with her evening classes and within six months was fully up to speed with her typing and shorthand. She had been successful in securing a job with the council. It was in a small typing pool, typing letters for all departments. Generally, those passed to Temperance were from the Housing department relating to unpaid rates. Usually reminding them of what was due, but sometimes more serious demands. Temperance was only expected to type what was written, then pass them back to the relevant director. She found it hard not to wonder and sometimes worry about the recipients, especially if it was a demand for a lot of money, or a threat for further action to be taken.

Her manager, an older lady called Miss Proops, would walk around the office looking over her shoulder to check Temperance was keeping up. She guessed Miss Proops was about fifty. She had her long grey hair pulled back into a bun and always wore a brown tweed suit.

The council seemed to employ men in the departments outside of the typing pool, but Miss Proops knew the senior managers in each department, and nothing appeared to intimidate her. She was like a strict schoolteacher, so Temperance tried to keep her head down most of the time. Her aim was to make no mistakes. Mistakes meant she had to do the letter again, which meant wasted paper, and sometimes wages docked.

Now earning a proper wage, Temperance was saving up to find her own flat to rent. She didn't mind renting with Elsie really but yearned for her own space. Elsie went out a lot, late into the night, and sometimes brought men home. She was quite untidy, and not very good at doing her share of the cleaning.

It had been eighteen months and Temperance felt it was time. There still was the problem of money though, and she had written to Vi a couple of times requesting help. Once Violet had sent her two English pounds, but Temperance had not even received a reply to her last letter. She wasn't going to be put off, she felt they owed her, so she sat down to write to her sister once more. She would keep on asking, until she had what she was owed. To compensate for what she had gone through. Her family owed her that at least.

24

NORFOLK - 2024

Sam pulled up first, outside the large 5 bar gate; the entrance to Spitalbrook. He turned off his engine and waited for Kit to catch up. The gate wasn't locked, and Melody got out to open it, pushing it wide open. It looked like a long drive, overgrown where grass grew, but mostly it was gravel and dirt, with bramble encroaching on both sides. Kit pulled up while Melody was walking back to the van, and Tilly jumped out quickly to join her.

'Shall we walk up the drive, Tilly?' Melody had already started forwards. She motioned to Kit and Sam behind her. 'Just follow us,' she called back, then linked arms with a hesitant Tilly, and encouraged her up the drive. Sam got back in his van, started the engine, and followed slowly up the track. Kit followed closely behind, carefully avoiding the overgrown hedge and shrubbery, a little worried about her paintwork.

It took several minutes to reach the farmhouse, and as it came into view, Tilly stopped. What she saw in front of her was a beautiful old building. A 17th century beamed structure with a heavy papering of ivy partly covering one corner, creeping right up into the eaves of the building. She tried to take it all in. She had never seen anything like it. A million miles away from her Georgie, or her mum's modern detached home. She turned to Melody, almost speechless.

'Wow Tilly. It's beautiful,' said Melody, clearly also enchanted by the character of the cottage. She waited for the stunned Tilly to respond. 'Don't you think Tills? Where's that big old door key the solicitor gave you? Come on, let's let the cars past and then get inside. I can't wait.'

Melody was excited and hurried forward to meet the drivers, with Tilly just behind her.

'It really is beautiful. I do love old buildings,' Tilly paused again, 'and how I wish Uncle Hector was here.' A sudden pang of something gripped her. Sadness, regret, Tilly wasn't sure which, but a feeling that something was missing.

'It really is beautiful, but just think, Hector wanted you to see it. To be the first one to go back. He would be so pleased. Go on Tilly, you get in front of us.' Melody, still in charge, pushed her friend in front of the small group.

She stood facing the peeling door, with her three friends just behind her. The thick coating of grey, dusty cobwebs told them everything they needed to know about the recent use of this majestic front door. No-one had been through it in many years it was quite clear. Yet there was good news. No visible barrier had been erected. No barricade to break through, simply a heavy old door. The window to the left was covered by a rambling rose which blocked most of the glass. A heavy, dirty net curtain could just be made out through the grimy pane, and then darkness. Whatever was behind the door, could not be seen from outside. Tilly rummaged in her pocket for the key. Large, cold and tactile, she held it in her hand, pondering. She could tell when she was handed it by the solicitor, that it was the key to somewhere special. Tilly was apprehensive, but at the same time excited.

'Come on Tilly, get the key out!' said Melody impatiently. Tilly didn't want to be rushed. This was like something from a film - Tilly wasn't sure if she was ready for a scene from The Addams Family but knew she couldn't put it off any longer with Melody at her heels. Tilly pushed the key through the web into the keyhole, wriggling it about to engage the teeth. It took some work, then when Tilly was on the verge of passing it to Melody to try, there was a rusty clunk and the lock turned. She turned to look at her friends, with a nervous grin.

'Time to take the next step Tills, and we are here with you.' Kit encouraged, also impatient to get inside, to see what work was ahead of them.

'Okay, don't rush me!' Tilly grasped the large round brass handle and turned.

'Well, there certainly isn't any danger of that Miss Brown.' Tilly ignored Sam's playful sarcasm and edged open the door, her friends surged forwards to get a first look inside. A shower of dust fell, dislodged from the door top, and more abandoned spider's webs clung at their clothing, as they all stepped over the threshold, into the sleeping cottage.

The door took them into a square hall, with three more doors leading off it. All closed. A window to the left was dark; curtains closed. It was too dark to see properly, and Sam stepped forwards and pulled back one of the curtains, releasing another cloud of choking dust.

'We have certainly got some cleaning to do,' said Melody stating the obvious. 'I think if we can get some light in, we will see the full extent of what we have to deal with, and then we can make a plan. Did the solicitor say anything to you about the electricity?' Melody was back in project manager mode.

'I think he said something about the main fuse switch being turned off, and if we turn it on, then we can get lights on and the hoover plugged in. I don't know where it is though.' Tilly was thinking she should have asked more questions at the solicitor's office.

'I'll try and find the fuse box,' said Sam keen to be useful, and to get out to explore more.

'Okay, you go and have a look for that. If you know what you are looking for?' Tilly was no more clued up than anyone else, and she was happy for Sam to take on the challenge. Sam went back out of the front door to see if he could see anything in an outside box. He said that it would have been added later. It would not have existed when the house was built, as it was too old.

'I think we should open all the curtains in here, and the doors too. Take it in stages.' Melody was voicing her plan as she thought of it. The others agreed, so Tilly took the door to the right, Kit the door next to it, and Mel the door facing the front door. No-one had commented on the piece of furniture, covered in a white sheet. From the shape it had to be an armchair, pushed up against the wall in the hallway, positioned under the window. Above them, the hall ceiling was matted with cobwebs, many hanging spookily to touch their heads. Tilly was the first to open her door.

'It's dark in here, but it looks like a lounge. More furniture covered with white sheets. More cobwebs on the ceiling. Well, everywhere actually.' Tilly made her way to the far side of the lounge. 'There is a window here, and another door.' She called out to her friends, before pulling back the dusty curtain, by now expecting to get showered in grime. 'And a small fireplace.' Tilly returned to the hall to see what the others had found. Kit was standing by her door, which was just enclosing the narrow staircase.

'It's a cute staircase hidden behind a door. I've never seen anything like this before. I didn't go up though. I thought we should finish exploring downstairs first.' Both girls turned to Melody who had gone through the last door, into a kitchen. A very tidy kitchen, as Melody pointed out, with no white sheets in sight. In fact, all rooms so far had been very tidy. Just extremely dusty. The house had clearly been 'put away' before it was locked up. There was a large Aga to the left of the door, against another chimney breast. Tilly assumed it was linked to the hot water system, and although she didn't know a lot about hot water systems in general, the back burner in her boat which heats her water, was the same in principle.

Melody pulled up a blind on the back door, to find Sam staring in, smiling widely, and gesturing at the ground. Thankfully the key was in the lock, and Melody was able to quickly open the door.

'I found it in a box under this ivy down here,' said Sam, almost before the door was opened. 'So I managed to flick the main switch. Can you try the light switch please Tilly? See if it works.' Sam was sounding pleased with himself, having completed his mission successfully. Tilly turned to find the light switch by the door to the hall. An old round white switch, she hoped was still safe. She flicked it down. Nothing.

'Try in the hall, or the lounge. This old kitchen strip light has probably had it.' Sam went through to the hall ahead of Tilly and flicked the switch by the door. A dim glow of light, under a pink dusty shade appeared, and the friends gave a small cheer. It wasn't going to make a huge difference to the visibility, but a new bulb would solve that, and it proved the electricity was back on. They were in business.

The friends proceeded to explore the remaining room - a beautiful big dining room. Tilly thought the perfect space for the wake, if they moved the furniture around a bit. She lifted some of the white sheets to reveal a shiny walnut dining room table, and 8 chairs, plus a matching sideboard. She suddenly remembered the reason why they were there. Uncle Hector's wish for his wake to be held in his old family home. A home that until a few days ago, Tilly had been unaware of.

'I've decided there is no time like the present to get started.' called Tilly to the others, 'so remove any sheets you find, and we can vacuum when we come back with a hoover. Let us then make a list of what we need to clean, and a separate one for a wake.'

She removed all sheets from the dining room and took them through the kitchen into the hall. Melody had found a brush under the sink and was sweeping a small pile of dust from the windowsill.

'Don't bother with that Mel, there is going to be loads of dust. Has anyone been upstairs?' With Kit out of view, she guessed the draw of the secret staircase had been too strong for Kit. Noises above their heads confirmed she was exploring upstairs. Tilly called up the stairs. 'What's it like up there Kit?'

'Lots more old furniture. As you would expect, beds, chests of drawers and wardrobes. All covered.' Kit then appeared in the narrow stairwell, grinning. 'The floor is very crooked, and you have to go through one bedroom, to get to the next. There was a curtain in the corner of that bedroom, with another door behind it. I didn't open the door.' Kit by now was back down in the hall, where she was greeted by a large pile of white sheets.

Tilly had returned to the lounge. The light worked but again was dim. She also tested the wrought iron standard lamp, with a large, frilled shade, that was hidden in the corner behind the sofa. It too worked and gave a little bit of extra light. She pulled back the curtains fully and noticed the writing desk at the back of the room. What had the letter said? Something about a key. She was also trying to recall that last conversation with Uncle Hector. How she now wished she had spent a little more time with him in those last weeks. She resolved that she would carry out his final request to the best of her ability and give him the best send-off she possibly could, back in his old childhood home.

A lovely black and white photo in a small wooden frame, was lying on its back on top of the writing desk. Tilly reached over and stood it up. It showed a young woman, between two boys. Too old to be her sons. The older boy had a wide familiar smile. It dawned on her, this was a photo of Hector as a youngster. Excited, she called to her friends.

'Look at this lovely picture Melody. I think it's Uncle Hector when he was a boy.' At that point, Tilly dissolved into floods of tears. She'd been holding in the emotion of the visit, together with the enormity of the challenge ahead of her, since they had arrived at the house. In the end, the simple black and white photograph had overwhelmed her, and emotions won out. The pressure to get it right felt huge. Melody hugged her friend, reassuring Tilly again that she wasn't on her own. Sniffing, Tilly wanted to explain.

'I..I..I'm not sure I can do it Mel.' Tears still ran freely, down her blotchy cheeks. 'It's too much.'

'You *can* do it Tills, and we are all here to do it with you. Come on silly, dry your eyes. I think we've done enough for today.' Melody had the perfect maternal comforting way about her, and Tilly gave a shaky sigh as she tried to compose herself. 'It's just a bit of cleaning, and we will be sorted. Spray a bit of Flash about, a wipe with a cotton cloth and it will look as good as new. Now dry those eyes.' Melody passed Tilly a tissue, as Sam and Kit joined them to find out the cause for a sudden outburst of Tilly emotion. 'I've made a list of cleaning things, and we can think about food and drink for the wake once we are back on-board Georgie.

'I agree, it's time we got back.' Kit wasn't the domestic type and was ready to get back to normal. 'I'll turn my car round while you lock up.'

They made sure the back door was locked but decided to leave the electricity turned on. Plans were still to be finalised for their return with a vacuum cleaner, and cleaning products. Something Melody was firmly in charge of. They pulled the big old front door to, and secured it. Tilly returned the key to the safety of her coat pocket, before getting back in the car with Kit. Sam closed the gate on the way out, and they left the sleepy, aptly named village of West Snoring, and headed back home to plan a wake.

25

NORFOLK - 1954

'Hello father, it's Violet. I am coming up to visit you this weekend. I am concerned about mother's health.' Violet needed an excuse to visit her father. 'I'd like to see the boys too. It has been a while.' Her father was non-committal and Vi ended the conversation.

She had received another pleading letter from Temperance. Her parents never asked after Temperance, and she didn't feel comfortable visiting her old home anymore. It wasn't the family home she knew as a child, and she thought often of her younger brothers Hector and Joseph. They were growing up without their sisters, and she suspected Temperance was not mentioned by her parents. She hadn't asked if she could visit. She gave them no choice and had stated it as a fact.

Violet planned to catch the train to King's Lynn then a local bus to the village. Ronald had offered to drive her, but she didn't want to involve him if she didn't need to. Anyway, he probably wouldn't approve of what she had planned.

Two days later and she was on the train, in a comfortable compartment with just one other passenger. She had a small overnight bag, but she only planned to stay the one night. That would be long enough. She had some sweets in her bag for her younger brothers, and the most recent letter. As the train wound its way into the Norfolk countryside, she took out the letter and read it again.

15th July 1954, Auckland, NZ

My dearest sister,

How I long to hear from you dear Violet. You will never know the loneliness I feel, and I thank God that you will never experience this isolation. When a family has turned their back on one of its own. It is a terrible feeling Violet, and that is truly how I feel. I have not asked you for much, and I am eternally grateful for all you have done for me, but I need more help. More money from father. Only you can get that for me.

I am trying hard to make a go of this new life, and I hope you are proud of me? I am close to getting my own flat, now that I have a proper job at the council. I want to visit the South Island too, so I am saving up to travel a bit.

Did you know there was an earthquake in Kaikoura last week? That is a place in the South Island. It was so strong that houses shook. I am waiting to feel one for myself. They say the small ones just make the pictures on the walls swing. Can you imagine such a thing Violet? There is also a volcano off the coast of Whakatane. One of the ladies I work with comes from Whakatane, and she told me about it. I'd like to visit that too. The Māori people call it Whakaari but the English speaking people call it White Island. It erupts regularly, and some people have been killed while working or visiting it. Don't worry, I don't plan to climb it, I would just like to watch from the safety of the mainland.

Violet, please try to find a way to send me more money. I was grateful for the two pounds you sent, but it isn't enough. I need to live. After what I had to endure, I feel I am owed that, at least. Please Violet, I implore you.

Your loving sister,
Temperance

There was a short wait for the bus at King's Lynn, but by early afternoon, Violet found herself standing at the big 5 bar gate: the entrance to Spitalbrook. The old family farm. 'Deep breath Vi, this is it.' She said to herself, as she took her first steps up the gravel drive, to the sprawling 17th century farmhouse, she had once called home. Thickly lined several deep, by overhanging beech and oak, the track was littered with years of fallen leaves, beech masts and acorn cups. From acorns and beech masts foraged by squirrels and hidden deeply in the undergrowth, a smattering of tiny saplings broke through the shrub layer. Each fighting for light beneath the aging canopy.

So many emotions washed over Violet as she walked that dirt track. The smells of the countryside hadn't changed. A fresh, slightly bitter scent of ivy filled her nostrils, and she breathed it in deeply. The woodland's musty dampness reminded her of childhood games of hide and seek. The crunching underfoot brought the realisation of her presence back at the old farm. A shout came from the side of the farmhouse.

'Hey. Hello there.' It was a young voice. Violet quickened her pace, as a young boy came through the garden gate and stood. As she got closer, she realised it was one of her brothers.

'Joseph, is that you? Hello. I'm your sister Violet. Do you remember me?' As Violet walked towards him, the young boy ran towards Violet and launched himself at her with real emotion, gripping her round the waist, cheek pressed firmly against her breast.

'Hello Violet. I'm Hector, not Joe. It is so good you are here. Joseph is back in the garden.' He drew back and gripped her by the hand. 'Come with me. Come on.' Eagerly her brother pulled her through the side gate, where Joseph was waiting. A shy boy, Joe held back. Violet approached him and put out her hand, aware he wasn't sure of her.

'It's our sister Violet, Joe. Give her a hug.' Joseph stepped forward, pressed by his older brother, and gave her a brief hug. 'Come on Vi, come in and see mother and father. This way.' Hector led the way round the back to a small door, opposite a burgeoning vegetable patch. Her father's work. It led into the kitchen. She was greeted by the familiar baking smell of her mother's kitchen, the black and red flagstone floor, and blackened fireplace. Nothing had changed there. Some washing was hanging above the fireplace, but no sign of her parents. Hector walked through to the dining area, beckoning her to follow. Her father was sitting in an old threadbare armchair, with a dog at his feet and a newspaper in his hand. He glanced up and lowered the paper a shade.

The room was the family's main dining area, with a further fireplace backing on to the kitchen. Worn yellow curtains hung at the window. The teacup and teapot prints, so loved by her mother when new, now faded and deteriorating with age and years of sun damage. A rough rag rug lay in front of the fireplace, protected by a heavy tarnished metal fireguard. A table of heavy oak, with barley twist legs, and 4 small matching chairs, was positioned under the window, and her father's armchair had the spot closest to the fireplace. No doubt in wintertime, it was the warmest spot. On the opposite wall, the door to the stairs was closed, as was the door to the lounge.

'Violet.' Her father spoke in acknowledgement of her presence, nodding as he did so. A smile was not forthcoming.

'Father.' Violet responded in return. She had been thinking about the purpose of her visit, all the way up on the train. She'd rehearsed many different scenarios and potential conversations. Violet decided she would need to choose the right moment, and that moment was not yet. 'I'll put the kettle on father. Would you like tea?' Deciding she needed some refreshment after her long journey, and to begin building bridges, this seemed the best ice breaker.

'I can do that for you Violet, you sit down with father.' Hot on her heels, young Hector was keen to help. Joseph hovered in the doorway as Hector went back to the kitchen.

'When you have done that, go and play, there's a good lad.' Violet's father was firm, but not unkind. Hector put on the kettle, then ushered Joseph back out into the back yard. He was very aware that defying his father would not be wise.

Albert Brown was an aging farmer. Now in his 50s, a lifetime of long working days, had left him with mobility problems. His work on the farm had changed and adapted as his health had deteriorated. Violet could see a change in her father. His face was drawn; almost gaunt, with a ruddy complexion. His eyes sunken. Albert had always liked a drink, and Vi suspected his alcohol consumption had increased. The kettle boiled and Violet made tea for the two of them. Her mother had not appeared, and Vi presumed she was lying down. She would see her later, but for now, it was her father she was concentrating on. She handed a cup and saucer to him, then sat down at the dining table. There was a short silence as they both took sips of the steaming tea.

'What are you 'ere for gal?' The broad Norfolk accent evident as Albert addressed his daughter. 'It has been a while. What is it you want from us now?' Violet wasn't surprised by his directness, but tried to stay calm, even though her heart thumped with increased anxiety.

'I was keen to see mother; to see how she is. I haven't heard from her for some time now father. And the boys. They need to be reminded they have sisters.' Trying not to stumble over her words, she knew her father wasn't stupid.

'And what else?' Albert Brown wasn't interested in frivolities - as he wasn't interested in his family if the truth were known. 'Why are you *really* here Violet. Is this your sister's doing?'

'You haven't even asked about Temperance. How she is, where she is, what she is doing to manage, to survive. Have you no interest in your daughter?' Violet couldn't help raising her voice, but the reality was her sister needed help, and this man had to acknowledge his part in her departure. Whether he would or not, was yet to be seen.

'Your mother is dozing in the lounge, so please keep your voice down Violet. I suggest you go up to your room and freshen up, then we can discuss what it is you want, after the boys have gone to bed. I do not want them upset.' Violet was almost speechless. Never had he shown such concern for his daughters. She finished her tea in silence, then took her small bag up to the spare room, where a bed had been carefully made up for her. She sat down and leant back for a few moments and fell promptly into a light sleep.

Violet awoke abruptly when a loud rap at her door was followed by one of her brothers calling her name.

'Hello Hector, I'll be right down.' Quickly gathering her composure, she changed into a clean blouse and joined the rest of the family in the dining room. The table now laid neatly for five. The strong smell of fish filled the room. Of course, it was Saturday, and they always had kippers for tea. She took her place at the end of the table, after pausing to greet her mother as she came in from the kitchen with a large plate of smoked fish. Both boys were seated on the far side of the table, sharing a chair, with napkins already tucked in to their shirt collars. A large plate of thinly sliced, thickly buttered brown bread, filled the centre of the table. Vi was momentarily taken back to her own childhood. So reminiscent of family teatimes, but with one person missing. It wasn't the whole family, without Temperance.

They ate in silence, and then all moved into the sitting room. A darker room, with two heavy, red, patterned armchairs, in front of the wide, inglenook fireplace. A rug on the flagstones, which almost covered the room, made it a cosier warm space. Floor length green lined curtains at the window, and a standard lamp with a frill edged shade. Nothing had changed with the décor since Violet had lived at the farm. It wasn't likely to change now either. Violet's mother had various health problems and had little interest in the home. Violet worried for her brothers. Her mother clearly suffered with 'her nerves' and spent a lot of time in bed. Perhaps Violet worried needlessly. Both boys seemed healthy, although Joseph was quite timid. She hoped their father wasn't using the strap to discipline them. She hadn't seen sign of it this visit, so was hopeful.

The boys sat down on the rug, and Violet instinctively knelt down with them. Hector pulled out his game of Ludo and started to play it with Joe. Both parents sat in their armchairs in silence. The radio droned from the sideboard and her father lit a pipe, his evening routine unchanged. Her mother picked up some darning. Her father's worn work socks, way past their usefulness, but old habits die hard. They had worked through the war to raise their children, and the 'make do and mend' mentality had very much stuck.

'Violet.'

'Yes Hector.' Violet was enjoying the time with her brothers and letting them get used to her company.

'Where is our sister Temperance?' That was not the question she had expected from her brother. It proved their parents had not made any effort to explain Temperance's whereabouts. She needed to think fast.

'She has gone away.' She glanced at her father, who had removed the pipe from his mouth and was looking at her. 'She is on holiday.' Her father nodded. She hoped that would be the only challenging question from the boys. She quickly changed the subject. 'I brought you both some sweets boys, you will need to check if it is ok for you to have them now.' Violet put her hand into her pocket and pulled out two small paper bags, bulging with toffees. Hector looked up at his father, who again nodded.

'Just one now boys and then save the rest for tomorrow,' he said. Both boys keenly tucked into the sweet bags, their game forgotten. 'Time to get off to bed now. Make sure you clean your teeth.'

Hector quickly put away the game then hugged Violet before saying goodnight to his parents. Joseph followed behind, copying his older brother's lead. It left Violet in the company of her parents, and she pulled an old rocking chair, closer to the fire. The chair was an heirloom, that had belonged to her grandmother. She remembered Gran living with them, when she was a child. She would sit in the corner and knit. Mostly socks, but also pullovers and tank tops. She died when Violet was seven. She remembered it well, because until that time, she had shared a room with Temperance. When Gran died, Violet got a room to herself. She returned to the present, and thoughts turned to the conversation she needed to have with her parents, or perhaps just her father.

'I want to talk to you about Temperance. She has written to me.' Violet waited for a reaction. There was none. 'She needs a bit of financial help to get herself set up in her own home.'

'No Violet. She has had all she is going to get.' Albert cut in sharply, without letting Violet explain any further. Violet's mother looked up at her husband. Concern etched on her face, but she didn't utter a word. It was clear who was in charge. 'No, she is getting nothing more, and that is my final word.' Violet was a little taken aback by quite how abrupt he was but not surprised. There was no point in pursuing it, Violet was clear on that. It meant she would reluctantly have to move to plan B. That would have to wait until the following day. Violet said goodnight to her parents and made her way up the uneven stairs to her room. Sleep eluded her for several hours as her troubled mind ached with thoughts of the challenge ahead. She eventually drifted off into a dream filled sleep, with the only comfort that she would return home to her beloved Ronald in a few short hours.

26

NORFOLK - 1954

After a night of little meaningful sleep, in an unfamiliar bed and with the help of a loud cockerel outside her bedroom, Violet was wide awake by dawn.

She felt as if her head had cleared overnight. Not quite sure how that had happened, considering the broken sleep, but she knew she needed to rise early, and act fast. She wasn't proud of her planned actions, but she felt she had no choice. She dressed quickly and quietly, careful not to wake the family. She could hear her father snoring loudly from the adjacent room and smiled inwardly. He was quite a heavy drinker at the weekends, and she didn't expect to see him before 10 at the earliest.

At the bottom of the stairs, she carefully unlatched the door, through to the dining room. The flagstones were cold on her stockinged feet, as she crossed the room, through the kitchen and into the back parlour. The room was dark, and the door always kept closed, but if she was quick, she could locate the savings tin and take a few pounds without anyone knowing she had been there. The far side of the room had a kind of heated cupboard, where her mother kept bedding and table linen. It was adjacent to the fireplace which had the backboiler producing hot water for the home. The piping ran through this cupboard and made it a useful warm space to dry damp clothes. She reached down inside the cupboard, to a small shelf. As she felt along the length of the shelf, her fingertips met with the cold metal of the money tin. Success. Still no sound from the rest of the house, her heart was beating faster as she carefully extracted the tin. It was a simple old biscuit tin. It had been in the house since well before the war. Rectangular, solid, it had originally contained Jacobs crackers. Decorated with Victorian city scenes, now tarnished and faded. The lid was firmly closed, but Violet was able to prize it open without a problem. As expected, it contained a bulging tired brown envelope; banknotes peeking from one side. Violet quickly slipped her hand in and took a small bundle of notes. She knew this was her father's money and that her mother had no knowledge of the cash. But Violet had always known it was there.

As a small child, she would hide in the parlour to escape the shouting, and had once witnessed her father stowing the box away when he thought no-one was watching him. She had later that day gone back to the cupboard, inquisitively exploring the hidden tin, and discovered the treasure within. She had never taken money from the box, until today.

Quickly she replaced the tin, closed the door and tucking the cash into her girdle, she left the parlour. Pausing in the kitchen, heart still racing, she listened in silence to see if anyone was stirring. Still nothing, she let out a sigh of relief and as quietly as possible, filled the enamel kettle, and put it on the hob. She sat back on the kitchen stool to wait for it to boil. A nice cup of tea would ease her guilt.

The boys were awake shortly after the kettle had let out its piercing whistle, and she could hear them moving around upstairs. Violet's mother appeared in the kitchen fully dressed, taking her housecoat from the hook on the back of the kitchen door.

'Good morning Violet. You were awake early; did you sleep well?' It was the first time her mother had spoken to her since she had arrived. Violet knew it was because her father was not in earshot.

'I was unsettled. A strange bed, that's all. Is father awake?' Her mother shook her head. 'Would you like tea, it is brewing in the pot?' Violet took two cups and saucers from the dresser and took the jug of milk from the larder. 'Let's take it through to the dining room table, where we can both sit down.

'I should get on, Violet dear. I have my jobs before church.' Her mother seemed anxious.

'You can come and sit down; a few minutes will not hurt. We haven't had a chance to talk mother. I'm concerned for your health.' Violet wanted to take the opportunity before her father appeared.

'You don't need to worry about me. I am under the doctor and he has given me pills for my nerves.' Her mother was clearly not keen to engage in conversation.

'And you haven't asked about Temperance. Don't you have any interest in her, mother? She is still your daughter, and very much alone.' Violet noticed her mother's face drop. She put her hand to her brow.

'Of course I have interest Violet, but she has made her choice. I cannot go against your father. What he decides, must be.' There was to be no breaking down of this barrier her parents had built. They drank their tea in silence.

By 9 o'clock both boys were downstairs tucking into a bowl each of porridge. Violet had explained to her mother that she would not be staying another night and, as it was Sunday, she would need to be back to King's Lynn for the midday train. Getting to the station, would take her an hour walking, and without a bus service, she had already resigned herself to make the journey on foot. She felt anxious to leave before her father surfaced, so collected her small bag from the bedroom. Her mother hovered by her side, as she checked everything was there, then thrust a small parcel of sandwiches into her hand.

'You will need something for the journey Violet.' Violet smiled and briefly embraced her mother - an awkward moment for them both. 'And Violet, please when you next write to Temperance, will you send my best regards?'

'I will mother, thank you. I have my small box brownie in my bag; please will you take a photo of me with the boys?' Violet really felt as if she didn't know when she would see her brothers again. A photo of them together would be the next best thing.

Her mother agreed, and when the boys had finished their breakfast, they all gathered in the front room for the photo. Hector put his arm around Violet's waist. At 14 he was already up to Violet's shoulder. Joe more reticent, stood slightly away from Violet, but she put her hand on his shoulder, and the picture was taken. Violet was keen to get away before her father appeared, so she said her goodbyes, with a tight hug from her brother Hector, who then insisted on walking to the gate with her.

As they walked the length of the gravel drive, Violet wondered if she would ever return to her family home. It had always held happy memories from her very early childhood, when it was just her and Temperance. When the boys came along, things had started to change, and she couldn't bear to think about it. Hector broke into her thoughts.

'Will you send me the photo please Vi? They had reached the gate.

'The photo?' Violet was momentarily confused by the question. 'Oh, you mean the photo mother has just taken of us?' Hector nodded. 'Of course I will Hector.'

'And will you come back to see us again?' Such innocence, Violet didn't want to disappoint her brother. She nodded, unable to lie outright. A nod didn't somehow feel like a lie. She had no intention of returning.

'How about when you are old enough, you come and stay with me? You would love the big city, I'm sure Hector. And Joseph, if he wants to.'

'You mean London? I'd love to go to London. Yeah, Joseph is a bit shy. He's ok though. I look out for him at school.' Hector was going to be the adventurous one, Violet was sure.

'I need to go now lad; I have a train to catch. Be good for mother.' As she walked away, she turned and waved, to see Hector swinging on the old gate, waving back. She kept walking and waving, until she could no longer see the gate, or her young brother.

Brushing away a silly tear, she strode forwards up the road, to Lynn, and ultimately home to her Ronald.

27

NORFOLK - 2024

Just two days later, Sam, Melody and Tilly had gathered a variety of cleaning products, filling Sam's van for the return visit to 'Spitalbrook'. Tilly had borrowed the Dyson from work and Melody had brought her Henry vacuum cleaner from home. Lois was with grandma for the whole day, and they had managed to get out early. No mean feat for Tilly, who was not a morning person. Melody had also thought of all the essentials for a full day at the house, with not only mugs, coffee, tea bags, and milk, but also a kettle and some bottled water. Kit had to go back to London to finalise things for her New York trip but was returning at the weekend. Sam had been put in charge of maintenance jobs and had his tools.

It was a beautiful bright and sunny late spring day. The journey was non-eventful, and the small group travelled in silence, while Radio Two blared out on the van's radio. Tilly started to nod off, but before she had a chance to get into a deep sleep, they had pulled up at the entrance to Spitalbrook. Sam made good time, going against the traffic and the threesome arrived at just after 9. Melody gave Tilly a nudge, to rouse her.

'We're here Tilly, jump out and open the gate.' The van had three seats at the front and with Tilly by the door, yawning, she slid back the door and stepped down, making her way over to the gate. It felt familiar being back so soon and Tilly was keen to get stuck in this time. She opened the gate, then followed Sam's van back up the drive.

Seeing the house again, gave her butterflies in her tummy. There was a fresh cherry blossom scent in the air. As the sun shone through the leaves it left a dappled pattern at her feet. To think, her grandfather had grown up here with his siblings. Her lovely Uncle Hector being one of them. It really was the family home, or at least, it had been at one time. Taking in more of the surrounding grounds this time, Tilly saw how far the fields of neatly cut grass spread out to both sides of the property. Bound by a simple wooden fence on one side and neatly cut hedges on the other three. Clearly someone was still managing the grounds, even if the house itself was not maintained. Perhaps it didn't belong to the house, but Tilly was just grateful there was nothing for her to do on the outside, to make it presentable for the guests. She hurried up to the front door, where her friends were waiting.

Once inside, Melody sorted out the kitchen bits and pieces, and they had a cup of coffee before starting. The girls put on rubber gloves and aprons, while Sam took himself off to sort out the lights and run the taps. He said the water would need to run for a long while to clear out the old stagnant pipes. The girls left him to it and set to work in the three main downstairs rooms. Tilly had brought with her special attachments to clean the curtains. Valerie had insisted she borrowed everything, and it seemed as if she was going to need them. Melody took her Henry into the dining room to start on the carpet, moving furniture to the sides to get to the whole of the carpeted area. It was wooden parquet, with a large, deep, maroon, patterned rug covering it. Melody wanted to get the rug up, so that she could polish the parquet, but they discussed it and decided it was too big a job with the limited time, so she stuck to just hoovering. Tilly came in with her curtain attachment, hoovering the heavy brocade fabric, removing the net curtain completely. Who has net curtains these days anyway, she thought. It brightened the room instantly and highlighted the surfaces which needed some polish, despite the covering of the white sheets. The curtains would need dry cleaning, to be the cleanest they could be, but in the time allowed, the hoovering had to do.

By one o'clock Sam was complaining of hunger pangs, so they gathered in the hallway with a couple of dining chairs, to eat their sandwiches, and assess where they were at with the list of jobs. Sam had successfully changed all the bulbs he could find, including the strip light in the kitchen, which had certainly highlighted the dated decor. The dining room had clean curtains and carpet, and Tilly had started polishing the furniture with a nice lavender scented spray. The ceiling cobwebs in all the rooms were now no more, much to Tilly's relief. She was not at all keen on spiders. Sam had run the taps and said they were now running clear. They had found a toilet outside, and one upstairs through the main bedroom. Sam had decided the outside toilet would be the best one to use at the wake and had cleared a pathway to it, but had said he couldn't clean the toilet, because he didn't know how to do it properly. Melody had to agree that he wasn't the best when it came to domestic duties. She took over and worked her magic, leaving it unrecognisable. Sam fixed the lock on the door, and Mel added smelly 'fresh linen' scented room fresheners.

The afternoon was focussed on the lounge, where the floor was stone tiles under another heavy, dark rug. Tilly did the same with the curtains, removing the nets to a black sack, and tried to ignore the writing desk, hidden behind the sofa. There would be time to explore its contents once they had finished the cleaning. She dusted and polished the heavy, oak, oversized mantelpiece. The fireplace was littered with years of crusty black bits. She swept the whole of the hearth with a dustpan and brush, carefully pushing the brush up the small chimney to dislodge any loose particles. The actual chimney flue had been blocked partially by some brown paper. Tilly pulled at it, dislodging a shower of black soot and the remains of a dead pigeon, which made her jump.

'I think we deserve a cup of tea.' Sam came into the lounge having finished the maintenance jobs he had found for himself. 'I've put the kettle on. How are you two doing?' Melody was on her hands and knees with a bowl of hot, soapy water and a sponge, cleaning the skirting board. She looked up at her husband and smiled.

'I think we're getting there love. Do you agree Tills?' Melody continued to clean.

'Yeah, I have hoovered these curtains and the sofa and most of the big rug. I can't move the sofa to do underneath it, but I imagine we will only need chairs and tables. I propose we push the chairs to the back of the room and pull the coffee table out in front of the fireplace.' Tilly had been thinking about the funeral and wake as she cleaned. The logistics of seating people together formally. She decided that wasn't a possibility, so a buffet laid out in the dining room, with chairs spread across the three downstairs rooms, seemed the best option. She had also been wondering how many people would attend. She didn't think it was likely to be that many but guessed some people from Sunny Days might want to come. Then there was her mum and David, the solicitor Ashley Coombs, her Aunt Gilly, and her two cousins. Plus, obviously Kit, Mel, Sam and herself. She would check with the solicitor, as he was organising the funeral. He would know numbers.

They stopped for tea, and tasty snacks in the form of homemade fairy cakes, provided by Mel's mum.

'Lovely cake Mel. Would your mum make some for the wake, do you think? I'll buy the ingredients.' Tilly spoke enthusiastically, with a mouth full of sponge.

'Of course she will Tilly, and you won't need to buy the ingredients. She loves cooking. Anything else? Sausage rolls perhaps or cheese straws? I'll get her to do both.' Melody's mum had been their old school cook when they were at primary school. She made the best shortbread biscuits, which they had with the school, strawberry flavoured, artificially pink yoghurt. They were the lightest melt in the mouth biscuits you ever tasted, and she was the most popular dinner lady because of them.

'Thank you, Melody. I will find out how many people will be there from Ashley.' Tilly stood up and put her sandwich wrapper into the cool bag Melody had brought with her. 'It's three o'clock now, would you say another hour and we will be done?' Sam and Melody nodded, so Tilly went back to the lounge. She stood looking at the writing desk, itching to open it. But it wasn't priority. Reluctantly, she accepted it would have to wait until after the funeral. Instead, she had a look through the sideboard drawers, where she found at least four clean, ironed tablecloths, and a full set of cutlery. In cupboards, either end, was a dinner service which was old and crazed. Tilly thought paper plates, or even a cheap Tesco value set would be better than the vintage family china. Another thing to check with Ashley about. She took the cutlery and gave it a good rinse in some warm soapy water. The tablecloths were a bit musty, but not bad enough that it would notice.

The girls finished off their jobs, cleaning paintwork while Sam mopped the hall and kitchen floor. The sky had clouded over, and it looked like a storm was brewing. They came together in the hall, to assess the results of the day's work, agreeing it was ready to receive visitors.

'Obviously, the whole house could do with a coat of paint, new kitchen and a general update, but that is someone else's worry for the future. In the time we had, I think we've done a good job, and it's now far more presentable. Have you put an air freshener in every room Mel? One of those little bottles with the sticks in it, we brought with us?'

'You mean the reed diffusers, and yes, I have put them everywhere. I'm leaving the kettle and mugs. They are spare, so can stay until the funeral. Everything else I've got in here.' Melody lifted up the big cool bag she had brought with her. They were ready to go. Tilly checked the back door was locked and ushered the other two out, so that she could lock the front door behind her.

Tilly felt odd. Like she was leaving a friend behind. She knew that her next visit to Spitalbrook would probably be after the funeral, and she wasn't looking forward to that day. She really wasn't sure she was ready for it. Was anyone ever ready? They got into Sam's van and drove back to Georgie. This time, both girls slept in the van. Evidence that they had worked exhaustively all day.

Sam dropped Tilly off at the canal, as the light was fading. The weather had held out, until that point, then the heavens opened. Marmite jumped down from the roof of the boat and joined Tilly, as she entered her floating home, and they settled down for a cosy evening together.

28

NORFOLK - 2024

'Hello love.' Celia met Tilly at the church gate. 'David is just parking the car.' She seemed to Tilly, unusually kind to Tilly, which was welcome, as Tilly still didn't know how she was going to get through the day. She had arrived at the local church, St Christopher, before anyone else, and had been in to speak to the vicar. The Reverend Susan Green was going to take the service. She wasn't sure how strong Uncle Hector's faith had been, but clearly it was what Hector had planned for himself and so a church service was to be an important part of the ceremony. There had been a few calls between herself and the solicitor, but thankfully, Ashley Coombs had dealt with all the arrangements, as he had promised.

Tilly felt like she had already done a day's work. She had got up at 6, and Sam had arrived at 6.30 to take her, plus four crates of carefully prepared food, in the van to Spitalbrook. Barbara, Melody's mum, had been true to her word and supplied them with a wealth of lovely buffet treats. Not only sausage rolls, scones and cheese straws, but also some individual cheese and tomato quiches, plus a whole box of the special shortbread biscuits, just for Tilly.

They were only expecting about fourteen people, give or take one or two. So they had decided to cater for twenty. It would be a small affair, but for Tilly, just as important to make it as perfect as if there were a hundred. The roads were clear, and they were at the house just after 7am. Sam carried the boxes into the hall, while Tilly dressed the main table and sideboard. At the last minute, they had decided to hire crockery and cutlery from a local catering company, who were willing to let them have just twenty place settings. In the absence of a fridge, Tilly got Sam to place the food items in the old larder. The plan being for the three girls to put everything onto platters once they returned to Spitalbrook for the wake. A 5-minute job, Tilly thought. She didn't want things to dry out and curl before everyone arrived. Sam and Tilly were in the van and back on the road by 8.30, heading home to prepare for the main event.

David arrived and joined Tilly's mum at the gate. He nodded to Tilly then took Celia's hand and they walked into the church. Tilly's Aunt Gilly and her older cousins Tris and Charlotte had arrived while Tilly was talking to Ashley. Gilly had smiled, but her adult children had almost glared at Tilly. She presumed they had got wind of the £10,000 and didn't like it. There had always been competition and jealousy in the Brown family, and Tilly wasn't close to her cousins. She didn't want any bad feeling on this of all days. She refused to let them upset her today.

Jane from Sunny Days arrived next, already dabbing her nose with a clean white linen handkerchief. Tilly had been holding it together until that point, but when Jane gave her a choked-up hug, Tilly wobbled a bit. Composing herself with a long, slow deep breath, she sent Jane in, to sit near the front, persuading her there were not going to be that many people and she was perfectly in her right, to sit at the front where she could see and hear the whole service.

Sam, Melody and Kit were the last to arrive, all together, just before the arrival of the hearse. Tilly had chosen not to arrive with Uncle Hector. The undertakers were very kind, giving her the option for another car and said it had all been provided for by Uncle Hector. But in the end, she decided it would be nice to greet people at the church, so wanted to be there early with plenty of time to do just that. Tilly and Ashley greeted the undertaker Mr Carter, together. A calm smiley man, who had gone through the process with Tilly at the undertakers the week before. He had reassured her that she didn't need to do, say or remember anything and that they had it all in hand. It was reassuring for Tilly. She had a reading to do, but that was her choice, and she didn't need to remember it off by heart.

Tilly took her place by her mother and David on the front pew. Ashley Coombs sat in the pew behind her. As the music started up, 'My Way' rang out echoing through the church rafters, Frank Sinatra in full voice, Uncle Hector's choice. The congregation all stood up, as the pall bearers made their way slowly up the aisle, carrying Hector high on their shoulders. Almost majestically on his final journey.

How her great uncle would have loved this attention from a small group of people closest to him, Tilly thought. Although it crossed her mind that perhaps a few of the family members could have done more with visiting in those final weeks and months. That wasn't for today though and, pushing this to the back of her mind, she focussed on the music. The flowers atop the eco-friendly bamboo coffin, were simple white lilies. All carefully selected by Hector himself, unbeknown to Tilly. Whilst she knew it would have been a very difficult discussion to have with him, she felt a mixture of sadness and relief that it had not been down to her. Ashley had already explained to her that the plans had been made long before his recent memory loss, and he reassured her that this was exactly how Hector wanted it.

As the music faded, and the pall bearers took their seats at the back of the church, the Reverend Susan Green took her place at the lectern, smiling reassuringly at her compact congregation. There was a tangible pause where silence took centre stage and all eyes were on the Reverend, before she began to address the few gathered.

'We are gathered here to not only celebrate the long and interesting life of our dear friend and loved one Hector Aubrey Brown, but to reflect on how he has impacted on our own lives. Each one of us will have a connection, and each connection will be unique to us as individuals. I was fortunate to be invited to visit Hector during his residency at Sunny Days. This is unusual for someone in my position. We so often know only what family members have told us about their dearly departed loved one. But in Hectors case, I visited him three times on his request and got to know a little bit about the man whose life we are here to celebrate today.

He told me in detail about his travels around the world delivering art pieces to the rich and famous. About his happy childhood at Spitalbrook where we will end our celebrations later today, and about his loving family, some of whom are here with us today. He shared funny stories about the care home in which he had made some close friends, George being one of them, and of his feeling that Sunny Days really was a happy place to end his days.

Hector explained to me that he was not scared of death. He wasn't 100% sure of what he believed came next, as he put it to me he 'sat on the fence' where religion was concerned, so he wanted to cover all bases, by allowing me to take the stand here today.' There was a ripple of laughter among the small group gathered. Tilly could well believe this to be Hector's view and could hear him saying exactly that. Susan continued.

'He told me that talking to a person of the cloth and doing the right thing - by which he meant having his funeral in a religious setting, would perhaps get him a ticket to upstairs.' Another ripple of laughter. The elderly organist then began the opening bars of Morning Has Broken and they all stood up, to a rustle of papers as the congregation fumbled through the order of service.

There was just one reading. That was from Tilly. She had chosen something short, which she read clearly, and without too much shake in her voice. She ended with her own brief few words.

'As the Reverend Green has already said, Uncle Hector had an interesting and varied life. Most of which I knew very little of. I wish, now, that I had spent even more time with him than I did. But I am glad for the visits I made and the chats we had. Sharing a cup of coffee while he watched birds on his bird feeder or reminisced about his siblings. Because I have learned that time is precious. We have just one chance on this earth, and we must value and appreciate that time, and our loved ones, be they friends or family. Those who are important to you.' Tilly looked across to Kit, Melody and Sam. Melody was wiping her eyes but mouthed 'love you' to her friend.

Tilly felt strong and knew then that she had no need to feel doubt or shame. She had made visits to Uncle Hector, and she knew he had appreciated her for it. 'Uncle Hector was a special man, and life is poorer without him. I will miss him.'

Tilly returned to her place on the pew and Kit gave her a reassuring squeeze on the shoulder. They stood to sing the final song Psalm 23. Tilly wasn't sure she knew this one, until the music started and then she realised it was the tune from The Vicar of Dibley. Just like Hector to pick something with a comical connection, she thought. The small group sang loudly, relief in their voices that they were close to the end.

The funeral ended formally with Hector's casket being carried out of the church accompanied by a tinny version of 'Time To Say Goodbye' the Andrea Bocelli and Sarah Brightman version. Tilly hadn't taken Hector as an opera fan, but clearly there was much she would now never know about her great uncle.

Surprisingly, Hector had paid for a plot in the graveyard. The group followed his coffin to the spot, tucked into the corner, by the moss coated flint wall on two sides, and the grave of a 'Bernard Hollingwell' who had died in 1923, on the other. It was difficult for everyone to get around the grave, but here more words were said by the Reverend Green, as Hector Brown was slowly lowered into the ground. Tilly felt comforted that there would be a place for her to visit, but that final descent of the coffin brought a rush of tears she hadn't quite expected. But she had this beautiful place to visit, for remembering and for paying her respects. Not that she needed a place. She would always remember Hector, but she felt it symbolised him as a person, and in time she would arrange for a lovely big headstone. Ashley said that was already accounted for in his finances.

And then it was over. Just the wake to get through and then she could relax. Tilly took a deep breath and brushing away her tears she joined her friends.

'Coming in the car with me Tills?' said Kit. Still feeling a little choked up Tilly nodded and climbed into the sports car. Leaving everyone milling about at the church, the young ones headed off to welcome their guests to the wake.

29

NORFOLK - 2024

'Was this going to be her final visit to Spitalbrook?' is what Tilly was thinking as they pulled up at the now familiar five bar gated entrance, to the old Brown family farmhouse.

'You ok love?' said Kit, with the engine still running. 'Hop out and grab the gate.' Tilly was already unbuckling her seat belt.

'I'll walk up behind you Kit.' Tilly knew that if this was to be her final visit, then she wanted to experience that atmospheric walk up the long tree and shrub lined track one more time. On her own, in the peace and quiet, even better. Kit drove very sedately ahead, and was soon out of sight and parked, leaving Tilly the solitary walk.

When Tilly reached the house, Kit was still sitting in her sportscar. Kit waved, and Tilly beckoned to her, getting out the ornate front door key for the final time. The girls went into the hallway and turned on the light. Tilly had dressed the side table earlier with a large bunch of lilies in a vase, placed on a cream broderie anglaise tablecloth. The pungent scent of freshly blooming lilies filled the room.

'It looks and smells gorgeous Tilly. You have worked real magic in here.' Kit was genuinely surprised at the transformation of the dusty cobweb filled hall she had encountered just a couple of weeks previously. Tilly felt a warm glow in the knowledge that her hard work was evident.

'It wasn't just me Kit. Melody and Sam helped a lot with the cleaning and preparation. Sam brought me up here early this morning with the food and flowers. We just need to put it all onto platters, then lay it out in the dining room.'

As the two of them made a bee line for the larder, Sam pulled up outside with Melody who joined them to help with the preparations. There were glasses laid out on the sideboard, with a variety of alcoholic and soft drinks in the dining room. Mainly red and white wine and a few beers, but Tilly knew a lot of the friends and family were driving, so tea and coffee was also on offer.

Melody had a list of things in order, that she knew she had to do. First was to light the old aga, which she had practiced once before. Then she filled the kettle and prepared a cafetiere. They had two trays with mugs laid out neatly on the enamel dropdown surface of the 1920s Easiwork kitchen cabinet. A jug filled with milk, next to a bowl of sugar and a neat pile of teaspoons were nestled behind. They really had thought of everything. Once she had finished hot drink preparation, Melody put the sausage rolls and quiches on a tray and into the main oven to warm, then added the cakes to a pretty oval platter they had found in the sideboard. Tilly was flapping, going from one room to another without achieving very much and Melody could see she was anxious.

'It's fine Tilly, we have everything covered, you really can relax now.' Melody's calm voice was soothing, but didn't make any difference to Tilly. She just wanted it all to be over. She had got through the funeral and her speech and now she just wanted to successfully finish the task she had been set, with a more upbeat celebration of Hector's life. A bit of mingling and then the will. Roll on 5pm was all that was on her mind, when a tap at the open door, brought her back to her senses. The first of the guests had arrived. It was her mum Celia and her stepfather David.

'Can we come in?' A silly question really, as Celia was by then in the hallway. Tilly came forward to greet her with an air kiss, followed by a light shoulder touch from David.

'Of course mum, come in. David.' She smiled and led them through to the dining room and showed her to the drinks.

'A coffee for me please Tilly, as I am driving.' David was polite, but too busy scouring the house for eye contact. 'Milk and two sugars, ta.'

'Of course. The kettle is on. Oh and Mum, you can help yourself. Glasses are on the sideboard in there. There is a bottle of white and a bottle of rose in the larder here.' They had to pass through the small kitchen to get to the dining room. 'You can help yourself.'

The remaining few guests trickled in, commenting on the farmhouse as they arrived. 'Lovely old features.' 'I love the beams.' 'What quaint windows.' All marginally more interesting conversation pieces than remarking on the weather. Which in fact had been unseasonably warm all day and for which Tilly was thankful. If there was a God, she figured he was watching over them today.

The warmed food was removed from the aga and placed on the table on large platters. The selection of finger food and some snacky bits were going down well amongst the guests. As the afternoon progressed, a lighter mood developed. There was a bit of laughter and small groups had formed. She saw her cousin Tris talking to Ashley at one point, which gave her a little concern, but it was nice to see Jane chatting to her mum. She couldn't imagine what they were talking about but was too busy with keeping tea and coffee topped up to try and join in, or even worry too much.

She found herself physically relaxing, the day was a success, and all fears she had been storing up for so long, now dissolved as a distant memory. She wondered why she worried about things unnecessarily. Yet she had no answer and would probably continue to be a worrier, however much she knew it was a waste of energy. She glanced at her watch, almost 3pm. Time to gather everyone in the lounge for the reading of the Will, which Ashley was going to oversee. She took a deep breath, filled the coffee pot and went off to find him.

Ashley was ready, as ever the professional, with his briefcase. Tilly had bought some bottles of prosecco to toast Uncle Hector's long and happy life and brought them through to fill the glasses. She grabbed a teaspoon and lightly tapped the neck of the bottle, to grab the attention of the guests.

'Hello everyone, can you all come into the lounge area, for the reading of the will. Bring your glasses, or grab a glass if you don't have one, so that we can raise a small toast to our dear Hector.' Tilly was happy with how the day had gone and at last felt at ease. This last bit a formality and then they could all clear up and go home.

The guests broke off conversations and moved rooms. Ashley stood by the fireplace, facing the group shuffling some papers. Tilly took the prosecco round and filled some glasses, half-filled others. Then a hush descended.

'Thank you all for coming. I think you will agree that Tilly and her friends have done an excellent job of preparing this old building to accommodate us all here, in the childhood home of Hector Brown.' There was a murmur of agreement in the room and lots of nodding. Jane who was standing next to Tilly, patted her appreciatively on the shoulder and others smiled. Tilly felt herself blush and nodded her thanks back. 'Now I just want to finish' continued Ashley,' by reading the last will and testament lodged with my firm of solicitors by Hector. He cleared his throat and then read:

'This is the last will and testament dictated to my solicitor Ashley Coombs, this 3rd day of May in the year 2024, whilst of sound body and mind (but old and tired - not senile) of I, Hector Donald Brown.

To my friend George at Sunny Days, I leave my walking stick with the ivory handle. It can be found in my room.
To the lovely staff at Sunny Days, I leave £100. I hope they will treat themselves to an evening out, and a few bottles of bubbly.
To the charity 'Cat Care', I leave the sum of £100
To my niece Celia Kennedy I leave my antique carriage clock. This was your grandmothers and she loved it dearly.
To my niece Gillian Fitzgerald, I leave my oak hall stand.
To my great nephew Tristan Arthur Fitzgerald, I leave my fish knife and fork set.

To my great niece Charlotte Katherine York (nee Fitzgerald), I leave your great grandmother's dressing table set and tortoiseshell mirror.

I leave the remainder of my personal effects together with the sum of £10,000, to my great niece Matilda Jean Montgomery-Brown. Tilly receives these items, on the condition that she carries out the wishes I have made clear in a separate letter addressed to her and lodged with Mr Coombs. It is not necessary for this letter to be read out in public.

There are to be no challenges to this will. It is short and sweet. These are my wishes.

Signed H D Brown.'

Ashley folded the papers and looked up. There was a stillness in the room, blank looks, and those of surprise. Wanting more maybe? An almost imperceptible sense of expectation hung heavy, with the only sound that of a dozen almost silent breathers. After a moment, Melody pushed through from the back of the group.

'Any more teas or coffees people? If not, I will start washing up. Sam love, could you put the immersion heater on please?' Well done Melody, Tilly was thinking. Sam went to the dining room cupboard and flicked the switch for the immersion. Kit and Tilly both moved to collect glasses and mugs, in the hope it would prompt people to gather their things and move on. Tilly noticed her cousin Tristan talking again to Ashley in the doorway. He was quite animated in his hand gestures, but she couldn't tell what he was saying. Thank goodness Ashley was here to deal with any controversy.

Celia and David left first. Not surprisingly, Tilly thought, although they did say goodbye, and complimented her on her speech and the organisation of the day. They clearly had no issue with the Will, which was a relief for Tilly, but David was successful and had provided her mother with security. She didn't need anything from Hector at this time in her life. Jane from Sunny Days gave Tilly a hug as she left.

'Well done love, it has been a lovely afternoon. Well, you know what I mean, as lovely as this kind of event can be. Your Uncle Hector would be so proud of you. Yes, so proud. Now he has set you another challenge. What a tinker - he is determined to stick around one way or another isn't he? Anyway, bye love. Bye now.' Tilly gave Jane a hug and said she would let her know about the donation to Sunny Days, or the solicitor would. Tilly wasn't sure about these bequests, but felt sure Ashley would have it all in hand. After all, it was his job.

She waved Jane off and noticed her Aunt Gilly and Uncle George were getting into their car. A giant, gas guzzling, 4-wheel drive, straight out of the showroom. They hadn't bothered to say goodbye. Her cousin Charlotte, with her husband Jasper gave Tilly a brief air kiss and followed them. Jasper worked for the same company as her uncle George. They drove a sporty soft top. Tilly didn't know about cars, but it looked expensive. Charlotte looked back and smiled. They had always been quite close when they were little and it didn't seem as if Charlotte bore any grudges. Tilly smiled back. Then Tilly saw her cousin Tris. Face like thunder, approaching her from the dining room.

'I want a word with you Matilda. Can we go outside.' Tilly's stomach did a flip. Then she straightened herself up and put her tea towel down.

'I'll just be a minute, Mel.' Tilly glanced round to see if she could catch Ashley's eye. She wasn't sure what Tris was going to say to her, but it already felt confrontational. 'Come out of the back door here, Tris, where it is quiet.' As she passed the dining room entrance, she saw Ashley was talking to Kit. She'd have to face her cousin on her own. Tristan at 6 foot 1 was quite intimidating, but Tilly took a deep breath and stepped outside, followed by her cousin.

'I really must protest, this is grossly unfair, and you have clearly been influencing our uncle.' Tristan could barely take breath as words of derision poured out of his angry mouth.

'I am as surprised as you are Tris. I can assure you he did not speak to me at all about his will and I had no interest in it. Just as you showed no interest in Uncle Hector, from where I am standing. You didn't visit, call or message. I think you are lucky he remembered you at all.' Tilly suddenly found some fighting confidence from somewhere and let rip at Tris. Taken aback, Tristan was briefly silenced, flustered at the retaliation from his younger, smaller and poorer cousin. Because Tilly knew that was how he saw her. His privileged upbringing hadn't allowed for circumstances such as this, where he didn't get exactly what he wanted. What he expected and what he assumed was his entitlement. He turned away from her.

'This isn't the end you know. Fish knives and forks, for goodness' sake, while you get ten grand. I don't think so.' Tilly wanted to protest and explain the reason for the money, but he had already gone. Striding to his parent's car. A spoilt boy in a man's body, not yet settled with a partner of his own, she just let him go. She didn't need this at the end of what had been, overall, a positive day of celebration.

On her way back to the dining room, she bumped into Ashley coming the other way with an almost empty platter of finger snacks.

'Let me take those from you.' Tilly must have looked or sounded a bit down.

'What's the matter Tilly, you look a bit upset. Is it emotions of the day, or something else? I saw that tall chap talking to you. I hope he wasn't rocking the boat?' Ashley didn't need to get involved, but Tilly was grateful to share the burden, after all she had kind of hoped he would be there before her chat encounter with Tristan.

'Oh yes, that. He's my cousin Tris. The eldest of the three of us. Uncle Hector's great nephew, then there is Charlotte and then me. His mum is my mum's sister. We were close when we were little, but when we reached secondary school age, they went to a private school. His dad, Uncle George, has a job in the city, in banking. ' Tilly didn't really know why she was telling Ashley all this, but it felt right. 'So they have a lot of money. A big house in Oxford and another one in Yorkshire, plus a holiday apartment in the Algarve. You know, Portugal?'

'Yes, I do know where the Algarve is.' Ashley was very patient. Perhaps he had a lot of experience of dealing with emotional customers. 'Was he causing a problem though, when you spoke just now?'

'He isn't happy with the Will, that is clear. I did try to put him in his place, but he is quite intimidating. I suppose I am just glad he has gone. Will you be sorting out the things from the Will? You know, for the Cat Charity and my cousins and mum and all that?' Tilly suddenly felt overwhelmingly tired. The day had been a big one and she had been running on adrenaline since early that morning; her tank was just about empty.

'Don't let him bully you. I did already have a word with him. I told him that the Will could not be challenged. I suspect he thought he would have a better chance with you. I need to go back to the office and open our copy of your letter, so that I can see what the conditions are to you inheriting Hector's personal items. All of which are still in his room at Sunny Days, incidentally. And £10,000. Lucky girl, he clearly thought a lot of you.' Ashley was reassuring and Tilly felt able to let worry of Tristan go.

'Oh, I don't know. I suppose I was the only one visiting him. We had some happy days together; he loved to reminisce about his youth, and I loved to listen. That is all he really wanted. Someone to listen and company. He did love it at Sunny Days though and his friends there. I'd like to go back and see them.'

'Let me see what the letter says and then I can sort out your money, plus the other bequests.' Tilly thought he perhaps wanted her to tell him what was in the letter - he knew she had read it. She'd had it for weeks, after all. But she didn't have the energy. He asked her if she needed a lift back, but Tilly didn't feel comfortable with that idea, so thanked him for the offer and for all he had done that day. She told him she would call him in a few days, when she agreed to drop the key back to his offices.

Then there were just four. Melody had done a good job of consolidating the remaining food, while Sam collected up the rubbish in a black sack, which he put in his van. Kit was on washing up duty. And perhaps pigs might fly, thought Tilly, seeing her friend looking uncomfortable in a pinny and yellow marigolds. How fortunate was she, to have such kind and loyal humans as her best friends?

They spent another 40 minutes tidying and putting away. All the things they had brought with them, were safely packed back in to cool bags and boxes. The cutlery safely back in the sideboard. Tablecloths in a bag to be washed at home. Sam had turned off everything that didn't need to be on and the door finally pulled closed and locked firmly.

'Group hug?' said Tilly. They gathered in a huddle of arms around bodies. 'Thank you so *so* much for today.' Came Tilly's muffled voice from within the scrum. They released their grips. 'I really mean it. I couldn't have done this without you. I love you guys.' Melody put her arms around her friend again.

'We love you too Tills, and we wouldn't have it any other way! Now we need to get back and have another look at that letter of yours. Focus on proper family tree building. '

'That's for another day Mel, I just want to get back home to a cuddle with Marmite, a nice gin and tonic, and a big bar of fruit and nut in front of the telly.' They laughed at the predictability of their friend.

Tilly got into Kit's car, and they slowly made their way up the drive, leaving Sam to sort out the gate.

'Bye Spitalbrook' Tilly said under her breath. 'What secret stories you could tell us, we will never know.'

30

NORFOLK - 2024

'The Will says I have to build his family tree, to solve the mystery,' said Tilly in dismay. Melody on the other end of the phone line, smiled to herself. 'What even IS that Melody'. As usual Tilly was getting worked up, before she needed to.

'Oh Tills, you know what a family tree is. Where you work out your parents, then their parents - that's your grandparents, then their parents...and so on.' Tilly grunted. It sounded like hard work, but she knew it was a hobby of Melody's, so she had figured she was the person to turn to for help, after she had been so helpful researching at the library with her. It was handy having a proper grown-up friend!

'Okay, so where do you think I should start - and will you help me? Pleeeeease Melly?' Tilly waited for a response, the line momentarily quiet. Melody couldn't possibly say no.

'Of course, Tilly, you know I will. Shall we meet this morning for coffee and we can start the plans.' Melody fortunately had the whole day to herself.

'I think there are other things I need to sort out first, or at least at the same time. I know getting started on this is important and I am grateful you have agreed to help me. There are a lot of other things going round in my head too. For a start, I need to take the key back to Ashley.'

'Oooh, Ashley is it now Tilly? You really are on first name terms.' Teased Melody, although she had felt they seemed quite familiar at the wake. Chatting like old friends at one point, she had noticed.

'Oh no Mel, there is nothing like that. For a start he is a stuffy solicitor and secondly, quite old.' Tilly really was on the defensive.

'Not that old Tilly. Plus, solicitors have an advantage of earning lots of money.' Melody laughed and Tilly realised it was all in jest.

'I genuinely think that staying friendly might be to my advantage. I must give back the key, and I don't know how I am going to fulfil the requirements of the will, if I don't have access to the house, and therefore the writing desk. Plus, anything else in there that might give me a clue as to where Uncle Hector's sister Temperance is now. Or was. I can't imagine she is still alive.' Tilly gave a big sigh, blowing loudly through her pursed lips in frustration. 'So, if I stay friendly with Mr Coombs...Ashley, I figured he might let me borrow it now and again.'

'Good point Tills, so, as I said, a meeting of minds at our favourite coffee establishment is in order.' Melody was solidly with her in this challenge, and she thought perhaps enjoying it.

'Okay, if you have time. Shall we say 10 o'clock at Brenda's?' Tilly glanced at her watch. It was just after 9. The girls firmed up their date and hung up. Tilly had half an hour to sort herself out, but first messaged Kit. Not sure of her plans but not wanting to leave her out. She knew Kit's flights had been moved, but with the funeral and wake to worry about, hadn't paid full attention to her friend when she had given her the final details. Pleasingly, Kit responded immediately to say she was going to be about for 5 more days and so would happily meet them at An Extra Slice at 10 o'clock. Tilly decided that would give her time to pop the key back to the solicitor's office before their coffee date.

~

'Hello, is Ashley…I mean, Mr Coombs available please?' Tilly had cycled up to the parade of shops and gone straight to the solicitors. The door being open, she went up to the first floor to find Angela on duty.

'Yes, it's Miss Brown, isn't it? I'll just see if he is free, please take a seat.' Angela was only gone a minute, when she returned followed by Ashley.

'Please come this way Tilly and take a seat.' He ushered her into his office. It seemed rude to protest, and she still had twenty minutes before she was going to meet the girls. 'Please take a seat. I presume you have brought back the key?'

'I have, yes. It's here in my bag.' Tilly rummaged around, then brought out the key in a crumbled used brown window envelope. 'There you go.' She placed it on the desk. He picked it up, lightly brushing her hand as he did so. Tilly felt herself blush.

'We have now read our copy of the letter and are fully aware of the challenge you face Tilly. The £10,000 that Hector so generously bequeathed to you, will be paid into your bank account immediately. The matter of his personal possessions, which is concerning your inheritance of all he had at the Sunny Days Care Home, I will make a judgement on, once you feel you have met the challenge set. Does that make sense to you?' Tilly nodded.

'To be honest Ashley, I am not really fussed about the possessions I might inherit, it's more that I want to try my best to fulfil his request. I tried when he was alive. We discussed his sister's disappearance, so I was aware that something odd happened. But I had no details. That is what I think I need to now go away and fill in. All those missing links. My friend Melody is going to help me build a proper family tree. We are meeting shortly at the café, so I need to get a move on.' Tilly stood up and held out her hand. 'Thank you again for everything you did to make things go smoothly for Uncle Hector's funeral.' Ashley took her hand gently but firmly and gave it a shake.

'It was a pleasure Tilly. Remember we are here once you solve the mystery! I don't envy you that, but sometimes people do put funny things in their wills. This is up there with the oddest I have dealt with, but I can see you are prepared to rise to the challenge set!'

Tilly left the office, collected her bike and pushed it the short distance to the corner café where her friends were already seated in the window, waving and making faces as she passed them. Her bike secured against the railings, she joined them, indicating to Brenda as she passed.

The girls hugged briefly, then got down to talking about what had to happen next. Tilly was pleased to see Melody had a notebook. She was going to take charge again, thought Tilly, in some respect relieved, but also keen to have some control.

'I've given back the key, so no need to go back to the solicitor until I've solved the challenges.' Tilly smiled and felt energised. One weight off her shoulders in that she no longer had to worry about losing that key. Yet, a much bigger challenge not quite faced head on yet. That was why she needed her friends.

'We can't do it all here Tilly. Let's have a coffee, and make an outline plan, based on what the letter says, then go back to Georgie and do it there. Can we have another look at the letter?' Tilly was already getting it out before Melody had finished speaking. 'Oh good girl, so, let's see exactly what he is saying, and let's break it down.'

Melody opened her notebook on a clean page and wrote:

1. *A key sits in the writing desk. Find out what it is for.*

2. *Find out what happened to Temperance.*

3. *Find the missing money. Is there a connection?*

'It doesn't seem much when you put it like that - just three questions.' said Kit, not quite appreciating what those three questions really meant.

'I think it is huge Kit.' replied Tilly, almost snapping. 'Temperance could be anywhere in the world. A key that Hector never even tried to find a home for, and well, as for missing money.' Tilly felt it getting on top of her before they had even started.

'Calm down,' said Melody, the voice of reason. 'That is why we are all looking at it together. Why we are here. Why we are friends. I see it being broken into three as a positive. We can take one bit at a time. Where do you want to start Tilly?' Mel and Kit looked to Tilly.

'I suppose I want to find Temperance. Her disappearance is the one thing that I had properly engaged with Uncle Hector about. It seems as if I might immediately need that box that his sister Vi gave him. He said it may have clues. I bet it's at the house, and I have just given back the key.' Tilly slumped melodramatically, her chin leaning heavily on an upturned palm.

'We don't know that, so let's find out what we do know. And that, I think, should be done back at your boat.' Melody was in the driving seat and the others agreed. Once they had finished their drinks, they gathered their bits, agreeing to go back to Georgie for the afternoon, where they could spread out with papers and plans, and their own unlimited cafetiere of coffee.

~

'So Tilly, I think we need to start by writing down everything you can remember from your chats with Hector, and what you know yourself about your family. Then once that is exhausted - which I suspect won't take long, we might have to speak to your mum, or any other relatives. Your Aunt perhaps?' Tilly made a face, as if to say she'd rather not, but didn't vocalise as much. 'Do you have a big A4 pad of paper, and some pens? Coloured preferably.' Melody was straight in.

Tilly found pens and paper, and once the coffee was starting to percolate, they settled at the table together. Starting with Tilly, the information, sketchy from memory, started to grow a tree. There was Tilly's dad, Trevor and her mum Celia. Melody encouraged Tilly to add all the relevant information to her chart and although a little messy to start with, Tilly's enthusiasm started to grow. Kit wrote down one side of the family, Melody the other.

'Now we can add the dates of birth for your parents. And your dad's date of death. Do you know them Tills?' Melody spoke softly, conscious of the subject matter.

'I know the dates, but not the years. Mum will be able to tell me those, so can we do that afterwards?' Getting keen to grow the tree so that it was of some use to help with her challenge, she wanted to push on. 'They were never married though, my mum and dad.'

'That doesn't matter, but all useful info. Okay, so the next generation back is grandparents - and in particular the parents of your mum - Uncle Hector is on the Brown side, isn't he?' Melody was a very calm, patient and methodical person, but she also sensed Tilly's urgency to deliver a result quickly. 'It may take a little research, but I can use my Ancestry membership to do that. Do you know what part of the country they come from?' Ever practical, Melody wanted to gather as much useful data as she could right from the outset.

'Well I guess it was Norfolk, at least from the time they were living in Spitalbrook where Hector grew up. So shall we assume the family are from Norfolk when we search your website?' Tilly sounded positive.

'You are getting the hang of it already Tilly. Anyway, let's get all the grandparent's details down. So do you know your dad's parent's names, or do we need to talk to your mum for that too?' Tilly paused for a moment, looking thoughtful.

'Dad's mum, my granny, was called Erin. I know that, because I always liked the name. She was from Wales. She had a lovely Welsh accent. Obviously, Gramps was Montgomery - and his name was Arthur. Haven't a clue when they were born or married. It's so sad I can't talk to dad about it, but they are not alive anymore either. Dad was an only child and I think they were quite old when they had him. I bet dad would have known. Anyway, mum might know or she may even have certificates.' Tilly felt positive that she could get somewhere now, with the help of her friend. Kit wrote furiously to capture everything as Tilly reminisced. 'My mum's mum I used to call Nanny Pops because when I was young, she had a lovely big ginger cat called Poppy.'

'I don't need the names of pets, Tilly, just people.' Melody tried to stay calm but glanced at her watch. She needed to keep an eye on the time.

'I know. Sorry, I'm just thinking out loud really. She used to live near my mum's sister, my Aunty Gilly. They lived in a care home. They didn't have dementia or anything like that, they just wanted to be somewhere with other people. It was a kind of care home for rich people. Like the one Uncle Hector was in. Quite nice really.' Tilly leant back and sighed. 'More coffee girls - oat milk Melody?' Both Tilly and Melody preferred oat milk in their coffee since being introduced to it at their favourite cafe. Kit stuck with regular milk or just had it black.

'Yes please, and have you got any of those nice coffee biscuits?' Melody was very at home on Tilly's houseboat.

'Coffee coming right up. Can you reach into that small cupboard beside you for the biscuits please Kit?' Tilly pushed their papers out of the way, and placed a tray with the coffee pot, milk jug (in the shape of a cow - a treasured charity shop find) and three mugs in front of her friends. Kit found the biscuits, and they sat back to enjoy their break.

'You know ladies, this is going to be more fun than I thought. Thanks for your help!' Tilly smiled at them both. Melody felt a pang of guilt at checking the time again and gave Tilly's arm a squeeze.

'You are very welcome' said Melody, 'that's what friends are for. I have another hour before I need to pick up Lois from nursery. After coffee, let's crack on.'

'You're on!'

Tilly waved goodbye to Melody and Kit, then climbed back down her small steps to the warmth of the cabin. They had made good progress, but Melody had left Tilly with a list of things she needed to find out from her mum. The whole first stab at family tree building had been an eye opener for Tilly. She was beginning to understand why Melody found the hobby so addictive and was keen to get to the next level. She decided there was no time like the present and picked up her mobile.

'Hi mum. Yep, I'm fine I just have a few questions I think you can help me with...'

31
CHRISTCHURCH 1970

3 Kauri Drive
Christchurch
New Zealand

April 1970

My Dearest Violet,

I am writing to thank you for the last money transfer. It has enabled me to move out to the South Island with a very nice gentleman Myles. He is 17 years older than I and is a widower.

You will no longer feel pressured to provide for me, but I am grateful for all you have managed to do.

I will not be a burden to you any longer.

Ever your loving sister,
Penny

32

NORFOLK - 2024

The call had been brief, as always, but Celia had suggested they meet up in person the following day, to explore the information Tilly needed, to make progress with her challenge. She also had some things to discuss with Tilly. That explained her keenness to meet in person.

Tilly had to work at the plumbers in the morning, until 1pm. It was an old-fashioned tradition to still have what Val called 'half day closing' on a Wednesday. Celia and Tilly agreed to meet in An Extra Slice at 1.30pm - a first for Celia. Her mum had also agreed to drive Tilly over to Sunny Days after coffee, to collect some, or all of Hector's personal items. Tilly had been corresponding with Jane since the funeral, together with Ashley, there had been a three-way agreement that Ashley would collect the items bequeathed to family members. As he had control of Hector's bank account, Ashley had also paid out the monetary donations and bequests. Jane had bagged up Hector's clothes which they had agreed would be donated to charity. Everything was still in Hector's room and could stay there for a while as there were no new residents imminent.

The morning was a drag, with just one visitor to the office: a double-glazing salesman. The building was quite tatty, to be fair, but Tilly sent him away saying the management were not there to discuss anything of that nature. He left his card, and Tilly filed it with a pile of others. She knew Val and Donald were unlikely to spend any money on the place, but it was there if they wanted it.

After whipping the hoover round, she locked up and headed past the parade of shops to the corner cafe. She couldn't see her mum's car and the café was quite busy. She found a small table for two in the corner and sat down, getting her notes out. Melody had given her a good set of pointers, so feeling organised she read through her questions. At 1.30 on the dot, her mum appeared. She seemed a bit flustered, but smiled, nonetheless.

'Hello Tilly, shall I get the coffees? Cappuccino for you?' Tilly nodded and Celia went to the counter to order.

Brenda brought their drinks quickly, plus two pieces of her own recipe chocolate brownie and, winking at Tilly, said it was on the house.

'Thank you so much Bren.' Tilly hoped her mum also appreciated Brenda's kindness. They settled with their coffees and Tilly looked down at her notebook.

'I have lots of questions that I hope you can help me with.' Celia nodded looking through the list of questions Tilly had noted down.

'I can help with all the dates, Tilly. I have always had an interest in history, as you know, so that won't take us long. You read them out and as I answer make a note.' Celia seemed happy to get stuck in, which relaxed Tilly and gave her hope for the other questions, which were in her head. Those she planned to add in at the end.

After a surprisingly relaxed half an hour, Tilly had the key dates for her parent's, grandparent's and on her mum's side, great grandparent's births, marriages and where relevant, also deaths. Not always a full date, but a year at least for the great grandparents. Tilly was amazed at how much her mum knew off the top of her head but felt saddened that she hadn't already known this about her mum.

'This is great mum. I am going to draw this out as a proper tree, which Mel can help me with. She is going to show me how to create an online family tree through a website she uses. But do you know anything about Hector's sisters? That is what I really need to find out.' Tilly still wasn't sure how this was going to take her to a point where she could 'find' Temperance, but in data gathering mode, and with her mum willing to help, she wanted to get to the nitty gritty. She felt her mum knew more than she was letting on, and there was still that case her mum had shown her, full of special things - and letters. Tilly just had to persuade her mum that now was the time to share, if she knew anything.

'You must remember Tilly, and now you can see from the dates, that there was a big age gap between your Grandpa Joseph; my father, and his sisters. He was 16 years younger than Violet. Hector was 14 years younger. I met her a few times when I was younger, but not Temperance. She had already gone before I was born, and sadly, was never spoken about. Then my father passed away at a young age, and I really didn't have any need or reason to stay in contact with my dad's family. Apart from Hector - but he was always travelling for his work, so not in this country most of the time, let alone close by. My mum's parents, your granny and grandad Poppy were still alive, and they were our family. So you see, we just lost touch, and never had any reason to go searching for people who we didn't really know anything about.'

There was a pause, while they drank their coffees, and Tilly took on board and digested what her mum had said. Perhaps she had a point, although that was still no reason for her seeming neglect of Hector in recent months.

'Anyway Tilly, I had something else I wanted to talk about.' Celia was looking down at her cup, she shifted a bit on her chair. Body language shouting change.

'Oh yes. What's that?' Tilly felt the mood had changed suddenly and was on the defensive.

'I've had a call from your Aunt Gilly. They are not happy that you have inherited that £10,000 from Hector, and Tristan and Charlotte have been left those two insignificant items. Apparently, Tristan is particularly unhappy.' Tilly flipped.

'Seriously mum. Is that all they care about? Money, and material things. No care about Uncle Hector. Well, I can't help what he chose to do, and anyway, those possessions are not mine until I meet the challenge of his will. I don't even know what he had, but I don't recall there being a lot in his room. Anyway, I am really not interested in doing it for gains, I am trying to do the thing that Uncle Hector asked me to do. To fulfil his final wishes as I did for the wake. I am pretty sure my delightful cousins would have no interest in it, if they knew there were hoops to jump through.' Tilly stood her ground, although it wasn't her mum making the demand for anything more. 'Perhaps he just needs to speak to Ashley Coombs. He is the executor after all.'

'Well I am just passing on the message. I am sorry about my sister's family. If it is of any consequence, I agree with you. And Tilly...' she paused. 'I am proud of what you have done for your great uncle. It is clear he was very fond of you, and you are showing a maturity beyond your age in the way you are dealing with it.' Celia looked up and smiled at her daughter. 'Really Tilly, think nothing more about it. I will call Gilly and tell her it is what it is. Hopefully they will see reason and not pursue it any further.' Tilly, feeling tense, tried a few deep breaths and nodded.

'I mean it mum; they can talk to Ashley. If you could tell them that please.' She pondered briefly on what she was about to do next. She had with her the letter, and as her mum did still seem to be on her side, she decided it might be the right time to share Uncle Hector's letter with her. If she was going to get any extra information from the historical papers in her mum's special things box, this might just persuade her.

'Okay, so Mum, I have the letter here that Uncle Hector wrote just for me. You know, with the extra challenge? Would you like to read it, then you can see why I am so keen to get my hands on any other information which might help with my search?' Tilly unfolded the letter and passed it to her mum. Celia hesitated at first, then took it.

'If you are sure love,' was Celia's reply. Tilly nodded. She wanted her to read it.

Celia took it from Tilly and read the letter; then read it again. There was too much to take in the first time, and even after a second reading, she wasn't sure she had captured it all. However, what stuck was a couple of things. Hector's impassioned plea for Tilly to find his sister, something about missing money, and the need to locate the home for a key! What an odd group of challenges.

'Personally Tilly, I don't think there was ever any money. Certainly nothing came down my father's side and he always said they were poor at home. Farming didn't make you rich and his father liked a drink. He knew that. No, I think that bit is a red herring. I will see what I have in the case. I haven't looked through my dad's stuff since he died. It was too painful. But maybe now is the time. The last of the Brown siblings has passed on, and we must try to move on. Shall we go to Sunny Days to collect Hector's belongings, then go back home to look in the case?' Celia was thawing, and a definite softer side was emerging. Tilly welcomed it and felt that at last her mum was coming round. 'I know I said you couldn't read the letters until they were passed to you. But I think this Will has changed things. I want to help you Tilly. Truly I do.' Celia was convincing.

'Yes please mum, and thank you, that would be really helpful.'

A happy mother and daughter left An Extra Slice in buoyant mood, heading for Celia's white convertible Golf, and a final trip to Sunny Days. Jane was waiting for them when they arrived.

'Hello Tilly. Lovely to see you again. Hello..em.' She turned to Celia. 'I'm Jane, I think I saw you at Hector's funeral.' Jane hesitated. Celia put out her hand.

'Hello Jane, yes, I'm Hector's niece. Celia.' They shook hands.

'Of course. Celia. Welcome to Sunny Days, I don't think I've seen you here before?' Celia looked a little embarrassed and smiled. She had clearly never visited Hector at the home. 'Follow me through to Hector's room.' Jane showed them along the corridor, by now a familiar route for Tilly, which took them into his room. 'Make yourselves comfortable and I will arrange for some tea and biscuits.'

They sat down by the French doors, and Tilly pushed them open wide, welcoming in the warmth of the late spring afternoon. A fragrant pink climbing rose, draped itself across the wooden arch, and hung loosely framing the window. The bird feeder was alive with a family of long tailed tits busily tucking in to a feast of fat balls and seed; clearly someone was still filling up the various feeders. Hector had so loved watching his birds, it brought a lump to Tilly's throat. The tea arrived and Jane placed the tray down on the coffee table.

'So ladies, dear Hector's clothes are in these sacks, and I think we have already agreed that these will go to charity.' Both ladies nodded. 'Everything else - small personal items are in the top drawer of his bedside cabinet over there.' Jane pointed to Hector's bed, which had been stripped of its cotton bed sheets and had been made up with a simple blue nylon padded eiderdown, that, quite frankly had seen better days. 'Everything else here, apart from the bed, belonged to Hector. Mr Coombs has already been to assess the items left in his will to family and friends. Those items are over there by the window. He has taken the walking stick for George and the clock is here for you Celia. Everything else is ready to pass on to those named in the will. What remains is for you Tilly. The furniture and the items in the drawer. Everything has been itemised, but Mr Coombs has that list and has said you can take your items with you, on trust.' Jane sat opposite the two, and Tilly glanced round. She didn't have room for furniture on her boat, but there wasn't a lot there. The bedside cabinet, a coffee table, Hector's armchair. They were the main things.

Jane wanted to give them some privacy and left the room. Tilly looked at her mum.

'It's sad, isn't it? Seeing that this is all that is left of Hector's life. You never visited, did you?' There was a pause, and a guilty silence sat between them. It was something Celia could not deny. They both looked at each other.

'I know I should have visited Tilly, but it just wasn't convenient for us. And I knew he was being visited by you, so he wasn't completely alone.' It was a poor excuse, and Celia knew it.

'There is nothing that can be done now, you have to live with that guilt. If guilt is what you feel mum?' Tilly felt like she was being the 'grown up', but in the circumstances there was nothing that could be done now.

'You are right, of course you are, but like I said, it was difficult. I'm here now to do what I can. Perhaps we can arrange for the furniture to be stored at my house until you have a house of your own?' Celia had always been hinting to Tilly that living on a houseboat really wasn't a life choice but a passing fad. Tilly pushed back.

'Mum, you know I have no intention of moving from Georgie, but yes, thank you while I think about it, if these few bits could be put in yours, I'd appreciate that.' Tilly wasn't budging on this matter, and Celia knew it.

'Okay, well let's take the personal bits from the drawer now, plus my clock and I will come back with David or borrow his four wheel drive to pick up the rest.'

'Sounds like a plan' agreed Tilly.

They collected the bag from the drawer. It was cotton, with a zip. Tilly decided not to look inside. She thought it might be too upsetting and wanted to do it in her own time. Celia picked up the clock which had been put into a Kellogg's cornflakes box. They went back out to reception and updated Jane on their plans. Jane was accommodating, saying there was no real rush but if it could be cleared in the next couple of weeks, that would be good.

'Thanks for coming with me mum. I wasn't sure how I would find it. In the end, it wasn't so bad. I just need to focus on the family tree for a while now and see what I can find out about Temperance and Violet.'

'Like I said before Tilly, perhaps it is a good time to have another look in the case. Do you have time to come with me now? You can stay for some tea, and I can drop you home later?' Tilly nodded. She felt suddenly like a little girl again, who needed her mum.

'Thanks mum. I'd like that.' They both climbed into the convertible, with the cloth bag on Tilly's knees, and the box at her feet. She glanced back for a last glimpse of Hector's final happy place.

'Bye bye Uncle Hector, I'll try my best for you.' whispered Tilly as her mum started the engine and made for home.

33

NORFOLK - 2024

Tilly and Celia sat up at the dining room table with the case between them. Whilst it felt like they had done nothing but drink tea or coffee all day, the first thing Celia did on entering the house, was to fill the kettle, and flick it on to boil. It seemed as if armed with a cup of tea, any job would be easier to tackle.

'So mum, to begin with, I want to get that airmail letter you wouldn't let me read, so that I can see the address and the date. I don't want to pry, but it does seem very likely that it will give me some giant clues.' Tilly had her notebook out already, keen to add to the data she had been given earlier by her mum.

'I appreciate that Tilly. I still feel a little uncomfortable sharing everything from the box though.' She rummaged to the bottom, biting her lip as she delved to pull out the brown paper bag. 'There is something else I remember though. My dad was close to his cousins - four spinster sisters. They lived in Crewe in Cheshire. He told me stories of the 4 girls visiting the farm in the summer, in their pretty dresses. By all accounts they were a more affluent family.'

'I've certainly never heard this story mum. Go on. What else do you know? Tilly felt a flutter of excitement. Like pages were turning on her mystery, and every page turn was welcome in this book.

'Well just that Tilly. The Spinster Sisters from Crewe. That's what dad called them.' She laughed, 'It could be a film title, couldn't it? Tilly wanted to know more.

'Do you at least know their names mum. I can't go onto the internet and google 'Crewe spinsters' now, can I?' At this they both laughed, and the mood relaxed.

'I know there was Gerty, Minnie and Con. I can't think of the last sister's name. But they were Smith. Cousins on my dad's mum's side. She had just one sister, Aunty Josephine. She married a miner and they lived in Wales for a while. Then they moved across to Crewe. I never met them; they were older than Hector and my dad. More Temperance and Violet's age, I would say.' Tilly raced to scribble down the extra information as her mum remembered things. 'That last sister's name might come to me. Ah, here is the letter we were looking for.' Celia pulled out the thin blue paper and hesitating, handed it to Tilly. Tilly took it and turned it over. It was firmly sealed - the letter had never been opened. She looked at Celia, questioningly.

'Can I open it? Break the seal?' Her mother nodded. Tilly carefully opened it along the 'tear here' line, conscious that she was holding potential gold dust in her hand. She silently read. It was short and addressed to 'Dear Mother'. What about her father, Tilly wondered. She read on and her question was answered immediately.

Dear Mother,

This letter comes with a genuine sadness for you, following the death of my father. Violet wrote and told me the news. I know you will be finding it difficult on your own and will be grieving in your own way for the man who has controlled your life for as long as you can remember. But I am sure you will manage with the help of your family. Indeed, I hope you embrace a newfound freedom.

I trust you have the support of Violet and the boys at this difficult time. I want to reassure you that I will not make any further demands on you. I am now settled with Myles, who is supporting me to live. I have stopped my job at the council and will focus on my family.

I hope you are able to enjoy what years you have remaining,

Your daughter, Temperance

Dated March 1971, it had a PO box address in Wellington, the capital city of New Zealand located in North Island. Tilly put the letter down after reading it through a few times and scribbled the address in her notebook.

'Well at least now I know where she was in 1971. There isn't a lot else in the letter. I wonder what she means when she says, 'I will not be making any further demands of you.' Tilly handed the letter to Celia who scanned it quickly.

'I really don't know any more than you Tilly. I think it gives you what you need though, don't you? Plus, the Crewe spinsters, of whom I have already given you the little I know.' Celia was already gathering back together the paperwork and filling the case with it.

'Are the sisters still alive mum? The ones in Crewe.' Tilly was thinking that if she could speak to these cousins, then as close cousins to her grandfather and to Hector, they would be able to tell her about the times when they were young together. About Violet. About Temperance. They may have even corresponded with her.

'Oh no Tilly. Well, at least I don't think so. They were much older, as I said. They were close to Violet's age, and she died, oh, what six or seven years ago. Come on, let's get this cleared away now and sort out tea. David is working late tonight. Then I'll drop you home.'

Tilly accepted it had been a small win with her mum, and whilst she would dearly have loved to keep delving through the small insignificant vanity case, she acknowledged that she had made genuine progress today. Not least with a whole new family branch to explore. Two more steps on the long family research ladder.

They had macaroni cheese together in the conservatory. It was still light, and Celia chatted about her garden, especially her new small vegetable patch. The topic of family seemed no longer on her mind, unlike her daughter's. Tilly made polite conversation, but her thoughts were elsewhere. She was keen to get back and start on her tree, do some internet surfing and most importantly, contact Melody.

'If you are ready to go back now Tilly, I'll grab my car keys?' It clearly wasn't a question, Tilly thought, but she *was* ready. She acceded and within 10 minutes they were in the car and heading back to the canal side.

'Thanks mum, for today.' Tilly waved as her mum drove away, then climbed on board. What she wanted now was a cuddle with Marmite and a catchup with her WhatsApp buddies.

Hey ladies...I've had an eventful day. Who is free for a coffee catchup tomorrow so that I can pick some brains?

Tilly sat back on her bed with her laptop propped on her knees and Marmite tucked in close to her side, purring enthusiastically like a muffled machine gun. With the message pinged off to the girls, she relaxed back to enjoy a lemon and ginger tea, some social media scrolling and eventually sleep.

34

NORFOLK 2024

Tilly woke with a thumping headache. She looked at her watch; only 6.35am. The sun was streaming in through the skylight and, as she blinked her eyes open properly, she saw Marmite's big green eyes staring back at her. That explained the heaviness on her chest. She gently hoofed him to one side and reached for her water bottle. Popping a paracetamol out of its packet she swallowed it with a long glug of water. Marmite miaowed pitifully, signifying his desire for breakfast.

'Okay gorgeous, I am getting up…as soon as you move.' As she sat herself up fully, Marmite was forced onto the floor, where he sat and watched her get dressed. Then raced ahead to the galley where Tilly fed him with his favourite rabbit flavoured meaty dinner. It smelt horrible to Tilly's sensitive nostrils, but Marmite wolfed it down.

Then it was her turn. Over a leisurely breakfast of blueberry pancakes, topped with honey, full fat Greek yogurt and a handful of seeds, she was checking her emails, when a message popped into the Best Buddies WhatsApp group from Melody.

Hello lovely. I've got stuff on with Lois at nursery this morning, but I'll be free at 2 if that's any good for you? Call me Mx.

Tilly smiled to herself. Perfect. She really needed to see Melody who would be able to help with the seeds of a plan currently germinating, in her oh so active mind.

With the morning to herself, Tilly had some jobs to do around the boat, and a list was swiftly drawn up. First was to water the plants in pots on top of the boat, which were looking particularly parched. Tilly had been neglecting all the things she loved about her life on board, since Hector had passed away. Or even before this, if truth be told. She had a small, raised bed, on her mooring. It was nothing but weeds and desperate for her time. She added 'weeding' to the list. She was also keen for time to sit down with her laptop. She had to explore the possibility that the spinster sisters from Crewe, might appear in a google search. It seemed a long shot, but at that moment it was Tilly's focus, and she was struggling to properly think of anything else. Any chance to find something more before her catch up with Mel would give them both a head start.

After an hour of internet searching, Tilly stopped to stretch her legs and put on the kettle. A coriander and fennel tea would perk her up a bit. The sun was bright and reasonably warm for the time of year. Tilly had a dahlia tuber she had picked up in a bargain bin at the supermarket, with the intention of planting it in a pot. With the newly weeded patch, she decided her raised bed would be as good as a pot and dug down into the soft soil with her bare hands. Fingers clawing through to break it up, leaving an adequately sized hole to accommodate the sad looking tuber. There was a small green shoot, so Tilly was hopeful. It wasn't in her nature to discard anything that might still have life or a use. A trait which proved inconvenient at the best of times, especially when her living space was so limited. She firmed the soil and gave it a good water. Something she was never short of, with her watering can living on the end of a rope tied to the side of the barge. Marmite came to show a bit of interest, pushing his damp nose against her ankle, then jumped away quickly from the splashes, as Tilly pulled up another can full of water from the murky canal.

Refreshed, Tilly returned to her desk with her herbal tea and a forgiving, or perhaps just forgetful Marmite by her side. Looking back at her notes, she reviewed where the previous hour had left her. In summary, her searching had thrown up a Gerty Smith, current Chair of the Crewe branch of the WI. She thought very unlikely, based on the estimated age of her Gerty. Then there was Minnie Smith, who had held the 1942 Cheshire long jump record for girls. Not very relevant, but interesting, nonetheless. Finally, the death notice of Freda Smith, who had died age 95 during the first wave of covid at The Shrubbery Care Home in Crewe. It was the most promising of the stories she had found, especially as the article finished by saying '…where Miss Smith resided with her sister.' What a shame it didn't mention her sister's name, Tilly thought. She scribbled down the details of the home, as a message popped into WhatsApp. It was from Kit. Of course, Kit was flying Saturday, it had clean gone out of Tilly's mind. She opened it and read.

Hey ladies, I'm sorry I haven't been in touch much since the funeral that's allowed, thought Tilly. She read on *Have handed keys over to a flat sitter, so heading to dad's tonight. Can be at the usual by about 3.30 if you can wait for me? Hugs, Kx*

Tilly felt that almost ever-present lump rise in her throat. One of her best friends was about to take a lifechanging step in her career, to travel halfway across the world, yet Tilly had forgotten all about it. What kind of friend was she? She hurried a message back.

Kitty cat, I am sooooooo glad you will be able to join us, and OF COURSE we can wait for you. That's ok isn't it @melody? See you both at The Extra Slice this afternoon.

She instantly received a thumbs up from Kit and a heart from Melody. Glancing at her watch, it was just before midday. Still loads of time before she needed to leave. No excuse not to be fully prepared, she gathered her laptop and charger, notebook and pen, and stashed it all into her rucksack.

The canal was alive with wildlife. Small damselflies in the prettiest fluorescent blue petticoats, flitted in front of her as she strolled by the waterside. She decided on the scenic route taking some fresh chopped up kale from her fridge, she treated the ducks on her way. Regulars on the bank, they were not shy in tapping barge owners for tit bits. A bit too tame for their own good, Tilly sometimes thought, but it didn't stop her from saving her left over veg for her feathered friends. She waved a 'hello' to her neighbours Nell and Karim Singh. They leased a small shop on the high street, selling an assortment of interesting herbs and spices, but they lived on a boat on the canal. A 17-foot barge, which they had paid to have professionally restored to a very high spec. Tilly had been on it a couple of times for parties. The Singh's loved a party, and their food was out of this world. Their large family had long since flown the nest, so Nell and Karim had chosen an alternative step into retirement, by selling up and sharing out their money to help their three children get onto the property ladder, leaving enough to buy their beautiful barge. They had even bought some of Tilly's decorated canal art pieces to adorn the top.

'How are you, lovely Tilly?' called out Karim, as she walked past.

'Good thanks, and you both?' Tilly paused.

'Enjoying life Tilly, enjoying life.' Karim nodded and beamed. His smile said it all. Life was good, and it pleased Tilly to see that. She continued on the canal path, then turned up into the main street.

Tilly arrived at An Extra Slice with time to spare, but spotted Melody sitting at an outside table, in the shade of a Norway Maple. Melody immediately stood up to greet Tilly, all smiles.

'Hello my lovely, how are you doing?' Melody was always so maternal, her caring nature oozing at every move.

'Oh, you know Mel, up and down. You are early. How are you? And lovely Lois and Sam of course?' Melody gave Tilly a big hug, assuring her that they were all fine.

They sat down opposite each other, and the chatter began. Tilly keen to update Melody on the day with her mum, spoke at speed leaving Melody struggling to keep up. Melody decided just to let her friend pour out her news, until Brenda appeared at their table.

'Hello girls, I haven't seen you for a few days. No Kit today?' Brenda was poised with her notepad to take their order. Whilst she was fond of the girls and often slipped the odd free left-over sponge slice, or fruit scone, she did have a business to run.

'Oh, sorry Bren, we,' Tilly stopped herself, 'actually not we, *I* was talking. So much to catch up on. And yes, Kit is joining us as soon as she can. Probably not for another hour though, so we won't get her a drink right now. I'll have my usual please.' Tilly looked to Melody.

'A latte for me please, with oat milk. Thanks Brenda.' Melody sometimes had a flat white, but always with oat milk.

'Coming right up ladies.' Brenda disappeared back into the building, and the girls laughed.

'I'm sorry Mel, it was just quite a full-on day yesterday. The boat is a mess, and tomorrow I'm at the plumbers, so I don't have time to do all the horrible jobs. I am so desperate to get started on this research.' As Tilly paused briefly to draw breath, her phone pinged. A text ping, not a WhatsApp ping. She glanced down.

'What is it Till? You look worried.' Melody didn't miss a thing, and Tilly hesitated, as she read the message.

'Oh, I'm not worried. No. Actually the opposite. Look, it's a text from Ashley.' Tilly turned her phone so that Melody could read it.

'I didn't realise you were texting this Ashley, Tilly. It seems very informal.' Tilly snatched her phone back, slightly flustered, and a little surprised at her own reaction.

'I haven't been texting him. It's the first time. I see what you mean though. But look what he is saying. That he is arranging for the £10,000 to be paid into my account, so that I can start my research. I mean, that makes it real, doesn't it?' Tilly looked at Melody who was nodding slowly.

'It does. It is real Tilly. You knew that was going to happen. It's good, isn't it? It will help if you need to start travelling. Like these people in Crewe that you have been talking about. It will cover train fares and accommodation if you have to stay.' Melody was really thinking sensibly. That is why Tilly needed her help to unravel the mysteries, if they could be unravelled. At that point Brenda arrived with the coffees and Tilly cleared the table. There was a short period of quiet as they sipped at the steaming drinks. Melody was the first to speak.

'I think, from what you have briefly told me, that the next step is contacting the Shrubbery Care Home to see if the name of the other sister matches either of the names your mum gave you. We could also look at the electoral roll. That will give more recent information of people in any one area. ' Tilly looked up, ears pricked like a new puppy.

'I haven't looked at electoral rolls have I, for the other searches? You know, when I was looking for Temperance?' Tilly scribbled something down on her notebook.

'No, we didn't need to, but they are available. It's just an idea. It's exciting that there could be some of Hector's cousins alive. A few emails, and you could be on your way to Crewe!' said Melody light-heartedly and they both laughed.

'Yeah,' Tilly paused again, thinking, 'and I don't even know where Crewe is!' She exclaimed and they both laughed again. 'With the PO Box address in New Zealand, I could also start searching on New Zealand records, couldn't I?

'You could, but it is quite old. Have you thought about using a genealogist in New Zealand to try and help you? You can pay them, because you'll have the money.'

'What money?' Both girls looked up to see Kit standing behind them. 'I got back sooner than I thought. What have I missed?'

The girls were so pleased to see Kit they jumped up and launched themselves at her; a group hug ensued, which was a little out of Kit's comfort area, but this once she let them. Then Melody insisted Kit sat while she went and got her a coffee, allowing Tilly free reign to update her on all the latest news and events. She was just finishing the story about the spinsters of Crewe and those she had found so far, when simultaneously Melody arrived with more coffee for all three of them, and a further text pinged on Tilly's phone.

'It's Ashley again.' Tilly looked at Melody.

'And?' said Melody

'Ashley? What am I missing?' questioned Kit.

'I hadn't got to that bit yet Kit. Ashley texted me earlier to say he was arranging for the money to be transferred soon. You remember, Ashley is Hector's Solicitor, that's all.'

'And I said it seemed quite familiar. Perhaps he likes you Tilly?' Melody was deadly serious.

'And perhaps he is just doing his job.' Tilly opened up the second text.

'So what does the second one say Tills?' Kit now pushing.

'Ok, it says *'Hello Tilly, I am writing to let you know that the sum of £10,000 has been deposited into your bank account ending 245 this afternoon. I am available to help advise you on how best to manage this money, if you would like to contact me. Ashley'* so, there you go, nothing more than business?' Tilly looked at her friends who were both smiling. 'What? Oh you two. Give it a rest' She laughed with them, and logged in to her banking app.

And there it was. A huge balance of £10,327.00. It took her back down to earth. This was real. The last time she had a large balance in her bank was before she bought Georgie with her inheritance, after her dad died.

'I must start taking this challenge seriously, and so do you two. No more nonsense about solicitors fancying part time admin assistant arty types. I want to find the Crewe spinsters, and then I want to find Temperance. I intend to succeed even if it costs me the whole £10,000.' Tilly looked at the balance once more, then logged out of the app.

'We are just teasing Tills. We are with you all the way.' Melody put her arm round Tilly. 'So now, you have a plan and some money, we need to find out what is happening with *this* young lady now, don't we?' She said turning her attention to Kit. Kit smiled, and they all sat back down.

'Right,' said Kit, 'how long have you got?'....

35

NORFOLK - 2024

'Yes, I know I am not family, but. Well... I might be.' Tilly was having a frustrating telephone conversation with the admin receptionist at The Shrubbery Care Home, in Crewe. 'I understand about patient confidentiality, but I have a *really* good reason for asking. Is there someone else I can speak to please?' Tilly found herself getting wound up trying to explain herself to the person on the other end of the phone.

They had agreed to get the Manager, and Tilly had been put on hold. Tinny classical music played, to fill the time. While holding, an idea came to Tilly, not quite in a flash, but more like a slow vision of fuzziness, piecing itself together until the picture was clear. Ashley. She would get Ashley to speak to them. They had to listen to him; he was a solicitor after all. At that moment, the music stopped - thank goodness - and a new voice, kind, with a Scottish lilt, greeted her.

'Good afternoon my dear, my name is Margery, and I am the home manager. Now, how can I help you today?' Tilly instantly felt more at ease.

'Oh hello Margery, thank you. I am searching for a distant relative, or perhaps several. I appreciate you can't break any confidentiality rules, but if I got my late great uncle's solicitor to call you, might that help? I just need to eliminate the Freda Smith who recently passed away, from my search.' There was a brief pause.

'I don't see why we wouldn't be able to help if you can ask the solicitor to call us. Can I just take a few details from you now please?' Tilly gave her name, the names of the three sisters that she knew, Hector's name and relationship to the sisters and finally Ashley's name. All she needed to do now, was speak to Ashley.

She proceeded to spend the morning at the plumber's office which, as usual, was uneventful. Paul had been there for quite some time, and they had chatted about her challenge. He seemed to have got the hint that she wasn't interested romantically, so it was refreshing to have a proper conversation with him. Tilly got the impression he wasn't that keen on eventually taking over 'Water Works Ltd' from his dad, at some point in the future, but was too scared to say. She discovered Paul had always wanted to be a pop star - or a singer at the very least. He told her that he had joined an amateur dramatics group locally and had a small part at Christmas in a musical show, which he had loved and felt at home with. Tilly had felt quite sorry for him, so encouraged him to keep going with the singing and to, perhaps, enter one of those talent shows you sometimes see on the telly. After all, someone has to get picked and it might be the way for Paul to get his big break.

Coming out of the plumbers, the most obvious thing to do was to go straight to the offices of Gently, Barker and Coombs, to see if Ashley was free. Approaching the now familiar glass panelled door, she felt a sudden pang of something. Excitement? No. Anxiety? Possibly. As with most things, Tilly was overthinking. Just go in and up the stairs, she told herself.

The door was unlocked, so that was a good start, and she advanced to the top and knocked on the door. Had a knock been necessary? She thought it probably hadn't and proceeded to enter. The room was empty. She had expected to see Ashley's secretary, Angela, in the prim high-necked blouse, sitting stiffly behind the heavy desk. But no. She took another step, when at that moment the door of Ashley's office flung open and a flustered Angela appeared.

'Er, hello. Can I help you....I er, don't think I have an appointment booked in?' As Angela sat down hastily behind the desk, she knocked over a spider plant, which spewed dry soil across her desk. Tilly noticed her blouse buttons were not done up correctly and surmised that Angela had been doing a bit more than taking minutes in Ashley's company. She smiled to herself and felt relief that her own thoughts had been correct. Ashley was clearly not interested in her, and that suited Tilly.

'I wondered if Ashley was free? Just for a minute. Sorry, I should have called, but as I was passing..' Tilly didn't feel she had to give the secretary all the details.

'Oh, no that is ok. He doesn't have another client for half an hour, if that is long enough? Go on through.'

Angela was by now composed, and sat down, having swept the spilt soil into the wastepaper basket.

'Thanks Miss Howard.' Tilly smiled and turned, as Ashley stepped out of his office.

'Ah Tilly, I thought that was your voice. Come this way.' He ushered her back into his office. 'What can I do for you today?'

They sat down and Tilly explained the situation. Ashley was pleased that she had started the search already. He wasn't sure how talking to someone in Crewe was going to help find someone in New Zealand, but encouraged her nonetheless, and agreed to make the call.

'Hello, The Shrubbery Care Home, how can I help.' Ashley managed to get put through to the manager, explained who he was and gave her the names of the three Smith sisters that were known to them. She agreed to look into their request and said they would be in touch. It was a good start.

'While I am here Ashley, another thing I've been thinking about, is visiting the old farm again. It's just something that Uncle Hector had said to me; I feel some clues may be there. He said about a key in the writing desk in his letter, and he had also said to me about letters sent to him from Violet. You know, his other sister?' Tilly hadn't properly thought this through, but as she was at the actual offices it seemed as good a time as any to see if she could borrow the key again.

'I see.' Ashley looked thoughtful. 'I think that would be ok, but only for a short time. We do need to have access to the property at all times, which means having the key to hand.' Ashley seemed reluctant. Tilly gave him her sweetest smile, knowing now that there was no danger of leading him on.

'A week max, and I promise I will bring it back.' Tilly would be able to do what she needed at the weekend. Hopefully with Sam's help.

'Okay, one week.' Ashley opened his drawer and pulled out the envelope, handing it to her.

'Thanks Ashley.' Tilly gave him a wink and left the office with a skip. Once outside, she took the quickest route back to her boat. Suddenly, she felt more positive and excited about the next steps. The potential to succeed felt very real.

36

CHRISTCHURCH - 1994

PO Box 14
Christchurch
South Island
New Zealand

17th July 1994

My dearest devoted sister,

I am devastated to bring you the news that my beloved Myles was taken from this world, and I am alone once more.

I know that it has been many years since we have corresponded, and that I told you the last time there would be no more, but I am again all alone in this world and feeling my age. As I am unsure of your current home, I am addressing this to the family home. I have some friends at the church. I am not a regular church goer, but it is a small community and they are kind to me.

I hope that this letter reaches you, and that you are well, and contented. It had always been a dream of mine, that I would return to the home country with my family, but it was not to be. Let it be known, dear Violet, that I have always thought of you, and appreciated your support and kindness at the most difficult times. I am truly grateful to you, in the knowledge that our secret will be forever buried within us both due to your loyalty.

Your ever-loving sister,
Temperance

37

CREWE - 2024

And just like that, she had a pass to visit the Care Home in Crewe where a 'Miss Gerty Smith' had resided until her death two months previously. All it had taken was a phone call from Ashley Coombs, and the reassurance that Tilly's intentions were all above board and legitimate. Unfortunately, they hadn't given him any more information than that, so Tilly had taken the bull by the horns, made the appointment and booked a train ticket, plus a room in a Travelodge. Mid-week it had cost just £35 so seemed easier than trying to do the return trip in one day.

As the train pulled in at Crewe station, Tilly suddenly felt a flutter of butterflies in her tummy. She was armed with her notes, questions and all the family history she was able to glean from the chat with her mum. It still didn't feel like it was enough to potentially walk into an elderly stranger's life, recently bereaved of her sister, and start asking questions. But it was something she had to do, and with her rucksack zipped and hauled over one shoulder, she swung open the train door and jumped out on to the platform.

Tilly had already checked the route and, as it showed it to be just twenty minutes on foot from the railway station with the Travelodge also nearby, she had decided to walk. A bonus it being a sunny day. The Shrubbery was easy to find. Set back off the main road with a long sweeping drive, the landscaped gardens were spectacular. Tilly appreciated a well-manicured garden, even if she struggled with her few pots. As she strolled up the path, she nodded hello to a gardener who was trimming the hedge. It didn't look like it needed a trim, but clearly it was of the greatest importance to maintain precisely everything in the grounds of a place named 'The Shrubbery'.

The doors opened automatically, and she found herself in a bright and airy reception area, with more plants trailing from shelves behind and beside the desk. A young man was sat at a computer to the back of the reception area. He got up when he saw her arrive.

'Good morning, my name is Danny, how can I help you today?' His smile was almost artificial; he had clearly been on a customer service training course, yet it was genuinely welcoming and put Tilly at ease.

'Hello Danny, my name is Tilly Brown. I have an appointment to meet the Care Home manager.' Tilly smiled back.

'Ah yes, we are expecting you. Please come this way. I will settle you in the visitor's room and then call Mrs Merryvale, to let her know you are here. She won't be long.' Danny showed her into a room adjacent to the reception and closed the door. Tilly slumped down on a smart blue upholstered chair. The kind you see in most clinical waiting rooms. Everything was extremely clean, which was good to see, much like Sunny Days when Hector was there. It was only a few minutes later that there was a tap at the door, and in rolled a very smiley lady, with red cheeks and her hair in a greying bun on the top of her round head. Tilly stood up.

'Hello my love, no need to get up for me. You sit yourself back down there, and we can have a chat.' Tilly held out her hand.

'I am Tilly, thank you so much for agreeing to see me Mrs Merryvale.' They shook hands and sat down.

'Oh none of that Mrs Merryvale nonsense, you call me Margery, or just Marg, everybody does.' She laughed, throwing her small round head back as she did so, and Tilly couldn't help but laugh too.

'Okay Marg, I will,' said Tilly.

'So let us get down to business then Tilly. After I spoke to you initially, I spoke to your solicitor. Ashley, isn't it?' Tilly nodded. 'So, I understand that you are researching your family, in order to try and trace an elderly relative, and you think we may have someone who can help you?' Margery was still smiling, which made Tilly hopeful, although she realised it was probably a permanent smile. How she envied people who could be so happy all the time.

'I really hope so. It started with me searching for the names of three elderly sisters. There was a 4th sister too, but I don't know her name. I just know three names, with the surname Smith, who all remained spinsters. They lived together in Crewe in the family home I believe. When I found a death of Freda Smith that occurred during covid, I thought the dates tied in roughly with my Freda. Then the newspaper clipping said she lived at this home with her sister.' Tilly looked up at Marg.

'Sisters' corrected Margery.

'So Freda who passed away, lived here with more than one sister?' Tilly found her heart beating faster at this news.

'She did love. She lived with her younger sisters Con and Minnie. Their sister Gerty died before they came to us. So we just have Con and Minnie with us now.' Margery continued to smile.

'They are the sisters I am looking for. Con must be the name my mum couldn't remember, but the others were Gerty, Minnie and Freda. Oh, this is wonderful. You knew, didn't you?' Tilly felt a bit silly. Clearly the home was not going to let any old stranger wander in to talk to their residents.

'We did a little research with the information you and Ashley gave us and decided that it all fitted and that you are a genuine relative. I think you are first cousins, twice removed.' Margery gave another hearty laugh. 'If you can understand that nonsense - our Danny at reception did the workings out for me. There is something I need to tell you though, before we go through to see them.' Tilly felt another jolt. Please no bad news, now she was so close.

'Minnie is not very communicative. She has dementia and has good days and bad days. Now, her sister Con, who is the baby of the family at 94, has all her marbles, and is excited to speak to you.' Tilly's eyes welled up. She wished she could control her emotions a bit better sometimes, but right now, they were brimming over.

'I'm sorry Marg, I don't know why I am like this. It's just...well...I am so excited. Lucky. Oh I don't know, all of those things. I can't quite believe I have found them so quickly. Thank goodness for the internet again.' Tilly clasped her hands together, then unclasped them in excitement.

'Calm yourself, love. They are lovely ladies, and they have asked to put their Sunday dresses on, just for you. Come. Let us go through.' Tilly got up, quickly brushing away an escaped tear. How sweet that they were able to dress up for her. This must feel like a special occasion for them as well as her. She followed Margery through the secure doors, and along a corridor. Very similar to the one Hector was in. Then stopped outside their door.

'They have interconnecting rooms. Minnie needs more help, and can sometimes be unsettled at night, but they spend each day together. Mostly in here, and sometimes in the day room with other residents. I will knock and then go in, you just follow.' Margery knocked gently then pushed the door open. The room was not unlike Uncle Hector's, with a large window looking out onto their own private garden. Both ladies were sitting in their own armchairs, looking towards the window. One of the ladies, looked frailer and more stooped, but they both looked up, and the stronger of the two, presumably Con, got up from her chair and turned to greet them.

'No need to stand on ceremony Con, you sit yourself back down love.' Margery encouraged, but the old lady wasn't going to be moved.

'I want to meet this young lady. And how do you do Miss Tilly. I have heard all about your search from Marg here, and I do hope my sister Minnie and I can help you.' As Con grabbed Tilly's hand in hers, Tilly felt the smooth warm aged skin against her own. Her grip was tight, and she held it long, looking straight into Tilly's eyes. She was a bit shorter than Tilly, but still upright. She edged back towards her seat, keeping Tilly's hand in her own. 'Minnie. Minnie dear, this is our cousin Joe's girl. Her name is Tilly, and she has come to visit us. Minnie? Did you hear me?' Con's voice was slightly raised, as you would to someone hard of hearing. Minnie had a more vacant look on her face. Con let go of Tilly's hand and patted Minnie. 'Sit down dear. We are looking forward to talking about the old days with you. Oh such happy times.' Con's face lit up at this point.

'That is wonderful Con. And I am looking forward to hearing about them too.' She got out her notebook and waved to Marg as she crept out of the room, not wanting to disturb the happy group.

'Now Tilly, where shall we start?'

38

CREWE - 2024

The sun streamed in through the French doors, lighting up the living room shared by Minnie and Con. A space in which Tilly embarked on a new journey of discovery with her newfound family. Never had Tilly dreamt she would feel quite such strong emotions, washing over her in waves as she explored a history she had only previously touched on with Uncle Hector. She presumed the feelings were because of Hector. It brought back those happy times sitting with him in his room at Sunny Days. It was almost history repeating itself. She felt she was being given a second chance to bring something to these dear old spinsters' lives.

The conversation was mixed. She let Con chat about anything and everything; they clearly didn't receive visitors as a rule, although Con had mentioned Nuns who visited occasionally, and with whom they said prayers and gave thanks for the lives they had lived. This clearly gave much comfort to Con. She wasn't sure about Minnie, who did seem to know Con, looking to her for reassurance constantly, never letting go of her bony hand. Con in turn held tightly to Tilly's hand.

When the flow of one-sided conversation slowed, Tilly saw her opportunity to bring the subject around to Hector, Violet and ultimately Temperance. A knock at the door, and refreshments were delivered by the young man Danny who had been at reception when she arrived. He brought a trolley with tea, coffee and a small plate of sandwiches, neatly cut into triangles and covered with cling film. There was a pot of tea with a knitted tea cosy to keep it warm, and three flowery matching bone china cups and saucers.

'Lunch is up ladies. Now, we have smoked salmon and cucumber, cream cheese, and plain peanut butter for you Minnie, because we know that is your favourite.' Danny winked at Tilly. What a sunny personality he had. Perfect for bringing a bit of happiness into the lives of these elderly residents. They had so little else to look forward to.

Tilly got up and poured the tea, shared out the sandwiches and moved the small table over, so that it was next to Minnie. Tilly was pleased to see Minnie tucking in to the sandwiches, albeit shakily. They were such a sweet couple. At least they still had each other. For Tilly without siblings, it had always been just her. But she hadn't felt lonely, it was all she knew. She was a bit spoilt if she were honest. Until she lost her dad, that was.

Snapping out of her self-pity, she sat back down with a cup of tea. They had offered her sandwiches, but she didn't feel hungry. Not for food anyway, just for information.

It felt like they were ready to answer her questions now. She planned to start slowly. As she started to talk about her grandpa Joe and Uncle Hector, Minnie stopped eating and looked transfixed, as intently she processed the words Tilly spoke. A realisation slowly emerged, and she lifted her hand as if asking for permission to speak. Her sister Con protectively reassured her, that they were talking about the old days and that she would probably have lots of different memories mixed up. Not to worry herself.

'Yes Tilly love,' she turned to Tilly, 'Minnie and I remember such happy summers on the farm with our cousins Violet and Temperance. Don't we dear?' She nodded at Minnie, who was still transfixed. 'There were chickens. We loved to collect the eggs, and Aunt Laura would cook them for our breakfast. We would pencil an initial on the egg so that we knew whose egg was whose. When we were younger, we would play hide and seek. The farmhouse was perfect for that. So many nooks and crannies. The great big fireplace, hidden cupboards, oh, so many places for a small girl to hide in. Then as we got older, and the boys came along, we would play with them. I used to push Joseph in his pram. There was a small stream that ran along the bottom of the field with the hay bales and once I let the pram go. It trundled down towards the water, but luckily Temperance caught it before it went in. She was a very fast runner. A slim sporty girl was Temperance. Joseph in his pram was a bundle of giggles, and shrieked with laughter the whole way, oblivious of the danger.' Con stopped, for a moment remembering those happy times so many years before. 'We were closer to Violet and Temperance of course. They were both nearer our age. We saw them every summer, and in the late spring holiday too. Until…' Con stopped again, but this time her face looked sad.

'Go on Con, I'd like to hear more about your time at the farm.' encouraged Tilly. 'But only if you feel able to.' Recognising something wasn't quite as it should be.

'Well, as we got older, things changed. It wasn't as much fun. Aunt Laura, our mother's sister, she was sweet, but very timid. Uncle Albert was a very stern man. Unkind to his daughters. If Uncle Albert was there, Aunt Laura rarely said anything – she always seemed afraid of him. We didn't like Uncle Albert, but thankfully he was usually working in the fields.' Tilly made notes, but so far, she didn't feel she had learned anything she didn't already know. These were all things that Uncle Hector had talked about.

'So what changed Con? You said you were close to Violet and Temperance 'until' but until what?' There was something she wasn't being told, and whilst she didn't want to upset the old lady, she had come to try and find out more about the circumstances around Temperance leaving. It was the whole point of the trip to Crewe.

'Well Tilly dear, that is just it. Something happened, and all of a sudden, our father said we were not to continue visiting. Forbade it. Just like that. We were not given any details. Oh, but we did so love going out with Violet and Temperance as they got older. We would stay at the farmhouse, and all of us six girls would walk to the local dance. Sometimes we would dance with a local gentleman from the village. Once, there were two boys who walked us back to the farmhouse. All six of us you know, plus these two boys. Oh, we did laugh as they escorted us. But that was the last time. In 1951 it all stopped. No more visits to the farmhouse. No more laughing, no more dancing. Our father forbade any further visits. No explanation. Well.' She stopped again.

'Well what Con?' Tilly was getting tense with anticipation. She felt Con knew more than she was letting on.

'Well, much *much* later, my sister Freda, she was the oldest, she wrote to Violet. They were closest. She had to do it in secret because of father. Freda told the rest of us girls; Minnie, Gerty and I, that Temperance had done something bad, and had been sent away to live. Overseas, she said. I didn't know what bad thing she had done, and we couldn't ask our parents, so we assumed she had been with a boy and, you know. Maybe he had got her in the family way.' Con put her hand to her mouth as she said it. Clearly the fear of scandal still haunted her.

'Oh no. How sad.' Tilly had heard this happened in the old days. But this was just an assumption by the sisters. 'But you don't know that is exactly what happened, or where she was sent to?' questioned Tilly. Con shook her head.

'Years later, when both our parents had passed, my sister Gerty tried to contact the family. She wrote to the farm and eventually had a letter back from Hector telling her that Joseph had passed young, and that Violet was living near London. He was travelling all around the world at that time, for his work. He used to accompany special cargos, valuable parcels and paintings to their new homes, I believe. He said that he didn't know any more about Temperance than we did but suggested we left well alone. So we did.' She looked up at Tilly. 'I am ashamed to say I wish I had done more. It is sad Tilly dear. Very sad.' Tilly agreed and didn't really know what else she could say.

'Thank you Con, I really appreciate you telling me what you know. I hope you didn't mind me coming here to see you, but I promised Uncle Hector that I would do all I could to find his sister Temperance. I think I know what I have to do next.' Tilly squeezed the old lady's hand.

'It's lovely for us to meet a cousin Tilly. For that is what you are. We have no other relatives we know of, having never married or had children. We were happy in our own way, at home with mother and father, but I do wonder what it would have been like to have followed another path. A husband and children. But it is no use pondering on what might have been. Our father was a strict man. A methodist lay preacher you know. He would go door to door to preach the message of the Lord. He liked us to stay at home with mother, and that is what we did. All four of us.' She sighed. It really did feel as if Tilly had opened some old wounds in her chat.

'I think that I should leave you both now to rest. If I may though, I'd like to visit you again, if you would like that. I wouldn't be able to come every week, but I could come every now and again. If you'd like. And I could write to you.' The ladies were both looking keenly at Tilly, and Con nodded eagerly.

'Yes please Tilly. We would love that, wouldn't we Minnie? It has been so lovely to have you here Tilly dear, and to get letters. Oh, that would be a dream.' Minnie nodded slowly, taking the lead from her sister. Tilly didn't really know what she was promising, but these two dear old ladies were family, and they had no-one to visit them. It was the least she could do.

On her way out, she caught Marg and explained that she would like to visit again. She was told that would be fine now she was registered on their records as a legitimate visitor. Tilly wandered out of the automatic doors heading to her Travelodge, feeling lighter in spirit. Whilst she may not have got an exact answer to her mystery, she had more evidence that pointed to Temperance heading abroad for a new life, and maybe a reason why. She pondered on the idea of searching for a child as well, although she imagined it would have been adopted. Well, at the very least her day had brought some comfort to two elderly ladies who were her own flesh and blood. For that she felt the trip had been a success. Tilly vowed that she would return.

39

NORFOLK - 2024

The Travelodge room had been a short walk. Passing a fast-food chain on her way, she had picked up a burger and chips meal deal before checking in. The room was adequate, and tiredness of the day had hit Tilly as soon as she arrived. After eating, she soon crashed out, enjoying the comfort of the large double bed, all to herself.

The following morning the train back was stop start, but Tilly wasn't fussed. It gave her the opportunity to collate her notes into some semblance of order, and to jot down the many ideas, flitting around in her head. She pulled out her notebook and opened it on a clean page, leaving a few pages blank in between the earlier scribbles. There was something special about a nice clean page. Not as good as the first page of a brand-new notebook but getting there. She headed up her blank page in a nice lilac thin tipped sharpie - 'Plan' then below it, in bullet points:

- Contact Ashley to update him
- Contact Sam and Melody about house visit
- Contact mum?
- Research online genealogists NZ
- Flight prices

She knew there was more to add and left a space while she started on the first item. Getting out her phone, she sent a brief text to Ashley:

Hi Ashley, thanks for chatting to The Shrubbery for me. I have had a very successful visit to the Care Home and met not one, but two elderly sisters who turned out to be cousins to my grandpa Joe and Uncle Hector. I had such a lovely day with them yesterday and they were able to chat about the old days. I hope to visit Spitalbrook this weekend and will drop the key back to you after the visit.
Regards, Tilly Brown

Now to think about the weekend. A WhatsApp message to Melody followed, asking if Sam would possibly be free at the weekend for a trip to West Snoring. She had an idea and was keen to explore the whole house when they had the place to themselves. That sent, she hesitated about messaging her mum. Perhaps she would do that when she had more idea of the next steps she planned to take. She didn't want her mum to know she was going to Spitalbrook - not until she had thoroughly searched the place for other possible clues. Tilly felt they had to be there somewhere.

There was nothing more she could do about the weekend, so she moved on to the next point. The Wi-Fi signal was quite good on the train, and when it wasn't she used her data. So, she relaxed back, with the carriage to herself, and proceeded to search for a genealogist in New Zealand who might be able to help her.

The time flew and when she pulled into the station closest to home, after one change and a short wait, her notebook was filling up. She had whittled it down to three different people who seemed to be doing research in New Zealand. She drafted a generic message and sent it off to all three.

Arriving back at Georgie, late afternoon, Tilly was delighted to be greeted by a very affectionate Marmite purring loudly, whilst pushing as hard as possible against her ankles. She had just unlocked the door and pushed her way in, when she received a message. Glancing at her phone she could see it was from Melody. She plonked her bag down on the bed and opened the message.

Have you remembered it's Kit's leaving drinks tomorrow night? I am guessing not, you numpty. No worries, you know now. Of course we are free Saturday to go over to the farmhouse with you. Speak tomorrow - 8 at the pub? Mx

Of course. Tilly thumped the heel of her hand against her forehead. How could she have forgotten Kit's imminent flight to New York. The excursion to Crewe, and the excitement of the prospect of getting into Spitalbrook to have a proper root through everything, had moved all other thoughts from her mind. 'Okay Tilly', she said to herself. 'Calm down and take a step back.' As she spoke, Marmite pounced onto the pew next to her, meowed his loudest plea for attention, which Tilly could not ignore.

'Okay boy, of course I couldn't forget you now, could I?' She left her laptop open on the table, and proceeded to shake some biscuits into his bowl before heading into the shower to refresh herself after the long journey.

As the evening drew in, Tilly received replies to two of the family historians she had contacted. The first said, very politely, that she couldn't take on searches for other people who were not living in NZ. The second was less dismissive, but no less positive, as the chap, his name was Frank, lived in the UK and wondered if she would like to meet. That was disappointing, as Tilly thought she had found people in New Zealand. His profile was misleading and his suggestion a little sleazy. It sounded like he was using it as a dating site. She decided she needed an early night, and that she would sleep on the next steps.

Friday morning was a beautiful early summer morning. Tilly thought she had heard a bit of rain overnight, but it could have been in her dreams as quite frankly nothing would have woken her. She had felt totally exhausted after her trip. Physically and mentally. She looked at her watch, surprised to see it was only 7am. That was the benefit of an early night - a longer day followed!

After rising, she prepared a generous portion of muesli, granola and fresh mixed fruit. With added sunflower and pumpkin seeds. As she tucked in to her healthy breakfast, she logged in to her emails. One more regarding the New Zealand connection was waiting for her. Interestingly, it had come in at 3.15am. That looked promising. She moved her bowl to one side and opened the message.

Good afternoon Miss Brown, or should I say good morning! My name is Drew, and I am also tracing the Brown family. From what you have put in your online tree, I think we may have a match and I would love to connect. Cheers, Drew.

Tilly suddenly sat up and read the message again 'I think we have a match' she read out loud. This was exciting. She quickly drafted a reply, and pressed send, perhaps a little too hastily.

Without much chance of a response until the evening Tilly decided she had to get on with her day. A new exhibition of her art was due to be displayed in the old methodist hall, near her mum's house. She had a couple of items of barge art to finish and any painting she could find time for. With the theme of 'In the Countryside,' it left her a wide range of subject matters to choose from. She loved sunflowers, poppies, hay bales and open landscapes with rolling green fields. She also loved very tiny subjects like bumble bees and dragon flies.

It was decided. Her day would be spent creating and she would allow herself a break from the family history research. A break from the challenge and a break from all things related to Hector Brown and his mysterious family. However important the challenge, Tilly needed headspace, and some 'Tilly Time' so there really was no better time to start, than the present.

40

NORFOLK - 2024

How satisfying it was to be able to create something from nothing. Art in many forms, poetry, even the odd story. This was Tilly's happy place, the thing she loved to do. Create something that would give joy to others. And it was something Tilly was very good at. A flare it was said she had inherited from her mother's side, although most definitely not her mother. She knew Hector had been an amateur artist, so she assumed it had skipped a generation. What she wasn't very good at was believing in herself. Even with Kit and Melody praising everything she did, oozing enthusiasm, she always had doubts. However, the previous afternoon had thankfully been very productive, and beautiful weather had meant sitting on top of the boat with her paints and easel had been the perfect way to feed her desire to create. The soft breeze permeated through the silver birch alongside the canal which added to the relaxed atmosphere and created the perfect ambience to paint. With her existing stock of finished watercolours, Tilly now had enough pieces for the exhibition, and that meant one less thing to think about.

Tilly turned on her laptop to check her emails and there sat a new message from Drew. A ripple of excitement ran through her. She couldn't wait to open it, telling herself under her breath to calm down.

Hey Tilly, it is so great that we have connected.
So how are you? I thought it would be a good idea if I told you a little bit about myself, so that you can see that I am genuinely researching my family and can be trusted (winking face emoji).
So, my name is Drew Bartholomew-Brown - you see that straight away we have a partly shared surname. I have only just begun my search to trace my grandparents and great grandparents. It has been easy on my mother's side as they have a family bible, but my father's is another story. I am looking to specifically research my grandmother's family which I believe is where the 'Brown' comes from. You would think most people would know their grandparents, but my father is an only child who says that he didn't get on with his parents, and so he left home at 18. He can't give me any information at all other than he had heard his father passed away in the 1990s, before I was born and that they lived on the South Island.

I grew up on the North Island and have only very recently moved out into a small flat here in Auckland. My parents are Nicholas and Jane Bartholomew-Brown, and they live at the very north of New Zealand in the Bay of Islands. I was born in 1993 in Auckland, New Zealand. At the age of 30 I am now feeling ready to explore more of my roots. I have done a DNA test and am waiting for the results. That is quite exciting. I have started to write down my family tree, and that is where I think I have a connection with your online tree. I may be wrong, but I think your Temperance Brown may be my grandmother, which means we are related! It's very early days for me, and I am definitely no expert, but I will be in touch again as soon as I have more information.
I look forward to your contact, regards Drew (smiley face emoji)

As before, Tilly read the message through again. Then once more. It did seem incredible what this Drew was telling her. She pulled out the notebook she had taken to Crewe and made a few more notes. It generated some questions in her mind. Why was Drew saying he was related to her? Why didn't he make his dad give him more information? Mind you, she hadn't found it easy with her own mum, so she supposed the relationship could be similar. It all seemed quite incredible. So incredible, that this time, Tilly decided he must be fake. He knew who she was looking for and had made up a story. Yeah, that was it. Really, what were the chances he was related to Temperance? Very slim, she decided. After getting her hopes up, she now felt this too good to be true message was just that. Pushing her laptop to one side, she decided to get on with her day.

That evening was Kit's farewell drinks and a chance to catch up with her besties, to tell them about the message and also to ask Mel about visiting Spitalbrook. Before that, Tilly had a three-hour afternoon shift at the charity shop booked in. She didn't really feel like it, but it had been a few weeks since her last stint, and she didn't like to let them down.

It turned out to be more interesting than usual as she was asked to look after Lucy, a local GCSE student who had chosen to do her work experience at the shop. Her interests were in recycling rather than retail. Quite a hippy young thing, Tilly thought her heart was in the right place. Young Lucy was keen once she had been persuaded that her job was to sort the bags of clothes donated, and not to try everything on and then make a little pile for herself! It meant Tilly was able to work at the front of the shop serving customers which suited her.

She finished work with plenty of time to get ready for the night out. She cycled up to the pub for 7pm where she had arranged to meet Sam and Melody, in advance of Kit's arrival. They had a few balloons and a 'Good Luck' banner to decorate the corner of the pub. Gez the landlord was easy going and had said they could do what they liked provided they cleared up afterwards. With quite reserved plans, they didn't think there would be a lot of tidying up later. As she arrived, she could see Melody already in the throes of decorating, a bunch of bright blue helium balloons bobbing by her side as she teetered on a bar stool to fix the banner.

'Hiya Mel, do you need help, where is Sam?' Tilly had expected to see Sam there with her. Straining to reach a high beam, Melody glanced down to Tilly and grinned.

'Phew, got that one on there now. What, oh yes, he has gone back to the car for the flowers.' She was quite out of breath. 'I've just about finished this now. He did help first, then found an excuse to get out of it, typical Sam. Grab my hand please Tills and help me down from this stool.' Tilly assisted Melody to the floor then hugged her friend.

'It looks great Mel; I think Kit will love it.'

The girls gathered the rest of the decorations together, spreading the balloons along the back of the corner seated area that had been reserved for the party. A 'whoop' from the door signified Kit's arrival, her family and a few other friends close behind. Tilly was the first to greet her friend, who was all smiles. An uncharacteristic hug from Kit demonstrated her excitement, at her impending trip. The girls sat down while Kit's dad put £200 behind the bar to kick start an evening of chat and laughter.

As the evening progressed, some of the family members drifted off, and finally the three girls plus Sam were left in the corner, sipping their drinks.

'Now it's a bit quieter, I need to tell you about the message I got back from Drew.' Tilly had been thinking about the message, wondering if her initial reaction might have been a bit hasty.

'Oh really, he came back to you? Come on then girl, tell us what he said, this is exciting.' Melody was keen. Kit looked puzzled.

'Sorry Kit, I didn't want to bother you with this, with so much New York stuff for you to think about. In short, I searched online for someone in New Zealand who might be able to help with my search for Temperance, and this guy Drew Brown sent me a message. I replied and he's now sent me another email. But I'm not sure now, whether he is genuine.' Tilly showed them the email on her phone and explained why she had suddenly felt sceptical. They all leaned in to read the message, and Melody shook her head.

'You're wrong Tilly, I think you should give him a chance. Find out a few more things about him - ask him some specific questions. Just don't be too quick to judge, he's given you quite a lot of information after all. I don't think someone would make all that stuff up. Why would he? Maybe consider doing a DNA test yourself. Then you will see if you have a connection!' Tilly made a face, still not convinced, but if anyone could persuade her it would be Melody. Her sensible friend.

'Okay, I'll think about it, but not tomorrow. I will make him wait a day or two. Talking of tomorrow...' Tilly smiled at Sam.

'What are you after Tilly,' said Sam playfully.

'I need to go back to Spitalbrook, and I wondered if you two could spare an hour or two tomorrow. Pretty please?' Sam and Melody looked at each other.

'Sam may be able to take you Tills, but I am busy all day, sorry. I've got a Mother's Union sale and I'm on the committee, so I need to be there. Is that ok love?' Melody smiled at her husband, who nodded.

'No problem, Tilly, what time shall I pick you up.' Sam was always amenable, and they agreed a pickup time at the canal.

The party came to a natural end, and the friends said their final farewells to Kit. A few tears were shed, but lots of hugs and agreements they would meet on facetime as soon as she was settled in her New York apartment.

Tilly cycled home, a little tipsy in the cool of the evening, her mind buzzing with ideas for her visit to Spitalbrook but not quite able to shake Drew Brown from her thoughts either. Something she would have to park for a day. Spitalbrook was her focus right now, and with Sam's help, she was sure she could start to unravel part of the mystery surrounding the Browns and their old family farm.

41

NORFOLK - 2024

'Thanks Sam. I really appreciate this. I promise I'll try to keep it as short as possible. Two hours max.' Tilly didn't want to take advantage of Sam's kindness.

'It really isn't putting me out Tilly. With Melody doing her own thing today, I'm free all day. My mum has Lois because my sister is visiting with her little boy George, so basically, I was at a loose end anyway. Tell me what you have planned.' So, while Sam drove, Tilly explained her main objective of the day. Finding the key and seeing what else was in the writing desk. Searching for letters, that might give her more clues. She didn't want to mention the fireplace until she'd had another look at it.

Traffic was clear with only one small hold up, and within a short time they were out in the open Norfolk countryside. There were fields housing pigs, in their small metal huts, interspersed with arable fields of potatoes and beans. The pair made good time, driving right up to the door and parking under the shade of a large beech tree. They were getting rather warm weather for late May which meant everything had grown at the front, although Tilly could see the lawns were still being kept tidy. She wondered who managed it all. Considering no-one had lived in the house for many years, the gardens were clearly still well maintained. She assumed rented out to someone local. She turned her attention to the key, fixing it in the large keyhole, and turning firmly. It gave a satisfying clunk and the door opened. Tilly turned on the hall light, before pulling back the curtains to let in the natural light. Sam followed.

'I've got my newspaper, so I'll just sit here by the window while you do your thing.' Sam smiled and opened his paper. 'If you need anything, just give me a shout.'

'Okay Sam. I'll shout when I need a cuppa and you can put the kettle on. The milk is in this bag, and there are still some tea and coffee bits in the kitchen, left over from the wake.' Sam gave her a thumbs up, and settled back into the big armchair, looking rather too comfortable Tilly thought. She turned her attention to the matter in hand. With her bag and coat hung up, her focus was to start in the lounge.

The room was gloomy. It brought back memories of Hector's wake. The chairs had been covered back over with sheets, and the curtains were closed. As Tilly pulled back the drape to let in a bright stream of sunlight, dust particles danced in the beam. She then went behind the armchair, to the writing desk. She had to move the chair forward, so that she could drop down the flap. The hinge on one side was a little stiff, and Tilly had to give it a bit of a push. It opened suddenly with a loud grating noise, revealing a crammed desk of, on first appearance, what looked like papers. To one side was a small drawer. A key was what she was looking for, so a drawer was the obvious place for it. Tilly gently teased it open. It too was rammed to the brim. She found she was shaking as she tugged at the small wooden handle, until it released with a jolt. Tilly took the drawer to the brightness of the window where she lifted the papers from the top and placed them on the sill. Some funny looking small green stamps. She looked a bit closer and read 'Green Shield' within a shield and 033p above it. It didn't mean anything to her, and she kept sifting through. What looked like an old petrol coupon turned up next. A small blue driving licence for Albert Brown. Some treasury tags, a small box of drawing pins, rusty ones at that and a lot of dust. A tarnished metal pencil sharpener, then finally at the very bottom of the drawer, a small bunch of discoloured keys. Did it include 'the' key she wondered? Tilly took them out and tried them one by one in the writing desk drawer. Three of the smaller silver keys fitted snugly. One in each of the two drawers, and a third fitted the main lock of the drop-down writing slope. This left one slightly larger key. Once golden bronze in colour, with an ornate decorated head, which included a cut out filigree leaf pattern. It looked more like a key for a box, and a special one at that. This must be the one Uncle Hector had been referring to. Tilly piled the other bits back into the box hurriedly. As interesting as they were, she didn't have time to go through them all now. Then her attention turned to the heap of paperwork in the middle of the desk. She grabbed a handful and pulled it out onto the desk, carefully placing the golden key on the top of the bureau. Bills, statements and an envelope with 'certificates' written on the front. That might be useful, she thought.

  After half an hour of wading through the contents of both large drawers as well as the middle section where the keys had been hiding, Tilly sat back on her heels, head spinning with thoughts of where to go from here. She had found a few letters, which were not from family members, and a few postcards. One from Uncle Hector to his parents from Paris in 1969. Another addressed to Hector and Joseph from Aunt Kit and Uncle David, sent from Morecambe. Yellowed around the edges, the picture showed a donkey wearing a straw hat, and 'Wish You Were Here' singing its cheery message to the recipient. She couldn't resist trying to decipher the small, neat writing, written she guessed, by Aunt Kit. *'We hope you are being good boys for your mother, while your father is away. Uncle and I will be home Tuesday and will visit with treats.'* Tilly was getting sidetracked. She stood up and stretched her legs, then called to Sam to put the kettle on. Hands on hips, she scanned the room. On the sideboard, the photo of Violet with her two young brothers caught Tilly's eye. She picked it up casually and stared at it. She could see Hector in the boy's young face. He wasn't smiling though, neither was her grandfather Joseph. They looked a little scared. She placed it back on the sideboard and went out to the kitchen to see how Sam was getting on with the coffee.

'Have you found what you came here for Tilly?' Sam handed Tilly a mug of steaming coffee and a packet of digestives. They sat down in the hallway, not wanting to uncover any more furniture.

'I found a key. Correction, I found four keys, but three fit the writing desk locks. The fourth is a little bigger and doesn't match. It looks like a key for a box of some kind. Here, what do you think?' Tilly took the key out of her pocket and passed it to Sam.

'Yeah, that does look like it would fit a jewellery box or similar. Quite pretty. So, was there anything else? You haven't said anything, but Melody told me you wanted to look at the fireplace for some reason.' Sam hadn't been concentrating fully on what Melody had said to him, only that it involved the fireplace and possibly alterations to it. He was fond of Tilly but did think she lived in a bit of a dream.

'I wasn't going to say anything Sam, but now you....' Tilly stopped, and gestured with her hand pointing upwards, almost spilling the coffee.

'Now you...what?' said Sam, urging her to finish her sentence. Why did girls do this? Melody was the same.

'I've just realised something about the photo.' Tilly put down her coffee cup and went back into the lounge. She picked up the photo in its frame and turned to face the fireplace. The three were positioned in front of a large, open fireplace, but the picture rail around the top of the room was identical, right down to the two existing pictures. Unchanged for perhaps 70 years. But the fireplace had changed. It was now much smaller. 'Look Sam.' She called him in.

'What am I looking at? It looks like a regular fireplace to me.' Sam didn't see an issue.

'I wasn't going to ask you to do this until I was sure, but now I am sure my hunch is right. I need you to try and chip a bit of the fireplace away, to see what's behind it.' Tilly was looking directly at Sam, and he could see she was serious.

'I want to say you can't be serious, but I can see you are. I really don't think it's a good idea Tilly. It isn't our house, and you can't just go messing about with the structure.' Sam didn't give a very convincing argument. 'Tell me why? What is it you think is there?'

'It was something the lady in Crewe said about the great big fireplace. They used to play hide and seek. There is no other large fireplace in the house and a large inglenook would be in keeping with the age of this house, and perfect for hiding things in. Now if that has been closed up, maybe that is where the money is hidden.'

'Oh Tilly, you are a dreamer. You've been watching too many films..' Sam gave her a hug.

'But no Sam, now I have proof. Look at this photo. See?' She passed him the picture of Violet and the boys, clearly standing in front of an inglenook fireplace, in the same position as this much smaller one in front of them. Sam nodded, reluctantly.

'You're right, it does look like it was once much bigger. I know there was a phase, probably a fashion, or possibly to make it warmer, when those big fireplaces were blocked up. It was normal. That doesn't mean anything is hidden behind it though, does it?' Tilly had to agree.

Sighing, she put the photo back. She felt frustrated that she hadn't found anything that showed she had met that part of the challenge. Whilst she knew it wasn't the main thing, she still had a hunch and was also not someone who would give up too easily. For now, she had to let it go.

'I'm going to have a quick nose in the other cupboards while I am here. Just to make sure the mystery box, or whatever the key fits, isn't lurking close by.' Tilly didn't want to go into a lot of detail with Sam. It was clear he thought her a bit silly with her romantic ideas. This romantic idea, however, had some substance. In his letter, Hector had said his sister Violet had given him a box. Yet there had been no such box in his room at Sunny Days, so might that box be somewhere in Spitalbrook? She had to use this opportunity to try and find it; he had told her it may hold a clue to Temperance's whereabouts.

She had already looked in the cupboards of the sideboard, which were not fruitful. The back parlour dominated by a more formal dining table, with chairs and a love seat, all draped with dust sheets also had an uncovered glass cabinet. There was a standard lamp in the corner and the gold and green striped curtains were closed. Tilly couldn't see anything else in the room, apart from a cupboard set into the wall in the far corner, blocked by a tall side table. She pulled back one curtain, to let in some light, then edged the table out and gave the door handle a tug. It clicked open. It seemed to be full of sheets plus a couple of towels; threadbare and worn. She could see space below the shelf, which was inaccessible and dark. Tilly got her phone out and turned on the torch. Leaning her head into the cupboard backwards, she shined the torch up. There was a narrow ledge up high jutting out into the cupboard space, but Tilly couldn't reach. She pulled one of the chairs from under the sheet and dragged it over to the cupboard to stand on.

'What are you doing now Tilly?' Sam's unexpected questioning almost knocked Tilly off balance.

'Sam!' she shouted, 'you made me jump. Now you are here, come over and make yourself useful.' Tilly beckoned him over. 'You are taller than me. Can you see that ledge up there?' She shone her torch into the cupboard.

'Just about, yes.' Sam seemed a bit tetchy. Perhaps he was getting bored. 'What do you want me to do?' Sam moved into the space Tilly had been occupying, knelt up on the chair and took the torch.

'Reach up - all along the ledge. Just make sure there isn't a box there. Please.' Tilly tried not to sound frustrated, but she felt so anxious to make a discovery of some kind, it came across as ungrateful. She was in fact very grateful to Sam, and to Melody for letting her have Sam for the day. 'I'm sorry Sam. Sorry for making so many demands.'

'No, Tilly. It's not a problem. I'm here to help, and I will do what you need. Right.' He reached up inside the cupboard and felt along the ledge. 'I can't feel anything up here love. Nothing like a box. Nothing at all.' Sam looked back to Tilly and saw the forlorn look on her face. Turning back to the cupboard, he shone the phone's beam of light down, beneath the shelf with the linen. 'But. Hey, what's that?'

'What is what Sam?' Tilly stepped forwards leaning over the chair.

'Let us move the chair out of the way. I can see the shadow of something under a sheet. A box shape. Can you grab the fabric?' Sam stepped back so that Tilly could get to the cupboard. She leant in and could just reach the sheet with her fingertips, managing to edge it back.

'Oh yes. There *is* a box. We need to get it. It looks like cardboard; a shoe box I think.' Tilly felt another rush of excitement, as she urged Sam. 'Can you reach it for me please my arms aren't quite long enough?' They swapped places again, and Sam pushed the sheets to the back of the shelf and leant down into the bottom of the cupboard. The shelf was slatted like a regular airing cupboard, and Tilly shone the torch down through the gap to help Sam see. He managed to grab it with one hand and drag it forwards so that he could grasp it with both hands and then edge it out through the gap at the front of the cupboard. As he brought it out into the light, Tilly was quick to take it from him. It wasn't heavy, faded brown in colour and as Tilly took it to the window to see it more clearly, faint pencil writing could be seen on the top. The lid had been taped down, but the tape was flaky and brown, no longer doing its job.

'Is it what you were looking for?' Sam joined Tilly by the window to view the treasure. 'It definitely doesn't need the key, so I guess we continue the search for that one another day.'

'You're right about not needing the key. I'm not sure if it's treasure though. I was trying to read what it says on the lid. I can see it now. 'Hector, from Violet'.' Tilly felt herself shaking. This was the box Hector had mentioned in his letter. She was sure of it. She lifted the fragile lid to find the box packed with post cards and letters. She puffed out her cheeks and sighed loudly.

'No luck?' said Sam, picking up the wrong signals.

'The opposite Sam. I am sure this is one of the things I was looking for.' Tilly put the lid back on the box, closed the cupboard door and pulled the curtain.

With the box safely in her bag she at last felt she had accomplished something. 'Come on Sam. Let's go home.'

42

NORFOLK - 2024

'Thanks Sam. I mean it. I'm so grateful to you. Give Mel a hug for me, I'll WhatsApp her later.' Tilly waved as Sam drove away, then hurried onto the boat, Marmite quick at her heels.

It was a bright warm Saturday, just perfect for painting. The idea of an arty afternoon briefly crossed her mind but moved on even quicker. Tilly had a small box of letters to interrogate, plus some serious work to do on her family tree, so the painting would have to wait. She also had a new potential relative to consider. A decision she had to make about whether to give Drew another chance. Her friends had been very persuasive at Kit's leaving do, and having slept on it a bit, she decided she may have been a bit hasty dismissing him out of hand. She *would* give him another go. But she wasn't a push over. She had asked for help, yes. He had offered, yes. But you hear such scare stories about people and the internet, she felt she was being wise to be wary, that wasn't unreasonable. Tilly couldn't help herself and fired up her laptop there and then.

A girl easily distracted, Tilly was known to jump from one thing to another, only to return to the original plan hours later. Her friends teased saying it was her 'blonde' genes. Not in an unkind way. She was intelligent enough, just found she always had too many things on her mind at any one time. The plan to read the letters was still at the top of her list; just edged down a smidge so that she could refresh herself with the contents of Drew's email.

The email opened after a few minutes. Tilly's aging laptop was slowing. Tilly usually got Kit to work her magic to speed it up, defrag is what she called it. With Kit now in New York she would just have to be patient as it slowly came to life. Lots more emails showed as unread; all spam. Unsubscribing to a chunk of unwanted messengers was another job on her 'to do' list.

Drew's email located, she read it through slowly, with a mind to send him a quick response, then to grab a sandwich before she got on with reading the letters, out in the sun. Careful not to reveal too much about herself, she began to type.

Hello Drew,

Thanks for your reply. I was surprised to receive one so quickly, so I appreciate your thoughtfulness.

I'm well and interested to see if we have a connection as you suggest. I'm currently in the early days of developing a family tree, so I can't confirm whether we are related or not. Cool about the DNA test; I'm going to investigate doing this myself. I guess this will be the most convincing evidence to prove our connection!

I will contact you again, once I have done more of my tree and can see where we fit together.

Kind regards,
Tilly

She pressed send, then only afterwards scanned back through what she had written and read it to herself. '*Where we fit together*' Oh my goodness, why did I write that?' said Tilly out loud. The email was on its way to New Zealand. There was nothing she could do about it now.

Tilly closed the lid of her laptop sighing and grabbed the box of letters. Marmite meowed loudly, curling himself around her ankles as she moved towards the door.

'Okay Marmite, just a few biscuits while I grab my sandwich. It isn't dinner time for you yet.' Yet another distraction. The cat placated with a few treats, she could come back to her original plan for the afternoon. Tilly took her camp chair out into the fresh air, with the box of letters tucked under her arm. Settled on one end of Georgie's roof under the shade of an overhanging willow, she opened the box and took out the first letter.

Tilly enjoyed reading the social chit chat in the letters which, so far, had all come from Temperance in New Zealand, with one from New York. She was slowly building up a picture of the mysterious Temperance, but so far, no new evidence of why she was there. The only real pattern, which was common to every letter, short or long, was a request for money. Sometimes quite desperate. Then Tilly found a letter, which had not been opened. An old airmail letter, so it was very clear it had not been cut through to reveal its contents. Tilly hesitated. It was addressed to Mother and Father, and the address was Spitalbrook. There was nothing for it, she just had to open it. Carefully, she slipped her long pink fingernail under the seal and gently edged it along the seam, tearing it slowly until the thin blue paper opened to reveal the writing inside. Dated 17th September 1968.

Dear Father and Mother,

I hope this finds you both comfortable. I have decided to write you a final and long overdue missive.

You may not be aware of the kindness my dear sister Violet has shown me, while I was forced by you, my own parents, to traverse the most desperate of times. I strove to build a new life for myself in an alien country, due to your unkindness. I am saddened that you have never felt able to contact me. This would have been my dearest wish, but it is clear to me now, that even though you did the most terrible thing to me, driving me from the home and from the family I knew and loved, you have never shown any remorse. This brings me much sadness. I have also been very unhappy that my existence has been wiped from the lives of my young brothers Hector and Joseph. They have the right to know both of their sisters, but I have had no contact with either of them, and can only assume you have orchestrated this. It is the most wicked form of punishment to both myself and my brothers.

It is only now that I feel strong enough to write and tell you my feelings. Now, with my husband Myles by my side, who cares deeply for me, I have the confidence that has been missing for most of my life.

I want you to know that I do not forgive you for the things you did to me, or for the way I have been treated. So I require nothing more from you. No more money and no contact. I have stayed true to myself and worked hard to support the family I have in New Zealand. I know I will be at peace with myself, should I receive the unfortunate news of your passing. I hope you are able to be at peace with yourselves.

Your loyal daughter,
Temperance Bartholomew-Brown

Tilly read the letter through twice then carefully folded the delicate paper, unaware of the tears rolling down her cheeks, until an involuntary sob caught in her throat. Dragging her shirt sleeve across her chin, she sat with her head back and took a deep breath. Head spinning with so many different thoughts. How Hector, and her own grandfather Joseph had clearly been denied access to their sister. How the emotion of rejection, for whatever reason, overflowed from the written page. Plus, the clear regrets as Temperance reached out one last time, to her parents. Then finally, the name. Bartholomew-Brown. The same as Drew's. It was clearly her married name, and the missing jigsaw piece Tilly was searching for, in order to give Drew's story some credence. She was sad but also lifted.

Not sure she could face any more of the letters after the emotion of this one, Tilly decided to email Drew back. She needed to apologise and send a much more friendly note, and to tell him she was definitely going to do a DNA test. Thinking back to the family tree which she had neglected, dismissing it as unnecessary, she now realised it was very necessary. As the whirlwind of plans were spinning around in her head, she hurriedly packed away the letters and went back inside to get the laptop.

By the evening, Tilly was feeling pleased with herself. She had got over the upset of the letter, sent an apologetic and much friendlier email to Drew, even suggesting his idea of a facetime meeting was a good one, she asked him when he would be free. Then she went on to Ancestry and ordered her DNA kit. A legitimate use of some of Uncle Hector's money, she thought. Another hour had been spent adding to her family tree, a husband for Temperance, and she assumed a child. As the name had been carried down, a son seemed likely, and this fitted with what Drew had said. This would be Drew's father. It was starting to slot into place. It still seemed a shame that Drew didn't have the actual evidence from his father, but as seen with the Brown family, a rift can have a devastating effect on a family. Links broken, sometimes never to be healed as seemed the case with Temperance and her parents. She would await Drew's response to both emails, before she thought about it any further, but it did feel as if she was getting very close to solving the puzzle. It would be good to be able to present the evidence to Ashley and then move on with her life. A life a little less exciting without Hector or his mysterious challenge sent to her from the grave. But a life, nonetheless.

It was by now just after 5 in the afternoon. Still warm, Tilly thought and satisfied she had earned some chill out time, she put her laptop on charge and got out her art easel and paints.

As Tilly collected her paintings together, she heard a tinny ringing sound coming from her laptop. When she lifted the lid fully, she could see a call was coming through from Drew. Panicking, she put her hands to her hair. It was no good thinking she could change her appearance now, and without further thought she clicked on the green phone symbol. A few seconds of blank screen, then a big smiling face appeared, completely filling the screen.

'Hey, Tilly. Hello there. Can you hear me?' Drew, surprisingly clear, was there on her screen talking to her. Tilly felt her heart racing. He had lovely big brown eyes, but fair hair. An unusual combination she thought, then mentally reprimanded herself. He's potentially your cousin, she said to herself.

'Hi. Yes, I can hear you loud and clear. I can see you loud and clear too, you are very close to the screen!' Tilly felt surprisingly at ease with her newfound cousin. Perhaps that is what it was like when you met long lost family. She found herself grinning widely. This was really quite exciting.

'Great job Tilly. You look beaut. You've decided to do the DNA test then?' Confidence oozed in Drew, and his extremely perfect face beamed at her.

'Yeah, I only ordered the test today, but since then I read some of Temperance's letters, and it seems like you are right about us being related. I think doing the test is immaterial now, but I will do it when it arrives.' Tilly had already forgotten about the DNA test she had ordered earlier that afternoon.

As they relaxed into a more regular conversation about hobbies, work and home life, Tilly learned that Drew liked to travel and had previously worked as a guide on Whale Watching tour boats from Kaikoura, a small town on the South Island. That he was a qualified electrician and worked for himself, and where he could he did extra work so that he could do more travelling. Tilly felt boring in comparison but didn't have trouble filling an hour chatting about her several jobs, her cat and her boat. It seemed that they at least had boats in common! Eventually, they ended their call, with Drew saying he was going to see if he could find out a bit more about Temperance and would tackle his father about it again.

Tilly felt altogether lighter. She had a smile on her face, and if she had been walking was sure there would have been a bounce in her step. She couldn't wait to message her friends. With the Best Buddies WhatsApp group open, she punched out a quick message.

Hey guys, you will never guess who I've just been chatting to! She added a big winking emoji, sent the message, then sat back smiling.

43

NORFOLK - 2024

Tilly felt time flying by. She had so many things to think about and worried that she was going to forget something important. She had recently received a nice, postcard style letter from Kit in New York, explaining how she was now feeling settled, and had started to make some friends. She described the block she was living in and some of the American diners she had been taken to by work colleagues, but she hadn't said anything about the job. It was early days though and Tilly felt sure her friend would say if there was anything wrong.

Receiving the card had prompted memories of Tilly's early family history search, when trying to trace Temperance. How she discovered her ship had sailed to New York, throwing her a curve ball when starting out on her research journey. Now, with evidence that Temperance had ultimately travelled to New Zealand, Drew and his connection had been on her mind. Since their Facetime chat, a couple of weeks had passed. In that time, Tilly had focussed her spare time on the family history and the many different tree building sites. She'd identified Temperance and Violet's dates of birth. The birth certificates had arrived confirming both women had been born at the farmhouse, Spitalbrook. Violet the eldest, was born in 1925 and Temperance followed on in 1927. It confirmed the names of her great grandparents as Albert and Laura, which she already knew. She had also found Violet's marriage to Ronald Stillman, and both of their names on the 1939 census. With this being before their marriage she could see Violet at the family home. There was a thick black line beneath her name, but no Temperance. It was odd she thought, as Temperance would only have been twelve years old at that time. She could see another black line, no entries for Hector or her grandfather. It was a reminder again, of her connection with these people, and made her anxious to receive her DNA kit, which was due to arrive very soon. She made a mental note to ask Judith at the library if she could tell her what the thick black lines meant.

Tilly had a busy two weeks working in both 'Cat Care' and 'Water Works Ltd' one week and running the plumbers single handedly the next. It was daughter Belinda's graduation in Durham, and Val, Donald and Paul all wanted to attend. Tilly felt it was only fair to offer to hold the fort, considering the flexibility they had afforded her. That was until she discovered she'd committed to working the whole week on her own. The graduation was to be on the Wednesday in Durham Cathedral, but Val wanted a day for the girls to get their hair and nails done beforehand. This clearly couldn't be done the day they travelled up, and then celebrations afterwards, meant they would not be returning until the Friday. It was too late for Tilly to rescind her offer, so a tiring week of almost full-time work followed. It just left Tilly the evenings in which to think about the other things on her mind. She needed to plan the next steps in her search for Temperance. Slowly it evolved, and once firm in her decision, she arranged to meet Melody at An Extra Slice to discuss it over breakfast the following Saturday.

The week dragged as the plumbing shop was so quiet. Tilly used the time to keep searching the internet for more historical evidence that Temperance had settled. What she wanted was a marriage, and then a child, but it seemed tracing her 20th century ancestors was a lot harder than the historical data obtained at the library.

On Wednesday the DNA test arrived, and Tilly's interest was piqued once more. Keen to get it done and posted back, she produced the required amount of saliva and deposited it in the tube provided, getting it back in the post that same day. Feeling more buoyed by this small action, work seemed less onerous, and time passed swiftly.

On the Friday, a familiar, but unexpected face appeared at the shop door. Tilly was surprised how good it felt to get a customer, even better as it was someone she knew.

'Hello Ashley, how may I help you?' Tilly was suddenly in professional mode now it was her turn at the other side of the desk.

'Good morning Tilly, how is business?' Ashley was in a suit and looked unusually smart, even handsome Tilly thought.

'In truth, it's very slow. But I am finding things to fill my time. How is business with you and how is Angela?' At this reference to Angela, Ashley visibly blushed.

'Oh, I can't complain. Angela is..er..fine. Yes, fine.' He smiled, and Tilly thought she saw a little twinkle in his eye. 'I've come in for a chain to go on the sink plug. Do you sell such things?' Ashley relaxed with the change of subject.

'We do.' Tilly got up from the desk and went to the corner where everything on shelves was held in untidy cardboard boxes; prices in childish handwriting, were scribbled on each box. She reached to the back of a low-down shelf and pulled out a small plastic bag from one of the boxes, containing a chain. 'Like this you mean, for a sink I assume not a bath?' Tilly placed it on the desk.

'Yes, that's it. It's for the office rest room. I've just got to work out how to fit it - DIY and me don't go well together!' Ashley laughed.

'I'm sure Angela could do it - 'Women's Lib' and all that. I suggest you ask her.' Tilly winked. 'That will be just £1.25.'

'A bargain. Thank you, Tilly. Now, on another subject, your uncle's will, how are you coming along with the challenge he set you?' Now Ashley was the one smiling. 'I'm only asking out of interest; I'm not putting pressure on. You know he left you that money, regardless of what you chose to do, but I was interested in how important it was to you and if you had made any progress?' Ashley seemed genuinely interested, and Tilly was keen to chat about her most recent discoveries and next steps, although careful not to mention the fireplace. It was too soon, if ever, for that.

'I am genuinely keen to complete his wishes. I have taken that very seriously I'll have you know. My research has been slow and steady, but I am making progress.' Tilly told him about the online contact with Drew, and her DNA test. Clearly, there was nothing to say about where Temperance was now, or if she had passed where she may rest, but she was working on that. 'I am meeting with one of my friends at the weekend and I think I have almost decided I want to go.'

'You want to go where?' Ashley hadn't followed her train of thought.

'To New Zealand. I think I want to follow in Temperance's footsteps, using the money Uncle Hector left me - it is what it's for after all.' Nodding, Ashley looked impressed.

'I have to say you really are taking it seriously. Most girls....I mean young women of your age would take the money and run. It's good you are so keen to uphold Hector's last wishes. I look forward to hearing what happens next in the "Tilly searches for Temperance" adventure.'

'Of course, I don't really expect to find her alive. She would be in her late 90s by now if she is. I just want to follow it through. I feel I am ready to take that next big step, on Uncle Hector's behalf.' Tilly found herself tearing up, and waved Ashley out of the shop before he noticed.

Shutting up the shop at 3.30pm, she was glad to be back on her bike for the short cycle along the canal to Georgie and the weekend.

~

It was a bright Saturday morning and Tilly arrived at the coffee shop first and sat down at their usual table. She was excited about what she planned to tell her friend, hoping Melody would be supportive. She had every confidence she would be. Tilly had only just caught Brenda's eye, when Mel appeared at the door, a little out of breath, but smiling as always.

'Hiya Tilly, sorry I'm late. Lois was being a little minx. Had it fixed in her head that we were going to see a lion today! Of all things, a lion, I ask you!' Melody rolled her eyes and raised her hands in an 'I don't know' gesture. 'So I dropped her at mum's who is now playing zoos with her. I have promised we will take her to a real zoo when we go on holiday!!' Melody slipped off her jacket, just as Brenda arrived at the table to take their order.

'Hello ladies, I haven't seen you for a while. I was worried that you had abandoned me now Kit has gone away.' Brenda winked at them, before taking their order. Neither particularly hungry, they ordered a toasted teacake to share, to go with their coffees.

Once Brenda had taken the order, Tilly leant across the table to hug her friend.

'Firstly Mel, I want to thank you for lending me your husband the other week. Sam was a star, and so patient. Did he tell you we found the key, and a few letters?' Melody screwed up her nose. Sam hadn't really been able to tell her very much about that day, even though Melody had tried to prompt him.

'Sorry Tilly, he told me he made the coffee! That was about it.' Melody looked apologetically at her friend. Tilly laughed.

'No need to apologise Mel, it means more for me to be able to tell you myself anyway. Plus, since then, I have sent off my DNA test.'

'Go girl! I am pleased to hear that you decided to do that. What about Drew - any more contact?' Melody put her head on one side, questioningly.

'Oh yes Drew. You know I told you we had that first Facetime chat?' Tilly couldn't remember who she had told, or what she had put into the WhatsApp messages. She didn't want to leave Kit out but didn't want to overload her either. Melody nodded. 'We had such a nice chat, it felt like we had known each other all our lives. I guess we must be related - you hear that don't you? About long-lost relatives.'

'You do. It proves we were right to encourage the contact with him. Right, what is the really big thing you want to tell me?' Melody was keen.

'Well...' Tilly's eyes sparkled and Melody leant forward, willing it out of her. 'I'm going to New Zealand. There, I've said it. I'm going.'

'Just like that? Seriously Tilly? I wasn't expecting that!' Melody was frowning slightly, and the creased brow look didn't suit her.

'I know it seems big, and sudden, but it really isn't. I don't know exactly when, but soon. As soon as I can organise it. It's the only way I can complete the challenge set for me by Uncle Hector. Then I can go back to my boring Tilly Brown life, but right now I am Matilda Jean Montgomery-Brown, private investigator, at your service.' Tilly put on her poshest voice to deliver the news, and both girls fell about laughing. 'And I have Drew to help me. I am comfortable that he is legit now. I haven't found a connection yet, but I'm confident I will.'

'Oh Tilly, I am so proud of you. I'm behind you all the way. What does your mum think?' Tilly's face went blank.

'Do you know what Mel? I haven't a clue.'

44

NORFOLK - 2024

The late summer village craft fair was almost upon them. Tilly had a variety of paintings prepared, priced and ready to display. She had paid £25 for a stall and her spot in the village hall, equidistant from the village and the canal, on a small estate of mostly bungalows, some council maisonettes and just a couple of two bedroomed properties, one of which Sam and Melody lived in, with Lois. She was hopeful for lots of visitors, to boost her coffers. The New Zealand trip would be funded by the nest egg left by Uncle Hector, but she felt she didn't want to waste the money. Fired up with excitement over the prospect of the trip, she was focussing on a bit of fundraising to enable some sightseeing in addition to the family history research.

After her catch up with Melody, Tilly had called her mum and told her straight that she planned to visit New Zealand. She didn't tell her about Drew, thinking Celia would be concerned about her meeting a stranger, or at the very least might put doubt into her mind. Tilly didn't want that. As a 26-year-old, independent young woman she felt it was no different to Kit flying to New York on her own. She had gathered the courage from somewhere and now was not the time to start doubting herself. So thankfully Celia had been supportive, saying it would be character building, and various other clichés, which made Tilly feel comfortable. No lies had been told; she just hadn't divulged everything about the trip.

Tilly had hoped her mum would have time to visit the village fair but realised it would depend on Dave. It was a reminder to Tilly how fortunate she was to have the independence she had. The thought of her movements being controlled by a man, made Tilly physically shudder.

The fair was in full swing when Melody, Sam and Lois appeared at her stall. Little Lois ran up to Tilly and clutched her round the legs, then put her arms up and pleaded for a 'carry'. Tilly swung the little girl into her arms. She was as light as a feather and the cutest little thing. Tilly adored Lois, and at times envied her best friend. But Lois was still not the best sleeper and when Tilly met with Melody, after a particularly sleepless night and saw the dark circles under her yawning friend's eyes, she was reminded that she wasn't ready for motherhood just yet.

While she stood chatting, Tilly's mum appeared behind Melody, smiling. Tilly tried not to sound surprised, secretly delighted to see her there.

'Hi mum, glad you could make it! Are you on your own?' Tilly knew she would be, but it seemed polite to ask about Dave, in a round-about way.

'Hello love. Yes, he is working through paperwork, but I said I wasn't staying in to waste this lovely weather.' A rather bold move by her mum, Tilly thought. 'Have you sold much?'

'I don't blame you mum. No, not yet, a few earrings but it's early days. There's been some interest in one of my large paintings and the woman was going off to find her husband, so I'm hopeful she will come back. I haven't offered to reduce it yet, but if they come back and are in two minds I have decided I can afford to reduce it by £10. That might be the clincher.' Tilly loved selling her own work, more than anything. She said there was a real satisfaction in earning money from something you had truly created from scratch with your own bare hands. 'You remember Melody don't you mum? And her husband Sam.' Melody turned to shake Celia's hand.

'Hello Mrs Kennedy. It has been a while, I know. How are you?' They shook hands and Celia politely passed the time of day. Melody had changed a bit since college days but wasn't unrecognisable. 'What do you think about Tilly's plans to visit New Zealand? Quite an adventure, and a stroke of luck hooking up with Drew.' Celia looked blank, and Tilly was furiously shaking her head at Melody making 'throat cutting' gestures with her hand. 'Er..yeah, Drew the..er..travel agent in town.' Tilly was now nodding over her mum's head as Melody stuttered her U turn. 'Who is..er..going to try and get her some flight details.' Phew, Melody had edged back up out of that hole she'd inadvertently dug herself. Sweating a bit, she decided it was time to move away. 'Anyway, nice to meet you, come on Sam, let's have a look round the whole of the fair. Come on Lois.' Tilly put Lois down and she ran to her dad who lifted her above his head and positioned the little girl onto his shoulders. She giggled and gave Tilly a wave.

'So you have already approached a travel agent then Tilly?' Tilly crossed her fingers behind her back.

'Oh, only informally. So that I could start to work out costs, that's all. No dates set yet.' Tilly puffed out her cheeks. Lying felt uncomfortable, but she hadn't even told Drew yet. He was next on her list, and then Kit. If her plan worked out, she might be able to afford to fit in a stop to see Kit in New York on the way.

Tilly enjoyed spending the rest of the day with her mum, who even offered to man her stall for a while so that she could browse the other crafts. Tilly got the impression her mum was standing up to Dave a bit more. It wasn't anything specific she said, but the way she had turned up on her own. Normally, if Dave was at home, then her mum stayed at home too. Celia also mentioned her special things box again, reminding Tilly it was there and available for her to access again any time she needed to.

'I've only just started to think about the trip mum, but since I've been doing the research on Uncle Hector's family, which of course is your family, I feel the only way to really find out what happened to her, is to head out to New Zealand. It is what Hector wanted; why he left me the money. It is enough to cover flights, and once I'm there, I just plan to backpack and stay in cheap hostels. It will be an adventure.' It felt good to be discussing something so close to them both with her mum, and Tilly felt the weight of guilt lift. Perhaps she would tell her about Drew after all, but not yet.

When the fair was over, Tilly was in buoyant mood. The potential customer had returned to become an actual customer, happily paying £85 for her landscape. The painting of a rainbow over the mountains surrounding Wast Water in the Lake District had been painted from a photograph Tilly's dad had taken before she was born on a holiday with her mum. She had also sold a small enamel jug painted in pink and blue plus a few pairs of bead earrings and a handful of hand painted greetings cards. In all a successful day. The day had remained warm and dry, which was as forecast for early September. In fact, they were expecting at least another week of unusually warm weather before there was any sign of autumn moving in.

Tilly enjoyed packing her things away slowly, making sure everything was wrapped then placed carefully into the large trolley she used for local fairs, where she could attend on foot. Her mum returned as she had almost finished the packing up, and they walked back to Celia's car together.

'So you really are set on this trip happening quite soon Tilly?' Wanting absolute clarity, Celia knew her daughter was prone to getting carried away with an idea.

'Definitely mum. I've been looking at flights, and…..er…actually, I have a confession to make.' She decided she needed to get the Drew little white lie nipped in the bud.

'Oh, what's that then dear?' They had arrived at Celia's car.

'I have actually made contact with a person in New Zealand who is going to help me with my family history research out there.' Tilly couldn't meet her mum eye to eye. 'It's Drew. You know, the one Melody mentioned? He isn't the travel agent he is someone who lives in New Zealand and seems to be tracing the same family. Our family. So it is possible, well, actually very likely we are related. We need to work out how.' There was a silence while Celia processed the news. 'Well? Say something mum.'

'I thought Melody seemed a bit tongue tied…you both did. So. What do you know about this Drew then? I can't say I won't worry, but you are an adult, and you are sensible.' Celia seemed quite relaxed about the connection, Tilly realised she had been wrong with her assumption.

'I'm going to be contacting him again tonight. We have spoken once, and he seems nice. Very friendly, but it is a bit difficult with the time difference. I haven't told him that I plan to visit; he thinks he's helping me from a distance. Which he is. I'll update you when I have some more concrete plans mum, thanks for coming today, I really appreciate it.' They awkwardly embraced, then Tilly saw her mum into her car, and waved her off.

It took Tilly half an hour to pull the trolley back to the boat along the canal side. She smiled as she walked, planning what she was going to say to Drew when she next made contact.

The idea of travelling all the way to New Zealand excited her. She wouldn't be sailing, but apart from the method of transport, she really felt like this would be following in the footsteps of Miss Temperance Brown, who headed out for new lands, in November 1951. Tilly had the idea of flying as close to the date in November as possible. It was to be genuinely following in her footsteps. There was no doubt about it, Tilly was now eager for the next stage.

45

NORFOLK - 2024

A storm was brewing, with very high winds and heavy rain predicted. Tilly had spent the morning at the plumbing suppliers, but hurried back along the towpath, as the winds began to pick up. She was keen to get home before the storm hit with a vengeance, to make sure everything was firmly tied down and more importantly that Marmite was safely inside the boat with her. He hated storms, especially high winds. The leaves were starting to fall from the many poplars and alder that lined the path, flying in her way and as the heavy drops of rain started to fall, Tilly pulled up the collar on her jacket and picked up the pace.

She managed to get home just before the heavens fully opened. Marmite was waiting for her at the door and greeted her with a loud meow. They both clambered quickly down the short wooden stairway into the comfort of her safe space, firmly clunking the door closed behind them.

Tilly secretly loved a storm. The earthy-mixed-with-mossy smell it conjured; the wildness of the trees flailing in the tumult, the people scurrying, pulling jackets down or racing to catch a lost hat. There was an excitement generated by the unpredictability of a storm. Of course, she loved to watch all this from the warmth of her cosy cabin, knowing she was moored securely as the ebbing of the water gently buffeted Georgie from side to side. Tonight, her thoughts were with New Zealand and more planning. But first she rustled up some tea before she settled to focus on the trip.

The storm was still raging at full pelt outside and Tilly had heard some of her plant pots rolling about on the roof. If they were the only casualty, she decided it wasn't so bad. With the washing up done and Marmite now settled on her lap, she had a list of things to do. The first was to power up her laptop. The second open emails to send Drew the message that she was definitely, or almost certainly if her sketchy mental etchings went to plan, going to be visiting in the not-too-distant future. It was a plan without definition. It crossed her mind that now she had decided on the trip, there probably was no need for Drew's help. After all, she had initially been seeking the help of someone located in New Zealand, never dreaming of visiting herself. She brushed that thought aside. She had now contacted someone who was also a distant relative, cousin or some such thing, so there had to be a win in there somewhere.

Tilly decided there was no time like the present to put through a Facetime call, but as the ringing started an email popped into her inbox. It was from Drew. What were the chances of that? She didn't have time to read it, before the connection clicked through and a grainy face appeared on her screen.

'G'day T..lly g..l.' The sound was broken up and a dalek-like voice came to her through the airwaves.

'I can't hear you properly Drew. It must be the storm.' He was shaking his head - clearly, he couldn't understand her either. For a few minutes, they struggled to converse and eventually gave up. Tilly felt disappointed. She hadn't realised how much she had been looking forward to chatting to Drew until that point. Coming out of the app, she returned to her emails and opened the one he had just sent through.

Hi Tilly,

Just had to message you straight away because I think I've found Temperance. Or at least, I have found an address for her. It may be old, but it's a start. Just thought you would be stoked to know. Let me know what you want me to do next; I am all yours to do with as you will! My other bit of good news is that dad responded to one of my many messages. I think he must have got fed up with me and relented. The bad news is he hasn't really said much, just that I am 'barking up the wrong tree' about my grandparents. Very frustrating, but I will keep on at him, as he clearly knows something.

OK, that is all I have for now. Hope we can catch up properly soon - perhaps you will have your DNA results so that we can compare how many centiles match! Exciting stuff.
Love Drew

The message just re-enforced her irritation with technology and their failure to be able to speak properly. She would have to tell him by email of her plan. Tilly growled to herself. Wringing her fists in frustration she started to type.

Hi Drew,
Sorry that we failed to connect. There is a storm raging here, and my Wi-Fi is not great at the best of times, being on a boat, but I have now received your email. I agree it's good news that you have located an address for Temperance. I would give you the next instruction, but I have something more exciting to tell you, which might mean you don't need to do anything

more. Well not yet anyway. I've decided to take a trip out to New Zealand to do some of the work in tracing Temperance myself. Of course, that means you are off the hook now, if you like. But if you want to meet me and we follow this little investigation together, to trace an ancestor and with it discover how we are related exactly, then that is fine too!

I haven't done any real research into flights or accommodation or anything yet, but I am looking at November, with a possible overnight stop off in New York to see my best friend Kit on the way. Let me have your thoughts.

Bye for now,
Tilly x

Once she had pressed the 'send' button, Tilly had a feeling of euphoria. Whilst there were no flights booked just yet, she felt like something had changed. She was going to New Zealand. She had made a commitment of sorts to Drew in the email. There was no time to lose, she needed to message Kit and then to find flights. She found herself smiling and humming as she punched the keyboard with gusto urgently determined to finalise her plans to make it happen.

'New Zealand' she sang, 'watch out, because here I come!'

46

CHRISTCHURCH - 2000

The town of Christchurch, on the South Island of New Zealand had been a growing and interesting town when Temperance first settled there. Temperance and Myles had then made it their home, until Myles' death in 1994, at which point everything changed. Temperance was on her own once more. Her home with Myles had been large and envied. It had reminded Temperance of the old family farm back in Norfolk. What she could remember of it. After Myles' death, Temperance had lost it all. Myles, she discovered had large debts, the house she had thought was his, had turned out to be privately rented. The landlord ruthlessly evicted her only months after his death. In mourning, and desperate once more, she had to return to the council, her income by then quite meagre.

The house allocated to her in the suburbs was a modest affair. Single story white wooden cladding. State housing wasn't lavish, yet even at her lowest point, Temperance tried her hardest to make the new small chalet into a loved home. Her depression on losing Myles and the home they had shared, consumed her. With pleasant friendly neighbours, who tried their best to engage with her, Temperance had a little support, but her spirits were low. As time went on and Temperance learned to live on her own once more, life became a little brighter.

One sunny December afternoon, some six years after Myles' passing, there was a knock at her door. Temperance heard it, but remained in her armchair, hoping it would go away. It could only be a salesman, she thought. She turned up the wireless and refocussed on her crochet. It was to be a blanket for her bed. All shades of purple, they reminded her of her sister. The sister she no longer had contact with.

Another knock. Louder this time. Temperance sighed and put down her crochet.

'Okay, I'm coming. ' Temperance spoke as she opened the door. Usually even tempered, she was slower on her feet these days and a little less patient when put under pressure. A well-dressed, older woman stood before her, smiling widely. Temperance thought the lady looked familiar but couldn't be sure and couldn't quite place her. 'Hello, can I help you?' There was a pause as the two women stared at each other.

'Hello Penny, it's me. Elsie. It has been a while, I know.' Temperance stared, still not recognising the unexpected visitor.

'I'm sorry. I don't recall an Elsie, do you have the right address love?' Feeling confused, especially as the woman knew her name, she started to close the door, but Elsie stepped forward, putting her foot in the way.

'Temperance love, it's me, Elsie.' She repeated, an element of pleading in her voice. 'You remember. From the boat.' Elsie paused, in the hope that Temperance recognised her. Without even a flicker of acknowledgement, Elsie had to continue. 'We shared a flat when we first arrived in the country. I taught you to type. You must remember me. Come on love.' Elsie hadn't expected such a blank reception and felt a pang of anxiety. Eventually Temperance responded.

'Oh.' Another long pause, before Temperance's face started to change. 'I see. Yes. I see, I remember a girl who got on the ship at Tilbury.' Temperance nodded; the corners of her small pink mouth, lifted slightly. 'Perhaps you would like to come in for a cup of tea?' She stepped back and let Elsie pass, then followed her into the lounge.

Elsie sat down on a low stool by the primitive gas fire, on one side of the small open plan lounge dining room. In the kitchenette, a paper-thin wall away, Temperance made them both a cup of coffee and brought it in on a tray then sat on her only armchair and turned to Elsie.

'I'm sorry love, you do seem familiar, remind me again who you are. My memory is not what it was.' Temperance had relaxed and sat back on her chair.

'I'm sorry Penny to confuse you like this. I looked you up in the local phone directory and saw you had moved from the house you lived in with your husband. I thought it would just be nice to say hello, that's all.' Elsie was feeling a bit awkward. She hadn't envisaged her old friend having deteriorated so, since their last contact so many years before. 'I visited you at your old house, oh, about twenty years ago. We had tea and cake in your lovely garden. Do you remember that?' Elsie sipped her coffee. 'I am sorry to hear about your husband. Is your son close by?'

'Oh Elsie. I did have a lovely garden in that big house. I'm sorry, I don't remember your visit. But I do remember the typing, and that very long boat trip. Yes, that was Elsie. Pretty young thing. So that was you. My first friend in New Zealand. How lovely to see you again. I do hope you don't think me rude, but you have changed a bit.' She smiled back with what Elsie could only describe as sadness in her dull eyes. 'Sadly, my…our son, he isn't close. He is very busy, so he doesn't really have time to visit me.'

Elsie finished her coffee and excused herself, saying she would visit again. Temperance closed the door on her old friend and returning to her lounge picked up her crochet and the memory of her visitor evaporated like it had never happened.

47

NORFOLK - 2024

At last, it was the weekend, and with a long list of 'must do' jobs, Tilly bounced out of bed feeling more energised than she had for a long time. With a steaming mug of hot tea, she sat down one end of the pew and fired up her laptop. It was 9am UK time; 2pm for Kit in New York. She didn't think Kit worked on a Saturday, so put in the call.

'Hey Kit…. Yaay, Kit, can you hear me?' The Facetime connection to Kit in New York was wavering in and out. Tilly waved furiously when eventually the fuzziness on the screen began to join and form a picture of her friend.

'Hi Tills, yes, I can see and hear you loud and clear. I was moving, but I am sitting down now. So, how the hell are you, my love?' Tilly thought that after just three months in America, Kit already sounded like she had a twang to her accent.

'I'm well Kit. Excited to be calling you. I have some news.' Tilly was positively bursting with the desire to share her plans with her friend.

'Come on then girl, out with it. I sure am ready.' Kit was definitely morphing into an American.

'I'm planning to come and see you.' The news tumbled out of her in true Tilly style. 'Er, I mean if that is ok, of course?' She waited momentarily for Kit to respond, seeing her friend open mouthed on the screen.

'Gee Tilly, I hadn't seen that coming. When? But of course it's ok for you to visit. Will you be on your own?' Kit paused. 'I mean, gosh Tilly, I have so many questions.' Tilly laughed.

'I thought that would surprise you.' Tilly said with glee. She proceeded to explain the reason behind her visit. That over, and logistics of an overnight stop in New York discussed, Tilly promised that firm dates and flights would be sorted out next. They eventually signed off agreeing they couldn't wait for November to arrive.

Tilly knew she needed to move positively to get the plans in action but decided it would have to be an evening job. She needed to tidy up, gather the information already gleaned from all sources on Temperance, the family and the tree, plus contact Drew again. Was she procrastinating yet further, she silently asked herself? There was an alternative to an online evening search. A visit into the village, to the travel agent crossed her mind. Get a professional to do it for her. She had already decided on November, but did actual dates matter? The money was there, so she just had to get on with it.

An hour later and Tilly was pedalling hard against the wind as her bike took her along the canal path to the high street, having decided on the professional option. Passing An Extra Slice, she waved to Brenda, who was collecting some dirty coffee cups from an outside table. Brenda waved back and beckoned her in.

'Not today Bren, I am going to book some flights.' shouted Tilly as she flew past and turned up towards the main parade of shops. Bike secured, she went straight into the travel agent, worried that if she delayed any further then her nerves would get the better of her. She knew she had to just do it. Bubbles of excited nerves filled her tummy as she pushed open the door.

Jenny, the pretty young estate agent, introduced herself, then invited Tilly to take a seat in front of her exceptionally neat desk. The chair was comfortable and inviting, Tilly suspected a tactic to make sure the customer stayed put, right through to a booking. She shrugged off her jacket and tucked her rucksack between her feet.

'So Tilly, what can we at 'Flights of Fancy' do for you today?' Jenny's teeth gleamed artificially. Her ample chest did so too, as it spilled from her tight low-cut dress. Tilly tried to avert her eyes, sitting up higher in the chair.

'I want to book some flights please. To New York to begin with, and then from New York to New Zealand.' There, she had started the ball rolling.

'Okay, that sounds simple enough. Dates?' Jenny tapped at her computer, not looking up. 'And is it just flights you want, or accommodation too? We can find package deals for you.' The tapping continued.

'Ummm....yeah, I haven't really decided exactly. Was thinking November. Just flights please. Is there a good time?' Tilly realised that perhaps a little more planning might have been prudent.

'November is entering the summer, so flights will be a bit dearer. I can get you to New York on Friday 10th for £240 with KLM from London Gatwick. How does that sound?' Jenny still didn't look up.

'Yeah, that sounds fine.' Tilly made a note. 'Then from New York to New Zealand a few days later please?' It felt very simple, so Tilly just relaxed and let Jenny do the work. She was glad she had chosen the expert route, as Tilly wouldn't have known the first thing about electronic travel authority, which Jenny explained later was essential to be allowed into both countries. Jenny sorted that out for her too, so earnt her money.

After almost an hour, Tilly left 'Flights of Fancy' with a printout of her flight details, a dent in her bank balance and a fluttering feeling in her tummy. It had been so much easier than she had anticipated. Jenny had given her some instructions about her boarding pass and accessing her tickets on her phone. She just had to go home and tell everyone!

The cycle back was more leisurely, with Tilly barely concentrating on the ride, her head so full of the day and the next steps. She was on a roll, ambitious to plump out the trips on paper with lots of detail. There was her mum to tell. Val at the Plumbers to tell. Melody and Sam to tell. Most important of all, she needed to tell Kit and Drew. It was going to be a busy evening.

48

NORFOLK - 2024

Tilly managed to square things with her employer, arranging an open-ended period off. Val said she would cover for her, but Tilly knew Val would probably go straight to an agency. Unusually understanding, Val seemed to recognise how important it was to Tilly, to be able to carry out this research for Uncle Hector. After she had completed the call, she received a message from Paul, who was excited to hear about her plans from the horse's mouth - limited as they were and wanted to pick her brains. They chatted briefly about travelling the world. It seemed that Paul was keen to escape the family business, even if it was just for a short time. Tilly told him it wasn't too late and left him to pluck up the courage to discuss it with his parents.

Her second challenge was to find a temporary home for Marmite. She didn't want him to go to a cattery for what might be a month - although she hadn't booked return flights, so was reassured by Jenny that she would be able to get flights home without a problem. In the end Melody and Sam came up trumps with an offer to look after him at their house. Tilly was happy with that. Marmite was a friendly cat anyway, but he knew Melody and would get lots of cuddles with Lois. A 'win win' for them all.

When it came to her mother though, Celia was concerned that Tilly didn't have a return ticket. Tilly explained all she could remember from her trip to the travel agent, saying she would copy the printout she had been given, so that Celia had all the flight details. That seemed to placate her mum as, in the end, there was nothing Celia could do but support her daughter.

Tilly settled down to send messages to Kit and Drew. The ball was properly rolling now, and Tilly felt super excited. The main thing for Tilly, was to focus on the reason for the trip. To fulfil Uncle Hector's final wishes, to find evidence of Temperance's final resting place and the whereabouts of the missing money. With all this in mind, she started to type:

Hi Kit,
Guess what! Flight to New York booked for Friday 10th November. I know I should have checked with you first, but I'm really hoping you can give me the Big Apple tour and a sofa to sleep on. I then fly out to NZ on Monday

13th. Sooooo excited, I just can't wait. I'll send you the flight details and times soon. Now must get on and tell Drew.

Bye for now, big love Tilly xxx

Now for the one she was a bit more anxious about. Tilly wasn't going to put any pressure on Drew. He only had to be involved if he wanted to be. As she typed Drew's email address into a blank email, an unopened message from Drew appeared, sitting in her junk. That was odd, she thought, but perhaps not odd. She had only messaged him the other day to tell him about her plan to visit. She had asked him some questions about meeting or not meeting. She clicked on the unopened message and with her hand shaking, eagerly scanned the words on the screen.

Hey Tilly,
That is fantastic news. Of course I want to still be part of your journey. This is our journey now, little lady, and don't you forget it. I'll await your next instructions, and I will be here waiting to meet you! I can't have my long lost cousin arriving in a strange country, without a welcome party now, can I? So you just get those flights booked and we can sort the rest out when you get here!

Drew x

What a relief. As usual Tilly read through the message several times. It was all good news, all going so smoothly. She couldn't quite believe her luck. She could send a quick reply, but what she really wanted to do was call Drew, as their last call had been so broken up. Before she had had time to think it through, she'd pressed the FaceTime button. It rang.

'Drew, hi it's me Tilly.' Obviously, she thought. Nerves speaking.
'Hey Tilly, aye, I can see it is you! Much better connection than last time, aye?' Drew was smiling broadly but looking a bit dishevelled.
'Oh, sorry Drew, what time is it? I forgot about the time difference, but I was so excited I wanted to tell you my news.' She was rambling again.
'That's not a problem Tilly, sleep is overrated anyway.' Drew teased. 'Come on, what is the news?'
'Very funny. Well anyway, I've booked my flights. I am going via New York to see my friend Kit. I told you that didn't I?'
'Yes, you did. That will be nice. Break up the journey a bit too.' Drew was relaxing back, and she could see he didn't have a shirt on, just what looked like pyjama bottoms. She felt herself blush, then chastised

herself for inappropriate thoughts about her cousin. They certainly had good looking genes in the New Zealand branch of the family

'Oh…er…yes. I will be flying out of New York on Monday 13th November. I will message you all the flight details. Do you think you will be free to meet me at Auckland airport? I mean…you don't have to..' Tilly was getting a little tongue tied, 'unless you want to. Of course. I mean..' Shut up Tilly, she said to herself.

'Wild horses wouldn't stop me from meeting you Tilly. I already can't wait. Then we can get out and find our ancestor Temperance. First stop that address I found. What do you say?' Drew really did have a way about him. It was impossible to say no, and Tilly found herself nodding eagerly.

'Yes please Drew. I would be lying if I said I wasn't anxious about travelling to a country so far away, all alone. But I didn't want you to feel you had to help me. I am nervous, excited, apprehensive and oh so many other adjectives. Sorry, I am rambling again. I am like this when I get excited.' Tilly stopped to take a breath.

'Tilly, Tilly Tilly, don't you worry your pretty little head. I am here. Gee, you think I would let you do this on your own. No, we are family. I am here for you. Send me the details, then go and enjoy the planning and I will see you in…what…about six weeks or so?' Drew really was making it very easy for her.

They ended their call, promising to keep each other updated. Not least because Tilly was still waiting for her DNA test results to come through, which Drew had reminded her about. Apart from that, Tilly wanted to go back to the library to talk to Judith again and to do some proper work on her tree to make it look like the one Melody had shown her of her own family. With the extra information from her mum to add, a bit more research could then be done.

It looked like the next six weeks would be extremely busy.

49

NORFOLK - 2024

It was the weekend, with just under a week to go before the off, Tilly was fine tuning her 'to do' lists. There were four and they each had a name. Charlie, Marmite, Temperance and Tilly.

'Charlie' was a list of the things she needed to do to the boat, before leaving it for what might be a month. Turning off electrics at the mains, plus the stop cock for the water. Making sure all bills were paid up front, telling her neighbours, securing her bike. Making sure her fridge was empty, so that she didn't return to anything festering, and the same with her fruit bowl and bread bin. Really boring but essential. Her neighbours Nell and Karim had a key and had said they would keep an eye out. They were a reliable retired couple who Tilly could trust.

The 'Marmite' list was much shorter. A note for Melody detailing Marmite's favourite food and what times he was normally fed. She had included the details of the vet and the fact that he was known as Marmite Montgomery-Brown. His flea and worming were up to date, so there shouldn't be any need for it, but it was there 'just in case'. She had put £40 in an envelope, which would cover his food. She didn't want to take advantage of anyone.

List 'Temperance' contained a reminder to herself to print out the tree and any other relevant information she had gleaned during her time researching the family. She would take her laptop with her but wanted a hard copy too. The last 5 weeks had been quite fruitful, and Tilly had spent several evenings at the library with Judith. Judith had been so interested in the search, she had taken it on herself to contact the New Zealand equivalent of the records office, to see if they could access information about someone's life that the general public could not. It had come about due to their inability to trace a death certificate for Temperance, or a birth certificate for a child around the time Temperance would have given birth. Assuming she was pregnant when she left the UK in 1951. Considering the relatively small population of New Zealand, they thought more than one 'Temperance' unlikely, although acceded they could be completely wrong in that assumption. Judith had been like a dog with a bone and didn't want to give up. Tilly left her to do whatever she could, being fully furnished with all data Tilly had been able to locate. It was very likely that Judith would continue doggedly searching even once Tilly had left the country. She had

Tilly's number and email address and they had agreed that Judith would keep her updated with anything new and relevant that she discovered.

The final list was 'Tilly'. And it was a long one. It started with a note to check the other lists. Then a detailed list of clothes, toiletries, notebooks, photos and flight information. Passport and cash in both US and NZ dollars, with a special over the body purse to keep it all in safely. All of which she'd had packed for the best part of the last two weeks. She had a notebook with key information on places in New York she wanted to visit, plus another one to cover New Zealand. That one wasn't so much 'must visit' places as a tourist, but more the places that might have any kind of link to Temperance. The main one being her last known address that Drew had discovered. Tilly had also been surprised by an offer to take her to the airport by Dave. It had to be her mum's doing, but she knew it would be churlish to turn it down. So, the final point on her list was to be ready to be picked up at 8am. The flight was leaving at 15:30 and they needed to be there two hours early. She was relying on Dave to have worked out the timings. All she needed to do was be waiting with her bags.

Tilly sat back with her bulging case at her feet and a medium sized backpack at her side. She had weighed the case numerous times, only now confident that it didn't exceed the limit. The new grey backpack, a treat to herself for the holiday had various useful pockets. She would be able to take it onto the plane with her and had already put inside a puzzle book, pens, another notebook and the latest paperback by her favourite author. She absolutely would not be short of notebooks!

Tilly had arranged for Marmite to be collected that weekend. It was the most convenient time for Sam. Poor Marmite was aware something wasn't quite right. Tilly had tried to keep his travel basket out of view, but in the end, she had limited space with her bags and case clogging up the lounge area, so it had been placed on her bed. After his breakfast, Tilly had kept the boat hatch closed, so that he couldn't go wandering. Marmite of course had made a beeline for the bed. After initially sniffing at the cage, realising that it wasn't something positive, he'd jumped down and wailed pitifully at the door to be let out. Tilly tried to comfort him; the fish treats taking his attention for a short while. He then returned to the door and growled quietly. Soon enough Tilly heard Sam's van and grabbed Marmite before he could escape and welcomed Sam into the maelstrom.

'Hi Sam, please excuse all the bags. Don't worry they are not all for Marmite.' Tilly closed the door behind Sam and then gave him a brief hug.

'Before I forget, Melody has sent this. It's a present for Kit, can you squeeze it into your case please?' Sam plonked himself down onto the only available space at the end of the pew.

'No problem. It's tiny, what is it, something home-made?' Tilly took the neatly wrapped parcel from Sam and balanced it on the suitcase.

'Yeah, I think it's something she crocheted. And this is for you.' Sam produced another small parcel from his pocket and handed it to Tilly. 'She said to tell you that she has made herself one too.' Tilly took it, smiling.

'Aww thank you Sam, can I open it now?' Sam nodded and Tilly tore at the tissue. 'A friendship bracelet. Oh, that is so thoughtful of Mel. Please thank her for me. I will message her anyway.' Tilly slipped it over her right hand and secured it on her wrist. A detailed pattern with tiny seed beads woven into it. Far more intricate than those they had made at school by plaiting threads. 'I won't take it off.' She grinned.

Impossible to put it off any longer, Tilly grabbed Marmite and took him to his basket. She was well practiced at this Olympic event, managing to fold his long stiff back legs with one hand, whilst avoiding the swiping front claws, then with a gentle shove the cat was in, and the basket lid secured. She carried him out of the bedroom triumphantly, then handed Marmite plus a rather large bag of cat 'stuff' to Sam. Litter tray, cat litter, food and a blanket he sometimes slept on. No doubt he would find somewhere new to sleep at Sam and Melody's, but it was there as a bit of home in case it helped. More pitiful meowing could be heard as Sam put him into the van, then waving he headed back home leaving Tilly alone.

'Ok Tilly, you're on your own now.' Tilly's self-pep talks gave her direction. 'Grab those lists girl. 5 days to focus. You can't afford to get this wrong.' It was going to be an anxious but exciting few days. She was ready to take it head on.

50

MID-FLIGHT - 2024

And she was off. It had been smooth sailing to the airport and Tilly couldn't believe she was at last on her way to New York. New York. The Big Apple, but most importantly to her friend Kit and the first step towards her search for Temperance.

With her small hand luggage securely positioned under the seat in front of her, Tilly felt able to relax. She had been lucky to get a window seat. As she put her head back against the seat, Tilly turned to face the window. The hazy reds of London rooftops already indistinguishable and clouds now filled her portal. Tilly felt comfortable without the slightest pang of anxiety. She went over the morning's journey in her head. She had spent the previous night at her mum's and Dave had driven her to Heathrow that morning. She didn't want a fuss, but he insisted on carrying her bag for her to the check in, then gave her a very unexpected hug. Once check in was complete Tilly had checked her emails knowing it was her last chance, noticing one from the DNA company. She had quickly downloaded the details but decided now was not the time for in depth analysis of that. She could do it once she had arrived, if she remembered. It just didn't seem that important to her anymore.

The plane had been on time, and she had got in line along with lots of other people to board her New York flight, just a slight flutter of excitement went through her as she'd climbed the steps, she breathed in the chilled fuel filled air. The person in the seat next to her; a middle-aged woman with full makeup, high heels and a very smart suit was quiet. She had very little luggage. It looked to Tilly like just a laptop bag and a tiny handbag. The prim lady had smiled briefly as they shuffled to their seats but was now lying back in her seat with an eye mask on. Her laptop at her feet. Odd, Tilly thought, as it was only just gone 3 o'clock in the afternoon, but perhaps she worked shifts or had been travelling since very early. There would be time on the eight hour flight to find those things out. That was assuming her neighbour didn't stay under the eye mask for the whole eight hours!

The arrangement was for Kit to meet her at the airport. The timings had worked out very well with the five hour time difference, she would be arriving at some time between 6 and 7pm New York time. Tilly had only ever flown short flights before, with her mum and dad. Italy for one memorable summer holiday when what stuck in her mind was the heat. It had been unbearably hot for Tilly. It was going to be the opposite to hot in New York. Tilly had been warned that November in New York could be heavy snow but thankfully snow or freezing weather was not forecast for the weekend. She assumed global warming had something to do with that, but was grateful, nonetheless. She rummaged about in her bag for her book, then relaxed into the journey.

Tilly was jolted from quite a deep sleep by the announcement that they would be landing at New York JFK in twenty minutes. Having spent the journey reading, eating and sleeping on repeat, Tilly felt it had been a short eight hours.

She had managed to extract limited information from her travelling neighbour. Her name was Jackie and she was travelling for work. She was gluten intolerant which meant she had special sandwiches. This last bit of information Tilly only acquired through eavesdropping when the food came round as Jackie hadn't volunteered it. It didn't matter now; she was wide awake and thinking about the next stage of her journey and that meant seeing Kit. Tilly tucked her book into her bag and sat back to wait for the landing. She could see the bright lights below her in the distance, lighting up the early evening darkness. Stop one was almost upon her, and the butterflies were rising. She could feel an immovable smile etched onto her face. New York, she whispered, bring it on.

51

NEW YORK - 2024

'Cooeee...over here.' Kit was calling and waving furiously as Tilly came through the arrivals gate, pulling her wheeled suitcase behind her. Tilly felt a little flustered with her rucksack over one shoulder and her winter coat tucked under her arm. She heard a familiar voice and looking into the sea of faces spotted the frantically gesticulating Kit, not difficult to see in her fluorescent green puffa jacket. She pushed her way through the dense crowd to Kit, and they hugged briefly, before Kit pulled away. Uncomfortable with overt displays of affection, Kit had never really liked even her best friends in her personal space. 'It's good to see you Tills, can I help you with that?' Kit took the wheeled suitcase from Tilly. 'Follow me. Stay close so that we don't get separated. It's a cab ride or ten stops on the subway.'

'Subway?' Tilly wasn't thinking. After the long flight she suddenly felt quite tired.

'It's the name for the underground. Come on, this way. There's a stop quite close to my apartment and you'll be able to tick 'ride the New York subway' off your long list of places to visit and things to do.' Kit strode out ahead, and Tilly could only follow.

It took another forty minutes to get back to Kit's apartment in Manhattan. It was a great location, and Tilly had asked how Kit could afford to rent somewhere so central. But it turned out the apartment along with several others in the block were all owned by the company Kit worked for. With regular student and apprentice positions, linked to the nearby Columbia University, it proved a perk of the job. There had been quite a lot of walking, but Tilly was in awe of the bright lights and buzzing atmosphere of the iconic city. Everything and more that she had expected, it was senses overload but did the job of waking her up. She didn't know where to look first, there was so much to see.

Thankfully there was a lift, or elevator to be precise, which took them up to Kit's 7th floor flat. Tilly was thankful they hadn't needed to climb any stairs and almost fell through the front door. Kit showed her to her tiny box room, where a single futon bed had been rolled out for her visit. Tilly dumped her belongings onto a small wicker chair hidden behind the door before Kit gave her a quick tour of the remaining rooms. She was then left to freshen herself up.

After a welcome shower, Tilly felt rejuvenated. She had managed to get a fair amount of sleep on the flight thanks to her uncommunicative fellow passenger.

'Phew, that was a lovely shower Kit, thank you. So, what's for dinner? My stomach thinks my throat's been cut. It's rumbling somewhat!' Tilly sat down next to her friend on the small sofa. 'Oh, and while I remember Melody sent you this. She made it.' Tilly passed Kit the small rather crumpled parcel and Kit opened it.

'Aw, sweet. It is so like Melody. Have you got one too?' Tilly held up her wrist and Kit slipped hers onto her own wrist. 'I must message to thank her.'

Relaxing together on the sofa, Kit had some suggestions.

'I have made an itinerary for us, which starts this evening.' Kit laughed at Tilly's shocked look. 'Don't worry, tonight it's just grabbing a dollar pizza slice on East 43rd Street. Get your shoes on. I'll share the rest of the itinerary once we are there.'

'Ok, sounds good,' said Tilly, stifling a yawn. 'I could certainly eat pizza right now. How far is that?' Tilly hoped that being back out in the fresh air and bright lights would wake her up a bit. She pulled on her trainers.

'Only three blocks. We will be there in no time.' They left the apartment together chatting furiously, their conversation carrying them all the way to the restaurant which Tilly was amazed to see was really called '99c Pizza'. Calling it a restaurant was being generous, as it was really a takeaway with a couple of bar stools up against a high bar by the window. The girls got their pizzas and an iced tea each and sat on the stools. Tilly tucked straight in.

'So Tilly, I said I would share the rest of the itinerary. You don't have to go with it if you have your own ideas, but I have tried to put the most touristy spots into the weekend, in an order where we can see them without too much doubling back.' Tilly was nodding with her mouth full. 'I'll take that as a yes. Ok, so the Rockefeller Center is our first stop tomorrow. We will go to the top to see the views; you can see right across New York. Then I've got a walk through Central Park, plus a boat ride out to see the Statue of Liberty.'

'Oh yes Kit, that I really must do. I also would like to do some shopping if we can fit that in, please?' Tilly had finished her pizza slice. 'I'm going to get another slice of pizza I really am starving. Would you like one?' Kit shook her head.

Once Tilly had returned, Kit outlined the remaining things from the list, agreeing that they would end the day at Macy's to accommodate her shopping needs. Kit had been given complementary tickets to a Broadway show for Sunday evening, another perk of her job. The Sunday itinerary had to be worked around being back in time to dress up for the show. Kit had deliberately packed most of the tourist spots into Saturday. It was going to be a whirlwind whistlestop tour of the Big Apple, but Kit wanted Tilly to go away with a good taste of the city. With the long flight to New Zealand the next day, she figured Tilly would have plenty of time to rest and recover.

They finished eating, then walked back to the apartment. Tilly changed into her pyjamas, then settled on the sofa with Kit who had opened a bottle of wine. They chatted a bit, but Tilly found herself struggling to keep her eyes open.

'I think I'm going to have to crash Kit. I want to be fresh for all the exciting visits we're going to do tomorrow. Thanks for today and for meeting me - I couldn't have found my way here on my own.' They hugged briefly.

'You're welcome silly. Sleep well Tills. I'll wake you at 8.' Tilly rolled her eyes and smiling took herself off to her bed.

As expected, Saturday proved to be a full and fast one. The girls were out of the door by 9, which felt early enough for Tilly although she had slept remarkably well. With the first stop the Rockefeller Center they did indeed see all there was to see of the New York skyline. Tilly picked out the Empire State Building and Central Park, somewhere they would be visiting. She took lots of photos, before they headed off to the café.

After coffee in the tower it was a packed day and using the sightseeing bus, they were able to jump on and off as they pleased. A respectful and emotional viewing of Ground Zero, followed by the famous Brooklyn Bridge. Every bit as impressive in real life as it was in photos. Eventually they took their scheduled trip from Battery Park out into New York harbour to visit a crown jewel of American landmarks - The Statue of Liberty. Tilly had been given varying reviews of the monument, from 'it's not worth it' to 'the best bit of the trip' but for Tilly it was at the top of her list, and she wasn't disappointed. They had the last visit of the day and Tilly took photos as the sun was going down. It felt very special. Then a bus straight to Macy's for a final hour of shopping, before walking back to a diner close to Kit's apartment for dinner. It was a burgers and fries joint, so nothing special Tilly thought. That was until she saw them. It was a good thing they had built up a ravenous appetite during their day, as they ploughed through a genuine mountain of food. A quadruple burger, with 4 types of relish and a huge bun the size of a tea plate, plus a bucket of fries that was actual bucket sized. A pint of fizz to wash it down, Tilly managed about three quarters of the meal, before raising her hands in defeat.

'It truly is delicious, but I don't think I can eat another morsel,' said Tilly, popping another chip into her mouth, her cheeks already bulging.

'We're in no rush. You did dive straight in, to be fair, like you hadn't been fed for a week.' Kit was laughing. 'And I warned you not to 'go big' didn't I? Everything is already big, without choosing to go even bigger.' The girls laughed. They started to relax after their busy full day, soaking up the atmosphere and the buzz of a Saturday night in New York City. Tilly still couldn't quite believe she was in America, but that she would also soon be heading out again. Who visited the USA just for a weekend? But this was proving to be one special weekend, with memories to last a lifetime.

When the girls had eventually eaten all they could, they made their way back along the brightly lit streets, to the apartment. Discussing options for the evening, they decided to go in and finish off the wine from the previous night in the company of each other and some relaxing music. Neither one of the girls were party animals and it was an opportunity for Tilly to find out a bit more about Kit's new job.

'I am loving it. There is a lot to learn. I mean a LOT. To start with I felt a bit panicked. A bit overwhelmed. I thought I had bitten off more than I could chew, and that is why I was quite reserved in our chats. But it turned a corner about two or three weeks ago and I am loving it. Greg has been very supportive with my training but also has shown me around. Advised on the best places to eat, where not to go at night etcetera.' Kit's face lit up as she spoke about the job. It was the first time she had mentioned any colleagues by name too, which was promising.

'This Greg, is he a colleague, or something more?' Tilly winked at her friend.

'Oh definitely just a friend I work with.' Kit was a bit too quick with her denial. 'He lives close, so it was convenient that he was made my mentor.' Kit changed the subject. 'And what about you and this Drew, who you seem quite fond of.'

'We are cousins Kit. He certainly got the handsome genes though. I haven't got round to working out the relationship exactly, but that reminds me.' Tilly dug about in her bag for her phone. 'Ah, here it is. My DNA results came through just as I was leaving the UK, and I didn't have time to analyse it. Drew has told me that we will be linked on Ancestry by the number of centiles in our DNA which match. It should do it automatically.' Tilly clicked through to the relevant webpage, to access the data. She was quiet for a while, so Kit left her to her research and went to the kitchen for another bottle.

'This doesn't make sense.' Tilly had logged in to her laptop to get the information on a bigger screen.

'What doesn't make sense? Here, hold up your glass.' Kit refilled both glasses with a chilled rosé then sat down next to Tilly on the small sofa.

'There aren't any connections which link me to Drew. Look.' Tilly passed her laptop to Kit, who scrolled through. 'I can see my cousin Charlotte on there, and she is showing as full cousin. If Drew is the grandson of Temperance, which is what he seems to think is the case, then we should show a connection as second cousins. So why isn't he showing at all?' Tilly continued to scroll down the list.

'I think you will have to ask him where he has got his information from when you see him. I don't really know enough about it, but I agree that you would expect to see him appearing if you were related. But remember, it is also reliant on computers.' Tilly sighed and put away the laptop, puzzled, but not enough to let it take over her evening with Kit. The girls chatted into the small hours, eventually crashing out, exhausting their conversation and wine stock. Their very busy day had eventually caught up with them and they took themselves to bed.

Sunday began a little later with a huge pile of pancakes for breakfast in a popular crepe and waffle shop overlooking Central Park. Tilly had chosen straightforward fluffy pancakes topped with strawberries and cream with a generous coating of maple syrup. Kit had her favourite banana pancakes with pistachio and chocolate topping. Even after the huge meal the night before, neither left even a crumb on their plate. They had been blessed with another bright day, unseasonably warm although there had been a heavy frost overnight. Tilly was drawn in watching families, groups of tourists, students and locals enjoying that special open space, so synonymous with New York. The crepe bar had a large picture window so the girls could enjoy the goings on, from the warmth of the inside. A slightly lighter schedule, they were able to take it easy, the remainder of the morning spent exploring the vast Central Park for themselves. Kit hadn't found time to explore it herself, so it was a treat for them both. With collars raised and scarves tucked in, it was the perfect place to get some fresh air and continue their chatter, conscious they had only a few more hours together.

At lunchtime neither Kit nor Tilly felt hungry. The pancakes had made sure of that. The day was full of walking and talking. They dropped into many gift shops - too many in Kit's opinion - before heading to the Metropolitan Museum for their timed slot. Kit had done an excellent job planning their itinerary and not a single minute was wasted. However, by the time they had completed their two-hour guided tour, it was time to accept they could do nothing more that day. Exhausted they grabbed a cab back to the apartment where they had 90 minutes to rest and get dressed for the night out. Tilly dug out from the bottom of her case the only dress she had brought with her, plus her black ankle boots. Not really knowing if she would need anything formal in either New York or New Zealand she decided it was safer to have something. A simple plain navy blue knitted jumper dress which came to just above her knee, was just right for the weather and could be dressed up with a long bead necklace and belt. Kit didn't wear dresses, but her black sparkly leggings were good enough for a night out. The girls hailed a yellow taxi from the corner of East 43rd street which took them straight to their Broadway show in proper New York style.

An unforgettable night of music and drama followed. Kit had been the envy of the office getting free tickets to The Lion King, one of the most sought after shows on Broadway. The show was jaw droppingly good and both girls were transfixed throughout. It finished off the most perfect weekend for Tilly. The girls wandered back arm in arm, a little tipsy after a few too many interval gins but buzzing with after show glee. Thankfully, Tilly's flight wasn't until 11.30 the following morning, so they could enjoy the whole of their last evening together.

'Do you know what Kit?' Tilly giggled as they rolled on towards the apartment.

'No Tilly, I don't know...what?' Kit slumped onto her friend, slurring a bit.

'I love you Kitty cat. I love you for making this such a special weekend. I truly do. You are just the best.' Tilly pulled Kit towards her in an ungainly hug, and they stumbled a bit, but managed to stay upright, laughing. Their friendship was proving it could stand the distance and they continued all the way back to the apartment arm firmly in arm, until they crashed out wearily to sleep off the indulgencies of their night out.

~

Tilly was up and ready by 9am, with her bag packed and taxi booked. Kit had been allowed to start work late, but Tilly insisted on getting herself to the airport, hence the taxi booking. At the kerbside, the girls hugged tightly, with Kit insisting Tilly was to get in touch, the minute she touched down in New Zealand.

Sailing through the departures, customs and all other checks, Tilly was settled in her upgraded Club Class seat by 11.15. With the prospect of a 15-hour flight ahead, she relaxed back in the unexpected luxury and proceeded to flick through the 372 photos she had taken during her whistlestop weekend in New York. With a few minutes to take off, she pinged messages off to Drew, Melody, Kit and her mum. Then with the phone in aeroplane mode, sat back to enjoy the very long flight.

52

MID-FLIGHT - 2024

The flight was undoubtedly long, but with the added comfort of Business Class, plus extra attention from a certain male flight attendant, Tilly felt thoroughly spoilt. She slept well, ate well and enjoyed many hours of inflight entertainment on an almost too wide widescreen tv. Seated next to her was a smartly dressed gentleman in full suit and tie. He had smiled politely when they took their seats, but no further exchanges took place for the first 4 hours of the flight.

Tilly eventually excused herself, to visit the toilet. With his long legs outstretched, it was impossible to pass without interrupting him. His reading material looked boring. From what she could make out, he was a scientist. She stood up and cleared her throat to draw his attention. He looked up and hastily pulled his papers down and his legs in, apologising profusely. Tilly noticed his New Zealand accent and edged past assuring him that it was fine.

Once back in her seat, Tilly smiled as she sat down and decided it was the right point to start a conversation.

'Hello. My name's Tilly. Are you on your way back home?' The man had put his paper away and had a glass in his hand.

'How do you do Tilly, I'm Nicholas. Yes, heading home after a tiring weekend in New York.' He held out his hand, and she shook it firmly. She had always been told by her dad that a firm handshake said something about a woman.

'Me too, although New York from New Zealand is a long way for a weekend. I hope it was worth it?' Tilly caught the flight attendant's eye as he passed and ordered a fizzy apple juice.

'Agreed. It was a business conference which I couldn't avoid. Thankfully, they paid for me to fly business class, otherwise I wouldn't have gone. What is the purpose of your visit to the land of the long white cloud - I assume not business?' Nicholas was warming. Tilly didn't have the energy to go into her trip in detail.

'A bit of tourism, because I have never visited New Zealand before. But I am also on a mission to do a bit of family history research, maybe even meeting long lost family.'

'Well there is plenty to visit if you are stopping for a month or so. But be wary of what skeletons might appear once you start digging. I avoid it at all costs.' He picked up his magazine, signalling that the conversation was over.

Tilly settled down to wait for her next meal. It felt like teatime and she was expecting eggs benedict, although the time zones were confusing her. She was keen to accept all complimentary drinks and snacks offered and to sleep in between. While in a half-asleep half-awake state, she found herself thinking or dreaming about meeting Drew, mixed with knocking on the door of a house, which, when she entered it became the inside of a library. She woke when her eggs benedict appeared, realising she could only have been dreaming for a few minutes. The hazy mind pictures faded as she tucked in to her meal and the remainder of her flight.

There was no further conversation with the mostly sleeping Nicholas and before she knew it, they were announcing the imminent touch down at Auckland airport. Tilly gathered her laptop, boiled sweets and notebook and tucked them safely into her rucksack. She was expecting to receive a message from Drew once they had landed but hadn't thought further about the meeting. She hoped desperately that they would get along, but there was still a seed of apprehension about that first meeting. It seemed an imposition to expect him to look after her, even if they were family.

It was dark as they landed, but Tilly could see the bright lights of the city below. The apprehension was replaced instantly by excitement, and she reprimanded herself firmly. This was going to be an amazing experience, and she felt it deep inside that something positive would come out of the adventure.

The airport arrivals lounge was very busy, and Tilly pushed her way to the front of the crowd to retrieve her case. Nicholas had got off quickly, clearly keen to get home. She saw him with his case, walking towards a taxi driver holding up a sign. She glanced at it, then back to the carousel, spotting her case, as her brain processed what she thought she had seen on the sign. As the realisation hit, she looked back, but he had gone. She closed her eyes to try and picture the sign; sure it had said 'N Bartholomew-B' then heard her name being called.

'Tilly. Here, over here Tilly.' Snapping out of her mixed thoughts, she turned towards the voice. There he was. Drew. Drew Bartholomew-Brown. She pushed through the remaining travellers. And then they were just a few feet apart. Drew stepped towards Tilly and hugged her tightly. Taken by surprise, Tilly stiffened, then relaxed and hugged him back.

'Drew, at last.' Tilly couldn't think what else to say. Stepping back and holding her at arm's length, Drew was every bit as handsome in real life.

'Let's have a look at you, young lady. Wow, you got the pretty genes.' Tilly felt her cheeks redden. 'Let me take your bag, it's late, but I've got us rooms in a local hostel. Don't worry, it's an upmarket one.' Drew grabbed Tilly by the hand and pulling her case with his other hand marched them through the busy airport and straight into a taxi.

After a twenty-minute drive on remarkably clear roads, the driver dropped them both outside a tall dimly lit building. Drew thanked the driver then once more took Tilly by the hand and led her into the building.

Drew did all the necessary booking in. It was late, but Tilly realised she was quite hungry, not quite remembering when she had enjoyed the eggs benedict but knowing her stomach was telling her it was a while ago. The rooms they had been allocated were adequate, each with a single bed, desk, chair and a small sink. They were in the same corridor of about a dozen, all sharing two bathrooms. One male, one female.

'There you go love, I'll leave you to freshen up while I find my room, then I'll come back and we can grab some chips. I assume you're not ready to crash out just yet?' Drew was kind in his concern for her. Tilly agreed that was a perfect plan and she sat down on the small bed, in a little bit of a daze.

In a local late opening bar, Tilly and Drew had found it easy to chat. Tilly said she felt she had known him all her life but was still puzzled about the DNA results. He agreed it was odd. Based on the information his mum had given him about his dad's family, his grandfather had been called Myles and his grandmother Temperance. Unusual names. He explained that his father just would not engage in talk about family, and his mother had only met them once, at her wedding. They lived in the very south of the South Island at that time and Drew's mum's family came from the Bay of Islands, at the opposite end of the country. They were clearly not a very close family, although he recalled his father mentioning once that his own father, Drew's grandfather had died not long after Drew was born. He never really mentioned his mother. It seemed crazy that Drew's father's mother was, in all likelihood, Temperance. Her Temperance. Yet Drew's father had little or no contact with her. Tilly had no experience of estranged families, but she knew it happened. Drew's father had clearly been estranged from his family for a very long time.

'I have tickets for a bus to get us down to Wellington in two days time via Rotorua. You will need tomorrow to recover from the flight. You'll probably sleep all day!' Drew laughed at Tilly's shocked look.

'Really? I feel ok. I'm sure I will be fine but thank you for doing all this. So, what's the plan in Wellington and are you sure you are ok to take this time off?' Tilly felt relaxed and was enjoying being taken in hand. To have someone else do the planning was a dream.

'Yes, I'm fine to have the time off and in Wellington we will just have a sightseeing day, before we catch the ferry across the Cook Strait to the South Island. It has all been planned. You don't need to worry your pretty little head about it.' Tilly overlooked Drew's slightly patronising tone. It was like having a big brother to take control, which was a big plus in her book.

'Ok then, I won't. I really am grateful to you Drew. I hadn't expected all this - although I probably was a bit naïve thinking I could just rock up in a city on the other side of the world, in the middle of the night, without any plans. Thank you so much for making this easy for me and taking the lead. Uncle Hector would be so proud of us.' Tilly's eyes glazed over as she thought about the reason she was there. It had been an eventful year, but she felt it had all been in preparation for this visit, with Hector's challenge at the forefront of her mind.

'It's absolutely no problem Tilly. I have enjoyed the planning, and the family research. It's as much a quest for answers for me, as it is a search for the missing Temperance for you. We are in this together girl.' He squeezed her arm and smiled reassuringly.

They finished their loaded chips and weak beer and went back to the hostel, where they parted with the agreement that Tilly would contact Drew when she was awake. Tilly wasn't convinced about jet lag, but as Drew was so insistent, went with it. Tilly promptly fell into a very deep sleep as soon as her head hit the pillow.

53

AUCKLAND - 2024

It turned out he was right. Tilly stirred at 9.30am local time, but after a quick visit along the corridor to the ladies, she returned to her room still quite dazed and fell back into a deep sleep until 11.

When she eventually surfaced, she managed to freshen up using the small sink in the room, then threw open the curtains to a bright sunny day. She grabbed her phone where she saw three missed calls from Drew. So much for their agreement that she would call him; she called him anyway.

'Hiya Drew, I'm awake now. Can't believe I slept in so late. Sorry.' Tilly couldn't stifle a yawn.

'Are you decent? Shall I come to your room, to update you on the day I have planned?' Drew sounded awake. More awake than Tilly felt.

'Yes of course. I'm clean and dressed.' Tilly ended the call and there was a knock at her door within a minute.

Drew arrived in an invisible cloud of musky aftershave, with a rucksack over his shoulder, smart grey chinos clung to his thighs, and he oozed sex appeal. Tilly patted the bed.

'Come and sit down while I finish applying my mascara. I can't go out looking like this.' Tilly smiled and leaned into the small, crazed mirror to complete her make up.

'You look lovely Tilly. Benefitted from a good sleep I hope?' He looked at Tilly in the mirror, her mouth open wide as she applied the blacked wand to her eyelashes. She nodded. 'Ok, so while you are doing that, I'll just go over the plans I have for today. We have lots of time. I have us booked in to a traditional Māori show in the city this evening. Before then, there is time to visit the museum. I think it is the best one we have.' She turned to him, zipping up her vanity bag.

'I'm ready. All sounds good. Please can we get a coffee and something to eat first.' Tilly picked up her own rucksack and they left the hostel.

On the bus heading into the city centre, Drew started to explain what he had discovered about Temperance from the voting records. She had an address in Christchurch until two years ago and he hadn't been able to find a death record.

'But let's spend the next few days just sightseeing. There is so much in this beautiful country for you to see. Actually, you haven't said when you plan to return?'

'That's because I don't know yet. It depends how well I get on in my search. I suppose a month is at the back of my mind. Will that give me time to see something of the country too, do you think?' Tilly looked to Drew for guidance but didn't want it to look like he was expected to plan her month for her.

'That will be just about the right amount of time to see the highlights.' Drew smiled encouragingly. 'Come on, let's get off here and get that coffee fix. I know the perfect place.'

For the third time since arriving, Drew took her hand and led her off the bus and across Dominion Road to the popular café, Forage. One of Drew's favourites he said she would like it. Any coffee boost, Tilly was happy and they were shown to a table in the window. It reminded her of An Extra Slice but on a bigger scale. They had a lovely selection of sweet treats, and she couldn't resist a large Danish pastry to go with her cappuccino. Drew had a cinnamon bun to accompany his americano. When it came it was almost the size of a tea plate.

As they ate and drank, they watched the passing bustle of locals and visitors, mingling busily in the popular central city street. After a short silence as they focussed on refuelling, Drew wiped the crumbs from his mouth and looked back at Tilly who was still only halfway through her pastry.

'We're lucky with the weather; it is warming up nicely. Just right for touring Tilly. I was thinking we could walk from here to the museum, then grab something to eat before the show.' Drew finished his coffee and got out a notebook.

'Oh, I'm glad you like a notebook too Drew, I have more notebooks than is healthy.' Tilly finished the last of her cake and coffee, brushing flakes of crisp, fresh pastry and sugar from the front of her hoody. 'I'm ready to go now - I can see you are eager to get going.' Tilly nudged Drew on the shoulder playfully and they gathered their bags.

'I do like a notebook, yes - I just wanted to check the times for the show. It's at 7 so not too late. Ok, let's go now.' They left the café, following the main road Drew took the lead. Tilly followed closely behind. Drew had a long stride. He was almost six foot tall with long legs, but Tilly had a quick pace and kept up as they negotiated the crowds. Then Drew took a left turn, into an interesting side street, which was less busy. They slowed down and proceeded to do a bit of window shopping as they walked.

It was a good time to talk a bit about themselves. Tilly decided not facing Drew would make it easier to dig a bit deeper into Drew's personal life, to find out about his home life, hobbies, passions and girlfriends. He had been keen to share details of the plans he had made to help her find Temperance, to fulfil the wishes of Uncle Hector, but he hadn't really said a lot about himself. Tilly was keen to prod a bit in that area. As they walked, they did start to converse and it felt relaxed. She found Drew so easy to talk to, perhaps too easy. He had a lovely smile, and she found herself having to detach herself from the feelings she was getting when she was near him. It reminded her of the DNA test results. It had to be explored again - she really needed to establish their actual relationship.

As they chatted, they walked taking in the famous One Tree Hill on their way to the museum. Tilly wasn't that fussed about a museum, but Drew had been keen to stress what an amazing museum it was and how it was full of all things that represented the best of New Zealand history. What Tilly was bowled over by was the building itself. It was equally as impressive as anything London could offer, so when she saw it, she couldn't help but feel excited to go in and explore. This gave Drew a boost as he had started to feel a little anxious at her deflated enthusiasm. They went in together finding the beautiful entrance majestic and welcoming.

'Wow Drew.' Tilly was almost speechless as she looked up at the high ceiling and detailed architecture of the Victorian building.

'I knew you'd like it once you got in here - everyone always does.' Drew had been many times but never bored of the museum. There was always something different to see. He was a real history fanatic.

They spent an hour and a half browsing the many rooms and collections. Tilly was taken with the Māori history represented by the many different carved tiki of all sizes, a large room containing a carved boat and many other artifacts. There was never going to be time to see everything, but Drew led Tilly around the exhibitions he had chosen in order, ending at an atmospheric restaurant. With ambient lighting and themed walls, overflowing with beautiful décor, Drew selected a table, and pulled out the chair for Tilly. She looked at him questioningly.

'Ooh, this is very lovely Drew, but haven't we got to get going? What about the show?' She sat down anyway; Drew just grinned.

'Don't worry it's all booked and planned. We'll eat here - because the show is here. Right here in the museum. I thought you might like that?' He was looking for reassurance that his plan was hitting the right spot.

'Oh wow Drew, yes! Yes, that sounds amazing. I didn't see anywhere 'show' like. But that means we have lots of time to eat, if there is no more travelling after this.' She picked up a menu and immediately looked at the prices.

'Exactly Tilly. I carefully guided you through the galleries on the opposite side of the museum. The show takes place in a large theatre towards the back of the building. No more than five minutes away. We can relax, eat, drink and talk about our day.' He smiled and Tilly couldn't help but smile back.

They both ordered Beef Wellington. A rather British meal, Tilly thought, but she fancied something homely and when she saw it on the menu, it took her back to being a little girl when her Nana Pops used to make Beef Wellington as her speciality. It was lovely on a cold winter's evening in England. As it was now cooling outside, in the New Zealand early summer, she thought why not? Drew said he had never had it but liked beef and was happy to try something new on Tilly's recommendation. They each had a glass of red wine and relaxed to enjoy their meal.

Chatting was easy, made even easier by the wine. Tilly at last was starting to feel properly at home in Drew's company. Perhaps it was their family connection. He never seemed short of something to talk about although rarely did he mention his family other than in passing. She really wanted to know if there was a special lady in his life, but she was finding it hard to broach the subject. Her second glass of wine made it easier.

'So do you have any special friends Drew? You know, people you are close to.' She took another sip and leant back on her chair looking intently into Drew's handsome face.

'Er, not especially. Well, I mean there's Jamie and Garth. We have been mates since we were tiny. But Garth is married now and his wife has just had a baby, so we don't see him so often. Jamie and I, well we have a beer together on a Friday. Not every Friday, but more often than not.' He smiled, not really catching Tilly's drift.

'Does Jamie have, er, a wife, or girlfriend?' Tilly was feeling a bit braver and prodded for more details. Realisation dawned on Drew.

'What are you really asking Tilly? Is it Jamie's personal life you are interested in, or is it in fact mine?' He grinned at Tilly turning the conversation around. She blushed giggling.

'Ok, yes, I just wondered if you have a girlfriend. Someone as charming and handsome as you can't be on your own at the age of twenty seven surely?' He leant forward putting his elbows on the table and firmly positioning his chin in his hands.

'Now, wouldn't you like to know? Come on, I'll get the bill. We need to take our seats; the show will be starting in fifteen minutes. You are going to love this.' Sidestepping the question, he pushed back his chair and paid the bill, while Tilly got her jacket on.

The show was a spectacle of Māori dance and chanting. Tilly was lost in the magic and entranced by the story telling. A truly traditional Māori show that Tilly hadn't been expecting on her first day in New Zealand. It was just an hour and the time flew. It was dark when they left the museum and Tilly shivered as they stepped out onto the main road. There were a few taxis queuing and the couple jumped into the first one. Tilly was feeling tired, the time change still affecting her, although she didn't like to admit it.

Back at the hostel they agreed that with an early bus to catch the following morning, it was time for an early night and they retired to their own rooms.

Tilly had enjoyed her day but welcomed a bit of her own space. She was tired but was also keen to catch up with her family and friends back home. Updating her friends and reassuring her mum were priorities. The time difference made messaging them online the easiest option. She settled down with her laptop to ping off a series of emails to Melody, Kit and her mum. She had sent them very brief 'arrived safely' texts on arrival, but nothing since. She didn't expect a reply due to the time difference.

The communicating complete, Tilly hadn't the energy to do anything more than undress and crash out. Teeth brushed and cold water splashed onto her face, she fell into bed and sleep followed swiftly.

54

ROTORUA - 2024

'I am so grateful to you Drew for arranging all this. You need to tell me what I owe you.' Drew waved away the suggestion. 'No Drew, I mean it. I was given money by Uncle Hector to specifically help me solve the mystery of the whereabouts of Temperance. I insist I pay my way.'

The pair were settled in comfortable seats facing each other, with a table between them and no-one else to share it. The bus slowly pulled away from Auckland bus station, next stop Rotorua. It was quite a new bus, fitted with a toilet, usb ports for charging and comfortable seating. With the bags secured in an overhead rack, Tilly shrugged off her jacket and proceeded to ready herself for the journey.

'Okay Tilly, but I'm not short of money and anyway it's my family too. But if you insist, then you can pay for the crossing when we get down to Wellington tomorrow. Regarding the now, I have booked tickets for the Rotorua experience.'

'Alright. But from now on we share costs. What is the Rotorua experience?' Tilly had got out her laptop together with her notes, ready to pass some of the four hours ahead of them.

'Rotorua is one of the most spectacular places to visit in New Zealand. An absolute must for all visitors. There are thermal pools, geysers and bubbling mud pools. I thought it would be the one place for you to see as a tourist before we get to the South Island. I've booked another hostel for the night.' Drew looked to Tilly for approval and was pleasantly surprised by her reaction. She had such a lovely smile when she used it.

'It sounds amazing; like nothing I can even imagine. Thank you again for being so thoughtful. So, we have a long bus journey, shall we plan our next step - you know, our search for Temperance when we get to Christchurch?' Tilly knew visiting tourist spots was lovely and was grateful to Drew, but she couldn't get Temperance off her mind. Once she had found her, or what had happened to her at the very least, then there would be time for touring. She turned back to Drew. 'I just want to go over what I know, and what you have found out.'

'Of course. Well, as I said yesterday, she seems to be my grandmother, but sadly someone I have never had any relationship with. She is your great aunt, being the sister of both your grandfather and your great uncle Hector.' Tilly nodded as he spoke and scribbled notes in her 'New

York/New Zealand' notebook. 'In my research, I've found her last known address in Christchurch. It matches the details you found in a box. At your mum's, was it? Or at the house? Anyway, you said there were some letters written by Temperance from a Christchurch address.' Drew got out his phone. 'Here, this is the address I thought we could start with. After that, if she isn't there, we will have to re-think.' He showed Tilly his phone, and the notes page. Tilly was satisfied with the simplicity of the plan and put her notes away. 'The positive is that we haven't been able to find a death certificate, so that indicates she is still alive.' Drew smiled across at Tilly, not wholly convinced by his reasoning, but anxious not to show it.

They passed the next few hours mostly in silence. Tilly had a book to read but was captivated by the scenery as they travelled south and barely did any reading. Drew put his headphones on. Familiar with the scenery of his home country he dozed on and off. As they pulled into Rotorua bus station both woke up. Tilly covertly wiped dribble from the corner of her mouth and rubbed the back of her neck. Sleeping on a bus always created unwanted aches. They both stretched, Drew audibly. They gathered their bags and exited the bus.

Once they had retrieved their cases, Tilly accompanied Drew to a motel type building behind the bus station, just a short walk away.

'It stinks Drew. What's that horrible smell?' Tilly screwed up her nose in protest, as she followed Drew into the building's reception area. Drew laughed.

'You'll get used to it Tilly. It's the sulphur. New Zealand is a very volatile and volcanic country. In Rotorua it all escapes through cracks in the earth's surface. Let's get our bags to the room and then we can get straight back out. We only have the afternoon to see it all. Come on.' He went to the desk to check in.

'Room Drew?' She followed him, pulling her case behind her.

'Yeah, sorry it's really busy in Rotorua, so I could only get one room. I hope that's ok. It's a twin - bunk beds actually. But we have an ensuite.' Drew grabbed the key from the counter and went through a door to the left of the reception. Tilly followed, processing this piece of information. Her conclusion, as she entered the room behind him, was that they were adults, she trusted Drew even though they had only spent two days together. So on balance one room made sense for the two of them.

'It's fine Drew. Providing I can have the bottom bunk!' She laughed and pushing past him plonked her bag on the bottom bunk claiming it as her own. Drew felt relieved. He had been a little worried about how to break the news to her that they had to share, so was thankful Tilly seemed okay with it.

Hell's Gate was one of the most popular attractions in the area and it swallowed up the rest of their day. They filled it exploring the natural geothermal wonders, which wowed the unsuspecting Tilly. She was particularly dumbstruck by the geyser, which spouted water high into the sky. Tessa their guide, explained in detail the Māori culture and their beliefs. She explained that the Māori people believe that New Zealand was fished from the sea by the daring demigod Maui. It was almost too much to take in for Tilly, but she was captivated by the stories. Tessa knew everything there was to know and brought the history and geography of the region to life. As they walked from one bubbling mud pool to vast expanses of steaming ponds they got talking to Tessa. At the end of the guided tour the older couples drifted off, thanking Tessa for the talk and some tipping her. Tessa turned to Tilly.

'Have you had a hangi since you arrived in our beautiful country?' Tilly looked puzzled, not having a clue what she was being asked and looked to Drew.

'Have I Drew?' Tessa and Drew both laughed.

'No, you haven't love. It's a traditional Māori meal where the food is cooked in the ground.' Drew explained.

'I was wondering if you would like to join us at the hostel tonight? We will be having a hangi with a few of the others.' The invite from Tessa was very welcome and Drew nodded.

'That's very kind Tessa, thanks. I think we'd love that. What do you say Tilly?' Naturally Tilly was excited to experience everything on offer, especially if it was traditionally Māori. Even if she still didn't know what to expect from a hangi, it meant they didn't need to feed themselves that evening. They agreed to meet later at the hostel where the hangi was to be held in the back yard.

Tilly and Drew returned to their room, feeling exhausted from their busy day. It was proving to be a full-on trip and Tilly still felt affected by the jet lag. She crashed out on the bottom bunk letting her eyes close for just a short while. When she woke, Drew was gently rocking her shoulder. Tilly yawned.

'Oh sorry, did I go to sleep? I just meant to close my eyes.' She noticed the strong aroma of musk bodywash mixed with a fruity aftershave. Drew looked clean shaven and was casually dressed in smart jeans and a rather flattering shirt, which clung to his biceps. She turned her gaze and got off the bunk quickly, realising they had a dinner date. 'Do I have time for a quick shower?' Drew nodded as he combed his wet hair into a slick side parting.

Tilly took her clean clothes into the ensuite and was showered and dressed in no time. They left the room in search of Tessa and the hangi. It wasn't difficult to find them. The general buzz of young voices, over a low playing hum of background music drew them to the group.

'Hey Drew, Tilly, great that you could come. The food is almost ready. Grab yourselves a beer and take a seat.' Tessa pointed to a table where there was a variety of cans and bottles. Tilly wondered where the food was. She couldn't see anything remotely like a fire, cooker or barbeque. A slightly older man was kneeling down behind the group. Tilly could see he was starting to scrape away some soil from a small area then as he pulled back a piece of sheeting she saw a cloud of steam escape from the hole. Fascinated, Tilly asked if she could get closer and Tessa encouraged her over to the edge of the hangi. The smell as the food was revealed was rich and inviting. Tilly felt her mouth watering.

'Can I help with anything?' Keen to be involved, the older man handed her a pair of gloves to put on, then coaxed her to kneel beside him. She could see silver parcels of food and helped to retrieve them from the hole. There was still heat coming from the stones which lay beneath the layers of parcelled up meat and vegetables, which were interwoven with greenery and sticks. Intrigued by this unusual method of barbequing Tilly carefully filled the basket then carried it to the table to share with the group. Drew had seen it all before but was pleased this bonus unscheduled event was giving Tilly an authentic Māori experience.

Tilly couldn't wait to tuck into her meal of moist succulent chicken, flavoured with fresh herbs, and an orangey pink fleshy vegetable they called kumara, was an explosion of new tastes to her tastebuds. She licked her greasy fingers and thanked Tessa for a lovely, unexpected treat. They settled to enjoy some gentle chit chat and friendly banter. Tessa was keen to travel once she had saved some money. London was the obvious destination, like so many before her and Tilly said she could always stay on her boat if she was stuck. Tessa thanked her for the offer, and they swapped details.

Eventually, the pair said their goodnights and headed back to their room. With a long bus journey to Wellington, they needed to be up early. Tilly felt like she was at long last, starting to properly relax and enjoy the trip. She settled into her bottom bunk. Drew checked the details for the following day and reminded Tilly of their need to be up early. Within minutes of their conversation, he could hear her gentle snore. Yawning himself, he set his alarm then put his phone on charge and settled down for the night. Not expecting to sleep well on a top bunk, he drifted off regardless.

55

WELLINGTON - 2024

The day was going to be a long one, yet they had no alternative but to ride it out. They both listened to music, read books, they even played cards to pass the time. Tilly dozed when she didn't think it possible to still be tired. The gentle motion of the bus just lulling her like a baby.

The journey would have been much quicker by car, but they eventually arrived in Wellington at just after 5pm. Drew had not booked a room in advance, unsure of their timings, but they had no trouble getting a very similar twin room in a Wellington motel. Tilly agreed that keeping the cost down with one room made sense, so that was to be their plan going forward. They then went for a walk into the city where they picked up a takeaway and took it back to their room.

The ferry crossing was booked for 8.30 the following morning. The 'Interislander' ferry would take them from Wellington in the North Island to Picton on the South, crossing the Cook Strait in three and a half hours, providing the weather behaved. Tilly was anxious to get the earliest ferry possible, even though Drew had wanted her to see something of the capital city. Tilly just couldn't shake her desire to reach Christchurch as soon as practically possible, so had managed to put him off. She convinced him there would be time to do the tourist bit after Christchurch, so he had reluctantly agreed.

After they had eaten, Tilly desperately needed to shower. Drew, allowing Tilly some privacy, wandered down to a small convenience shop he had spotted earlier, to buy some beers and snacks. It was a balmy evening, and he walked at a leisurely pace. The motel was high up overlooking the city of Wellington and as he walked down the slope he took in a vast panorama of the capital, lit up in the darkness by many thousands of homes and businesses giving it life. He marvelled at the unexpected beauty of the capital at night, before making his purchases and heading back.

'Hey Drew, I feel a whole lot better now I'm clean. That journey was a slow one today.' Tilly was rubbing her blonde curls with a towel when Drew entered the room. 'What have you got there? Ooh, are we having a party for two?' Tilly was definitely in high spirits, which Drew liked.

'Just a few beers, why not make it a party!' Drew winked at Tilly, went through to the small lounge area and flicked on the radio. 'I'll shower in the morning before we leave. I'm afraid it will be another day of travelling.

Perhaps we should have just flown down from Auckland.' Drew hadn't realised quite how keen Tilly was to get to Temperance. How he prayed they would have some positive outcome when they got there, or Tilly's disappointment would be hard to bear.

'Oh no Drew, I have enjoyed the scenery, and Rotorua was amazing. I'll be happier once we get to Christchurch to check out that address.' Tilly followed him into the lounge area and picked up a bottle which Drew had already opened.

'Do I take it you don't want to stop at Kaikoura on the way then? It's the top spot for whale watching, plus dolphins and seals, not forgetting the most amazing mountain views.' Drew sounded subdued. Tilly noticed and went over to him.

'You've been so kind and thoughtful. I know how important Kaikoura is because of your connection, so of course we must stop there. I assume we can't get to Christchurch and visit Temperance's address the same day?'

'No, it would be the best part of the day to get there if we do it in one go. I have friends in Kaikoura who will put us up and take us out on a boat to see if we can spot a whale. It's something I never tire of. That first glimpse of the arch of the back, or tips of the flukes. They are such spectacular creatures.' His whole demeanour changed as he spoke so passionately about this one love.

'Okay, okay you've convinced me.' Tilly had found a full day of travelling very tiring. This would give her the opportunity to do something for Drew; she could tell how keen he was for her to experience this.

'Great. I'll go online and book the Coastal Pacific train to Kaikoura for tomorrow and then continuing the next day on to Christchurch.' Drew was clicking away on his phone as he spoke. Within minutes it was done. It left them an evening of relaxation.

There was a small sofa, where they sat quite close watching a comedy that Drew said wasn't the best New Zealand had to offer but was all he could find. Tilly was feeling a bit giggly after her bottle of beer and buoyed by the extra confidence, she broached the subject of girlfriends once more.

'So Drew.' She took another beer from the coffee table.

'So Tilly.' He turned to her and smiled, knowing what she was about to say.

'When I asked you before about whether there was someone special in your life, you changed the subject.' She had shifted herself back on the sofa and turned to him, taking another long swig of her beer.

'Is there someone special in *your* life Tilly?' Again he avoided answering the question, although Tilly saw a mischievous glint in his eye.

'No, I have Marmite my cat for company.' She didn't hesitate in telling the truth.

'Oh yes, Marmite. But a stunning young woman like you must have them queuing at the door.' Drew grinned, knowing he had completely turned the tables on Tilly. He noticed her blush but still couldn't stop gazing at her. She really was the prettiest. Those Brown genes had a lot to answer for.

'I don't have time for boys Drew. Anyway, I know what you did there. Answer my question, now you know my position. Come on, we are cousins after all.' Tilly started to put her foot down.

'Damn it, yes we are. Well to be honest Tilly I am the same as you. There was a girl, Josie, but we weren't serious, and she met a new guy and went travelling. I was always too busy. There's still time, we're young.' He finished his beer.

'Yeah, we are. We need to look at that DNA again. I have linked your Ancestry family tree to mine now, so the DNA link should appear. I can't understand why it isn't showing a connection.' Tilly stood up. 'Anyway, I think I need my bed if we have another early start.' Clearing away their rubbish, Tilly gave Drew a brief hug. 'I'm so glad I'm not doing this on my own Drew. Thank you for being here. What an amazing stroke of luck that I sent that advert out for someone to help me with my search, only for you to be the person to respond. It was fate, clearly. Bringing long lost families together.'

'I'm glad you sent that advert out too Tilly. God works in mysterious ways' said Drew, as they took themselves off to bed, with an alarm set for an early start.

56

CHRISTCHURCH - 2024

The ferry was slightly delayed due to high winds, but they eventually got going and once out in the strait it was much calmer. At Picton, they picked up the train without any delays, thankful that they had allowed extra time. Their trip to Kaikoura was beautiful, as the train took them along the coast. Tilly had the window seat and marvelled at the scenery once more. Rugged coastlines and mountains of breathtaking beauty. New Zealand had it all.

They disembarked at Kaikoura where a taxi whisked them away to the coast. Then an afternoon of whale watching left Tilly a little bit more in love with the land of the long white cloud. She had felt a little queasy as the small orange vessel had started its journey out into the open sea, but after a hysterical shout from another passenger as he spotted their first whale, her nausea vanished. Tilly was captivated for the next hour by the peace and majesty of the creatures as they gracefully rose to the sea's surface. Their giant sperm whale eventually blew water from his blow hole, then tipped his whole body forwards, tail flamboyantly raised in a graceful act of a final bow to its floating audience. Tilly knew this was an experience she would never forget.

Back on solid ground, Tilly was consumed by a euphoria she could not describe. Drew understood it and walked in silence with her to their accommodation for the night. The couple Heidi and Seth, old friends of Drews were warmly welcoming, showing Tilly to her small room. It was comfortable enough, but Tilly was concerned that Drew had to sleep on a sofa in the lounge. He insisted he was fine for just one night and they enjoyed a tasty vegetarian meal of spicy bean chilli, large chunks of garlic bread and a bottle of red wine between them.

Tilly excused herself early and headed to her bedroom. Her anxiety heightened in the knowledge that they would be in Christchurch the following day; she needed some alone time. It meant Drew could catch up with his friends too. They needed a bit of space. She relaxed further when she heard laughter coming from the lounge and settled down to sleep.

The final leg of the journey, travelling through the picturesque vineyards of the Waipara Valley eventually brought the pair to Christchurch at midday. Tilly saw the sign for Christchurch as they pulled into the station and let out an enormous sigh.

'You okay Tilly?' Drew had noticed her emotion filled reaction to their arrival.

'Oh yeah...er, yes of course. Was I really that loud?' Tilly laughed, a little embarrassed that she had drawn his attention. 'I guess it is relief that at last we have made it to our main destination. Thanks Drew.' She smiled at him.

'Come on then, grab your bags, we need to get off.' Drew was up but thankfully the train was in no hurry, and they had plenty of time to gather their belongings before disembarking. The sun was out, and an almost cloudless sky gave Tilly a positive feel about the day.

They arrived at a smart looking motel within a ten minute walk from the station. Drew had continued with managing their bookings which suited Tilly, but had insisted on paying for this one, and had paid up front for two nights, with the option to stay longer. That was dependant on what secrets Christchurch held. Tilly was buoyed with positive energy as they followed the ground floor corridor to their room.

Drew went first and opened the door into a spacious double-bedded room. A double bed. That was not what they had booked. The room was large, with a futon under the window, a tv and luxury bathroom. Tilly followed, manoeuvring her suitcase awkwardly past Drew, who had stopped in the doorway.

'Come on, move please. I can't get past you...oh, ah. Is this the only bed?' Tilly had spotted the problem and felt a little deflated.

'It's ok, I'll go to reception and get us moved, or an extra room. I'm sure it will be fine. They must have got it mixed up.' Drew, flustered by the mistake, dropped his suitcase and quickly retraced his steps along the corridor. Tilly sat down on the bed. It really was a lovely room, but not suitable for them, she had to admit. A little reluctantly perhaps?

Ten minutes later Drew came back into the room looking even more stressed.

'What's the matter Drew?' Tilly could see he wasn't happy. It could only mean one thing.

'They're fully booked. They can't move us, and they can't give us an extra room. It's my fault. I didn't notice when I was booking that the room was double, I just selected the '2 persons' drop down box when I did it on my phone. I'm so sorry Tilly.' He sighed loudly, his body language displayed the frustration at his mistake. 'Anyway, the futon opens out into a bed and they said they will bring us extra bedding. I'll sleep on it.' Drew walked over to the window and looked out. Hands firmly in his pockets.

'Well done Drew, you sorted it, don't be so hard on yourself. We'll manage. It's a luxury room after all, look at this beautiful bathroom.' Tilly wandered from the bathroom, back to the large picture window, which looked out onto the motel courtyard garden. Drew turned to face her, still looking forlorn. She felt like giving him a hug.

'Come on, we've got a job to do. Shake off this mood. I am not worried, so you shouldn't be.' He shrugged, but accepting the situation unfolded the futon, in readiness for the bedding.

Their plan for the afternoon was to find somewhere to eat, then to head straight to the last known address Drew had found for Temperance Bartholomew-Brown. It was a long shot as it had come from an electoral role that was six years old. Tilly had everything crossed for a positive outcome. Her whole year she felt had been building up to this moment.

They found a cosy corner café offering delicious home-made quiche and salad. Tilly knew she was gulping her coffee and tried to slow down; her desperation to locate that address palpable.

An hour later and they were on their way to a suburb in the south of the city; Sydenham. The roads were long and straight and Tilly was walking at top speed.

'Tilly, slow down a bit. You haven't said what you are going to say to her, if she is there.' Tilly stopped suddenly and looked at Drew. He could see the anguish in her face.

'Sorry. I didn't realise how quickly I was walking. Actually.' She took a deep breath, 'I'm feeling a mixture of anxiety and excitement. I don't think I know what I am going to say. Yet. Oh Drew, I do hope she is there.' Drew gave her arm a reassuring squeeze.

'Not far now. We'll play it by ear. Come on, it's just two more roads then to the left, then number thirty two.' Drew was the one to now pick up the pace. He felt that same mix of emotions. They walked on together.

They stood and faced number thirty two. A shabby white wooden building. The front door was clean and the brass door knocker, letterbox and doorknob all shone as if recently polished. There were nets at the window, plain but neatly hung. Someone was living there. Tilly stepped up and lifted the door knocker, paused briefly then gave a sharp rap. It echoed through the house. She stepped back next to Drew and waited.

After what seemed like an age, they heard someone moving inside. Eventually the door rattled, then eased open as much as the security chain would allow. Tilly's heart pounded against her ribs.

'Yes?' The shaky voice of an elderly woman slipped through the gap.

'H..hello there.' Tilly struggled to keep the shake from her voice. 'My name is Tilly and I'm looking for someone who used to live at this address. Or maybe still does. Can you open the door please?' Tilly had been holding her breath. She slowly exhaled.

'Who? Who are you looking for?' The lady cleared her throat, sounding stronger, sensibly not keen to open the door to a stranger.

'Of course, if you can help in any way, I would be grateful. I have come all the way from England to try and find my great aunt Temperance Brown. I think she lives here. Or did once.' Before Tilly had finished speaking the old lady had opened the door and stood facing her. She was tall for an elderly person, stood upright. Tilly waited for her to speak.

'You are looking for Penny? I am sorry but she couldn't remain here without help, she had to move. I took over her tenancy last year. My name is Elsie. I'm Penny's oldest friend.' The old lady smiled kindly. Clearly thinking of her friend.

'Hello Elsie.' Tilly put out her hand and the old lady took it in her own. 'I am really pleased to meet you. Are you able to tell me anything about Temperance, I mean Penny?' Ever hopeful, Tilly had noticed Elsie had used the present tense when referring to her friend. Could it mean Temperance was still alive?

'I think that you and your young man had better come in. I will then tell you what I can.' Elsie stepped back to let them both through. 'Just go through love, to the left and sit down. I will put the kettle on and we can have a nice cup of tea.'

Over that nice strong cup of tea, Elsie proceeded to tell Tilly and Drew the story of her meeting Temperance way back in 1951 when they both chose to leave the United Kingdom for a new life. Once Elsie started talking, it was hard to stop her. She explained how they had travelled together on the SS Magnificent, what they had done on that long journey and how they had lived together in Auckland when they first arrived in the country. Eventually losing touch when Elsie married and moved away. Tilly was engrossed, visualising the two young women as they travelled on the high seas. Snapping herself out of the unrealistic romantic picture she had created in her mind, questions started to fill her head.

'You taught Temperance to type, when you were on the ship? That gave her the skills to enable her to work when she arrived here.' Elsie nodded, she felt a connection with the young couple who had appeared from nowhere to take interest in her. Elsie loved to have people to talk to. She had missed that in recent years.

'I did love. I don't know how she would have managed if I hadn't. She didn't seem to have any kind of plan.' Elsie's memory from those distant days was phenomenally clear.

'Do you mind me asking, what she was like? I mean, how did she seem, on the boat, was she happy?' Tilly wanted to see if she could find out whether Temperance had been pregnant. She didn't know quite how to ask this elderly lady about something so personal.

'Penny was a sad young thing. Oh yes, she was sad. Very private. We were friends, but she didn't confide in me and I didn't ask. I respected her privacy. But it was clear that something had happened at home. That poor girl was very unhappy to begin with. I think I helped with that.' Her face lit up as she remembered something.

'Do you think she was...er, in trouble in any way?' Tilly tried to skirt around actually saying the word pregnant. Elsie was shaking her head. 'I was wondering, perhaps she might have been in the family way?' There, she had said it. Elsie looked at Tilly.

'Oh no Tilly. She definitely wasn't. But I understand why you might ask. She was clearly trying to escape from something. I never did find out, because it upset her to dwell on the past. It didn't matter to me. We built a friendship, we supported each other and we learnt about living in a strange land, together. That's all. No, there was no child.' Tilly felt a sinking feeling. She wasn't sure why as it didn't affect what happened next. The big question was on the tip of her tongue, when Elsie answered it for her.

'Temperance is now in the Christchurch Twilight Care Home, not far from here on the edge of Christchurch. She has quite severe dementia. I visit her and sometimes she remembers me. Less so in recent months.' Elsie looked sad. Tilly had her heart in her mouth, realising that she hadn't heard a thing after 'care home'. Tilly's mind was working at 100 miles an hour as she processed this information. Temperance was alive. She was alive and that meant she might, no she *would* be able to visit and talk to her. She felt exhilarated. Her promise to Uncle Hector was going to come true. She had all but found Temperance.

'Elsie, I honestly am so grateful to you for telling us about Temperance and her journey.' stuttered Tilly in her excitement. 'Do you think I would be able to visit Temperance at the home? I really *really* want to see her. I can't tell you how much.' Tilly's euphoria evident.

'I'm sure you would, love. It's lovely there. They are kind and it's homely. She is in a happy place.' concluded Elsie.

Tilly didn't want to appear rude, but once she knew of Temperance's whereabouts all she could think of was finding her. Ten minutes later, after clearing away the teacups and promising Elsie they would stay in touch, they said goodbye. As they walked briskly back down the road, Tilly grabbed Drew by the arm.

'I can't believe it. She's alive. I just can't believe it. I am buzzing Drew; I'm just so excited.'

'I can tell Tilly. I'm excited too, but I think this is going to be a job for tomorrow. We need to wander back to our room and perhaps chill out for a bit, before finding something to eat then getting an early night. I feel quite shattered after the day's events.' Drew didn't want to dampen her enthusiasm, but they'd had back-to-back busy days, travelling and sightseeing. He needed to rest, even if it was on a futon! Tilly agreed. She had wanted to get back and check her emails, catch up and send messages to the guys back home, plus luxuriate in a nice hot bath.

When they got back to their room, Drew was relieved to see his futon was now beautifully made up with plump pillows and a sumptuous, billowing duvet. It looked extremely inviting so he threw off his jacket and splayed himself across the bed. Firm but comfortable, he closed his eyes telling Tilly to wake him at 7. Tilly laughed, placed her bag on the big double bed, then turned on her laptop before going to run herself a hot bath. There were lots of complimentary toiletries for her to choose from, so with White Linen bubbles creeping up the walls of the bath she nipped back to check her emails. With Drew snoring gently in the corner, she undressed and slipped on the towelling robe provided. Glancing quickly at the emails, filtering the junk from the genuine messages she saw one from Judith the librarian. She clicked to open it:

Hi Tilly,
I hope you are having a wonderful time on your travels and are making some progress with your search. I have found something exciting in the New Zealand archives. Basically, I found the marriage certificate for Temperance and Myles. On it, he is showing as a widower. This must mean he was married before. I'm still searching but as soon as I find anything more, I will get straight back to you.
Bye for now,
Judith

Tilly read it through briefly, then put her laptop on charge. Her bath almost full, she gently lowered herself into the steaming bubbles. Her skin stung as the heat bore deeper; she slowly exhaled and sunk down under the foamy surface. A warm blanket hugging her tired and aching torso, she felt sleep calling her.

57

CHRISTCHURCH - 2024

Both Drew and Tilly slept like logs. Without the need to get up early for onward travel, they had turned off all alarms and allowed themselves to sleep.

Drew rose first after a surprisingly good night on the futon. After showering, he stopped by Tilly's bed and gazed at her still sleeping peacefully. Her features were perfect but not at all like his own. They shared their blonde hair, but that was where the similarities ended. Tilly began to stir and Drew moved swiftly back to his bed where his clothes were piled ready to dress. He picked them up and took them back to the bathroom, just as Tilly opened her eyes.

'Morning sleepyhead,' he said smiling as she peered at him through one open eye.

'What time is it?' she croaked, clearing her throat.

'I don't know, but there's no rush to get up. I'll make you a coffee once I'm dressed. You keep dozing.' She didn't need telling twice and rolled over.

The morning was bright, and a sharp shaft of sunlight streamed in through the window, bouncing off the mirror back into room. Once awake Tilly couldn't get back to sleep. She lay with her eyes closed listening to Drew in the adjacent room; in her head she was planning the day ahead. The day that hopefully, she would meet her great aunt Temperance and complete the circle.

While Tilly washed and dressed, Drew went to the café on the corner of the road and collected bacon sandwiches and coffee. He still felt awkward sharing the same space with her while she was dressing, although they had undoubtedly built a close friendship. A little too close perhaps, in the short time they had been in each other's company. But it felt so normal to be with Tilly, like they had known each other all their lives. He assumed it was their family bond and wondered what their relationship would have been in different circumstances. When he returned to the room Tilly had tidied and made both beds. They sat on the end of the big double bed to eat their takeaway breakfasts.

'I want to go straight to the care home Drew; it's all I can think about.' Tilly brushed crumbs from the bedclothes onto the floor and stood up. 'I'm going to call them now and see when I can visit. Will you come in to see her too Drew? Please?' Drew nodded.

'Of course. I'll do whatever you need me to do. Go and make the call.' Tilly took herself out into the corridor and dialled the number.

'Hello, my name is Tilly Brown and I would like to make an appointment to visit one of your residents. Today if possible.' Tilly's voice was shaky. She couldn't conceal her nerves.

'G'day Tilly, I am Shani. I'm sure that can be arranged. Our residents do love to have visitors. Can you tell me who you want to visit please?' Tilly relaxed and explained who she was to Shani and how she had travelled to New Zealand to find her distant relation.

After she had hung up, Tilly explained to Drew how lovely Shani had been. Helpful, interested in her story without making any demands. It had resulted in an appointment at 2 o'clock, after lunch but before the afternoon tea and cake round. She said they were both welcome. Tilly couldn't wait.

They had three hours before the appointment and Tilly was on a high. They took a walk down to the harbour where Drew bought some chips, but Tilly couldn't eat. They sat on a concrete wall, watched the boats bob in the harbour and chatted about their trip so far. Drew squeezed Tilly's arm reassuringly. He knew she couldn't voice what was really on her mind, but he wanted her to know he was there for her. Sharing the scraps with a few seabirds they then turned back to retrace their steps towards the care home.

They were met with a large modern single-story building, with an imposing glass front. An ornately carved archway framed the entrance and beautifully manicured gardens. Tilly and Drew stepped up to the door, which slid open automatically, a blast of air-conditioned air hitting them in the doorway. Tilly walked up to the clean, glass desk behind which sat a glamourous blonde fiftysomething. She stood up to greet them.

'Tilly I presume. Welcome to Twilight Care, I'm Shani.' They shook hands, limply Tilly noted. 'We spoke on the phone. Please come with me and I will show you to the visitor's room.' Shani wasted no time with idle chatter, taking them straight to a brightly decorated side room. 'Sit here while I go and check that Temperance is awake and okay to see you now. I'll only be a minute. Make yourselves comfortable and grab a glass of water from the cooler.' She then disappeared.

'Are you okay Tilly? Do you want me to come in with you, or would you prefer to be on your own?' Drew sat back in the nearest chair, while Tilly sat opposite him on the edge of her seat, wringing her hands and staring through him. 'Tilly?'

'Oh, what? Yes…er no. I don't know. What do you think?' She refocussed questioning eyes on his.

'I'll come but I'll stay in the shadows. If you know what I mean. You'll be fine once you're in there.' Drew aware of the enormity of this meeting for Tilly, decided he needed to be the man to support her. Plus, Temperance was, after all, his grandmother.

As promised, Shani was back in no time and led them to the common room. She explained that Temperance liked this room with other people, but that she had put Temperance in a seat to one side where they would have more privacy. Tilly thanked her as she led them in and then left them.

There had been no introduction, but Tilly assumed Shani had told Temperance she was there to see her. The old lady was sitting in a large armchair, facing them as they approached. Tilly noted her carefully set white curls, her neat appearance even though she had received no warning of the visit. It was nice to know that at 94, she still wanted to take pride in how she looked. Nice that the staff made such a fuss of their residents. It felt very homely and that pleased Tilly. There was one large chair next to Temperance and a hard chair set back.

'Hello Temperance, may I sit here with you?' Tilly sat down without waiting for an answer. She noticed a smile creep slowly across the old lady's face.

'Vi, is that you Violet?' Temperance fumbled for her glasses which were hanging on a chain around her neck. She managed to sit them tentatively on the end of her nose, then leaned towards Tilly. 'It is you. Oh Violet, how I have longed for you to visit me. This is just wonderful.' Tilly felt awkward, not sure exactly how to react. Whilst she didn't want to upset Temperance, was it wrong to go along with her belief that her long lost sister was visiting. Dementia, Tilly knew, did strange things to a person's mind. She looked to Drew for guidance. He shrugged but also nodded. He was saying go with it.

'How are you, Temperance? I saw Elsie yesterday, and she told me you were here. Are they looking after you?' Tilly relaxed into conversation. She figured if she didn't say who she was, then they could still have a chat and no harm would be done.

'It's lovely here Vi. I have lots of friends. I have Stan, over there.' She pointed to a sleeping grey haired man, newspaper open on his lap and a cold cup of coffee by his side. 'We sometimes have our afternoon tea and cakes together.' She was smiling now, thinking of cakes. Tilly felt emotion brimming, a wave of something rising through her and spilling out, just about eye level. She dabbed at the corner of her eye with a tissue, again let down by her heightened response to all things relating to elderly people. She just couldn't help wanting to nurture them in their twilight years, appropriate for this particular care home. 'He's 98 you know, is Stan. We don't have many men.' She sat back and seemed to disappear back inside herself. Thoughts, Tilly presumed, whirring as she worked out what to say next.

'I travelled all the way from England to see you, Temperance.' Tilly felt that this, at least, was true.

'From the farm Vi? Oh Violet, the farm.' She then dropped to a barely audible whisper. 'Our secret, Violet. Our secret is still safe, is it?' Tilly's heart jumped into her mouth. What should she say to this? Whispering, Temperance leant close to Tilly. 'Just between you, me and the fireplace. Please Vi, do the right thing won't you?'

'I..um...yes Temperance,' Tilly hesitated, 'but when you say our secret, what exactly do you remember? It was a long time ago, after all. Perhaps more than 60 years.' Temperance was looking straight at Tilly, a slight frown creasing her already lined brow. She put a finger to her lips, indicating that Tilly was speaking too loudly and whispered again.

'Thank you love, just keep schtum. I know you will.' She tapped the side of her nose and sat back. It was then she seemed to notice Drew, who had inadvertently leant forward to try and hear the whispers. 'Nicholas. Is that you, my Nicholas? Come closer boy. Oh, my Nicholas, what a joy.' The old lady tried to get up from her seat, her voice rising with excitement. Drew got up out of his seat, moved towards her and crouched down by the chair. She took his hand.

'Don't try to get up.' Drew hesitated, not knowing how to address her. Her hand was warm, but he could feel her veins through the paper-thin skin. She gripped him tightly.

'Why did we never get along Nicholas? You were such a bonny child and oh, how your father loved you so. He would be proud to see the handsome man you have grown into. Oh yes. He would be so proud.' Tilly was watching, with confusion. It was clear that to Temperance, Drew looked like someone else, her son, she presumed. Tilly's brain was whirring, why did Nicholas ring a bell.

'Well, I am here now.' Drew was playing along, as had Tilly. It was a surreal situation. The old lady seemed happy and from Tilly's point of view, something key had been confirmed for her by this conversation. She couldn't have wished for more and would explain it to Drew when they left. At that point, Shani and another lady came in with a trolley. It was tea and cakes. Temperance seemed to lose interest in the pair when she heard the trolley and looked across at Stan who had also been roused by the sound. It must be the highlight of their day, thought Tilly. At that point, her phone dinged, and she saw 'Judith' flash across the screen. She pushed her phone down into her bag and got up.

'We will leave you now, to enjoy your tea. Thank you for the chat.' Tilly knew their visit had been short, but she realised that an enormous weight had lifted from her shoulders in that short time. She leant down to give Temperance a kiss. It seemed only appropriate. Drew did the same. Tea and cake had definitely become the main focus, and so they made their way out of the common room and into the fresh Christchurch air.

58

CHRISTCHURCH - 2024

Outside Tilly looked at Drew with tears in her eyes. Tilly wasn't sad, she just couldn't help the waves of emotion that swallowed her up at times like this. Drew pulled her to him in a big hug and held her while she silently sobbed.

It was a slow walk back and, to begin with, neither Drew nor Tilly could find any words. They walked in silence until Drew spotted a coffee shop and pulled Tilly in. He was the first to speak.

'So Tilly, what just happened back there?' Drew seemed confused. Tilly had begun to relax a bit as they walked, so was beginning to feel more like herself. They chose a table in the window, where they could still enjoy the sun and ordered coffee, sandwiches and cake. It turned out that meeting long lost relatives was hungry business.

They both tucked into their generous portions, before Tilly pushed her plate to one side. She knew they needed to dissect what had been said and to whom, so that they could do a proper postmortem on their meeting with Temperance Bartholomew-Brown. Tilly knew she had some explaining to do but was also keen to hear what Drew had to say. A second ding on her phone, showed a message from Ashley Coombs. It reminded her she still had a message from Judith to read.

'You're popular today.' Drew smiled. Tilly couldn't help but smile back. 'Nice sandwiches?' he asked.

'Fine, thanks. But I think we need to talk about more than sandwiches, don't you?' He nodded, taking a gulp of coffee then unceremoniously spat it back into the cup because it was too hot. Tilly laughed.

'Oh no, here, have some of my water.' She handed him her bottle, then got out her phone, flicking open the email from Judith. Half reading it as she spoke. 'Right, so that was the weirdest visit to a care home resident I have had this year. And I've had a few - I thought I was becoming quite the expert, but I did not expect that.'

'You must resemble her sister Violet, Tilly. When she last saw her, she would have been in her late twenties or early thirties, from what you have already told me. That could be the reason she thought you were her - well, that and the dementia.' Tilly nodded.

'Her long-term memory is still vivid. Her memory of the farmhouse and the fireplace. I had a theory about that fireplace. She pretty much confirmed it today.'

'What is your theory then? Drew continued to eat.

'That is where the family money is. Hidden behind the big inglenook fireplace. I am sure of it, but getting into the house, to then knock out the fireplace is going to be nigh on impossible.'

'Why do you need to? Just let it stay a mystery.' Drew didn't understand where Tilly was coming from, so she needed to convince him, to perhaps convince herself she was right.

'I need to, because it was one of the things Uncle Hector wanted me to do. It was in his Will. *"Find Temperance and find the missing family money"* it said.' Tilly suddenly grinned. 'I can't believe it; we actually found Temperance. Bless her. She seemed happy in her own little world. I don't know why I got upset.' Then she remembered the text from Ashley. 'I can let Ashley know. I don't need to wait until I am back home to tell him. I will send him an email later. His text is only asking me how I am getting on, so it's going to be great to be able to say I've found her.' She looked back down at her phone and started to read the message from Judith.

'And she thought I was my dad. I think that confirms she is my grandmother.' Tilly looked at him puzzled.

'Why your dad?' Tilly wasn't cottoning on.
'Nicholas is my dad. She was really pleased to see him, er, me. It was odd being someone else. So, in turn, I guess that confirms that we are cousins!' Drew didn't sound overjoyed with that fact, although he didn't really know why. To have Tilly in his life was lovely, but as a cousin?

'I find it sad that my dad can't appreciate how much it would mean for her to see him.'

'Er, no.' Tilly was still looking at her phone.

'Er no, what? What are you talking about?' She didn't look up.

'No, we are not cousins. We are not related. Look, Judith has just sent me something she found online.' Tilly seemed particularly pleased.

'Okay well don't look so pleased to not be related to me!' he laughed. 'Come on then, explain. We have just been to visit your great aunt who is also my grandmother. My father's mother, and..' but he couldn't finish his sentence. Tilly had got up and come round to his side of the table, pushing her phone under his nose.

'She isn't your grandmother. She's your *step* grandmother. Look, Judith has found the marriage of Myles, who was your grandfather, to Rebecca Oolong in Christchurch in 1955. Then the birth of Nicholas, your father, in 1960.' Drew was looking now with interest, but also still confusion. 'Then Rebecca died in 1963 - she hasn't said how she died. But he married

Temperance in 1968. Your dad Nicholas would have been a little boy.' They sat back in their chairs and looked at each other.

'I think I need another coffee Tilly. Or something stronger. It's a lot to take in.' Tilly agreed.

Heading back towards the hotel it felt different. Tilly felt different. She walked by Drew's side perfectly in step, but something had changed. When they got back to the room, she threw off her jacket and laid down on the bed, mentally drained. It hadn't been a long day, yet the revelations of the last couple of hours left Tilly with questions.

'Coffee Tilly, or shall we just go out and get drunk?' Drew grinned. She saw a twinkle in his eye, and opted for the pub.

'I think I want to get changed if we are going to go out out!' Tilly felt the need to pretty herself up. She had a soft pink lacy top she hadn't worn and with her tight black jeans, knew she looked good. She locked herself in the bathroom and an hour later emerged, like a swan perfectly attired and made up.

'Wow Tilly. You look stunning.' Drew couldn't take his eyes off his cousin. Who now wasn't his cousin. Until now, it had been okay to comment on her good looks, so where did he stand now? She still looked good and he couldn't help himself. 'Take my arm, young lady, we are going to go out and celebrate our newfound knowledge.' Tilly smiled and was only too happy to.

After two and a half hours in the pub, Tilly was feeling happy and a little bit tipsy. She had drunk two double gin and tonics, without anything more than a shared bag of peanuts to eat. Sitting beside each other on the bench seat, Tilly leant on Drew.

'So Drew, we are not related at all then. How do you feel about that?' Her elbow slipped and she fell forwards onto him, knocking the glasses. He'd had three pints and felt a little wobbly himself. There was a pause, as he looked into her eyes and considered how to respond.

'Shall we get some chips then head back. I think we've probably had enough.' He edged Tilly out of her seat, slipped his jacket over her shoulders and led her out of the pub by the elbow.

Once they were outside, with a chill in the air Tilly shuddered. The evenings were still quite cool as far south as Christchurch.

'Here, snuggle up to me and I'll keep you warm.' Drew pulled her in and with his arm over her shoulder, steered her on the path back. They looked like an ordinary loved up couple. The friends, now aware of the non-existent blood relationship, relaxed into each other.

'You didn't answer my question.' Tilly slurred. They stopped at a mobile burger van and bought two portions of chips. Drew turned to Tilly.

'I don't know how I feel. I like you Tilly. I mean, who wouldn't, you are gorgeous? When I thought we were cousins, I was proud to have you in my family and I'm so glad we found each other. But now..' He couldn't take his eyes off her cornflower blue eyes, shining even in the darkness of the evening.

'What now Drew?' Tilly wasn't sure what she wanted to hear, but she knew her feelings had been unchained. The knowledge had released something in her.

'Well. Now ...' He paused, then smiling widely, gently leaned down and brushed her lips with his own. She stood still, absorbing his scent and warmth. Savouring the moment in her tipsy state. It was a lovely feeling. 'I think we should go back to our room. Agreed?' She nodded slipping her arm in his and they continued back to the motel.

Tilly pushed open the door to their room and flopped down onto the double bed. Her head still a little dizzy; she wasn't sure if that was the alcohol or the effect Drew's kiss had had on her. He followed joining her on the bed and they sat for a moment in silence, not touching.

'Something changed today Tilly. I feel tingly when I am near you.' Drew lifted her chin with his hand, tilting her face towards his, he gently kissed her again. She didn't resist, it felt natural. She pulled him closer, and they fell back onto the large double bed, bodies locked.

A sudden need for closeness, for comfort and reassurance, took them by surprise. The physical act of love making released pent-up feelings they had both managed to suppress. In time, sated and happy, they drifted off together into a deep sleep.

59

CHRISTCHURCH - 2024

Drew woke first; memories of the previous night flooded back. He was in Tilly's bed, he was naked, and lifting the cover, he saw she was too. He flushed with embarrassment and slowly slid out of the bed without waking her. He gathered his clothes, from the four corners of the room, then crept to the bathroom where he hastily dressed.

When Tilly woke, she was alone. The curtains were still closed and it looked quite dull. Her memories of the previous night were hazy until she realised her pyjamas were still under the pillow and the other side of the bed was crumpled. She could smell the scent of a man on her covers, then it all came back to her with a jolt. It added extra tension to her already thumping head, so she reached out to her bag for some paracetamol.

With Drew apparently absent, Tilly dressed. She felt wobbly. That was the result of too much alcohol, something she wasn't really used to. But also confused by her feelings. She needed to talk to Drew about what they had done. They needed to move on today and she couldn't have a silly slip hang over them and spoil the remainder of her trip. As she pulled out her laptop to update her family history details with the information obtained by Judith, Drew appeared at the door, knocking as he entered.

'Are you decent?' he said playfully.

'Yeah, come on in.' Tilly saw he had coffee and pastries. What a perfect travel companion. Drew passed her a cappuccino and a warm paper bag containing a welcome croissant. She patted the bed beside her and, choosing not to mention the previous evening, showed him the information on her laptop.

'I wanted to get everything down that Temperance had said yesterday, plus the information Judith had gleaned about our…er, actual relationship. I wanted to have another read in the day, with a clear head.' She put her hand to her head. 'Actually, not such a clear head. Anyway, so now we know. Your actual grandmother died when your dad was only three. That is sad, isn't it?' Drew nodded.

'It may be the reason dad doesn't like to talk about the family. It makes sense, I suppose.' He sat down to look at her screen with her. 'So does that say my grandmother died in childbirth?' Tilly zoomed in on the death certificate that Judith had emailed her.

'So sad. Yes, and we presume the baby died too. So your dad Nicholas. Oh my goodness...' Tilly had just had a deja vu moment, or certainly a flashback to the airport arrivals. 'I think I might have been travelling with your dad on my flight over. It definitely was a Nicholas.' It had just dawned on her, as she put two and two together.

'There are lots of people called Nicholas, Tilly,' said Drew laughing.

'No, it wasn't just that. When I got to the arrivals lounge and I was looking for you, I saw someone holding up a sign that said "N Bartholomew-Brown" but I didn't get a chance to see who they were picking up because at that point you found me. I think I chatted to your dad without even knowing!' Tilly couldn't believe it. The conversation had certainly dissolved any awkwardness between them and she didn't feel the need to mention their night together, if he didn't.

'I'd be amazed if you got much chat out of my dad. He isn't much of a conversationalist at the best of times. But he does travel quite a lot for work and he doesn't drive. Next time I see him, I will update him on everything we found out - and I'll mention you - my non-cousin!' He gave her a friendly shoulder nudge and they both laughed.

'Yeah, he didn't talk much. In fact, I tried to force him to talk to me. It was a long flight. In the end he went to sleep.' She turned off the laptop. 'Drew, we need to pack up and leave today. I've done what I came to New Zealand for. I found Temperance, with your help. Now I need to go home.' As she voiced this inevitable fact, Tilly felt sad.

'You are not going home yet Tilly. I still have lots of New Zealand to show you.' Drew was emphatic and a little panicked. 'Plus, I'm not ready for you to go back yet.' Sounding a little emotional, Tilly looked at him. He was starting to pull things into his bag and looked up at her. She could see the sadness in his eyes.

'Come over here and have a hug,' she said beckoning. As they hugged, she felt his heart beating hard against hers. 'I have to go Drew,' she whispered, 'but of course, we can carry on our little tour. As friends, yes?' He agreed. But for Drew, he knew it was going to be hard. Just friends.

They checked out of the motel by 11 and walked to the closest café to plan their next move. Seated in a large corner sofa with space for their rucksacks, Tilly pulled out her New Zealand notebook while Drew got more beverages. She felt as if she had survived on caffeine since stepping on New Zealand soil.

'Drew, I think I need to see Temperance one more time before we move on. You can visit her any time, but once I have flown back that will be it.' She sat across from Drew; she felt making a little bit of physical distance between them might dampen her feelings.

'I understand that Tilly, although it is unlikely I will visit. Unless I can persuade dad to, that is. We can walk down there after coffee and see if you can go in now. I'll let you go in on your own. Now though, I think we need to plan the rest of your trip and you need to book a flight home.' Drew shuffled uncomfortably on his seat. 'I will miss you Tilly.' He paused and took a deep breath. 'I know that you regret last night. But I don't.' She looked at him but didn't say anything. That confirmed to Drew, that she had regretted their night of passion and he felt embarrassed. 'Right, well we need to get down to Queenstown, then Milford Sound. It's beautiful there but will probably be wet.' He felt hot and knew his face had coloured.

'I think I'll try to get a flight home in a week. Is seven more days enough to see the best bits left of New Zealand?' Tilly felt a sudden flutter of butterflies at the thought of leaving. Was it leaving New Zealand, or leaving Drew? She wasn't sure. Such confused feelings she hadn't expected out of the trip.

'Er..yes, a week should do it, I guess.' Drew hesitated.' So, I suppose you need to book that first and we can take it from there.

Tilly managed to get a good price, for a direct flight in just under two weeks. Drew felt a heaviness, knowing their adventure was almost at its end, although grateful for a few extra days. He put on a smile for Tilly, assuring her that he would make the next 10 days exciting for her.

With the bookings made, they gathered their bags and walked to the Twilight Care Home. There was a bench outside, and the day was warm, so Drew said he would sit outside with their bags, while Tilly went in to see if it was ok to visit. Shani was on the desk and remembered Tilly immediately.

'Hello love, everything okay?' Smiling she came round the desk.

'I'm moving on today and will soon be flying home, so I wondered if I could have another five minutes with Temperance. It will be the last time I see her. I know she doesn't know me, but I have been in contact with some of her elderly cousins in England. We didn't speak about them yesterday and I thought I would see if talking about them would trigger memories of her childhood.' Tilly knew she was talking too quickly, justifying her visit, which wasn't necessary, but she did it anyway. Shani was more than happy to welcome her in and took her straight to the common lounge where Temperance was in a chair next to Stan. She left Tilly at the door as before, to make her own introductions.

Tilly approached tentatively but was pleased to receive a big smile from Temperance.

'Hello, come and have a seat here next to Stan. What was your name again love?' Tilly was taken aback. It was a very different welcome to the previous day.

'I'm Tilly. I am your great niece - my granddad was your brother Joe. Do you remember Joe?' Relaxing, Tilly sat opposite the two elderly residents. The old man looked up.

'I'm 98. Still got nearly all my teeth.' Stan smiled, bearing a toothy grin, proud to share this piece of information with Tilly.

'Ah, yes, very good Stan. I'm 28 and I hope I still have my own teeth when I am 98!' She looked at Temperance who was still smiling and noticed they were holding hands. So sweet she thought, then thought of Drew outside.

'I had two brothers, Tilly love. Joseph and Hector. They were still young when I had to leave. I didn't get to say goodbye.' she sighed. Mentally Temperance was much sharper than the previous day. It was like conversing with a different person. Tilly didn't want to make her sad but if she had any more clues to share about the missing money, it was going to help Tilly with the final part of the Will. She had an idea, so thought hard about how to phrase her next question.

'Temperance, I am interested to know if you had a happy childhood, growing up on the farm. Did you meet with cousins?' How could she get the conversation around to money? It was challenging, but that wasn't going to do it.

'Yes we had some lovely visits from our Crewe cousins. Those girls would stay with us each summer. Long hot days in the dusty fields after harvest. Sleeping in the barn up in the rafters, on hay bales. Gerty and I were close. We enjoyed the local dance.' Her face lit up as the happy memories returned. 'All six of us girls were allowed to go together. Afterwards, Gerty and I would sing, arm in arm, as we walked back to the farm.' She was smiling as she reminisced and Tilly warmed. It fitted with the memories Con had shared. Young women enjoying their youth.

'Were there young men at the dances? Boyfriends?' Tilly was fishing, but she didn't really know what for. It still wasn't addressing the money question.

'Er...yes, oh but father didn't like it.' Her face changed as she recalled her father. 'He would say no-one was to touch me. No-one. He was.....'She frowned. 'I don't remember any more.' Temperance turned away and addressed Stan. 'You ok love? Tea will be round soon.'

'Tea will be round soon' repeated Stan.

'You moved to New Zealand when you were quite young? That was an expensive move, coming all the way out here, to the other side of the world?' Tilly hoped her line of questioning would prompt Temperance to remember back to the time she had arrived in New Zealand 70 odd years before. Temperance looked thoughtful.

'Hmmmm. So Tilly, you are my family, aren't you?' Tilly nodded as her great aunt rubbed her chin. 'It's the first time I have had a visit from anyone who is related to me. In all these years, I have only ever had letters. Vi, my sister. Do you know her?' Tilly shook her head. 'She looked after me. You know, made sure I was alright out here. She kept me supplied. You know?' Tilly didn't really know but nodded anyway. She wanted Temperance to keep talking.

'I had Elsie, she taught me to type.'

'Oh yes, we met Elsie. You were friends back then.' Temperance nodded. 'And you lived together in Auckland.' Again, Temperance nodded, more slowly this time as the memories returned.

'We both worked as typists. I had to earn money. That was the hardest part, the money. I had so little. Once I started earning my own money, I was able to start to build a life. Vi helped.'

'Helped how?' said Tilly. 'From back in the UK, she helped you?' Temperance was nodding.

'When she could. She sent me what she could. It wasn't easy for her, but she was the only one.' She had turned back to look at Stan.

'You mean she sent you money? Couldn't your parents send you money to help you?' Tilly noticed Temperance's countenance change at the mention of her parents.

'There was nothing they could give me to make up for what happened. Only Vi helped, yes, she sent me the money. She was the only one.' She turned to Stan. 'I think our tea is on its way now.' Then back to Tilly. 'It has been lovely to meet you. Very kind. Kind to visit me. You take care now love.' Tilly realised the conversation was over. Temperance had been polite, but when it came to her parents, there was clearly a problem. It had to be behind the reason she had left England. She would probably never know about that, or the money now.

'Thank you, Temperance. I'll leave you to enjoy your tea.' There was no sign of the tea trolley, but Tilly knew it was time to leave.

Outside, Drew was reading his book. When Tilly appeared, he stood up. He had missed her, just in those twenty minutes while she was inside the care home. He smiled, her blue eyes smiling back at him. He let out a big sigh.

'Everything okay Tilly?' Eyes brimming again with tears, she gave him a brief hug.

'I'm ready now. Ready to move on.' She picked up her rucksack and pulled it over her shoulder. She had done what she came to do.

'Come on Drew. Let's go.'

60

SOUTH ISLAND - 2024

On the bus south, heading to their next stop, Queenstown, Tilly relayed to Drew, the conversation she'd had with Temperance. He listened intently, because he enjoyed Tilly's company. He gazed at her face as she spoke. Pert, pale, pink lips. Fair eyebrows neatly shaped, rising then frowning in animated expression. But his interest stopped there. He hadn't found a real connection with Temperance, so the content of what she was saying passed over him. He decided it wasn't surprising. There was no genetic relationship between him and the old lady, which was probably the reason his father hadn't been interested in her either.

Tilly was so glad to have finally solved the mystery of the elderly Aunt's whereabouts, so while Drew slept, she used the journey to relay a few messages back home.

Hi Ashley,
Thanks for your message yesterday, it was very timely. You will not believe it, but I have actually found Temperance. She is alive and well, settled and happy in a very nice home for the elderly called 'Twilight Care' in Christchurch. I am sure you will be able to check this if you need to. I met with her twice, and we chatted. She has some memory problems, but apart from that seemed very well and content where she is.

I am moving on with my friend Drew, who has been showing me the sights here in New Zealand. I'll be flying home in ten days time and I'll arrange to meet with you properly once I get back.
Best wishes,
Tilly

Then she messaged the girls together. She knew they would be keen to know all about Drew as well as the trip and her search for Temperance, but she wasn't ready to spill all the beans in an email.

Hi girls (and Sam!)
Just to let you know that we found Temperance, who is very elderly and living in a care home. I have visited her twice and had a chat. Despite her

dementia she has been able to talk about her childhood at the farm, from which I have gleaned more details. I'll fill you in when I get home.

I hope Marmite is behaving himself Melody, and New York isn't missing me too much Kit! Home in 10 days!
Bye for now, big love,
Tills xx

Finally, she needed to message her mum, who had only emailed her once since she had arrived in New Zealand.

Dear Mum,
I am sending you this brief email to let you know that I will be flying home in ten days time. I'll send you the full details nearer the time.
My trip has been a successful one and I found Temperance living in a care home in Christchurch, which is a large town on the South Island of New Zealand. I visited her twice and now I am going to do a bit of sightseeing before heading back north to Auckland.

Looking forward to seeing you soon.
Love Tilly xx

Drew and Tilly then embarked on a seven day whirlwind tour of the South Island before heading back to the North. In Queenstown, they tried everything from white water rafting on the Shotover River, to visiting the Kiwi birdlife park. They stopped short of bungee jumping at Arrowtown but did some gold panning there, where Tilly was delighted to find tiny flakes of gold she was able to take home in a small bottle.

Moving on to Milford Sound they treated themselves to a scenic cruise around the sound, delighting in experiencing it during a particularly heavy downpour, which made the many hundreds of waterfalls all the more spectacular. They saw dolphins and a distant albatross, which they had been told was very rare. For Tilly it felt like the holiday of a lifetime, that she was desperately in need of to shake off the tension of the previous weeks. Experiencing it with Drew was an unexpected pleasure. She figured that most people do not plan a holiday with someone they have only just met, yet it had proved the perfect pairing.

Drew continued to plan their travel, book rooms and find the best experiences. He wanted to make the most of his last few days with Tilly. Dwelling on the future without her there was only going to spoil the time they had left. Whilst there was still very clearly an electricity between them that Tilly could not deny, she was making every effort to remain on a platonic footing. She limited her drinking to just one glass of anything alcoholic, if they did visit a pub, but more often she stuck to soft drinks. Drew did the same, afraid to upset what they had together.

The ten days flew by. Of course they did. Both Drew and Tilly avoided all conversation relating to anything post Tilly's flight home. It was a subject they had both involuntarily put off limits. They decided to fly back to Auckland from Christchurch. Their plane touched down leaving just sixteen hours until her flight home was due. An evening in Auckland, with a final night at their very first hostel, but this time a twin room, not two separate ones.

'Can you believe everything that has happened in the last three and a half weeks Drew? It just doesn't seem possible.' Tilly was nursing a lager shandy and enjoying a pub lasagne. Drew called it the last supper. He was very down but trying hard not to show it.

'What doesn't seem possible, is that I am never going to see you again after today.' Drew couldn't hide his emotion. Sadness filled his eyes as he stared straight at Tilly, willing her to change her mind about going home. Something he knew she was not going to do. 'I am going to miss you Tilly Brown.' He tried a smile. It half worked.

'I know you are.' Tilly reached out and gripped Drew's hand. He squeezed hers back, then pulled it away. It was too painful for him, the temptation. 'You can come and visit. You said you want to travel.' Tilly was putting on her bravest face. She was going to miss him dreadfully. She had never experienced these types of feelings for anyone before. It had just all happened at the wrong time and in the wrong place. 'Don't be sad.' He looked down at his pint and took a sip.

Her flight was midday and Drew was there to see her off. He clung to her at the gate and she clung back. As they parted, he whispered in her ear.

'Don't forget me Tilly. If you want me, I'll come to you.' Drew pleaded with his eyes and, staring back at him, Tilly found her throat dry unable to reply.

She reluctantly pulled away, briefly waved, then passed through the barrier, without a backward glance. Her antipodean adventure was over; she was going home.

61

LONDON - 2024

The twenty-eight-hour flight left Tilly feeling drained. Now she understood about jet lag. Something she really hadn't experienced on her flight out. During her six hour change over in Singapore, she had managed to contact her mum and both Dave and Celia were there to meet her at Heathrow. She was surprised at how pleased she was to see them both. The comfort of familiarity. She also hadn't anticipated the feeling of relief and sense of completion on returning home. Her objectives met; she could relax. For a little while anyway.

They dropped her back at the boat and Dave carried her bags through into the small galley area. The temperature outside almost freezing, meant it felt slightly damp inside. Tilly was keen to get the wood burner going and Dave volunteered to do that for her, while she sorted out her bags.

'Right love, we'll be on our way. It's warming up nicely now.' Dave called through to Tilly in the bedroom. 'Give us a call if there is anything more you need.' Tilly thanked Dave, they briefly hugged, then closing the door she made straight for her bed.

It was dark when she eventually woke up. Blearily she glanced at the clock radio, which showed 03:17 in luminescent green. She was fully dressed but cold. Dragging the extra blanket over herself, she was asleep again in minutes.

It was late the following morning when the monotonous sound of a telephone ringing, eventually dragged Tilly from her sleep. Scrabbling around for a few minutes as she located, first her slippers and then her phone, the caller had rung off. It was Melody. Tilly hadn't been up to messaging anyone when she got back, but now she was awake, she had to get back to reality. She called Melody straight back and arranged for Sam to drop Marmite off at 1pm and fixed a time to catch up with Melody the following morning at An Extra Slice.

That left her with one final appointment to arrange. A meeting with Ashley at the solicitor's office. She wanted to make it official so texted him. He was quick in coming back to her, saying he would be at the office all week and had lots of availability. She suggested after her meeting with Melody, which meant just one trip up to the high street the following day. All she needed to do now, was wait for Marmite. She felt her eyes closing again. Damn that jet lag. She pulled herself out of her lethargy and put the kettle on. A strong coffee in hand, she opened the fridge. It was bare. She took a loaf of bread out of her miniature freezer. Beans on toast was a quick tea for later. It meant she could put off shopping for one more day and snatch another 40 minutes snooze before Sam arrived with Marmite. Coffee drunk, her bed beckoned.

Marmite was ecstatic to see her. Sam said he had been no problem but really wasn't suited to being a house cat. They had found it hard keeping him away from the front door, his little nose pressing at it at every opportunity. The handover complete, Marmite was only too happy to settle down as close to Tilly as possible, purring loudly to express his feline delight in her return. Tilly decided the most sensible way to pass the afternoon was to watch some television. She figured it would get her body clock back to normal. After some cheesy beans on toast (she had carefully removed the mould from the aging cheese's edges before grating liberally over her piping hot beans) she had an early night. A busy day followed. She wanted to be at her best.

Melody was at the café first and had ordered their regular coffees in advance. Brenda, who had insisted they were on the house, beamed widely as Tilly arrived, puffing from the cycle ride. She really did need to get fitter. After a clinch with Melody, they settled down with their coffees. Tilly summarised her trip, as best she could. It wasn't easy. As she started to recall the trip, Melody interrupted.

'So, meeting with this Drew. What was he really like Tilly? You were quite vague in your emails.' Tilly wondered why Drew's looks and personality were the most interesting part of her trip.

'We got on really well. But meeting Drew wasn't the objective of the trip Mel; finding Temperance was.' Tilly tried not to sound defensive but knew she had failed on that score. 'Would you like to hear about my visit to Kit? Sorry. I should be thanking you for looking after Marmite. I hope he wasn't any trouble?'

'He was no trouble. You know that and of course I want to hear about our best buddy. From the Instagram pictures it looks like you had an amazing time. You packed so much in to just a weekend. It was exhausting just reading about it.' They both laughed and the tension was broken.

'I'm sorry Melody, so much was packed in to my time away, it's hard to isolate one small part of it. To be honest, I don't remember a lot about the time in the run up to meeting Temperance. I was so anxious about finding her, everything else is just a blur.' Tilly felt this was mostly true but intermingled with a small white lie. She remembered clearly everything about Drew. Their first meeting, their travelling, his consideration and kindness, his frustration when he got it wrong with the room booking, plus of course the night they spent together. Right now, Tilly hadn't decided whether she was going to share this last bit of information with Kit and Melody. Certainly not yet anyway. 'What I wanted to talk through with you, above everything else, is something I discovered from Temperance. I mean.' Tilly paused. 'Something I think I discovered when speaking to her.'

'Go on, I'm all ears.' Melody didn't seem offended by Tilly's evasiveness, so Tilly pressed on and explained about the secret and its link to the fireplace.

'So you see, I still need to get back into the house, to explore behind that fireplace. It has been my hunch all along. I'm worried that once I have reported back to the solicitor, that will be the end of our connection with the farm.' Tilly couldn't help but show some emotion. Melody picked up on it yet didn't really have an answer.

'It can't be helped Tilly. You can report back to Ashley what you have found. Which you have already done when you messaged him. Then move on. Your challenge is over.' It was what Tilly didn't want to hear, even though she knew it to be the case.

'I know.' Sighing, Tilly drank her coffee, and after some encouragement proceeded to fill Melody in on all the exciting bits about New Zealand, her disappointment that her adventure was now over suppressed.

Tilly and Melody parted with hugs, promising to catch up once she had finalised her business with Ashley.

She arrived at the offices of Gently, Barker and Coombs Solicitors at just before 3pm. Opening the door she was instantly greeted by the familiar musty smell of the damp 1970s carpet. At the top of the stairs, the door to the left was propped open and Angela was sitting prim and upright behind her dated desk. Her glasses balanced on the end of her nose, she looked up and beckoned Tilly forward.

'Take a seat Miss Brown. Mr Coombs will be with you shortly.' Tilly sat down in the high-backed leather chair and picked up a newspaper. Ashley appeared within minutes and ushered her into his office, indicating to Angela that they should not be disturbed, to which Angela mumbled something under her breath. Clearly not happy.

'It's really good to see you Tilly, grab a seat.' They both sat down, then Ashley spent several minutes searching through papers in his drawer, eventually pulling out a folder. 'Sorry about that. I knew I had Hector's folder to hand somewhere.' Tilly thought it would have been more appropriate to keep files in a filing cabinet but waited, keenly, to hear what he had to say. She wondered if there might be something for her to sign, to finalise Uncle Hector's affairs. 'It was great to read your message Tilly. I have to say, I am really impressed at your dedication to complete Hector's requests. I know I have said that to you before, but I really am.' Tilly smiled, it was nice to have her perseverance appreciated. 'I did get Angela to do a quick check with the care home and they confirmed that Temperance was a resident.' At this news, Tilly was a little taken aback. Whilst she had suggested this was an option for Ashley, she hadn't really expected them to follow it up.

'O-kay' she said slowly, not sure how to react. 'Did you think I was lying?' She couldn't help challenging him.

'Oh no, nothing like that, but you will appreciate that with something as important as a bequest from a Will, we must be seen to do all the necessary checks.' His tone had turned uncharacteristically authoritative. 'You know, audit, and all that.' He waved his hand in the air as if to brush it away as unimportant.

'I see. What else do you need me to tell you?' Tilly felt her heart rate increase.

'The Will requested that you fulfilled two challenges. Hector had left it to me, to decide whether you had made a full and genuine effort to meet those challenges. The first and arguably the most important of those two, was to find the whereabouts or final resting place of Hector's sister Temperance. You did an incredible job, aided by the money left to you by Hector for that purpose. I am very happy you have fulfilled that clause. Now, to the second clause and the whereabouts of the family money. Were you able to glean anything?' Ashley was looking straight at Tilly. She felt unnerved but took a deep breath and composed herself.

'I am not one hundred percent sure Ashley. I did try to ask Temperance, but her dementia meant she couldn't comprehend everything I said. In fact, in the first visit, she thought I was her sister Violet.' Ashley listened intently. 'She told me Violet had sent her money. Well, she implied money had been sent. So I think that is where the money went. I don't have evidence, but it is the best I could do.' She was hesitant to mention the fireplace. Would she always regret it, if she didn't ask him for that one last chance to visit the house? Conflicted she couldn't decide.

'It sounds reasonable. We will probably never know, but I'm happy you used all available resources, and that is all he'd asked.' Tilly lifted her hand. 'Sorry, did you have something else?'

'Yes. I…er…um. Well, I don't know how to put this, but there is one other thing.' She hesitated further. Did she ask if she could go back to the house, or did she just tell him about her hunch?

'Go on Tilly. You know me by now and I don't bite. You know that much about me.' He smiled encouragingly.

'I just wondered if I would be able to go back to the house one more time? The thing is…' As she said it, she realised it still wasn't going to be easy to excavate a bricked-up fireplace, without someone knowing.

'Actually, it doesn't matter. Forget I said anything.' She shook her head. She felt a bit deflated.

'It's okay Tilly. I understand your emotional connection to the house. It was Hector and Temperance's childhood home and the place where you said your final goodbye to him. I get that.'

'It isn't that. No. Like I said, it doesn't matter.' She brushed it off.

'Well, I am pleased to say that after due consideration, I am happy that you met the requirements of the Will. The challenges set by Hector were not easy, but you gave your best to solve them.' Tilly nodded.

'Is there something for me to sign?' Leaning forward she expected to be handed a pen. Ashley shook his head.

'There is something here in this folder, which hasn't been opened. It says it is to be given to you if you manage to complete the challenge set.' It was a brown manilla envelope. Nothing special, stuck down with tape. Tilly took the item handed to her and, for a moment, just looked at it. On the front it was addressed to Matilda Jean Montgomery-Brown.

'Can I…can I open it?' Ashley nodded.

'Go ahead. I have consulted with my partner and we have agreed that you have met the challenge. I do know what this contains, it's the final part of completing the estate. If, in our opinion, you hadn't completed the challenge, then there was an alternative envelope for me to open and this one would have been discarded.' He was nodding to Tilly, so she hooked her nail under the tape and pulled back the flap. Inside, there was a yellow parchment folded in three. She removed it and read:

I am fully confident that my dear niece Tilly Brown, will be successful in the challenge I have set her. If you are now reading this addition to my Will, then this has indeed been the case.

Also made this 3rd day of May 2023, whilst of sound body and mind, I, Hector Donald Brown, as a result of a successful completion of the conditions in my letter of 3rd May 2023 pass on to my great niece Tilly, the Deeds and therefore full ownership of the Brown family Farm, 'Spitalbrook' in the village of West Snoring, Norfolk, together with any other money remaining in my account, once my debts are paid.

This is to be passed on to Tilly once she has satisfied the condition that she makes a full and genuine effort to discover the whereabouts of my sister Temperance and the missing family money.

I appoint my solicitor Ashley Coombs, of Gently, Barker and Coombs Solicitors, to take an unbiased judgement on her success or otherwise.

Signed H D Brown

Tilly read it. Then read it again. After the third time of reading, she looked up at Ashley. He was nodding to her. Stunned, she eventually found the ability to speak.

'What does it mean Ashley? What does it mean the deeds of the farm are mine?' Tilly looked blankly at Ashley, not able to take in the words on the page.

'What it means Tilly, is that Hector has left you everything. He was the owner of Spitalbrook, the Brown family home and he has left it to you. So yes, you can go back to the house, because it now belongs to you, together with the fields surrounding it. I'll have to check what his bank balance is, but that too will be transferred to you, once our expenses have been deducted.'

Ashley reached back down to his drawer and pulled out the familiar brown envelope containing the big front door key.

'If you could just sign here for now, the key, and therefore the house, are all yours. We can sort out the full deeds and transfer of ownership once this has sunk in. I can see you are still absorbing the news. Congratulations Tilly. You are the new owner of Spitalbrook.'

Tilly cycled back to Georgie and Marmite, to process what had just happened, her mind a complete fog of confusion. It seemed as if her life may have just changed forever.

62

NORFOLK - 2024

Tilly slowly cycled back along the frosty canal path, her head still awash with thoughts, the first of those being that she needed to tell someone her news. News. That word didn't seem big enough, conspicuous enough, exciting enough to describe the act of inheriting a house! Not just inheriting a house, but a home. Effectively, her family home. It hadn't previously crossed her mind that the farm was owned by Uncle Hector. She just hadn't thought about it. Even when planning to go back and open the fireplace, the actual farmhouse owner had not been considered. A flicker of shame ran through her. She pulled up at the boat and parked her bike.

Tilly decided to WhatsApp the girls very briefly. A simple, clear statement of facts.

Hi Ladies,

As you know, I am back from my travels and earlier today visited Ashley Coombs at the solicitor's office, to update him on the outcome of my visit to New Zealand. Once he was satisfied that I had met the requirements of Uncle Hector's Will, he presented me with something I can scarcely believe. A second part to Uncle Hector's Will. In it, he says that he is leaving me Spitalbrook plus its contents and the remainder of his money. Can you believe it? He has left me his house!

I know it is a lot to take in; I am still struggling to get my head around it myself, but I wanted to tell you two first. You are my besties and we share everything don't we? I still need to complete the paperwork fully at the solicitors, but Ashley gave me the key. Please Melody, tell Sam I would still really like to explore behind the fireplace. I am even more convinced that the money is there. I didn't tell Ashley that, but now it's mine, I will be able to do it, without any guilt. Must contact mum and Drew now.
Catch up soon?
Love Tills xx

Having said she needed to contact her mum and Drew, she decided a call to her mum would be more appropriate than a text. They had only spoken briefly in the car coming back from Heathrow and she had been pretty tired. Marmite had climbed up onto her lap the minute she sat down, which made messaging difficult. She dialled her mum's number and it was answered instantly.

'Tilly love, is everything okay?' Her mum sounded anxious.

'Hi mum, yes fine. More than fine, in fact.' She pushed Marmite's pressing nose away from her ear. 'I am just about over my jet lag now, so must arrange to come over and tell you all about my trip properly. New Zealand is so beautiful.'

'I'd like that Tilly. When suits you?' Celia was trying not to sound pushy, but Tilly knew she had worried while she was away.

'Not sure yet, but I have something else to tell you that couldn't wait.' Tilly felt impatient to get to the point.

'That sounds ominous. Go on,' said Celia.

So, Tilly shared her news with her mum, explaining that it was completely unexpected, as part of an addendum to Uncle Hector's Will. After a long silent pause, her mum, clearly also stunned by the revelation, cleared her throat.

'I'm pleased for you Tilly. But I suggest you prepare yourself for a challenge to come from your cousin Tris. Once he finds out, there will be hell to pay.' Celia didn't sound very pleased for her daughter. Tilly guessed her nose had been put out of joint, being passed over by her uncle, but it couldn't be helped. Tilly hoped once her mum had digested the information, she would be happy for her.

As soon as she came off the phone, there was a message waiting from Melody. Messaging Drew would have to wait.

OMG Tilly. You own a house!! Go girl. Sam says when do you want to go? Free tomorrow if you are!
Mxx

A lump rose in Tilly's throat. A homeowner? That hadn't quite registered. She already had a home. Georgie was her home. But going to Spitalbrook to explore, she was definitely up for. She sent a quick response, and within a few minutes the plans to visit the following day were set.

~

'Are you absolutely sure you want to do this?' Sam was poised with hammer and chisel in hand.

They had made good time, with the house being exactly as they had left it. When Tilly had taken out the large metal key to open the door, it felt different. She opened the door, this time as the new owner of Spitalbrook.

'Definitely Sam. Yes, I am 100% sure. I know it's very soon, but you *know* I have wanted to do this since our last visit. Maybe even the one before.' She smiled at Sam and Melody looked on. 'I still have a bit of money that Uncle Hector left me. I will use it to renovate afterwards, I'll pay you.'

'No Tilly that's not what I mean. Payment is not necessary. I just wanted to check you were sure, before it was too late. Now you two stand back. There's going to be a lot of dust.' Sam pulled on his goggles and dust mask, then began to chip away at the edge of the brick work. Tilly and Melody took themselves out into the kitchen to chat over a cup of coffee.

After half an hour of loud hammering, Sam appeared looking for a hot drink and opinions from the girls.

'I've made quite a neat hole on one end. It looks a mess. I reckon two more hours and I will have the whole fireplace out.' Tilly wanted to have a look, but Sam said it was too dusty without a mask for protection.

A couple more hours passed with Tilly cleaning in the upstairs rooms, while Melody made some notes about jobs she thought should be priority for Tilly once she had taken on the house as her own. That was assuming she did that. After their chats, Melody was unsure Tilly was yet capable of plans. She was so focussed on the money she expected to be behind the fireplace, she couldn't think any further ahead. Melody got out some ready-made sandwiches and put the kettle on. They had a small electric fire which they had switched on in the dining room and Sam joined them, coated in an even layer of fine orange brick dust.

'Okay, it's done, but no Tilly.' He put his hand out to stop her, as she started to move towards the door. 'You need to let the dust settle before you go in. I have opened the French doors. Give it ten minutes.' Groaning she sat back down.

After the longest ten minutes of Tilly's life, during which she asked Sam numerous times if he had been able to see anything inside the fireplace, the time to see for herself had come. With Sam leading the way, and Melody bringing up the rear, Tilly edged into the cloudy room. Melody opted to remain in the hall, saying it was still too dusty for her. The fireplace area was unrecognisable. Sam had done a neat job of chipping away the bricked in 'modern' fireplace. He had stacked the pile of rubble neatly outside on the patio. Tilly stood facing the open inglenook, searching for somewhere that looked like a hiding place or shelf. Leaning in, she coughed taking in a lungful of dusty air.

'Here Tilly, take this and put it over your mouth.' Sam shook out a clean white handkerchief from his pocket and handed it to her.

'Thanks Sam. What do you think?' She still couldn't see anything.

'These big fireplaces often had a bread oven and other shelves, up inside. It might be open, or it could have a small metal door to access it.' As he spoke, he reached up inside, to the right of the flue. 'I can feel something metal, shine your phone torch up inside here for me.' Tilly crouched down inside the inglenook and aimed the beam of her phone torch upwards. As she adjusted her eyes and focussed on the crumbling brick lining of the fireplace, she could make out a ridge.

'I can see something, move your hand please Sam.' He stepped back and let her move into the space. She was smaller and could stand up inside the fireplace. 'I can feel the metal. It feels flat, like a lock on some wood. I think it's a box. A wooden box. There is definitely a ledge. If I edge it forwards, can you help lift it down?' Sam moved back in and between them, they lifted the box down into the light.

It was bigger than a shoebox and had the appearance of a writing box without the slope. Solid wood and securely closed.

'It's locked,' said Tilly, stating the obvious. 'The key!' she exclaimed.

'The key?' questioned Sam, not following.

'You know. It was part of the original challenge. What was the key for, it said? We never did find a box that it fitted. Do you remember when you brought me here and we found the keys in the writing desk? That ornate key that didn't fit any other drawers or cupboards. That's the one I need to try on this box.' She put it down and leant over the sofa, to drop down the writing desk flap. The key was in a small drawer and she quickly retrieved it.

'My heart is racing. Call Melody in.' Sam pushed the lounge door open, and Melody joined them. 'I want you to be here Mel. This is going the be the one - I feel it in my bones.' Tilly placed the old key into the lock of the box. It slid in smoothly. She looked at them both, before gently turning it. A soft clunk confirmed they had found the home of Hector's mystery key.

63

NORFOLK - 2024

The clunk was soft but the hinges quite rusted, clearly a hidden bread oven in an inglenook fireplace, once a very warm dry place proved to have let in some damp in the previous 70 years. As Tilly tried to lift the lid, it seemed stuck fast.

'Hold on Tilly, I have a screwdriver here, we should be able to lever it open. Those hinges look thoroughly rusted shut.' Sam pulled the screwdriver from his still open toolbox and wedged it into the crack between the lid and base. The girls leant forward as he twisted the tool firmly. There was an audible splitting of wood, as the hinges came away at the back, but he was able to get his fingers in the gap and ease it open.

At first there was silence. Tilly twisted the now open box to face her. All she could see was a piece of old, slightly mouldy linen which fitted the rectangle of the box like a small cover. Tentatively, she lifted it. It began to disintegrate on one side, its age showing. Beneath it, was more material, wrapping around something and just visible, the corner of a faded envelope.

'What is it Tilly? I can't see any money.' Melody was whispering. It seemed appropriate.

'I'm not sure, but perhaps there is some in this envelope.' Tilly eased the envelope out. It was sealed, with a large 'x' on the back, like a kiss. She turned it over, and in faded pencil, she could just make out what looked like 'Dear child'. Tilly looked at the others blankly, and they returned her with the same puzzled gaze.

'That isn't fat enough to have any money in it. Have another look in the box. Take out that material. It might be at the bottom.' Melody was drawn in. The suspense almost unbearable. Tilly put the envelope down on the table and returned to the box. Removing the fragmented linen, she could see thin silky pink material, wrapped around something.

'It's so fragile, I think I need to lift the whole lot out, can you just hold the lid there Sam, please? Thank you. And Melody, put your hand under this end, then we can lift it together. I'm not sure what it is.' Tilly pushed her hand gently down behind one end of the wrapped item and started to lift it. But then felt something she didn't like the feel of and a shiver went through her. 'Oh no.' She gasped and let it drop. 'Oh no Melody.' She put her hand to her mouth.

'What is it Tilly? You look like you've seen a ghost.' Melody took her hand out of the box.

'I c...can't do it. I felt. Oh my goodness Melody. Sam. I think it was a skull.' The friends gasped, and Melody stepped backwards.

'What do you mean a skull?' Sam was less squeamish than the girls. 'I can see a rounded shape under that pink silk; it is probably a ball. That letter, it might just be a time capsule. You know, where children hide things to be found in the future. Do you want *me* to lift it out?' Sam was being far more sensible, so whilst Tilly's head had gone to a very dark place, Sam had hit on the more practical answer. Of course, that made sense. As children the sisters had probably hidden something which they then kept as a secret between just the two of them. It made complete sense. Tilly released the breath she was holding.

'Yes please Sam. I don't know what I was thinking. But remember whatever they put in there, it will still be fragile, so please take care.' She watched, as Sam put both hands into the box and lifted out the whole parcel of fabric, wrapped in what looked like a pillowcase. As he did so, his hands too, felt the shape of the contents, his face then turned grey as he quickly placed it on the table. Light in weight, it crumpled in a heap. A small bundle of fabric encasing something else. Something he had also felt clearly through its thin casing.

'I...er, I am not sure about it Tilly. Actually, I don't think you should unwrap it any further.' She looked at him and could see the fear in his eyes.

'I was right. Oh my goodness Sam. I was right. It isn't a ball; it's a tiny skull.' Her eyes welled up and she began to shake.

'Look, let's all calm down.' Melody the voice of reason. 'Why not open the letter?'

The small group stepped away from the tiny, crumpled bundle and sat down on the sofa, still covered in a white protective sheet. Melody reluctantly took the letter on Tilly's instruction and carefully opened the envelope. It didn't take any effort, the glue having deteriorated years before and she removed a single sheet of white paper, folded in two. Melody looked first at the shaky writing, then read it out loud.

My darling child,

I have sent prayers to our heavenly God, to protect and keep you in his Heaven until we meet again.

I did all I could to ensure you were spared, yet God chose to take you early from me. Your tiny face and body, not fully formed, you could not survive dear one, but you should know that you were loved by me, your mother, as

I was loved by my sister Violet, your Aunt and her caring husband Ronald your uncle, who tried in vain to keep you with us.

You will sleep peacefully, my child, in the safety of the place that should have been your home.

Your ever loving Mother Temperance

As Melody's voice petered out, Tilly, with tears streaming down her face, let out a loud sob and pressed her face into Melody's shoulder. Melody held her tightly, whilst silent tears of her own ran uncontrollably. Sam hugged his wife, as they sat in silence, the letter falling to the floor. It had delivered news unthinkable and left the small group shocked in its wake.

When Tilly had stopped her sobbing, Melody went to the kitchen and put on the kettle. They needed some sweet tea to treat their shock. Sam returned to the bundle on the table. After suggesting that one of them had to at least check that this did contain the remains of a baby, he was willing to do that job. Tilly didn't want to leave the room, so stood at the door. As he unrolled the parcel, the pillowcase opened and revealed the small skull, and tiny fragmented bones together with lots of dust.

'Can you tell, Sam?' Tilly's anxious voice, from the back of the room, searched for answers. She wasn't sure what she wanted from him.

'It is barely recognisable Tilly. If you mean can we tell if it was a boy or girl, no. But there is a bit of pink lace in the bottom, together with the pink pillowcase, so a girl I would think. If you are happy, I'll wrap her back up and put her back in the box.' Tilly nodded.

'Thank you, Sam. Thank you so much. For everything.' She sat back down, thoroughly drained.

Melody came in with a cup of hot, sweet, steaming tea for each of them. They sat in silence and drank, engulfed in their own thoughts. Gradually Tilly managed to calm herself, bringing those thoughts into some kind of order in her own mind.

Accepting that there really was no money after all, Tilly's mind returned to the contents of the box. 'We need to give her a burial. The baby.' As she voiced her thoughts a lump caught in her throat, but her tears were spent. The others nodded. 'This really wasn't what we had expected today. I am so sorry Sam for making you do this for me. I was so sure there was something hidden. I was right about that and about the bricked-up fireplace. I never dreamt this was her secret though. Poor Temperance. It must have been on her mind her whole life.' Tilly sighed. 'I need to tell Drew. But as far as everyone else is concerned, I want this to remain a secret. Is that ok?' Melody nodded, and Sam agreed.

They spent an hour tidying the dust and dust sheets away. The pile of rubble was left on the patio, which Sam said he would remove but that there was no rush. Tilly had so much to think about now she had inherited the property and land, but it would all have to wait now. Her priority was planning a proper funeral for the baby. Sam replaced the box where they had found it and they left the house.

Tilly felt much better when she got back to Georgie. The shock of the discovery of a baby's remains started to have some logic attached to it. Temperance was not pregnant when she travelled to New Zealand, but she had been. Her parents, but Tilly thought it was likely to be her father, had not accepted the situation and had sent her away. Or maybe, Temperance had left of her own accord, because of the way she was treated at home by her father. Clearly, the baby had been born too soon, and reading the letter it indicated her sister Violet and Violet's husband Ronald had helped her. It comforted Tilly to know that Temperance had not had to endure it alone.

She called Drew. It was the first time she had spoken to him, since they had parted in Auckland. Although it was early morning in New Zealand, he answered instantly.

'Hi Drew, how are you?' Tilly saw his lovely smile and felt another pang of emotion. She knew it was just because of the day she'd had, but what she would do for a big hug from him at that moment.

'Hello lovely, how's it going?' At that point, Tilly couldn't help herself and burst into tears.

For a few minutes Drew hung on, while she scrabbled around the boat to find tissues. She then composed herself for the second time that day and updated Drew on everything. Firstly, her visit to the Solicitor with the revelation of her new inheritance, then the visit to Spitalbrook with Sam and Melody. Drew was naturally surprised and intrigued. When it came to the box hidden behind the fireplace, clearly shocked at their discovery, understanding then the reason for Tilly's overwhelming display of emotion.

'Oh Tilly love, I wish I was there to give you a big hug. I miss you.' Drew's plea was heartfelt. He wanted to step through the screen to be by her side, having felt empty since the day she had left him in Auckland.

'Aww Drew. Thank you. I'm fine, I really am. It has just been one of those days.' She sniffed and dabbed her reddened eyes. In truth, she missed him too, but it seemed pointless to say so. 'I just feel so sad for Temperance. I needed to tell someone. We are going to give the baby a burial, somewhere in the grounds of Spitalbrook. It feels like the right thing to do.' She could see Drew nodding. 'I am still struggling to get my head round the fact that the farm is mine. I have a lot to think about.' Tilly gazed into the screen.

'You do Tilly. But I feel honoured you chose to tell me Tilly, above your mum. I'll keep your secret, don't worry on that score. I think Hector and Temperance wanted this for you. It was destined to be.'

'It still feels unreal Drew.' She couldn't say what she wanted to say to him, so just smiled. His eyes lit up, as he smiled back.

'Give me the address and I'll send you a housewarming present.' Drew wanted to give her comfort. A nice card and flowers might go some way to do so.

'You don't need to do that. But it is an easy address to remember. Spitalbrook, West Snoring, Norfolk, England. That will get to me. Well, if I'm there it will get to me.' She laughed.

'That's better Tilly. Much better to hear that laugh of yours. It lights up your pretty face.' Tilly blushed. It was always nice to receive compliments from Drew.

'I'll let you know when, I mean if, I move there. I am not sure. But I will let you know when I plan the little funeral. That way you will know to expect a sad me when we chat.' She smiled at him again.

'I'm always here for you. You know that Tilly. Any time, day or night.' The screen froze, leaving Tilly unable to say a proper goodbye. Eventually, she cancelled the Facetime call and sent him a message to say bye.

Tilly certainly had a lot of thinking to do. That was very clear.

64

NORFOLK - 2024

Christmas was almost upon them, with all the usual hype. Tilly had managed to get stuck back into the admin at 'Water Works Ltd' which had been mostly left undone while she was travelling. Something that hadn't surprised Tilly one bit. It hadn't taken her long to get it all up to date, but her mind wasn't on work. She had chatted to Paul and told him about her inheritance. She hadn't told him that she had also inherited money, which meant she may not need to work there anymore.

Completing the paperwork with Ashley at his office, the deeds were now in her name. That meant Spitalbrook was officially her responsibility now. It made her grow up very quickly. Perhaps she had done that when Hector had died earlier that year, but this home ownership really did make her sit up and take life more seriously. She was genuinely coming around to the idea that her future may not be on Georgie, but thirty miles up the road in a farmhouse called Spitalbrook.

She had met with Melody, Sam and Kit at An Extra Slice, a few days after her meeting at the solicitors. Kit had made a surprise visit back for Christmas which Tilly decided was the perfect time to update them all with her plans. She also shared the news that she had inherited, after expenses and inheritance tax, £272,670.00 from Uncle Hector's estate. When Ashley had told her, she had nearly fallen off her chair. He had promised her that it was not a joke. Hector had been a very wealthy man. So the coffee and cake were on Tilly. She had other news to share.

'Thanks everyone for coming today. I have thought long and hard about this and didn't want to just put it in a text.' Tilly took a sip of her cappuccino. She wasn't sure how her friends would take her news.

'Thanks for the coffee and cake Tilly. What is the big news?' Kit had heard snippets of news, but it was nice to be back in their old haunt with her best friends, being part of it again.

'I've decided that Marmite and I are going to move to Spitalbrook. There, I've said it.' Tilly looked to her friends for a positive response. The three faces were blank as they took in the unexpected news, then all three leant over to hug and congratulate her.

'Well I didn't see that coming Tilly,' said Melody, the first to congratulate her. 'You'll definitely have to get a car though – and perhaps get some refresher driving lessons.' She winked at Tilly, perhaps not so willing to lend out her husband every weekend.

'Oh I'm definitely going to do that. Believe it or not the refresher lesson is already booked,' said Tilly triumphantly.

'Ooh, get you. What other secrets is the new grown-up Tilly keeping from us?' Sam teased. 'You know I'm happy to drive you and help out with jobs.' Tilly hugged him. Her friend couldn't have married a more generous man.

'Yes, I do know that. Actually, I was wondering if everyone would be free next Saturday? I know it's just before Christmas, but to do the burial, and then perhaps a small celebration in the house. I'll get everything we need, but Sam if you could drive me?'

'I can drive you Tilly.' Kit had her car now she was back home for a month.

'Thanks Kit. With all of us, it will be like that first time we visited Spitalbrook. I appreciate you all. Sam, do you think that you'll be able to dig a hole for us when we get there. Thankfully we haven't had any freezing weather so I think it shouldn't be too hard. There are tools.' Sam nodded. Did he ever say no to Tilly?

The week went quickly. Tilly had contacted Drew that same day, to warn him that in their following Saturday evening chat she might be a little subdued. He said, as he always did, that he was there for her, as a support to lean on, however she was feeling. It was comforting to know.

The week flew and Tilly had spent it planning the day. Kit picked Tilly up at 10. They had agreed to meet Sam and Melody at the farmhouse, but they had to take Lois to her sister's first. Tilly wanted to be there ready to receive her first guests, so timings were perfect. Kit was up for pulling a few dustsheets off furniture, although cleaning and housework wasn't her forte.

Tilly laid the dining room table with a small buffet of bits she had bought in the Co-op the previous afternoon. Using one of Uncle Hector's newly laundered tablecloths, the display looked inviting. She brought a small bouquet of fresh flowers with her to place on the grave. It felt odd that here she was preparing for a second wake that year, in the same dining room where they had celebrated Hector's life. Soon to be her dining room.

Sam arrived and went straight out to dig the hole. Tilly had marked a spot underneath an old Yew tree at the edge of the vegetable patch, in view of the kitchen window. She chose it because she knew that Yew trees were often in church graveyards. It seemed appropriate. The ground was naturally soft in this spot.

'Okay Tilly, it's done and ready. Shall I get the box?' Tilly nodded, momentarily lost in thought. Was this the right thing to do? Or was she overthinking it? 'Thank you, Sam. Let me get Melody and Kit. It's lovely and bright out there. The perfect day for it.'

'It's bright, but chilly. Keep your coats on girls. Follow me.' Sam took the box and the girls followed him, leaving by the back door. Tilly tweaked the serviettes, grabbed the flowers and followed. When they reached the freshly dug hole, they stood one on each side.

They shuffled a bit in silence, looking to Tilly. Eventually, Sam spoke.

'Shall I?' Sam held up the box, waiting for Tilly to give the nod.

'Go ahead Sam, lower her down.' Sam had positioned a strap across the hole to lower the box down. It was a snug fit, but after a small bump, was lowered until it would go no further. Tilly felt that familiar lump rising in her throat. She had written a small tribute and fumbled in her pocket to retrieve the folded page from her favourite notebook. It was pink, without lines.

'So, I just wanted to say a few words.' She cleared her throat, and took a deep breath, before letting it out slowly between pursed lips. 'This is in memory of a small life, snatched before she had taken her first breath. We have gathered today, to right the wrongs of the past and to give this tiny life the proper burial she deserved. A traditional eulogy would reflect on life experience, but she had no life to reflect on. However, I have met your mother, tiny girl, and she has borne a strength that is admirable, to get herself through her long and challenging life. She has not sought pity for her traumatic early years, or for the trauma she must have suffered in leaving you here. So this dedication is for you, our tiny Penny, and for your mother Temperance. May you rest in peace.'

Tilly whispered 'Amen' under her breath, dropped her head, gently brushing away a tear as it ran over her cold pink cheek. Her friends did the same, standing in silence together. Tilly took a white carnation stem from the bunch, and dropped it into the hole, which Sam had agreed to fill once they had completed their service.

The other girls left Tilly and went indoors. Overcome with emotion once more, she stood by the tiny grave alone. Memories of her meetings with Temperance, her meeting with Elsie, the cousins in Crewe and her cousin Drew, who turned out not to be her cousin, all rushed through her. They opened feelings she found almost impossible to manage. Not impossible, just almost. This ended a year of challenges, inconceivable at the start of the year. Her thoughts were broken into by a shout from the house. It came again.

'Tilly.' Kit was calling her name.

'Coming.' Tilly shook herself out of her dream state and walked back to the house. 'Yes Kit.'

'There is someone at the door. I didn't like to open it - it isn't my house, after all.' Kit stood aside. Mel looked on from the kitchen.

'Oh, a visitor. Who could possibly be…' Tilly pulled open the door and stopped.

'Drew? Oh my goodness…DREW!' She launched herself at the man who stood at her front door, behind an enormous bunch of yellow roses, suitcase at his feet.

'Hello Tilly. I can't stop thinking about you.' He paused. 'I think…..' He looked over Tilly's shoulder at the faces of her two best friends, staring back at him. Tilly stood back and looked at him. Speechless.

'I think I'm in love with you.' Drew, handed her the roses, picked her up and twirled her round.

'Oh Drew.' Tilly laughed. 'What took you so long?'

The End

SPITALBROOK

Printed in Dunstable, United Kingdom